THE
MALADY
IN
MADEIRA

BOOKS BY ANN BRIDGE

Peking Picnic
The Ginger Griffin
Illyrian Spring
The Song in the House
Enchanter's Nightshade
Four-Part Setting
Frontier Passage
Singing Waters
The House at Kilmartin
And Then You Came
The Dark Moment
A Place to Stand
A Family of Two Worlds
The Lighthearted Quest
The Portuguese Escape
The Numbered Account
The Tightening String
Julia Involved
The Dangerous Islands
The Selective Traveller in Portugal

WITH SUSAN LOWNDES

The Episode at Toledo
Facts and Fictions
The Malady in Madeira

THE MALADY IN MADEIRA

ANN BRIDGE

McGRAW-HILL BOOK COMPANY

NEW YORK

For
GEORGE AND THEO
(who took me up the Paúl da Serra)

The author wishes to express her indebtedness and grateful thanks to:

Town and Gown Travel Bureau, Oxford, for information about steamers and planes from Lisbon to Funchal;

Messrs. Horns, Radio and TV specialists, South Parade, Oxford, for details of radio transceivers;

The Refererence Department of the Central City Library, Oxford, for questions answered;

The Aeronautical Information Department of the Board of Trade, for charts of Funchal Airport;

The General Manager, Oxford Airport and No. 3 Group (Oxford), of the Royal Observer Corps, for details of the flight range, speed, and load of the Hawker Siddeley 125 ("The Dominie");

"A Person from Porton," for essential information about nerve gases;

Jane Bannerman, for patient help in correcting anachronisms about Madeira, which I last visited in 1947;

The late Wilfred Grabham of Funchal, for botanical information.

THE
MALADY
IN
MADEIRA

1 "I SHOULD DEFINITELY go, Mrs. H." Philip Reeder said, getting up and putting another log onto the library fire at Glentoran; it was late July, but one is usually glad of a fire in the West Highlands at all times of the year. As he sat down again he picked up a letter from the arm of his chair, and handed it back to his elderly guest. "They say they can have you '*in*definitely', and your doctor most definitely wants you and your respiratory tract out of these islands this winter, so I should take Pauline Shergold at her word and go and 'settle down' there, as she suggests."

"Honestly, Mrs. H., I think Philip's right" Edina Reeder said. "This last was your third go of congestion, and in the summer at that."

"It seems an awful imposition, to 'settle down' on anyone actually for months on end" Mrs. Hathaway said. Her nice, kind old face wore a worried expression. "Especially with a maid" she added—"and I have to have someone now. Being old is the greatest possible bore!" she added briskly.

Mrs. Reeder laughed.

"I dare say it may be—presently."

"No, but my dear, Watkins is apt to be troublesome in other people's houses—and she's not getting any more adaptable. She's getting on, too!"

"I should scrub Watkins, and take someone else" Philip Reeder said bluntly. "Not that she's any trouble here" he added rather hastily, noticing his wife's expression; "but I can imagine she might play up in places she wasn't accustomed to."

"I should be rather nervous of going so far afield with a total stranger" the old lady said, looking worried again.

"I've got it!" Edina exclaimed. "Mrs. H., I see your point about the devil one knows being better than the devil one doesn't know, but you needn't risk either! Take Madame Bonnecourt—she's bored to tears here now that Bonnecourt has had to go to Spain; I expect she'd love it, and I'm sure *she'd* be no trouble. She's thoroughly European, which no one can accuse Watkins of being!"

Mrs. Hathaway laughed.

"But my dear, could you spare her for so long? I thought she helped so much in the laundry and the dairy."

"So she does—but we managed before she came, and we shall manage while she's away" Edina said cheerfully. "My hankies and undies won't look nearly so nice, but I can thole that. I'm sure she'd make a perfectly good maid, and she's such a nice person."

"But good Lord, Edina, how long do you expect Bonnecourt to be away?" Philip Reeder broke in. "Won't he be back for the stalking? We shall be in a fearful fix if he isn't."

"The letter from London said 'an indefinite period'—surely he showed it you?" his wife replied crisply. "Anyhow I know Colin thought it might be a long job. You'd better rout round for an extra stalker, I'd say."

"What hell!" Reeder exploded.

When, some three years before, Bonnecourt, who in his native Pyrenees combined the roles of climbers' guide, smuggler, izard-hunter and O.A.S. agent, came under the suspicion of the French Sûreté, Edina's brother Colin Monro had learned with astonishment that, like himself, the Frenchman was employed by British Intelligence as well; he had been hastily smuggled out of France and given shelter, and a cover-job, as stalker at Glentoran. There he had made himself invaluable, not only as a stalker, but in supplementing the deficiencies of the aging shepherd in looking after the hill sheep, so Philip Reeder's dismay was quite understandable; however his wife showed little sympathy.

"You knew from the start that if London wanted him he would

have to go—that was always the understanding" she said flatly. "I think we're almighty lucky to have had him for so long. Anyhow even if he does come back before Mrs. H.'s Madeira jaunt is over, I'm sure he can manage perfectly well by himself." She got up. "Mrs. H., shall I run down to the Stalker's House and throw a fly over her? I shall just have time before lunch."

"Yes, do, my dear, if it isn't a bother—though I don't know what poor Watkins will say. Oh dear—I'm not sure."

"Leave Watkins to us" Edina said firmly. "She can go to her dreary old sister at Aldershot on a retainer basis. She's no pity!" She gave her old friend a reassuring kiss, and went out. She returned at lunch-time with the agreeable news that Madame Bonnecourt had always wished to visit Madeira, which she understood enjoyed *un climat plutôt bénévolent,* and that nothing would give her greater pleasure than to *soigner la personne de Madame Hattaway* for as long as required.

"I think she's really delighted at the idea" Edina said, helping herself to more rabbit pie. "The only thing she had on her mind was her chickens, and she's going to let Olimpia look after them." Olimpia was the Reeders' Spanish cook. "After all, no one could call the climate here benevolent exactly. So now you can write to Pauline Shergold, Mrs. H.; we'd better start enquiring about boats. There must be some line that calls at Madeira."

"Quite a lot of boats put in at Funchal" Philip Reeder said. "There should be no difficulty about that. I tell you what, Mrs. H.—if you get berths while Julia is still at Gralheira she might come across and join you for a bit."

"That would be *lovely!*" the old lady said. "Pauline knows her; they were at the same school for a time. And she was going to make quite a long stay at Gralheira with Nick and Luzia."

"I wonder how Nannie Mack is getting on in Portugal?" Edina speculated.

"Oh my dear, in that marvellous house!—I'm sure she'll be perfectly happy. And Nick and Luzia have put in so many baths and basins that Julia says there is boiling hot water everywhere now. Not but that there always *was* hot water, even in the old

Duke's time; but having it brought isn't quite the same as turning on a tap whenever one wants to."

"How did Julia sound when she wrote?" Edina asked.

"Oh, quite cheerful—she always does write cheerfully. Only she said she missed 'the dear Duque', as she calls him, rather badly; she said it was odd, since one saw him so little except at meals, what a difference it made his not being there in the background." Mrs. Hathaway paused, and sighed. "That made me fear that she was feeling the same about her Philip—he was away so much of the time, but he did appear at intervals, and he was there in the background, too."

"Yes, I'm afraid she took a bad knock over that" Philip Reeder said. "Pity about the old Duke being dead. We'd hoped getting out there would make a break, and take her mind off it."

"*Really*, Philip!" his wife said, impatiently.

"Really what?"

"Such a bromide!—'Take her mind off it.' What a way to talk!"

"Well, you advised her to go, didn't you? I thought that was what you had in mind."

"Oh, never mind! Mrs. H., have a peach—or cheese and oat-cake? There's no pudding today."

"Why, is Olimpia out?"

"Yes, she's gone to the movies in Machrahanish."

After lunch Mrs. Hathaway went off to lie down—since her recent illness this was insisted upon by her doctor. The Reeders lingered over their coffee in the library.

"I'm sorry I snapped at you" Edina said, presently. "It's just that the whole thing is so wretched, it's like touching a nerve in a tooth whenever it's mentioned. After all that havering, and rubbing off one man after another, to be *so* happy at last, and then to go and lose him, when they'd only had such a short time together."

"Yes, I know. No harm done" her husband said, reaching out and taking her hand.

"Such miles away, too, and not hearing till ages after it had happened. I'm not clear exactly where it was, even. Do *you*

« 4 »

know? Colin was so vague, to me—he said Afghanistan, but he'd got on his untruthful face, and he jerked his thumb out."

Philip Reeder gave a brief laugh—he was familiar with his brother-in-law's habit of pushing his thumb out of joint in moments of embarrassment or emotion.

"I suppose they have to be a bit cagey in his job," he said, "though I must say I think Colin overdoes it, in his own family. The mission was definitely in Central Asia, and if Colin said Afghanistan to you, it was almost certainly somewhere else! Colin did let out to me that the cover-story was to be big-game shooting of some sort—it often is, but that doesn't give one much of a clue. As a matter of fact I did hear a bit more when I was in Edinburgh last week; something rather odd—I meant to tell you, but then Mrs. H. had that bad turn, and with Bonnecourt going off like that in a hurry, I forgot."

"Monster!" his wife said, without heat. "What was it, and who from?"

"I ran into Watherston in the New Club—he's in the same line of business—and he said how sorry he was about Jamieson, and what a loss he would be to the Service. And then he went on to say that he'd met a man who'd been in Philip Jamieson's party, quite a youngster, I gathered, and when he was talking about it he said that Philip had wandered off without his respirator—and then he got into a frightful stew, and said 'Forget that!'—and shut up like a clam! Funny idea, to wear a respirator when you're shooting yaks, or ovis ammon, or whatever they were supposed to be after."

"I don't suppose they were really after any animals" Edina said, frowning a little, "if the young man got into such a fuss; though I suppose one might wear a respirator at great heights, mightn't one?"

"Not unless they were using oxygen. No, it's very queer."

"But was it being without his respirator that killed Philip J.?"

"Oh no—he was shot, as Colin told me all along; Watherston said there were several rifle-bullets in him when they found the body. But Watherston got the impression that Jamieson had walked into some sort of ambush in broad daylight. Such an odd thing for him to do; he may have been a bit of a bore sometimes, but he wasn't in the least stupid—on the contrary, he was fearfully good at his job, and he had lots of experience."

"How very peculiar" Edina said, still frowning a little. "That was *all* Watherston told you?"

"Yes, I think so. I could see he was a bit dissatisfied with the whole story, and so am I—you see, Philip had a queer sort of intuition about danger, sometimes—remember how he guessed that there was a booby-trap attached to that last satellite-tracker he found in the Scillies, after that poor dotty old chum of Mrs. H.'s got killed?—Professor What's-his-name?"

"Burbage" Edina said.

"That's it—Burbage. Well, Julia and he had found all these others in the Hebrides, *and* in Ireland, before, and there was nothing wrong with any of them; but something gave him a funny feeling about that particular one, so when the Navy sent to fetch it he took the boffin from the patrol-boat along—and by God, there *was* a booby-trap attached, with enough dynamite to blow up a church!"

"How ghastly! I never heard that."

"Well, that's how it was—Philip told me about it himself; and as I say, it makes this ambush business more peculiar than ever."

"I wonder if Julia heard about the respirator" Edina speculated.

"I've no idea. Colin may have told her, as he was there; he might easily tell her more than he told us."

"Yes, of course. Where is he now?"

"I think he was going to have some leave—they were all pretty shaken up by Jamieson's death. And—don't mention this to your mother, or Mrs. H.—but Watherston got the impression that Colin wasn't in terribly good odour in London just now."

"Why on earth not?"

"They seemed to think he'd boobed in some way after Philip was killed—of course he was in charge of the party then."

"Boobed how?" Edina asked, frowning again; she might readily enough adopt a rather condescending attitude to her younger brother herself, and indeed usually did; but the idea of official disapproval roused her protective instincts.

"Well, he seems to have decided that the important thing was to get poor Philip's body out, instead of following through for whatever they were after; anyhow he didn't bring back the expected results, so the whole expedition was a failure, and Philip's death a pure waste."

"*What* results, for goodness sake?" Edina asked impatiently.

"I honestly don't think Watherston knows that himself. It was something madly hush, and very important—at least London attached tremendous importance to it. And as they didn't get it, whatever it was, and Philip was killed, poor wretched Colin's image is a bit blown upon."

"What bores they are!" Edina said. "Oh well"—she got up. "At least if Colin's on leave he'll be there when Aglaia's baby comes—it's due the week after next." As she went out of the room, "A *re*spirator!" Philip Reeder heard her mutter to herself.

Enquiries were duly made about passages to Funchal for Mrs. Hathaway and her attendant; Edina Reeder, with characteristic ruthlessness, sent Mrs. Hathaway to stay with some neighbours, the Monteiths, for a few days, and in her absence despatched Watkins back to England, with a suitably golden handshake, for five or six months. "I couldn't have Mrs. H. subjected to all that selfish old creature's moans and complaints" she told her husband, when he seemed slightly taken aback by this arbitrary action. "And she didn't really mind. I told her that no one in Madeira spoke any English, and that they'd be right out in the country, which they will, and that Mrs. H. would probably go out by air—you know nothing will induce Watkins to fly. When she asked if there were no steamers, I reminded her about the *Lakonia!*—and after that she seemed quite cheerful." Philip Reeder laughed. "Now I'll go and fetch Madame Bonnecourt up; she's all packed and ready." And by the time Philip Reeder brought Mrs. Hathaway back from the Monteiths the Frenchwoman was installed in the house, cheerfully preparing to *soigner la personne de Madame*. "I must say she makes a marvellous maid" the old lady said that evening at dinner. "Watkins never pressed my *petticoats;* and she washes gloves beautifully."

"Watkins is a lazy hound" her hostess replied, with finality.

A day or two later there was a letter to Edina from Colin Monro. He and his wife had been involved in a car crash, and Aglaia's long-awaited baby had been born dead—"It was a boy, too" Colin wrote sadly. Aglaia was in hospital—"but she's going to be all right; she only got slight concussion. It was just the shake-up that was too much for the mite, they say." And he asked his sister to tell Mrs. Hathaway—"and Julia, if you're writing. Don't anybody write to Aglaia yet."

Before she even told Mrs. Hathaway Edina rang her brother up; always practical, she wanted to learn more first.

"Well, Ag will be in hospital—oh, University College—for about another week."

"And then shall you take her away? You know you can always come here."

"I'd like to *get* her away" Colin said rather distressedly. "You see there's the nursery all fitted up, and the cot by her bed for it to be in at night—she was determined to nurse it herself—all that sort of thing. But I've got to go off again myself, worse luck."

"Botheration! When?"

"Next week."

"How maddening! May one know where to?"

"Oh, Spain again—I'll be seeing old B., I expect."

"Well, let Ag come here if she'd like to. Will she be able to travel alone, or can you bring her before you start?"

"Actually I think she's probably going to those cousins of hers in Madeira; it so happens that they're in England. They were supposed to be dining with us the very night of the smash."

"Lawks!"

"Quite so!" Colin said, with a brief giggle, which slightly reassured his sister. "Thanks frightfully, Edina, but I think Madeira will probably be the best bet; they've got a charming house down in the South, near Madalena do Mar—she and I were there last year, and she loved it. Penelope breeds pigs and things, and it's so hot and lovely; and all these Portuguese comics about the place, it will make a more complete change for her."

"Yes, of course. What a good idea. They'll take her out, I suppose?"

"Well no, actually; they've got to fly home tomorrow. He's in a shipping firm there, and he must get back."

"Oh well, Mrs. H. is going to Madeira as soon as she can get a passage; you'd better get Aglaia's shipping cousin to put them on the same boat," Edina said cheerfully.

"I'll do that thing! What boat is Mrs. H. going on?"

"We don't know yet."

"Oh well, Terry will fix it up for them both! He's in with all the shipping lines—he used to be with old Thalassides."

"What, Aglaia's millionaire grandfather, that left her all the money?"

"Of course—but there's no need to go on about that" Colin said rather petulantly; he was always a little touchy about his wife's enormous fortune.

"Well, tell your shipping chum to fix a cabin for Madame Bonnecourt too, next to Mrs. H.'s" Edina swam on, ignoring his petulance.

"Why, what on earth is *she* going for?" Colin asked in surprise.

"To maid Mrs. H. I've disbanded Watkins pro tem—she'd have been more useless than ever in furrin parts, silly old creature."

"What does Madame Bonnecourt say to this?" Colin enquired.

"Thrilled to pieces at the idea of getting out of the rain and into the sun!—and Mrs. H. was frightfully good to her when she first came here, and was rather adrift; now she adores her. I'm much easier in my mind now that I know there will be a *sensible* person to look after precious Mrs. H. on the voyage, and while she's out there; this last illness really has aged her quite a bit."

"I'm sorry. Still, she had to get old sometime—perennial as she has always seemed! Where will she be staying?—Reid's?"

"Oh dear no! She's going to the Shergolds'—some sort of relations of hers."

"Oh yes, up at the Serra—a nice place, and fresher than Funchal."

"Why, do you know it?"

"Yes—Ag and I stayed a night with them last year, and went

up the Pico do Ruivo. But tell Mrs. H. to take some warm things —it can be quite chilly up there, in the evenings especially; it's a completely different climate from Funchal."

"Not sunny?—Madame B. will be disappointed."

"Oh yes, sunny all right—only don't let them leave all their tweeds and woollies at home, because they may be glad of them."

"I'll remember; thanks for letting me know. Well, I suppose I'd better ring off. Give Aglaia my love—she'll know how sorry we all are."

"No, wait a second." There was a pause.

"Yes?" Edina asked.

"Have you heard from Julia?" Colin asked, rather hesitatingly.

"Mrs. H. had a letter a day or two back."

"And did she sound all right?"

Edina guessed what prompted these questions. Ever since a boy and girl affair between the cousins, years ago, Colin had preserved a deep devotion to Julia Probyn, which neither her marriage to Philip Jamieson, nor his to Aglaia Armitage, had altered; his feeling for Julia, his sister guessed, would always be one of the most important things in Colin's life. And now he and Philip Jamieson had been on a mission together, and he had returned, and Philip had not. She decided to suppress the fact that Julia had admitted to missing the old Duke, with its implications of unhappiness.

"Oh yes, quite all right" she said; hurriedly recalling some items in Julia's letter from Gralheira, she passed them on—the hot water, and some estate improvements that Nicholas Heriot was introducing on his late father-in-law's Portuguese estate. "Mrs. H. is half hoping Julia might come on to Madeira too" she said then. "She thinks there must be boats from Lisbon—are there? You might ask Mr. Armitage that too."

"Of course there are—or you can fly to Porto Santo and go on in a launch."

"Ah, with Nannie Mack and the Philipino I expect she'd rather go by boat" Edina was saying, when the sound of a gong boomed through the house and down the telephone to London. "Oh, there's lunch—I must go" Edina said, and rang off.

As she went downstairs to the dining-room she debated with herself as to when would be the best time to tell Mrs. Hathaway about the baby's death. Better let her eat her lunch first, she decided—this would upset the old lady very much. Indeed she would really rather have put it off till tea-time and let her get her afternoon nap in peace; but the papers came soon after lunch, and Mrs. H. was apt to take her own *Times* up to her room with her. So over coffee in the library she said, without preamble—"Mrs. H., I've got some sad news for you."

Mrs. Hathaway looked up, a little anxiously.

"Not about Colin?" she asked.

Now why did she say that, Edina wondered, even as she said quickly—"Not him himself. It's the baby—it was born dead."

"Oh *dear!*" the old lady exclaimed. "What happened?—and is Aglaia all right?"

Mrs. Reeder repeated what Colin had told her, and his injunction that no one was to write to his wife just yet.

"Does Ellen know?" Mrs. Hathaway asked then. Ellen Monro was Edina's and Colin's mother, and lived in her own establishment in one wing of the house.

"No, I haven't had time to tell her yet—I was still on the telephone when the gong went. I'll go across in a few minutes, before the papers come."

"Yes, you should do that" Mrs. Hathaway said, measuredly. "She will be dreadfully disappointed. How is Colin taking it?"

"He's very sad, of course, especially as it was a boy; but at the moment he's thinking more about Aglaia, naturally."

"Yes, of course. Is he going to take her away now?"

"He can't *take* her, because he's off on another job; but she's going to Madeira too—you're to do the taking, Mrs. H.!" Edina said cheerfully. She explained about the Armitage cousins, and how Mr. Armitage was to be laid on to get them all onto the same boat.

"Oh, that would be nice, if this person can arrange it" Mrs. Hathaway said. "We can try to cheer her up, and she can look after us."

"I wonder is she'd be much good at doing that" Edina said,

though not unkindly. "She always seems rather an ineffectual little creature, to me."

"She's very pretty" Philip Reeder remarked.

"Oh yes—couldn't be prettier! P'raps that's why."

"Why's she ineffectual? Do the two things go together?" her husband asked, amused.

"Oh well, the very pretty do have everything easier than other people—a sort of automatic head start over the rest of the world" his wife replied airily. "Anyhow, I've always had the impression that Aglaia was rather wet."

"We don't really know her very well, do we?" Mrs. Hathaway observed mildly.

"No, we don't. Somehow I've never found it easy to get to know her. There's that immense prettiness, and tininess—and of course charming manners and all that; but I never felt I could get through to anything solid underneath."

"You suspect a soft-centre chocolate, in fact?" Philip asked.

"Yes, an absolute fondant!—sweet and melting, but nothing to chew on."

"Well, Mrs. H. will have a chance to find out a bit more on the boat" Philip said, "if this shipping type is able to fix them all up."

"Will she be *near* the Shergolds in Madeira?" Mrs. Hathaway asked.

"Not very, I don't think. Colin spoke of having spent the night when he and Aglaia went to them."

"The whole place is so small that they can't be very far away" Philip Reeder pronounced. "I believe the whole island is under forty miles long."

"As small as that?" Mrs. Hathaway asked.

"I believe so."

"That reminds me" Edina put in. "Colin told me to tell you and Madame Bonnecourt to take some warm things, Mrs. H. He says that up at the Serra, where the Shergolds live, it can be a bit chilly, especially in the evenings."

"Oh dear" said Mrs. Hathaway. "I thought Madeira was a case of summer frocks all the year round."

"I expect it will be quite warm enough" Edina said. "He just said it wasn't as hot as Funchal, up there."

"It was kind of him to think of it—he is a kind boy" the old lady said. "It's always better to be forewarned. Anyhow" she added cheerfully, "it is so nice to be going to a *new* place. I expect we may come in for all sorts of surprises."

2 SOME THREE WEEKS later Julia, Nannie Mackenzie, and Luzia Ericeira, now the wife of Nicholas Heriot, were inspecting a pleasant double cabin on a Portuguese boat at Lisbon docks; it had two bunks, and its own lavatory and wash-basin.

"Well, you and the Philipino will be all right here, won't you, Nannie?" Julia said.

"Yes, Madam; very pleasant" Nannie replied.

"Muito bem" Julia said to the purser. "Now, Luzia, where am I?"

The man led them a little way down the passage, and bowing, threw open a door with a large *A* on it, leading into a small drawing-room with two sofas, several armchairs, and some small tables; another door led into a bedroom with a proper bedstead —the walls and even the ceilings of both rooms were covered in quilted satin. Julia stood still, aghast.

"Oh but Luzia, I don't need all this splendour!—and it will cost the earth. Ask if I can't have an ordinary single cabin?"

Luzia spoke to the purser in Portuguese, and then turned back to Julia.

"This is the best suite, but they wish you to have it, as you are our friend—it will not cost you any more" she added, with a little sigh.

"Oh, well—if it's like that" Julia said; she knew what an extraordinary position the Duke of Ericeira had held in his own country. *"Muitissima obrigada"* she said to the purser. She went on now into the bedroom, where a door opened into a bathroom beyond. "Perfect!" she said. "I'll tell Nannie about the bathroom" she added; "she hates showers."

An hour later the boat sailed on its two-and-a-half-days journey to Madeira. Julia took leave rather sadly of Luzia Ericeira, once, long ago, her pupil, and ever since a close friend. In fact Philip Reeder had been quite right—her long stay at Gralheira *had* helped to take her mind off the loss of her husband. She had known the place before she knew him; it, and the people there, belonged to quite a different part of her life; in a curious way she had been able to slip back into it and almost forget the recent past, even with the presence of her little son as a reminder. Small Philip Jamieson was now a sturdy child of three, and already so much an individual on his own account as to do surprisingly little to recall his father, especially in these different surroundings; what Julia dreaded was a return to London and the double set of chambers in Gray's Inn, where she and her husband had lived so happily during the brief periods when he had been at home— since much of his time had been spent on missions abroad for British Intelligence. Soon, when she returned to England, she would have to give up the chambers, she had already decided: it had been a terrific wangle Philip's getting them anyhow, as a reversion from two legal uncles; a widow with a small child would not be welcome in those austere masculine precincts, and they were too full of memories for her to wish to hold on to them. But that uprooting would be a painful business, which she was in no hurry to embark on; that was why she had jumped at Mrs. Hathaway's suggestion that she should join her at the Shergolds' in Madeira, followed up as it was by a warm invitation from Pauline Shergold herself. She had always meant, sometime, to go and stay with Pauline, and see this strange place about which her former school-friend was so enthusiastic, but somehow she had never got round to it; now was the perfect opportunity. As the boat steamed down the Tagus estuary she found herself in a mood of happier anticipation than she had thought possible. A new place was to Julia the sort of stimulus that drink is to some people—she was relieved, now, to find that she could still react to it.

The boat was large, since it continued its run from Madeira to Portuguese Africa; the food at luncheon was admirable. To reach the dining-saloon they had to pass through a large circular lobby off which passages opened, and flights of stairs led to upper and lower decks; swing doors on both sides gave on to the port and starboard promenade decks. The lobby was furnished with green cloth-covered benches round the walls, and a few chairs and tables; at these Julia noticed with surprise that people were sitting, for the place was draughty, and yet smelt unpleasantly of stale tobacco-smoke; it was also very noisy, with a constant coming and going of stewards and passengers, the banging of the swing doors, and a distant clatter of glasses from the bar along the main corridor. After lunch they explored the boat a little, and found a pleasant small saloon evidently intended for the use of children, since it contained two play-pens, some boxes of bricks, and an old-fashioned rocking-horse; small Philip had never yet encountered one of these objects, and rode on it triumphantly till Nannie Mackenzie bore him off to the cabin for his rest.

Julia went on deck. The coast of Portugal was fading behind them; she could just make out the blunt blue shape of Cabo da Roca, the most westerly point of the mainland of Europe, and her mind went back to many adventures in that small and well-loved country, and to calm and happy weeks spent there as well. It was interesting to be going to see Madeira, the first of Prince Henry the Navigator's discoveries, the first settlement made overseas by that tiny nation which, little more than a century later, had colonised a third of the known world. But the wind was chilly—they were now in the open Atlantic, and the sun had gone in; she went down to her luxurious suite. And there, quite suddenly, a wave of loss and unhappiness swept over her. Almost automatically she had picked up her despatch-case; this was the time when she usually wrote to Philip—and now there was no Philip to write to! She put the case down again. Oh, why had he had to die? Why should he, the one in the party with most experience, have been the one to walk into an ambush? It wasn't *like* him—as Philip Reeder had done, she recalled her husband's curious instinct for danger, and his intuition about the mined satellite-tracker he had found in the Scillies. She remembered too her walk with him on Tresco, in a fierce wind, when they had seen the Russian trawler which first drew their suspicions to that point on the further island—how happy they had been, before they were even engaged, and in spite of their anxieties about Mrs. Hathaway's poor silly old Professor. Julia buried her face in her hands.

She soon pulled herself together—it was no manner of good giving-in, even to grief. She re-did her face, and then went to see if the child and Nannie were ready for tea; they were not, and she went to wait for them in that noisy, draughty lobby. In fact there were very few people there now, but she noticed a little group of four nuns sitting on the rather comfortless, wooden-armed, green chairs; they wore a head-dress that was new to her, with little goffered white frills inside the sort of hood which framed their calm, healthy faces. Curious, as always, Julia went over and got into conversation with them—she wanted to find out what order they belonged to. They were quite ready to talk, and soon volunteered the fact that they were "Dorothéesses", as they called it, members of a teaching order; they were going out to found a new house and a third school in Angola. Their eager cheerfulness and simplicity helped to restore Julia, and when the child and Nannie Mackenzie appeared she was able to make jokes over their tea, and then invigilate another ride of small Philip's on the rocking-horse while Nannie got his bath ready. Afterwards she heard his prayers, and told him stories while he sipped his mug of Cow-and-Gate milk, and Nannie had an early supper; that helped to fill up the time till it was reasonable to go and have a cocktail before dinner. On the way to the bar she encountered the purser, who came in with her, and after the manner of pursers made trivial conversation. No, the boat was not very full; it was not the season for many tourists. Yes, the weather was fine and the sea calm; it would probably be calm all the way to Funchal. Did the Senhora suffer from *mal de mer?* Julia said no, never. Ah well, on this part of the trip few passengers suffered; it was usually calm between Lisbon and Funchal.

She went to bed early, and fell asleep quickly; about one she awoke, trembling all over, from a nightmare—as so often now, it was about Colin: he was in some sort of danger, and there was something she ought to do to save him but, as happens in nightmares, one trivial mishap after another was preventing her. She switched on the light and lit a cigarette. It was curious, she thought, how since the news of his death reached her her nightmares were no longer about Philip; before that they had always tormented her on his account. She finished her cigarette, put out the light, and tried to go to sleep again, but it was no good—she was broad awake, restless and unhappy. The cabin was rather stuffy, and she decided to try a turn on deck; putting a coat on over her dressing-gown, she went out.

In the circular lobby the lights had been turned low, but they were still strong enough for her to see some dark shapes lying on the green benches round the walls. What an odd place to sleep, she thought, and tiptoed nearer—it was the four nuns bound for Angola, and as she stood in surprise one of them opened her eyes; seeing Julia, she smiled at her. Julia went over, and sitting down asked in French, in a whisper, why on earth they were sleeping there. The nun explained that they were travelling third class—there is seldom any luxury travel for religious orders—and instead of being put all together, or at least in pairs, as their rule enjoins on journeys, they were scattered about in four different compartments; so they had decided to sleep all together in the empty lobby. They were quite all right, the nun said cheerfully; much better than in the stuffy, crowded emigrants' quarters down below, where men and women were talking, smoking, drinking and singing all night long.

This made Julia really angry. She roused them up and swept them all off to her V.I.P. suite, where Reverend Mother was installed in the bed, and the others on the two sofas and a couch made of three chairs pushed together; they were thrilled with the bathroom and wash-basin, pulled out little plastic toilet bags from under their cloaks, and all had a good scrub even before they settled to sleep. "But what about Madame?" Reverend Mother asked, earnestly.

Madame had her own ideas about turning this incident to

« 18 »

good account; the nuns were going to have proper accommodation for the rest of the voyage to Africa, or her name was not
Julia!—and she had already decided on the best way of ensuring
this. She went into the bathroom and put on a cardigan over her
nightdress, and taking her burberry, and a cushion from one of
the chairs, she reassured the good nun, and went out and bedded
herself down on one of the green benches. It was not at all bad;
with the burberry round her feet, and wrapped in her coat, she
was quite warm enough—she fell asleep at once.

She was waked soon after six by a bustle of stewards, come to
clean the lobby; they stared at her in amazement. She told one of
them to bring her some morning tea. When it came she sat up
and sipped it, and lit a cigarette, watching the men Hoovering
the floor, emptying the ashtrays, and polishing the tables—to
the steward who came to take away the tray she said to charge it to
Suite A, and to let the purser know that she would like to see him
when he was about. After the men had left she took a comb and
compact out of her hand-bag, and tidied her hair and face; she
had barely finished when the purser came hurrying in—he
looked at the sofa-cushion and the burberry still wrapped round
her feet, but it was clear that the stewards had already told him
that they had found her asleep there.

"*Minha Senhora,* what is the matter? Why did the Senhora
sleep out here? Was the Senhora dissatisfied with her bedroom?"
He twisted his hands nervously, looking very unhappy. "We
wished the Senhora to be most comfortable, as she is a friend of
the deceased Senhor Duque, and of the Senhora Condesa."

In her slowest tones Julia told him that, no, her cabin was de-
lightfully comfortable, and she was most grateful for it. But she
was exceedingly dissatisfied with the accommodation provided
for the four nuns who were going to Africa. "I come out to go on
deck and take the air, and find them sleeping here; when I enquire, I find that they are among the emigrants, in *mixed* quarters, and not even all together. Does the Senhor not know that
the rules of religious orders require that nuns should be together
on a journey?" Unhappily, the purser muttered that he was vague
about this—possibly it was so. Julia assured him that it was

indeed the case. "I could not let this situation continue" she went on, "so I put them in my cabin, naturally. What else could I do? These are the servants of God, who leave their home to do His work in a distant land; they are worthy of the very best treatment—far more worthy than I. I hope the Senhor can assure me that he will this morning give them accommodation together, where they have proper washing facilities, and in privacy?—such as it seems do not exist in the quarters where they were put." The wretched purser began to murmur something about tickets.

"But the Senhor told me himself, last night, that the boat is not full; will the Company lose any money if these devout women sleep in two first-class cabins, whatever price was paid for their tickets?" Julia asked relentlessly. "I should like the Senhor's assurance that this will be arranged immediately." And as he still hesitated—"What would the Senhor Duque have wished?" she asked. And later that morning, when she had dressed and breakfasted, the purser came to her suite and invited her to go with him to inspect two pleasant two-berth cabins, next door to one another, in which he proposed to install the nuns; they collected their modest cabin-luggage from down below, and settled in with happy cries of pleasure and gratitude. "We shall remember the Senhora in our prayers" Reverend Mother said.

"Yes, do please; do pray for me" Julia said. She hurried away; tears had started in her eyes at the thought of how much she wished to be prayed for.

The weather, as the purser had foretold, remained calm throughout the short voyage; the further out into the ocean they went, the milder it became—it was very pleasant. Julia made the acquaintance of the Captain, a short, cheerful man; he had heard about her intervention on behalf of the four nuns, and thanked her for it. "This should not have happened, especially with the boat half empty—but these *religieuses* are so modest." Modesty was surely an attribute of their profession, Julia pointed out, laughing a little—he laughed too. "I am glad that you were here to concern yourself with them" he said.

Julia liked the Captain; he was intelligent and well-informed;

they got on very well. He asked where she was going to stay, and she told him; it seemed that he knew the Senhor Shergold a little —"He works in the Bank, I think? I have seen him sometimes when I was ashore." On the last morning, when they were approaching Madeira, he invited her up onto the bridge, and pointed out the new airport, built out almost into the sea, a few miles to the east of Funchal, and on their right the low island of Porto Santo, which before the airport was built had served as an air-strip for plane services to Madeira—"This was not convenient, since the passengers had to go on to Funchal by launch." It was on Porto Santo, he added, that Zargo and Teixeira, the discoverers, first landed. "But it is said that even before them an Englishman came here, with his bride; they were eloping and put in to a bay called Machico—the Senhora should go and see the place; it is not too far from the Serra, where she will be staying."

"Did they settle down?" Julia asked.

"Ah no, Senhora; they perished! The island was uninhabited then. This is so strange about Madeira, that till the fourteenth century it has no human history—no mediaeval ruins, no Roman remains, nor Iron-age sites, as in Portugal."

Julia was struck by this—it had never occurred to her that there was any part of the Western world so wholly without a past. She was beginning to ask how the original discoverers came on it, when with a brusque "*por favor*" the Captain stepped hastily past her to the starboard end of the bridge, putting a pair of field-glasses up to his eyes as he did so. He stared intently for a few moments, and then gave an angry exclamation. "Again!"

"What is it?" Julia asked—her immense grey eyes were as myopic as they were beautiful, and all she could see was the shape of a small ship steaming tranquilly along some distance away.

"It is a Russian trawler" the Captain said, still angrily. He offered her the field-glasses—"If the Senhora can adjust them?"

In fact Julia was well accustomed to adjusting field-glasses, and soon had them focussed on the ship whose presence so vexed Captain Almeida. To her surprise its rigging was cluttered with all sorts of curious objects which she did not in the least connect with trawling. "What are those funny gadgets on the masts?" she asked. "One is like a shallow bowl. Can they *fish* with that?"

"That at least can lead them to the shoals!" Captain Almeida replied sardonically. "It is a scanner—radar. But you may well ask what the rest of their equipment is for—much bigger fish!" He went on to explain that a year or so earlier there had been a NATO air and sea exercise in the waters round Madeira and the Azores, and that two or three Russian trawlers had dogged them during the whole operation—"With their instruments they could check and record everything; at the end Moscow will have known as much about the results of any experiments as the NATO commanders themselves!"

"Can't they be stopped?" Julia asked.

"Only if they enter territorial waters—the sea, unfortunately, is free, even for spies and saboteurs!" the Captain said bitterly.

"But why is that boat here now? Surely there is no exercise going on at present?" Julia pursued, puzzled.

"Ah, *Minha Senhora,* that is what many people would like to know—it is what they call a sixty-four-thousand-dollar question! But recently she has been constantly about here—this is the third time that I myself have seen her."

"And always the same one?"

"Always. I know her number—fortunately the Russians use the same numerals, at least, as the rest of the world!"

Julia put up the field-glasses again, and stared through them. "0263" she murmured. "Well, she is an ugly brute."

Just then the trawler made a sharp turn to starboard, and swung out to sea again. "Ah yes—she knows the limits well enough" Captain Almeida said vengefully. "But what impertinence!"

Julia stopped watching the trawler at that point; as they approached the land she was more interested in Madeira, which lay spread out ahead of them, a long bronze-green shape rising like the back of a whale out of the sea, dotted here and there with white villages down near the shore; as they came nearer she could see that the lower slopes were criss-crossed with the brown lines of the walls supporting the minute terraced fields. Now they came in close to Funchal itself, white pink-roofed houses piled up against the steep hillsides in a pretty confusion, with the grey mass of the Pico Fort standing out prominently among them. Close to the land the air was soft, and suddenly sweet with a vague flowery scent; it was very warm. Julia bade the Captain farewell, and went down to say goodbye to the nuns; then she collected Nannie and small Philip, gave a steward orders about the luggage, and they stood on deck to watch what went on.

The boats on the African run are too large to tie up at Funchal; they cast anchor a little way out, and the passengers are taken ashore in a launch. Nannie Mackenzie looked about her approvingly, as the small vessel came towards them over the water—"It looks a clean pretty place, doesn't it, Madam? And it's lovely and warm."

Pauline Shergold was waiting for them with the station-wagon; she was tall, and her chestnut-bronze hair caught the light with a coppery gleam as she stood among the small crowd on the quay. When they stepped ashore—"Well, *at last,* Julia!" she exclaimed. "I am glad you've made it this time. And this is Master Philip? He's bigger than Susan, but he's only three, isn't he? And this will be Nannie Mackenzie, of course. Well, you'll find quite a nursery party up at the Serra, Nannie, and Marta speaks quite good English now."

"How old is Susan?" small Philip piped up.

"Four! And I'm sure you're at least an inch taller—we'll measure when we get home. Now, are you car-sick, Philip? If so, you'd better sit in front."

The Philipino denied ever being car-sick, and this was confirmed by Nannie, who was already feeling reassured by this stream of cheerful chat. While Mrs. Shergold was seeing to the luggage at the back of the car—"What a sensible lady!" she muttered in Julia's ear, "You can see she understands children."

As they drove steeply uphill through the sunny little town Julia fairly gasped at the flowers, which bloomed on terraces, fell in cascades over garden walls, and smothered the houses and trees. All visitors to Madeira gasp when they first arrive, and no wonder; flowers from all five continents thrive together in that

mild and equable climate, and grow larger than anywhere else
—dahlias will run up to eight feet or more. "But that's a *red*
bougainvillea!" Julia exclaimed, as they passed a house which
was positively curtained in brick-red blossom.

"Yes, isn't it nice?—much prettier than the purple. The
flowers here are one of the things I wanted you to see, only you
never would come," Mrs. Shergold said, driving the car with
great dexterity up streets whose steepness surprised Julia almost
as much as the flowers beside them. "Of course we don't have all
these tropical things up at the Serra" she went on; "that's quite a
different climate. I hope you brought plenty of woollies."

"Yes, Colin told us to. How is Mrs. Hathaway?" Julia now
asked.

"Oh, in fine form; they had a nice trip out, and I think it really
did her good. And what a delightful person that maid of hers is."

"Delightful? Watkins?" Julia said incredulously; she had not
heard of the new arrangement. Mrs. Shergold laughed.

"Oh Lord no! Horrible old Watkins! No, she's got a French
maid, an absolute charmer, who *really* takes care of her, and is
the most wonderful needlewoman."

"Goodness!—she can't have brought Madame Bonnecourt?"

"That's the one."

"But how on earth did she get rid of Watkins?"

"Oh, Mrs. Reeder fixed that—rather arbitrarily, I gather"
Pauline Shergold said laughing. "But Mrs. H. is rather thankful
that she did, I think; I'm sure I am."

"So am I" Julia said fervently.

Beyond the town the road, still climbing, emerged into the extraordinary landscape of tiny terraced fields which is so characteristic of Madeira—minute patches of vines, wheat, sugar-cane
or sweet potatoes, clinging precariously to the slopes; at one turn
of the sandy road they came on two peasant women, who were
spreading onions out to dry along the verge—in fact the onions
impinged so much on the roadway that it would have been difficult to pass another car. *"Demasiado!"* (Too much) Mrs. Shergold called out of the window at them, shaking her head; the

women only laughed. "They *will* do that," she said—"You can't stop them."

Higher still they passed large plantations of eucalyptus and pines—both foreign importations, Mrs. Shergold told her guest; now the angle of the road eased off a little, and above them, to their left, stretched wild open country, rising to high, almost bare peaks, one of which was identified for Julia as the Pico do Ruivo, the highest point on the island. "We'll go up it one day; it's quite an easy walk" Mrs. Shergold said.

The house stood just where the plantations ended and the open country began—a grove of tall eucalyptus trees enclosed the whole place, and their strong medicinal smell filled the air. "This should be good for Mrs. H.'s chest—no need to inhale!" Julia remarked, as they got out of the car.

"Where's Susan?" young Philip demanded—"I want to measure."

"They'll be back for tea—I expect they've gone picking bilberries" Mrs. Shergold said. "Antonio*h*! *Bagagem!*" she called loudly; a shirt-sleeved gardener appeared and carried the luggage indoors. The house was large and cool, with spacious, rather bare rooms; upstairs Mrs. Shergold showed Nannie Mackenzie her quarters, a bedroom with a cot for the child, and a sunny sitting-room. "I'm afraid you'll have to use Mrs. Jamieson's bathroom, Nannie; we aren't all that well off for baths. But you've got your own basin."

"Perfectly all right, Madam" Nannie replied, looking about her with approval.

"And the day-nursery is here next door" Mrs. Shergold went on, throwing open another door. "Julia, you're down the far end of the passage, next to Mrs. H. and us—we keep as far away from the row as we can! You and Mrs. H. have to share a bathroom too. Ah, that's right, Antonio—show him which is Nannie's stuff, Julia."

Julia's own luggage was then brought along a broad corridor and through a baize swing door—"That keeps out *some* of the noise" Mrs. Shergold explained cheerfully. "I expect Mrs. H. is resting still" she went on, showing Julia into a rather small room. "Sorry this is so minute, but I've turned the biggest double room into an upstairs sitting-room for her, for when there's a crowd in —a lot of people tire her, sometimes, I think."

"You are *good,* Pauline!" Julia said impulsively. "This is perfect for me." She went over to the window and looked out at the garden below. "Oh, how lovely! It's quite like an English garden."

It was, almost. In the wide borders late phlox, day-lilies and red-hot pokers stood jumbled together, a hedge of sweet peas rose beyond the lawn; there were beds of roses. But there were also huge groups of blue and white agapanthus, and white and blue hydrangeas. "Do they stay out all the winter?" Julia asked.

"Oh Lord yes. Now I expect you'd like to throw your things out, and then come down. The brats eat upstairs, except lunch. I'll show you the bathroom and the loo." She did so, and went away.

Julia did a little hasty unpacking, and then made her way back to the nursery end of the house. The stairs were the far side of the swing door, and as she went through it Julia realised what her hostess meant by "the row"—shouting and laughing, what seemed a mob of children came running up, followed by a short dark woman whose frizzy black hair and splended rows of teeth betrayed some African blood. On the landing the young Shergolds swarmed round her—"Oh, are you Philip's mother? Where is he?" Julia, firm and calm, insisted on getting them sorted out by name: twin boys of seven, Marcus and Henry, Theodore, aged five-and-half, and Susan; all three boys had their mother's bronze-auburn hair, but Susan's small face was surrounded by a fair frizzy cloud. To her amusement the nurse, Marta, made no attempt to quell their clamour as they jumped round her, shouting their names, each trying to outshout the other.

"All right—now I've got you taped you can come and see Philip—but only two at a time."

"Why?"—in chorus.

"Because I say so." They gaped at this; Marta tittered. "Come on, Susan and Theodore." She led the two smallest into Philip's nursery. "Nannie, here are Susan and Theodore, the smaller half of a gang of ruffians!—you'll have to be much tougher here even than at Glentoran. Now Philip, when you've said how-do-you-do we'll measure you and Susan."

Philip advanced shyly, holding out a small fat hand—rather to Julia's surprise the two smaller Shergolds shook it quite politely. "Now, Theodore, which do *you* think is tallest, Philip or Susan?"

"Susan!—I'll bet an escudo!" Theodore pronounced.

"Well, we'll soon see. Stand back to back, you two." She took a picture-book, which Nannie Mack had just unpacked, off the table and laid it across the two heads.

"There's not a lot in it, Madam" Nannie observed.

"No, there isn't, Nannie. Where's Philip's ball?"

"Susan's taller! Susan's taller!" Theodore began to shout.

"Wait and see." When the ball was produced Julia laid it in the middle of the book; it rolled gently forward and fell off over Susan's face. "There you are, Theodore."

At that moment the door opened a crack and two bronze heads peered through. Julia went over. "Clear off! I said two at a time." She closed and locked the door; at once a loud hammering began. "They are little devils!" she said laughing; she went through into the night-nursery and out into the corridor, where she administered a smart slap to each sunburnt face.

"I say! What's that for?" one twin protested.

"Making a filthy row, and being little hooligans" Julia said tranquilly. "Now unless you're perfectly quiet you won't see Philip at all today—is that clear? All right, now wait here, and when the others come out you can come in."

"But *we* want to see the measuring."

"All right, Susan can stay till you've seen it." She returned by the way she had come, ejected Theodore, and let the twins in.

"I say, that's smart!" Marcus exclaimed, when the book and ball were demonstrated again.

"Yes, well there can only be half a centimetre in it, if that" Julia said. "Now, that's enough for now. And remember, you are only to come in here if Nannie Mackenzie says you can, and you're to go out the moment she tells you. Now where's Marta? I want her to meet Nannie and Philip."

"I'll shout for her" a twin said—as he opened his mouth for that purpose Julia clapped a hand over it.

"Oh no, you won't! Go and fetch her." Again slightly to her surprise he did as he was told, and ran off grinning. When Marta came and the introductions were made, the Portuguese proved, indeed, to talk odd but perfectly comprehensible English, but it was in Portuguese that she told her charges to go and wash their hands and get ready for tea.

"She seems a nice person" Nannie said.

"Yes—but not exactly a martinet!" Julia said, causing a discreet giggle from Philip's nurse. "Well, 'begin as you mean to go on!' as they say. I'm sure you'll be able to handle them, in your own quarters, anyhow. Tell me if you have any bother."

"Oh, most children soon get to know where they are" Nannie Mack replied oracularly.

Having done what she could to organise the well-being of her own little party, Julia went downstairs, wondering on the way why someone as sensible and efficient as Pauline Shergold should let her children run riot to such an extent. She soon learned. Her hostess was sitting on the verandah before a tea-tray on which a silver kettle was simmering over a spirit-lamp.

"Mrs. H. will be down in a minute or two" she said. "I won't make the tea till she comes, if you aren't dying of thirst; she likes it absolutely fresh-made. Have you seen the creatures? I heard them come in."

"Yes, we met on the stairs. I took them along to meet Nannie Mack and the Philipino; he *is* taller than Susan, but only by a hairsbreadth."

"Were they frightfully rampageous?"

"Well yes, a bit" Julia said.

"I expect you're wondering why on earth I let them be so rowdy" Mrs. Shergold said, lifting the lid of the kettle and peering in; she turned the spirit-lamp a little higher.

"Well yes, a bit" Julia repeated, with her usual frankness.

"It's to save trouble," Pauline Shergold said flatly. "No Portuguese nurses can bring themselves to keep children in order—keep them clean, yes, but obedient and mannerly, no. That's why people like the Ericeiras always have English nannies. But you can't keep one here, it's too isolated; I did try, twice, but they were miserable, and that's no good, for them or for the children."

"No, of course not" Julia said, much interested.

"The only way to make them behave according to our standards would be for me to do it myself, and that's simply not on" Pauline said calmly. "There are too many other things to do."

"Such as? Do tell me; you see, I suppose at some point I shall have to take a bit of a hand with the Philipino myself."

"Well, the garden, for one thing; Antonio is only a labourer, really, and Gerald does love it, so that's not absolutely pure selfishness—though a good bit, I expect! And I'm trying to put in a bit of work on the botany here, which is frightfully interesting and peculiar."

"Oh, is it? Peculiar in what way?"

"Because of Madeira being a volcanic island risen out of the ocean, never part of any mainland; so that all its native vegetation can only have been sea-borne, or air-borne by birds. There's a current called the Canaries Current that's supposed to have brought most things."

"Fascinating! Like having no archaeology" Julia exclaimed.

"Exactly. Well, of course most of it has been worked over, but there are a few puzzles still to be cleared up—and that seems to me more worth while than pestering the children, and tormenting myself, to drill them into what are, after all, rather arbitrary standards of behaviour. If you ask me, I think a lot of what we call 'manners' in the young were invented by bored Victorian nannies for their own convenience!" Pauline pronounced flatly. "'Be seen and not heard' isn't normal for young animals. Of course there are certain things which are quite basic: if I ever catch them being untruthful, or unkind, they're for it. But as a matter of fact I practically never do. Of course I realise they may be a bit of a nuisance to other people—if they play you up at all, just slap them."

"I did slap the twins" Julia said.

"Did you?—oh, good! Tell Nannie Mack to beat hell out of them if they're any bother to her. But I shouldn't think they will be—they'll know better! Hullo, here's Mrs. H."

3 JULIA WAS RELIEVED to find Mrs. Hathaway in good order. She had been very much disturbed to hear in Portugal of this latest attack of congestion of the lungs, especially since it had come on in the summer; now, seeing her old friend happy and content in Madeira, and tenderly cared for by Madame Bonnecourt, her anxiety was largely removed.

"Dearest Mrs. H., I hope you mean to stay right on through the winter" she said when they were alone.

"Well, dear child, that is what kind Pauline insists on" the old lady said—"and really I think perhaps I shall. You see she has given me my own sitting-room, so I need not be on top of them all the time; and at last I have managed to persuade her to let me make a little contribution to the house-keeping. I said I would visit for a month, and after that we would either be p.g.'s, or go to an hotel! So she gave in."

"The children don't disturb you?" Julia asked.

"Oh no—they're out so much of the time. Pauline has this theory about letting them holler" Mrs. Hathaway went on, using an antique expression which delighted Julia, "but of course they will have to drop all that when they go to school. They're lovely children, really—only it is such a shame that the boys should have their mother's glorious hair and poor little Susan just be that colourless pale blonde, like Gerald. It doesn't matter for a man, of course; but the boys don't need that wonderful *brun châtain*—it's no *use* to them."

Julia laughed, and asked after Aglaia. "Such misery, her losing the baby. Is she fretting very much?"

"Yes, I'm sure she is, but she is very brave, and puts a good face on things. She's a sweet child" Mrs. Hathaway observed thoughtfully. "I wish I knew why she's so worried about Colin."

"Why on earth should she be worried about *him?* This is just a routine job, in Spain; he's done it before." Julia's face clouded as she looked out over Mrs. Shergold's brilliant rosebeds, thinking of the so *un*routine job—she still did not know its exact nature —from which her own husband had not returned.

"I don't know at all. But she *is* worried; all the brightness goes out of her little face when his name is mentioned. I thought you might have heard something—you know all those people so well."

"No, not a thing" Julia said. "I've been in Portugal for two months, of course. Colin just wrote that he was going back to his old job in Spain for a bit, and there's nothing to that—it's what he was doing when I was out at Larège, and the baby came in such a hurry."

"Well, do try and find out when she comes" Mrs. Hathaway said.

"*Is* she coming?"

"Yes, Terence and Penelope are bringing her up this weekend."

"Oh good. Well, I'll certainly try, Mrs. H."

Julia wondered a little, later, as to why Aglaia should be worrying over Colin. In fact she had rather avoided his and Philip Jamieson's colleagues in London, after the shattering news of her husband's death; when officially summoned she had paid one brief call on Major Hartley, and been given Philip's wallet and wrist-watch and, almost worst of all, some unopened letters of her own which had only reached the expedition when he was already dead. Stiffly and numbly, she had received the official condolences—it still seemed so impossible that Philip could be dead—and had asked a few questions; but very few. She had been connected with Intelligence so long that not to ask questions had become almost second nature, and, told that the death had been instantaneous, that his body had been taken to India and buried in the cemetery at New Delhi, she had left it at that. Colin she had only seen once or twice; understandably he was fearfully distressed, and of him, too, she had asked very little, except to arrange for a tombstone in that unknown, far-away cemetery—she had remembered, with searing pain, how Philip had wished, in the Scillies, to have a tombstone put up to the Russian sailor murdered by his colleagues, after he had himself tried to murder Mrs. Hathaway's silly, much-loved, old Professor Burbage. Partly, she had not wished to add to Colin's unhappiness; she realised that the mere sight of her must cause him distress just then. But nothing, in any of these interviews, had given her the least impression that there was anything in the present circumstances of her cousin to call for worry.

At the time, however, any speculations were interrupted by the arrival of her host; they heard the sound of a car in the drive on the far side of the house, and a moment later Gerald Shergold came through onto the verandah. He was a short, stout, cheerful man, with a round merry face, and just the same pale frizzy hair as Susan's cropped close to his head, giving an effect of irrepressible marcel waves—in fact there was altogether something irrepressible about him. He greeted his newly arrived guest with— "Well, at *last* you're here, Julia! I do call you Julia, don't I? I don't believe I've seen you since our wedding-day."

"Oh yes you have, Gerald—you and Pauline came to drinks at Mrs. H.'s flat once, when you were over."

"And how long ago was *that,* may I ask? How many children had we got then?"

"None—Pauline was expecting the twins, I think."

"There you are—over seven years ago! Well, we'll forgive you for abandoning us now you have come. No drinks yet? It's quite time—I'll get some." He went into the house, where he could be heard bellowing for *"As bebidas."*

"The children get it from their father" Mrs. Hathaway remarked, with quizzical tolerance. "But he's a dear, really."

Next day Pauline Shergold suggested taking Julia for a walk; but first she spent some time giving Antonio minute instructions about digging and dunging a bed for vegetables beyond the flower-garden. "He *must* finish it today" she said as they set off, "so that we can plant out the cabbages. We get water tomorrow."

"What on earth do you mean? Don't you always have water?"

"Goodness no, not for the garden—only two or three days a week, so one has to arrange to do all planting on water days." As they walked down the drive she pointed to a small open channel which emerged from a narrow conduit under the road; it was damp but empty. "That's where our water comes in" she said; "each house has one."

"But where does it come *from?*" Julia asked, much intrigued.

"From the main *levada,* up the hill; we're going there now—the *levada* paths are much the easiest walking."

So Julia had her first introduction to that odd and ingenious system of water-supply, peculiar to Madeira and parts of the Canaries. As they struck up the open slopes their path crossed several of the small channels and presently, ahead of them, across the dull greyish green of the hillside they could see, winding like a ribbon, a line of blue and white, following the contours of the mountain—as they approached it Julia saw that this ribbon was formed by the masses of hydrangeas and agapanthus planted beside the broad, well-kept path which ran alongside the *levada* itself. This was an open channel some three feet wide and about as deep, through which a deep stream of clear water poured with a rapid, steady flow; a few yards along it Pauline Shergold showed her guest a neatly made wooden sluice, connecting with a lesser channel on the further side of the path—"That's where the men let out the water for all our district" she said.

"But why isn't it sent down through pipes?" Julia asked.

"Why should it be? Pipes would be fearfully expensive."

"But don't the sides of these open runnels fall in, and block them?"

"Not unless some person, or animal, uses a great deal of force. Feel." She knelt down and held Julia's hand against the wall of the main channel.

"But it's as hard as rock!" Julia exclaimed.

"Exactly. That's the thing about tuff—it practically turns to rock when it's exposed to the air. But before that it's almost as easy to cut as cheese; that's why all these channels are made so neatly and precisely. Tuff is God's great gift to Madeira."

"What *is* tuff? I never heard of it."

"Some form of volcanic residue—ash mostly, I believe. But it has these invaluable properties; easy to cut, completely durable when cut, and *cheap.*"

"Wonderful" said Julia. As they strolled along, she asked where the water, rustling gently beside them, came from. "There's such masses of it—how many gallons per second, do you suppose?"

"This *levada* has about fifteen—some have as much as eighteen." Mrs. Shergold went on to explain that the north side of the mountain range which forms the backbone of the island traps the moist airs from the Atlantic and condenses them into innumerable streams and springs; these are caught and led into the *levadas,* which bring the water round the slopes to irrigate the dry, southern side. "It's been brilliantly done—a marvellous piece of engineering, really. But the supply isn't unlimited— that's why we only get water so many days a week."

Julia was charmed by this simple way of distributing water. "Only I should have thought it might get polluted, in the open like this—animals and all that."

"Hardly any animals on Madeira graze loose; they're generally either led or tethered to a spike driven into the ground, if they aren't kept in stalls. Except the sheep up on the Paúl da Serra" she added—"they do graze in the open, but then there are no *levadas* up there; it's above them."

"What is the Paúl da Serra?" Julia wanted to know.

"Oh, it's a fascinating place—a high, high plateau down in the South. They say it was once the crater of a volcano, but if so most of the walls have crumbled away; now it's just a bare open space with nothing on it but sheep and bracken, with the most marvellous views. It's fearfully hard to get up, too, the sides are so steep—that's why the sheep don't stray. You'll see it one day —we're sure to be going down to the Armitages, and their house is a good jumping-off place for it."

Julia was still slightly preoccupied with the well-being and contentment of Nannie Mackenzie and small Philip, and the following day, when her hostess was intent on supervising the planting-out of the cabbages, and watering the garden from the now freely flowing channels which criss-crossed it in all directions, she joined the nursery party, who were going bilberrying. Small Philip was strapped into a light folding push-cart, which Julia had prudently taken with her to Portugal for use on Nannie's walks at Gralheira; Marta exclaimed at its handiness— "*Tão bom!*" she said. Marcus and Henry begged to be allowed to push it.

"One at a time" Nannie said firmly—"You first, Henry, and only walk, mind; if you start to run he'll have to come with me. Give me your tin."

"Why?" Henry asked—but he surrendered the metal pannikin which, like all the others, he was carrying.

"*Think!*" was all the reply Nurse Mackenzie vouchsafed.

"To have his hands free?" Marcus asked.

"Yes—and not to make a clatter" the Scotswoman said, taking the pannikin along with her own.

The little party proceeded some considerable distance up the slopes beyond the road, on small narrowish paths; Marcus was allowed to take his turn at propelling the push-cart, but Nannie refused to let Theodore try—"Not on these rough little paths; you can in the garden." Presently they turned off to the right, along a more level path, till among a group of tall bushes Marta called a halt.

Picking bilberries in Madeira is as peculiar and unexpected as so many other things on that singular island. When the Portuguese woman said "Here we peeck" both Julia and Nannie Mack, for a moment, looked around them, puzzled. Instead of a low, dense green growth, covering the ground and bearing the small bluish fruit, here was only bristly grass and pale shards of rock on the dusty soil; then as the children, pannikins in hand, sprang off the path and set to work, they saw that the bilberries in fact grew on the bushes, which were six feet or more high. "Goodness, how convenient!" Julia exclaimed—"No stooping!" Small Philip was released from his chair, and given a tiny pannikin by Marta, and he and Susan began picking together;

Julia noticed with pleasure that the twins adjured Theodore to leave the lowest berries for the two little ones to pick—perhaps there was something in Mrs. Shergold's unusual ideas of discipline, she thought. She watched them all for a little while, and then began to pick herself; the berries were large and juicy, and tasted much like the home variety—why, she wondered, should the plants that bore them have developed to such a size? Perhaps Pauline knew.

She wandered on, picking here and there, but mostly enjoying the sun, the mild air, and the occasional glimpses, on the slopes close above, of the blue and white line which showed where the *levada* path ran across the hillside. Soon she was out of sight of the nursery pickers, and presently out of earshot too; rounding a corner, happy and careless, suddenly she came to a dead stop. Lumbering leisurely down the path towards her came an enormous boar covered with dark spiky hair; immense tusks projected from either side of its mouth. Julia had never seen a wild boar, but this was so totally unlike any domestic pig that it could hardly be anthing else. She was rather frightened—would it be savage? Somehow she must prevent it from getting near the children; she must warn them—but if she turned and ran, would it run after her? Rather halfheartedly she clapped her hands, thinking as she did so what an idiotic way of trying to scare a wild animal that was. However, the boar peered at her out of its tiny eyes, half-buried in hair, and then obligingly turned downhill off the path; as it went it stepped on an ants' nest, and paused to root in this with its snout and lick up the swarming ants and grubs—Julia left it thus peacefully occupied, and hurried back to the others. She took Marta aside and tried to tell her what she had seen—she didn't want to frighten Nannie Mack, nor to arouse the curiosity of the twins; but the words "a wild boar" seemed outside the range of Marta's English. What *was* the Portuguese for wild boar? *"Porco"* she said hopefully, *"muito grande"*—and with a burst of inspiration—*"real!"* She knew that since the middle ages, when all game belonged to the Crown, wild duck, at least, were called *pato real*.

Luckily this form of penny dropped. Marta took the tidings

very sensibly, and asked how far away the creature was?—but she agreed that they might as well start for home; the pannikins were three-parts full already.

"We'll come again tomorrow" Nannie Mack told Philip and Susan, as she strapped the little boy into his push-chair—Julia wondered whether she would have said so if she had known why Marta had suddenly pronounced that it was time to go home. Back at the house she told her hostess what had happened.

"Oh, the tiresome old creature! He's come down again, has he?" Mrs. Shergold said calmly. "He's after the berries, of course."

"He wasn't eating berries, he was eating ants" Julia remarked.

"Yes, I daresay. You were rather lucky to see him, Julia—isn't he a splendid animal?"

Julia agreed. "But do they never go for people?" she enquired.

"Oh yes—he might easily make a dash at one of the children, if they teased him. I'll get Gerald to send some of the men from the golf-links up to scare him off."

"How will they do that? He didn't seem a bit afraid of me."

"Oh, beat tin cans, or set fire to a patch of grass and chase him with burning twigs. Anyhow Luzia has got nearly enough jam made. But we'll see to it."

"Pauline, how did wild boars get here, if Madeira rose up out of the sea? They can hardly have been carried from the mainland on that current, like the plants and things."

"No, they weren't" Mrs. Shergold said laughing. "Pigs were brought by the early colonists, and then some escaped and ran wild. But over the centuries they have reverted completely to the wild-boar type; they are *quite* wild, now. I'm glad you saw him —there aren't so many of them about, and they don't often come down as near to civilisation as this; but they do love bilberries! By the way" she went on, "Terence and Penelope Armitage are coming up tomorrow for the weekend, and bringing Aglaia."

"Are they? Oh, good. I should like to meet them."

"Have you never? Oh, they're rather fun. Penel is frightfully tough—equal to everything! It sometimes surprises me rather that she and Aglaia get on so well, for nobody could call *her* tough."

"I've seen so little of her that I don't really feel I know her very well" Julia said. "But she's so gentle and sweet, I should think it would be difficult *not* to get on with her."

"M-m—yes, perhaps. All the same I think it's hard for very efficient people not to get impatient with ineffectual ones, sometimes. However! I shall be interested to see what you make of Penel; she isn't naturally a patient person at all. Anyhow, I thought we'd all go over to Santa Ana on Saturday, and walk a bit; over on the north slope there is still some of the native forest left—it's the wet side. Now you *are* here, I want you to see as much as possible."

The Armitage party arrived on Friday evening, and Julia studied these relations of Aglaia's with interest. Terence was an enormous man, very tall and very broad, in fact with practically a prize-fighter's physique; he spoke very slowly in an unusually soft, gentle voice, and gave a general impression of absent-mindedness, almost of bookishness, partly due no doubt to the fact that he was shortsighted, and wore large, dark-rimmed glasses. But all this was in startling contrast to his build. His wife was dark, tall, lean and muscular; she spoke crisply, and all her movements were rapid and energetic. Beside her Colin's tiny wife looked almost like a doll, with her minute hands and feet, and masses of palish golden hair; the only big thing about her was her eyes, which were dark, dark brown, and immense—the casually caressing manner which Penelope Armitage employed towards her was rather like the way in which an affectionate but careless child might treat a favourite doll, Julia felt. She was at once touched and distressed by Aglaia's manner to herself; it was self-effacing, no, actually timid—she guessed at the reason, and went out of her way to be nice to the little thing, and engage her in conversation. To Mrs. Hathaway, Julia noticed, Aglaia turned with a happy assurance, an eager warmth—well, that was no wonder; the old lady's *bonté* was so marked and strong as to reassure anyone.

Next day they all, except Mrs. Hathaway, drove over to Santa Ana in the Shergolds' Landrover and the Armitages' car. From the col where the road crossed the backbone of the island Julia saw, for the first time, the northern slope—a remarkable sight.

The *ribeiras,* the valleys carved out by the rivers, were so steep-sided, and so densely covered with vegetation that the ridges between them looked, as Pauline Shergold said, like wedges cut out of a green cake. Down near the sea they got out and walked, seeing this rich growth from close to—the glossy leaves of myrtle and wild laurel glittered on the steeply hanging slopes, interspersed with heaths and ferns; here and there the tree-heath, *Erica arborea,* rose to a height of thirty feet or more, on trunks as thick as a man's thigh. "There!" Pauline Shergold said to Julia, patting one of these massive boles; "that's what I specially wanted you to see. Some heather, isn't it?"

After walking for some time through this damp, fragrant undergrowth they made their way back to the cars, and drove eastwards to a point beyond another village, where they again got out and climbed up an open valley beside a stream bordered with silver-blue *canas,* the tall reeds so much used in Portugal for fencing; here there was some cultivation, and Julia commented on the beauty of the contrast between the reddish soil and rocks, and the silver-blue patches of field-cabbage—"and the reeds too; just the same colour, but such a completely different foliage. It's enchanting." At the head of the valley they came out onto the sea-face; to their left the cliffs fell away below them almost vertically. "There's quite a fair path along this stretch" Gerald Shergold said, "and then we can cut down by another valley which will bring us back to the cars. It's only about three miles. That all right for you, Julia?"

"Perfect" Julia responded cheerfully. But after about half a mile she began to wonder if it was so perfect. The path, barely two feet wide, now skirted the very edge of the cliff; a small water-channel rather less than a foot broad ran along between the path and the slope above. Presently they met a peasant carrying a bundle of sugar-canes six feet long on his shoulder; to let him pass Gerald stepped into the water and stood there—Julia did likewise. "Where's he taking that?" she asked.

"Down to the road—every so often a lorry comes up and takes the canes down to Funchal to the sugar-factory. You must see that sometime." A little later they encountered another peasant with an even more eccentric load: he appeared to be carrying a dead pig, or goat—it had no head—slung from his shoulder on a stick.

"What on earth has he got there?" Julia enquired.

"Wine. That's going down to Funchal too, to make Madeira" Gerald replied, stepping into the channel again. "Goatskins are much the most practical way of transporting wine on these paths."

"Oh well, I never did care much for Madeira as a drink," Julia said, causing her host to laugh—in fact, as the man passed them a strong smell of goat was perceptible.

A little farther on Gerald's "fair path" became even narrower, and splashes from the water-channel beside it made the surface muddy and slippery in places; the cliff fell away to the sea below them with dizzying abruptness. "Don't go so fast, Gerald—I can't skip along this like you do" Julia said.

"Have my stick—we ought to have given you one" he said, turning back to her. "Hullo, what goes on?"

Julia too looked back. The rest of the party had come to a standstill a little way behind them; they heard Penelope say brusquely "Oh nonsense, Aglaia; it's perfectly safe."

"I don't *like* it" Aglaia said faintly. "How much more of it is there?"

"Only about a mile—come on. Hold onto my stick, if you like."

"I—I don't think I can do it; it makes me feel sick" Aglaia faltered.

"Everyone does it" Penelope said, still brusquely. She was immediately in front of Aglaia; they were all strung out like beads on a cord, Pauline behind Aglaia, and Terence Armitage bringing up the rear. He now stepped into the channel. "Watch out, Pauline," he said in his slow, gentle voice; "I'm going to pass you." He held her arm as he did so; his great bulk so filled the space between the slope above the tiny path that this was a wise precaution. "I'll take Aglaia down, Penelope" he said, still gently, still slowly; "there's no earthly reason why she should walk here if she doesn't like it." Rather to Julia's surprise, his wife subsided. "Now, stand by me in the water, Ag dear" he went on, "and let Pauline pass. That's right—on you all go. We'll meet you at the bottom." When Pauline had passed him he took off his jacket and spread it against the slope above, which was also mossy and muddy. "We'll sit here and have a cigarette," he said pleasantly to his little cousin, "and then take our time going down."

The rest went on, Julia half regretting that she had not had the enterprise to say that she would rather turn back too; the whole proceeding seemed to her both unpleasant and risky, though none of the others seemed to mind it in the least. She was greatly relieved when, at the head of the next valley, the horrid little path left the cliff and turned inland. But how *nice* Terence Armitage was, she thought; he had done it beautifully.

They didn't at once go down; Gerald led them across to the valley's farther side, where three bare-legged men were treading grapes in a small, roughly constructed, wooden *lagare* in the open air; several of the goatskins, empty and deflated, lay on the ground beside it. "There, that's the first stage of your un-favourite drink" he told Julia.

"Doesn't she like Madeira?" Mrs. Armitage asked in surprise.

"Not all that much" Julia admitted.

"Oh, but that's practically treason here!" Pauline said gaily. "For goodness sake keep quiet about it when you meet the Funchal people, or they'll have you deported! It's our bread and butter."

"It's our bread" her husband corrected her.

"What puts the butter on it?" Julia asked, as they turned and began to walk down the valley, which was again ornamented with the straight silver-blue spears of *canas* along the bottom, and patches of the rounded shapes of field-cabbage on both sides.

"Sugar—and now tourism," he said.

"And the sprinkling of brown sugar over the butter is wicker-work and embroidery" Pauline added. "I'll take you to get some when we go down into Funchal."

"You'll ruin yourself!" Gerald warned her.

That evening Julia made a point of seeing all she could of

Aglaia, sensing, rightly, that she might be feeling that she had made rather a fool of herself on their expedition. At one point, when they were alone, she said abruptly—"I *hated* that path along the cliff. I wished afterwards that I'd had the courage to say I wouldn't go on, as you did."

Aglaia turned her little face up to her, glowing.

"Courage? I felt an awful coward. But don't you think it was rather dangerous, p'raps?"

"Yes—I think we ought to have been roped" Julia said laughing.

"Was there much more of it?"

"I suppose a good mile—it seemed like *ten* to me. No, you did quite right, Aglaia. I suppose people here get so accustomed to these giddy little paths that they don't realise how frightening they are."

Aglaia was obviously encouraged by this; she talked much more freely to Julia than before, and the following day she actually suggested that they should take a turn in the garden together. They strolled across the lawn, and walked along beside the hedge of sweet peas. Suddenly—"There's something I want to ask you" Aglaia said.

"Ask away."

"When you were in London, I expect you saw the people in the Office" Aglaia said.

"Yes, of course" Julia responded, surprised that Aglaia should mention that miserable interview when she had been told about her husband's death.

"And did you get the impression that they were blaming Colin for—for any of it?"

"No" Julia said slowly. "No, Aglaia, no one said anthing about Colin at all, except of course that he had had to take over, and had brought Philip's body back to India. Why?"

"Well, they *are* blaming him," the girl said. "I'm not quite sure what for, because of course he can't say much, and he doesn't like talking about it." She turned aside, and began to pull at a spray of bloom in the hedge; her tiny hands were trembling. Julia was slightly shocked that Aglaia, in the first open reference to her own appalling loss, should be concentrating so entirely on Colin; but she realised that the girl was seriously troubled, and tried to overcome her feelings.

"How do you know that they are blaming Colin?" she asked. "I mean, are you sure about this?"

"Oh, it was Hartley's manner, when we met him, and then little things that people have let drop—and now his being sent back to this dim job in Spain! Yes, I know they feel that he failed in some way." She turned back to Julia, her cheeks scarlet, and burst out—"After all, it wasn't *Colin's* fault that Philip left his respirator behind."

"His respirator?" Julia was completely puzzled, as well as more shocked than ever by Aglaia's reckless words. "What do you mean? Philip was shot" she said, rather repressively.

"Oh, I'm sorry! I oughtn't to have said that—please forgive me" Aglaia said, her brown eyes beginning to fill with tears. "Only I am so worried about Colin."

"Well, now you must tell me everything you know" Julia said slowly. "Why were they wearing respirators, to begin with?"

"It was something to do with what they went to find out about —that's all I know. They were supposed to wear them all the time; it was dangerous not to. And Colonel Jamieson did go out without his that last morning, and I know Colin thought that was why he got shot."

Julia was utterly mystified by this, and greatly distressed. She questioned Aglaia closely, but could get no more out of her: they had to wear respirators all the time, Philip Jamieson had gone out without his, and so he had been shot; in the end she was convinced that that really was all Aglaia herself knew. But alone, she puzzled over it endlessly. What did one wear respirators *against*? Well, in the first War, gas, of course—but why should one expect gas in Central Asia? And if gas, improbably, had killed Philip, why was he shot as well? It didn't add up—it didn't make sense, she told herself wretchedly. And why had Major Hartley said nothing about the respirator to her? Alas, the answer to that did make plenty of sense; obviously the use of respirators was connected with "what they went to find out about," to use Aglaia's words—in fact it must be the key to that particular mystery, and she could only conclude that this was something considered too important and too secret for even her to be told.

Julia felt rather rebellious about this. She was Philip's wife—surely she had the right to be told all the facts about his death? After all, she had worked with and for Intelligence for years; it was not as if she were an irresponsible outsider. She thought of writing to Colin, guardedly, to ask him for the facts, but decided against it; it would only worry him—and the more so if he anyhow felt himself to be under a cloud. And was Aglaia right about that? Here she thought of writing to Major Hartley, if only to get some reassurance; but again she decided against it. Any hint of indiscretion on Aglaia's part would do Colin still more harm. That was the worst of Intelligence work: all your nearest and dearest somehow got drawn into the net, got involved, if only by implication, through your connection with them. She remembered how this aspect of his profession had worried Philip, for fear of its effect on their married life. Oh well, he and she had got by all right; their life had been perfect. Only now it was over—so soon, so soon! But learning about the manner of his death wouldn't bring him back, and any attempt to find out could only harm the living—Colin and poor Aglaia, who must be worried almost out of her wits to have spoken as she did. No, there was nothing to be done—except help those two in any way that she could.

4 "THAT WAS PENELOPE" Mrs. Shergold said, coming out onto the verandah, which she had left to answer the telephone, a day or so later. "She wants us to go down this next weekend, and go up into the Paúl da Serra on Saturday or Sunday. Mrs. H., will you come too? She'd love it if you would, but it's rather a long drive."

"How kind of her! How long a drive is it?"

"Well, it's between two and three hours on from Funchal, rather depending on how many hold-ups you get! The road is frightfully twisty, and so narrow, often, that if you do overtake a flock of goats in charge of a small child, you may have to follow it for half an hour."

"Do you know, Pauline, if it isn't inconvenient I really think I'd rather stay here" the old lady said. "You have made me so comfortable that I'm disinclined to stir! Will Mrs. Armitage mind?"

"I'm sure she won't; she just wanted you to come if you cared to. It's apt to be rather a hot drive, too. You'll be all right with Madame Bonnecourt, and you can ask Marta for anything you want. Don't let the children pester you."

Julia and Mrs. Shergold drove down together on the Friday morning—Terence Armitage was going to bring Gerald with him in the evening. Beyond Funchal the country was all new to Julia, and much of the road seemed rather alarming—steep cliffs above, a vertical drop below; an endless succession of hairpin bends as the road contoured round the *lombos* or ridges and the *ribeiras,* more ravines than valleys, which cut up the coast here, where the mountains press down on the shore; moreover, the road was very narrow much of the time, and to pass even a large car meant driving nearer the lip of the cliff than she found at all pleasant. Pauline Shergold tackled it with the same insouciance which she had shown on that horrible little path the previous Sunday, driving at a speed which seemed slightly reckless to her guest, constantly pulling up short, with a scream of brakes, when rounding a corner they encountered some obstacle. Mrs. H. was well out of this, Julia thought to herself.

At one point Pauline slowed down on a fairly open stretch, saying—"There's something I want you to see." She indicated a very peculiar tree with thick succulent-looking leaves and stems, standing a little above the road.

"Is it a cactus?" Julia asked, peering at it.

"No, it's a dragon-tree. It grows nowhere in the world but here and in the Canaries now; it used to grow on the mainland of Europe ages ago."

"How do they know it did?" Julia asked.

"Because it's been found fossilised! That's what's *so* odd about this place—human-wise, it's so relatively modern, but such an archaeological museum as regards its plants."

Presently the mountain chain raked back from the coast, giving gentler slopes; here, in open country and surrounded by vineyards, stood the Armitages' *quinta,* a big, simply built house overlooking the sea, with a large group of farm-buildings adjoining it on one side, a rather new and unfinished garden on the other. As they drew up Aglaia came out onto the steps to greet them.

"Mrs. Armitage is at the farm—she said we were to go and find her. Luzia will get someone to take the luggage in" she added, as a maid appeared. Pauline Shergold briskly threw out their cases and put the car in the shade, before they walked under a trellis of vines to the farm-yard, where hens scratched in the dust and small pigs ran about among farm implements; there was a lot of squealing, of which the most piercing emanated from a piglet which a tall dark man in shirt-sleeves was holding up and exhibiting to Mrs. Armitage, a look of deep concern on his tanned face.

"I will reflect, Manoel, and let you know presently" she told him, and turned to her guests. "There you are—good. Too bad about Mrs. H., but I know how old people get dug in!" As they walked back under the vine trellis—"Poor Manoel; he is in such a fuss" she said laughing. "You see these grapes?"—she indicated the green bunches which hung just above their heads. "They haven't turned colour yet, and the local theory is that the young pigs shouldn't be what he calls *crustato* till they do!—but he was showing me that it's high time they were done."

"*Crustato?*" Julia asked, puzzled.

"*Castrato* is what he means, but he always calls it '*crustato*'" Mrs. Armitage said, still laughing. Suddenly she stopped. "Oh, I forgot to ask him about his boy. Take them in and show them their rooms, Aglaia—I won't be a moment." She turned back into the yard, where they heard her calling "O Manoel!"

Over drinks before lunch, on a wide verandah overlooking the sea, Pauline Shergold enquired about Manoel's child—"Is it that nice little boy of his with the funny name, who's such a dab with a catapult?"

"Marcusinho? Yes, that's the one. Well, I think it's probably only a cold, but he is wheezing frightfully, like a railway engine! —and his mother says he complains of headache. If he isn't better tomorrow I shall send for the doctor—he's been like this for a week now" Mrs. Armitage said, with her usual decision.

The two men arrived early, and Julia readily accepted her host's invitation to go for a stroll before dinner. Below the garden and the vineyards they came on some plantations of trees with immense leaves—"Goodness! What on earth are those?" she exclaimed.

"Banana-trees. Have you never seen them before?" he asked, amused.

"Well, I suppose the one at Kew. But fancy their growing here! —I thought they were tropical things."

"Did you never hear of Canary bananas?" Terence Armitage asked, now openly laughing at her. "We're not so far from the Canaries, you know."

"No, of course not—that current. I don't know why I was so surprised."

"I see Pauline hasn't done her stuff yet about showing you the gardens here" he said. "They're full of tropical things. At one *quinta* alone there are over a hundred different species from all over the world, growing well, more than half of them from the tropics."

"How does that happen? I mean, it isn't all that hot here" Julia said.

"It's the steadiness of the temperature; the annual mean is between sixty-five and sixty-seven Fahrenheit, and it never falls below fifty. Plants are amazingly adaptable if they aren't subjected to any extremes."

"I never knew that" Julia observed—"I mean, one notices their adaptability more when they are subjected to extremes." She was thinking of the fragile crocuses and soldanellas that she had seen in Switzerland, coming up within a yard of the winter's melting snow. But he took her up on it in a way that surprised her.

"One does that with *people,* certainly" he said, turning to peer at her through his horn-rimmed glasses. "How do you find Aglaia?" he asked abruptly. "She's been subjected to extremes lately, poor little thing."

"Do you mean losing the baby?" Julia asked—she wanted to be sure of her ground before she went very far.

"Partly that, of course—it was tragic for her; he wanted one so much. He's your cousin, isn't he? Do you know him well?"

"Yes, *very* well" Julia said, with slow emphasis.

"Well, I'm Aglaia's cousin" Terence Armitage went on, "but I don't know her very well—at least not till this time. Now I think perhaps I'm beginning to."

"Yes?" Julia said, wondering what was coming.

"Well, for some reason I think her nerve is getting broken" he said, again peering at her through his glasses in his earnest way. "I think losing the baby has to do with it, though it was in no manner of way her fault."

Julia was a little disconcerted by this approach. She wanted to hear what he was getting at, but she wasn't sure that she was prepared to discuss her cousin Colin and his relations with his wife, about which she in fact knew very little, with an almost total stranger, much as she was inclined to like him. To gain time—

"Is that why you were so especially nice to her last Sunday, when she was frightened?" she asked.

"Exactly—if I was nice. I don't think being with Penelope is very good for her" he said frankly. "She's so efficient, and so completely sure of herself, that she is apt to have a rather depressant effect on people who are unsure."

"Yes, I can imagine that" Julia said, still hedging; what she wanted to say was "So what?"

"Well—look—I don't quite know how to say this" he went on, looking so earnest and troubled that Julia couldn't help warming to him a little. "I mean, *your* 'extreme' is so much worse than—than anyone's, that I don't like even to breathe on it; and yet it comes into it, so I can't help myself. I wondered whether she had spoken to you about her worry over Colin and—and the expedition?"

Ah—at last they were at it. Julia was rather relieved—and he had done it much more elegantly than poor Aglaia.

"Yes, she did" she said rather slowly. "She wanted to know what I expect you want to know, whether I had heard any official criticism of Colin in London; and I can only tell you what I told her—that I hadn't." She paused. "I only went to the Office once" she went on, "and neither then, nor beforehand, was I told what the object of the expedition was. In fact Aglaia knew more than I did; they never told me that Philip wasn't wearing a respirator when he was shot. She seemed to think there was some connection."

"Thank you very much—it is most good of you to tell me that. I hope you'll forgive me for having brought it up, but I am troubled for her. She is desperately worried, and very unhappy."

"Yes, I realise that" Julia said a little grimly, remembering her shock at the way Aglaia had spoken to her. "But I don't quite see what we can do to help her."

"I wondered"—Terence hesitated. "I wondered if it would be possible to find out if she is exaggerating? I mean whether this idea of hers that Colin is in some sort of disgrace is perhaps mistaken."

"I thought of that" Julia said. "There are one or two people I do know well enough to write to. But on the whole I decided against it."

"Should you mind telling me why? I know nothing whatever about Intelligence, you see, except that Colin works for it."

"Not a bit" Julia said, smiling a little. "I decided that it wouldn't be at all easy to frame any enquiry in a way that wouldn't reveal the fact that Colin, at any rate, felt that he was being blamed, and was *talking* about it! And that would only do him more harm. Of course if it were even *guessed at* that his wife was complaining about it, it would practically put paid to his career!" she ended rather sharply.

"Which is exactly what she *is* doing!" Terence Armitage said, with a sudden grin. "Yes—I see. It makes it a bit difficult."

"It isn't an easy life" Julia said. "One's belongings are involved, willy-nilly, and have to be as discreet as the agents themselves—at least they ought to be! I don't think she realises that. Do you think you could make her see it? Do you know if she has talked to anyone else?"

"I don't think so—not to Penelope, anyhow—she's not on very confidential terms with her."

"Goodness, Mrs. H.!" Julia exclaimed suddenly.

"Mrs. Hathaway? What about her?"

"Aglaia moaned to her too about being so worried over Colin" Julia said—"I remember now; and then she—Mrs. H.— asked me about him. Oh look, Mr. Armitage, this has got to stop! You *must* tell her to be more careful."

"I can try" he said rather doubtfully. "But on the whole, do you think it might be an exaggeration on her part?"

"That depends, surely, on whether Aglaia is a person who does exaggerate" Julia said. "And that I simply don't know. Do you?"

"She takes things hard" Terence Armitage said. "Anyhow, it's something that you got no impression that Colin was being blamed. Did you tell her that?"

"Not in so many words, no" Julia said. "When she mentioned the respirator business, we talked about that."

"Don't you think it might help her if you did?"

Julia considered.

"No—I mean, it might help her, but I think it would be better if you told her that yourself, as coming from me. That will give you an opportunity to rub into her how unwise it is for her to go on talking about Colin being blown upon, to all and sundry."

"You and I are hardly all and sundry" Terence objected mildly.

"Perhaps not." Julia laughed a little, reluctantly. "But in this context Mrs. Hathaway *is*" she added firmly. "If Aglaia really wanted to injure Colin, this is the way to go about it! The Office would certainly blame him for having talked, whether they are blaming him for anything else or not."

"All right—I'll have a talk to her. Thank you very much" he said again.

They had left the banana plantation behind and were now out among the vineyards again, so that they had an unobstructed view of the sea. Their path followed the indentations of the coast, and as they rounded a small headland they saw a smallish ship whose superstructure was garnished with the same sort of peculiar objects as the trawler whose presence had so annoyed the Captain as Julia's boat approached Funchal.

"Oh, look at that!" Julia exclaimed. "Can you see its number?"

"I'm not sure." He stopped, and fumbled in his jacket pocket. "Yes—I've got it" he said, pulling out a small telescope; he adjusted this, pushed his spectacles up onto his forehead, and put the thing to his eye.

"Is it 0263?" Julia asked, quite eagerly, for her.

"Yes, it is" Terence Armitage said. He took the telescope down, pulled his spectacles back into position, and turned and stared at her. "How on earth did you know that?"

"We saw her when I was coming in on the boat—Captain Almeida knew her number, and he lent me his field-glasses, so I saw it myself. He was furious with the Russians for prowling about here like that."

"Had he seen her before?"

"Yes; more than once, he said. Have you seen her before?" Julia enquired.

"Yes—also more than once."

"But what on earth is she up to, now that there's no NATO performance going on?"

"I don't know. No one seems to know. Of course she might really be fishing."

"Don't the Portuguese mind?—the authorities here, I mean?"

"There's not a great deal they can do about it, however much they mind, so long as she keeps outside territorial waters" Terence Armitage said, in his slow, calm way, amusing Julia. She looked out at the sea again.

"Would you say she's outside territorial waters now?" she asked. "She looks pretty close in to me."

"I don't suppose the Russians bother a lot, down here" he replied. "There's no one to take any notice, except the village policeman, and he only carries a truncheon, which has a rather short range! Come on—we shall be late for dinner."

"Does no one ever report her?" Julia asked.

"I shouldn't think so. I think she probably *is* fishing—what else could she be after?"

"You never had any satellite-trackers planted here?" Julia persisted.

"Satellite-trackers? Whatever put that idea into your head?"

"Oh well, we found quite a lot in the Hebrides, and off Ireland, *and* in the Scillies" Julia replied offhandly; "and it was a Russian trawler who planted those. We met her; only she wasn't carrying any of these peculiar doings in her rigging. She scuttled herself in the end," she added.

"What happened to the crew?"

"They were picked up. Anyhow, I shall recognise a satellite-tracker if I see one up on that place we're going to" she added gaily. "Oh, what *is* that bird?"

"That's one of our specialities—it's a wagtail."

"But it's all chestnut-coloured—how very odd!"

"Yes, it's only found here—and occasionally in the Canaries."

"I wonder if that got fossilised, like that tree. Oh well, the colour wouldn't show in rock, I suppose, so one would never know."

"You are absurd" Terence said laughing. "Now, tell me about your satellite-trackers."

They left early the following morning for their expedition. The men carried haversacks with lunch, and Penelope insisted on everyone's taking a torch. "For going through the tunnel" she explained. "It's rather slippery, so it's much easier if everyone has their own light." She produced a whole drawerful of torches, and tested each one before handing them out; Julia and Aglaia were a little puzzled by this mention of a tunnel, but Penelope Armitage wasn't a person one argued with, and they obediently pocketed their allotted torches. They drove for some miles across open country to a village on the slopes of the central range; here they paused while Penelope left a message summoning the doctor to see Manoel's boy, and drove on up onto the Lombo do Salão to a place where one could turn a car—always an important consideration in Madeira. A smaller track led on up a broad ridge, which they followed for some distance till it merged into the hillside; here a large *levada* appeared suddenly from the face of the mountain, out of a dark hole, and wound away across the sunlit slopes. They followed the water into the hill by a path channelled out of the solid rock, but Julia and Aglaia soon saw why it was desirable for each person to have a torch; the surface of the path was uneven and, like the walls and roof of the tunnel, dripping wet; the noise of the water, dashing and roaring along in the darkness close beside them was deafeningly loud in that enclosed space—so loud that it quite confused the senses. It was all rather strange, and, after the heat and sunshine outside, very cold; Aglaia clutched Terence's arm. "May I hold on to you?" she shouted—"Yes" he bellowed back. That tunnel is half-a-mile long, and to Aglaia it seemed interminable; presently, far far ahead of them, they saw a minute speck, a literal pin-point of light. It grew and grew as they approached, until at last, now facing the daylight, they could see their surroundings clearly—the dripping rocks of walls and roof, the wet path, the bright racing water beside it.

"Splendid bit of engineering, isn't it?" Gerald Shergold said to Julia, as they came out into the open air.

"Yes, marvellous. Rather gruesome, though" she said, pocketing her torch and shaking the drops of water out of her tawny hair. "I'm frozen!"

The tunnel had led them through right into the heart of the central range, which forms a sort of backbone to the island; where the *levada* entered the tunnel was a different world from where it left it. Instead of the hot, dry, southward-facing slopes they found themselves in a confusion of mountains with streams and waterfalls on all sides, among vegetation even richer than what they had seen down near Santa Ana a week before, with immense ferns above soft mosses among which cinerarias, silver-leaved and pale mauve, bloomed freely. "Goodness, who planted those, right up here?" Julia exclaimed.

"No one—they're wild" Pauline Shergold said laughing. They struck eastward along a rather indistinct track, rising all the time; soon they were above the dense vegetation and out on grassy slopes interspersed with screes and boulders, above which rose a pale silvery wall of apparently vertical rock.

"The Serra's at the top of that" Penelope Armitage said to Julia.

"How on earth do we get up it?" Julia asked, glancing at Aglaia, whose small face already wore an alarmed expression.

"I've ordered hammocks for you and Ag; I thought you might prefer it. We shall climb" Penelope said calmly. "I hope to goodness the men have come."

They had. As the party approached the foot of the rock wall a group of wild-looking men got up out of a patch of shade and came towards them, holding out a pair of light string hammocks, like fishing-nets; while two men held the ends Julia and Aglaia obediently lay in these, and other men wrapped the nets tightly round them, fastening them with bits of twig thrust through.

"I feel like a parcel" Aglaia said, with a nervous giggle.

Julia felt like one too when her hammock-bearers tackled the rock face. It was broken by shallow gullies and small chimneys, up which the rest of the party climbed, using hands as well as feet; Julia and Aglaia were slung across the gullies and hauled up the chimneys with what Julia, at any rate, recognised as considerable skill and great strength. But the laughing men who carried her seemed indifferent as to whether the bundle she had become was right-side up or not, and to be dangled head downwards over space gave her the most complete feeling of physical helplessness she had ever experienced—she was distinctly relieved when they reached level ground at the top and, still parcel-like, she was undone and set free.

"Well, was that all right?" Mrs. Armitage asked, as she stood up and shook out her dress.

"Yes, fine. What a clever idea" Julia replied. "Did you invent it?"

"Oh no; they always take tourists up in hammocks."

"Well, I suppose I could have climbed it, but this was much quicker" Julia said politely.

The Paúl da Serra is a remarkable place. On all sides the ground falls away sheerly, so that from it one looks over the rest of the island, spread out like a panorama, golden-buff to the south, a green tangle of mountains to the north, and on both sides the ocean; to the east the peaks round the Grande Curral, the great volcanic cirque, rise higher still beyond the Encumiada Pass. The plateau is fairly level, slightly undulating, and covered with grass and bracken; they walked forward across it, leaving the men with the hammocks, smoking, and still laughing, sitting down to await their return.

"I thought you said there were sheep up here" Julia said to Pauline Shergold.

"Yes, there are, lots; they must be further on." And after about a quarter of a mile they came on a group of them in a hollow by a spring—small and rather leggy, with long, straggling, untidy fleeces. "Goodness, don't they shear them?" country-bred

Julia asked; it was the end of the summer, and she would have expected to see sheep neatly shorn.

"They'll do that in a few weeks, when they've finished getting in the grapes and the sugar-cane. No winter here that you'd notice, remember" Terence Armitage told her.

"Oh no, of course not." She continued to peer at the group of sheep; though they were round the spring they were not drinking, but stood turning their heads from side to side, and uttering deep wheezy coughs. "Is there something wrong with them?" she asked Terence.

"I don't suppose so, except that they seem uncommonly tame; usually they scoot off as soon as they catch sight of one. Scram!" he shouted, and struck his stick against a rock. But the sheep paid no attention whatever; they still stood, coughing, and turning their heads idiotically from side to side; occasionally one walked a few steps, in an uncertain fashion, and then stood and coughed again.

"Terence, there *is* something wrong with them" Gerald Shergold said, standing still; the rest stopped too, and all stared at the sheep.

"They've certainly got a filthy cough" Terence said, peering at them through his glasses; he went over towards the little group to get a closer view, and stood still again—one of the creatures, moving in that dazed way, came in his direction—when it was within about a yard of him it stopped, and then, hesitantly, turned round and shambled off.

"Funny, that" Gerald said. "It only seemed to notice you when it got close to. Let's try the others." And indeed the rest of the sheep stood, or nibbled at the grass, quite unconcernedly till any of the humans came within about a yard of them—then, uncomfortably, they moved away.

"What on earth can be wrong with them?" Pauline said.

"Hadn't we better tell the shepherd about it?" Julia suggested.

"There is no shepherd; they're on their own up here" Penelope replied brusquely. "Look, Terence, we ought to see if the rest are all right. There may be something wrong with this pool."

"What could be wrong with it?" he asked, going over to the water.

"How do *I* know? But we can take some down later on in one of the thermoses and get it checked," his wife replied impatiently. "Come on—let's spread out and look for the others."

"Hold on a moment, Penel" Terence said, as she started off with her long rapid stride.

"*Now* what?"—but she stood still.

"I don't think anyone had better go on their own" Terence said, in his slow gentle tones. "If the clouds come up, we shan't be able to see two yards, and it's frightfully easy to fall over the edge. Let's go in two parties; we can spread out a bit while it stays clear, and see what we find."

"Ah, and how far do we go?" Gerald Shergold put in. "Right to the far side?"

"Hardly necessary, I should have thought" Terence said; "if we go half-way it ought to be enough to find out if these are the only ones affected."

The Paúl da Serra is nearly four miles across from east to west; a very faint track runs roughly along its centre.

"All right" Penelope agreed. "Let's walk for forty-five minutes, and then come back and meet here. We can leave the haversacks. How do we divide up?"

"I'll take Ag and Pauline, and Gerald and Julia go with you. Got your whistle? All right, so have I. Let's go."

The two groups set out, one walking to the right of the old track, the other to the left; Penelope marshalled her party like a tank commander, about a hundred yards apart, taking the outside post herself. In less than ten minutes Julia shouted, "Mrs. Armitage! Here are some more."

Gerald and Penelope came over to her. There were about forty sheep in this group, and they were behaving exactly like the ones near the pool: wheezing and coughing, turning their heads from side to side, and occasionally taking a few steps in a dazed way.

"I can't understand it" Gerald said.

"They may have been to that pool too" Penelope said.

"They're quite near it. Come on—let's see what we find further on. Spread out again, you two."

Julia, amused by her ruthlessness, obediently moved some distance away from Gerald. But the further they walked, the more sheep they found, and all in the same strange condition—wheezing, turning their heads from side to side, and all totally oblivious to the presence of human beings until they were within two or three feet of them, when they seemed to try, slowly and awkwardly, to escape.

"This is nasty" Gerald said. "They don't seem able to see properly."

"Yes—we'll have to do something about it." Penelope looked at her watch. "Thirty-eight minutes; that's quite near enough. Let's go back."

"It's as though they'd been doped" Julia said, still staring at the last lot of sheep they had come on, who were now nibbling at the grass again.

"But how on earth could they *be* doped, up here? And who would want to dope them?" Penelope asked. It was not a question any of them could answer.

"Obviously we must check on the water in the pools" Gerald said, as they retraced their steps.

"Yes—but we can't do that before Monday; everything will be shut. Oh what a bore!"

"Is there a vet down this end of the island?" Gerald asked.

"No, only a sort of old wiseacre—well, he is quite knowing about animals, as a matter of fact, but I shouldn't trust his opinion on a thing like this. No, Terence will have to get Pereira from Funchal to come and have a look at them."

"Who do they belong to?" Julia wanted to know.

"Oh, to a whole crowd of people, all round about. We must let the priest at Calheta know on our way home."

"Why on earth the priest?" Julia asked.

"He'll broadcast it at Mass tomorrow. The pulpit is the great channel of communication here!" Penelope said, a sudden grin making her rather harsh face charming for a moment.

Before they were half-way back, clouds swirling up from below engulfed the plateau; with frightening suddenness great white wreaths of mist swept across the grass and bracken towards them.

"Let's get back onto the track" Penelope said—"We shall go faster, too."

In fact they only just found the track, indistinct as it was, before the mist was all round them, chill and clammy. "I see what Terence means about people not wandering about up here on their own" Gerald remarked, turning up his jacket collar. "Does this track go right by the pool? I can't remember."

"Fairly near it. In about another ten minutes I'll start whistling."

5 IN FACT they heard Terence's whistle just as Penelope was about to use hers, and a few moments later the two parties converged in the mist, and walked along the track together, comparing notes. The others had found just what they had found: quantities of sheep, all dazed, all wheezing. "It must be some epidemic" Terence said; "they're definitely ill. We must get Pereira down here as soon as we can."

"Yes, and we must check on the water. Now where has that pool got to?"

They soon found it, and sat down to eat their lunch. Penelope Armitage hurried them remorselessly over their sandwiches and cake; as soon as one thermos was empty she went to the far end of the pool, partly filled it, swilled it out, emptied the contents onto the grass, and washed the cork. Then she came back to the nearer end and filled it again. "Get as clean a sample as possible" she explained. "Now, second cups, anyone?"

Julia, Gerald and Pauline all had second cups; but there was no temptation to linger—the mist was chilly, and concern about the wretched sheep affected everyone. When his wife made to empty the second thermos onto the grass Terence caught her hand. "Hold on, Penel—the men would love that."

"They'll have to go without it this time. Anyhow there's hardly any left" she replied inexorably, and repeated the routine of rinsing out and refilling the flask.

"You'd better mark the corks" Gerald observed. "If the water turns out to be poisoned you'll have to get new ones."

"So I shall—good idea. Give me your knife, Terence." With

the blade she scratched a mark on the plastic top of each cork. But the mention of poison had given Julia a fresh idea.

"Mrs. Armitage, would it be worth asking those men with the hammocks if they've brought anyone up here lately? I mean, someone must have put the poison in the pool, if it *is* poisoned, and if they put some in all the pools they'd have had to bring up quite a lot. So they might have used the hammocks."

"We can try; they're pretty woolly-minded as a rule" Penelope said with her usual brusqueness.

"We will certainly try it; it's an excellent idea" her more polite husband said.

"Anyhow do for goodness sake stop calling me Mrs. Armitage. It gives me the fidgets!" that lady said, as she hastily stuffed cups and sandwich-papers into the haversacks, along with the thermoses and the remains of the cake. "What's wrong with Penelope?"

"Nothing—nor with Julia!" Julia said cheerfully. "Thank you very much."

In fact the hammock-men, questioned about recent visitors to the plateau, responded with some rather striking information. Yes, about a week ago, or rather more—anyhow it was *not* the Domingo (Sunday)—they had taken a large number of *turistos* up onto the plateau; *muito curioso,* they had stayed up there all night! *Sim,* they had effects to camp out with; many, many bundles, and *large. Sim,* they were undoubtedly *straneiros* (foreigners); but Terence Armitage's painstaking endeavours to find out what their nationality might have been were of course quite fruitless. Well, some were dark, but others, on the contrary, were fair. No, their speech was very strange; the men thought it was not English—Terence spoke a few sentences in English, slowly and loudly, but this only produced bursts of laughter. Penelope asked in what money the men had been paid?—predictably, it was in escudos, and they had bargained *much,* the men said, looking rather disgusted.

"Then it can't have been Americans" said Pauline Shergold. "They never bargain."

"French would, like mad" Julia put in.

"Yes, but why should either French or Americans come up here and camp out all night to poison the wretched sheep?" Penelope asked impatiently.

Terence went quietly on with his enquiries. From what direction had the party come? Up from the north side, they did not know from where; two men had come up the day before, and had ordered the hammocks, and the men, to be there next day during *as tardes* (the afternoon) and to be ready to take them down *a manha d'amanha*—the following morning. Impossible of course to establish the exact time, but the men were clear that they were expressly told not to come at all early.

"Well, we shall have to make enquiries down on the far side, of course" Terence said. "Such a large party must have been noticed."

Julia seldom employed her rather moderate Portuguese in the presence of those who spoke it better, but on this occasion she addressed herself to one oldish man and asked him if these *turistos* had smoked at all? The reply interested her. *"Sim"* the man replied, and here was another most curious thing—the *cigarros* these *turistos* smoked were *brown!*—brown, and very small. Now "cigarro" in Portuguese is the word not for a cigar but for a cigarette; cigars are called *charutos,* as Julia knew. She looked very thoughtful.

"Well, we'd better go down; this is getting us nowhere" Penelope said. "I told you they were completely bat-witted." Julia and Aglaia were once more parcelled into their hammocks and slung down the rock wall; at its foot they were undone, the men were paid off, and the party made its way down the open slopes, where they left the mist behind, into the forest, and back through the noisy echoing tunnel. At the far end they emerged into brilliant sunshine, and began to walk down the ridge to the cars. On the way Terence said to his wife "Penel, I've been wondering— might it be a better plan not to tell the Cura about the sheep till the vet has been? I mean, if he gives it out at Mass tomorrow, all the owners will go storming up in the afternoon."

"Well, why shouldn't they?"

"Only if it were some infection, and they bring the creatures down, their goats and cattle might catch it."

"Ah, and however much the Cura warns them, someone will be sure to take a drink from one of the pools, if it *is* poisoned," Gerald Shergold put in. "He's right, you know, Penel; much better get Pereira, and hear what he has to say, before you give the alarm—and get the water analysed."

"Oh, all right. But we'd better see old Dr. Fonseca, and find out what he thinks of Marcusinho."

They drove down to the little town, and paused there to seek out the doctor; to Penelope's vexation he was still absent—he had returned, been given her message, and had gone out again.

"What a bore he is! Now we shall probably miss him!" she said crossly.

Which was precisely what they did. Both the Armitages kept a sharp look-out on all cars, passing and parked, but there was no sign of Dr. Fonseca's old Peugeot on the way back; at the house Luzia, the maid, informed them that the doctor had been, had seen the boy, and had left again. Penelope, swearing mildly, went across to the farm; she came back some time later looking worried.

"What did Fonseca say?" Terence asked, getting up and pouring his wife a cocktail.

"Oh, thanks. He seems to have been rather stumped; by what I could make out—but you know how vague Manoel is" she said, sitting down. "He certainly listened to Marcusinho's chest, and told them there was nothing there; and he hasn't got any temperature to mention—I took that myself. And yet he's got this fearful wheezy cough, and complains of terrible headache; he keeps moving his head about on the pillow."

"What did the doctor tell them to do?" Terence asked.

"Oh, the usual things—he gave him a purge, and told them to keep him in bed, and only to give him slops. But he seems quite *ill,* to me; obviously the pain in his head is really bad, and it seems to have affected his sight—he didn't know me till I was quite close to him." She emptied her glass.

"Rather like the sheep" Aglaia was ill-inspired to say. Penelope rounded on her.

"It isn't funny!" she said sharply.

"It wasn't meant to be—oh, I am so sorry" Aglaia said, almost tearful at her tone. "I only meant it all seemed a bit alike."

"Yes, well leave it for now, Ag dear" Terence said, kindly but firmly. "Penel, didn't old Fonseca give the child anything for the pain?"

"Yes, he left them *dois asprini,* and told Carmen to melt one in warm water; but he wouldn't take it," Penelope said. "I *wish* I hadn't missed him—Carmen is so witless."

"Have you any *ripe* grapes?" Pauline Shergold asked.

"Yes, the white ones on the house are practically ripe—but what on earth for?" Penelope asked impatiently.

"To get the aspirin down—peel a grape, take out the pips and put the powdered aspirin inside, and it slips down without their knowing. That's how I dose the brats!"

"Come and show me how" her hostess said, springing up. "I must do something about that pain." She and Pauline Shergold left the room together.

"Well, I shall have a bath; being near sheep always makes me feel as if I'd got ticks" Gerald Shergold said.

"Ah yes—why not?" his host replied. "I think I'll just go and telephone, if you'll excuse me" he said to Julia. "I might catch Pereira at home. Ag, put a bit more gin in the cocktail-shaker, will you, and give Mrs. Jamieson another drink—I'll make fresh ones before dinner."

Aglaia got up and did as she was told, tipping three glasses of gin into the jug used for filling the shaker.

"Oh, won't that be rather strong?" Julia exlaimed.

"Oh, p'raps it will—I'd better put in some more Vermouth."

"But not the dark!" Julia protested. "Use the white French—and only one glass," she added.

"So sorry—I always forget. I'm no good at making cocktails" Aglaia said plaintively. Julia got up and helped her, cutting some more lemon-peel to add to the brew before pouring it into the shaker; after agitating it for a moment or two she poured out a little and tasted it. "That's all right" she said. "Give me your glass."

"I'm sorry I vexed Penelope so much" the little thing said then. "I didn't mean to. Only it did seem so funny, the boy wheezing, and not being able to see her till she was close to—just like the sheep! And moving his head about on the pillow. Of course the sheep had no pillows!" she said, with a small giggle, "but they might have had headaches too—they wouldn't be able to tell us!"

"I think she only snapped at you because she's so worried about the child" Julia said.

"But don't you think it's funny?" Aglaia said.

"Do you mean peculiar? Yes, I think perhaps it is" Julia said slowly. "Of course if he's been up on the Serra. . . . Is he big enough to go so far?"

"Well, he's ten or eleven, and he rages about alone all day long."

Julia said nothing more—she sat frowning a little, as she did generally when she was thinking at all hard. She very much wanted to talk to Terence about the party of foreign tourists who had spent the whole night up on the plateau, and had smoked what she could only suppose to have been Russian cigarettes—and to see if he shared the wild suspicion that was beginning to form in her mind. Only why should the Russians want to poison half-wild sheep?—if they had been poisoned?

At this point Terence came back into the room, looking gloomy.

"Pereira's away—gone to Lisbon for a veterinary conference. But he'll be back on Monday's plane, so we ought to be able to get him down here on Tuesday."

"Doesn't he have an assistant?"

"Not really, no—just a sort of clinician who works in the lab; really only a boy. He did have quite a good one, but he went off to the mainland." He turned to his little cousin. "Now, Ag dear, don't you want to go and get a bath, before the others come in?"

Aglaia took herself off, greatly to Julia's relief. She began at once.

"Terence, I found out something rather odd about those tourists who spent the night up there."

"What was that? I saw you having a private natter with that old fellow" he said, filling his glass.

"I asked him if they had smoked, and he said yes, and that they'd smoked *brown cigarros.*" She watched his face.

"You're sure he said *cigarros* and not *charutos?*" he asked.

"Positive. *Charutos* would be brown in any case."

"H'm" Terence said slowly. "That's rather interesting."

"Yes, isn't it?" she said, with intention. He looked at her through his glasses for a moment or two.

"Have you mentioned this to anyone else?" he asked then.

"No."

"Well, I think it might be as well not to. I'll get over to Seixial first thing tomorrow, and find out if they were seen. They must have come up either from there or from São Vicente, and someone might have noticed what boat they came off. I see we're thinking of the same thing" he added, with his engaging grin.

"Yes, but why on earth?" Julia asked.

"We shan't know why till we know *what,* and we shan't know that till Pereira gives an opinion on what's wrong with the sheep —if he's able to; and till the water's been checked."

"About the sheep—you know I'm not absolutely sure that Aglaia isn't onto something" Julia said, rather tentatively.

"What do you mean?" he asked, but quite pleasantly.

"Could you find out if the boy had been up onto the plateau? She says he runs about alone all the time, so I suppose he might have done. But it certainly does seem a curious coincidence that he should not only wheeze, and move his head about, *but* not recognise Penelope till she was quite close to him."

"I shouldn't think there was much in that" he said. "I wish we hadn't missed Fonseca; I should have liked to hear what he said."

"When will he come again?"

"No idea—I haven't seen any of them. I don't suppose he'll come unless we send for him," Terence said.

"Have you talked to Aglaia yet about Colin?" Julia asked, dropping the unfruitful subject of the boy.

"No—I haven't really had much chance today. I will sometime."

"Well, that's a marvellous tip of Pauline's" Penelope Armitage said, coming in. "The grapes slipped down at once, aspirin and all!"

"How does he seem?"

"Oh, just the same. I don't like it—he seems so dazed and silly. I think I'll ring up Fonseca after dinner, and make him come over tomorrow. I'm going to have a bath now. What about you, Julia?"

"Yes, I'd love one."

"Come on up, then." She swept her guest off.

Next day the party rather dispersed itself. Terence set off after an early breakfast to pursue his enquiries on the far side of the island; he took Aglaia with him, "for the drive", he said; Julia hoped also to talk some sense into her about Colin and his affairs. The Shergolds seized the opportunity of driving down to the extreme western tip of the island to look for wild-flowers; it was really out of reach from their home if one wanted to have a long day there—they too breakfasted early, and took sandwiches with them. Penelope Armitage stayed at home to see Dr. Fonseca, and Julia remained with her, saying, untruthfully, that she was a little tired; in fact she was hoping somehow to manage to see Marcusinho herself. Aglaia's idea that he and the sheep were suffering from the same thing, fantastic as it seemed, nevertheless stuck in her head. But it was hard to judge from someone else's account, especially that of anyone as hasty and impatient as Penelope Armitage; any form of questioning always irritated her.

In fact Julia was lucky. After a belated breakfast she helped her hostess to peel two or three more white grapes and pound up an aspirin in a table-spoon; when the dose was prepared Penelope was just setting off for the farm when the telephone rang— she answered it with an irritated exclamation.

"*Sta?* Yes—oh yes, Aunt Sally. Hold on a minute, will you?" She set down the saucer with the grapes, and put her hand over the mouthpiece.

"Julia, would you take this across to Carmen? He ought to have had it already; this is an old aunt of Terence's, who'll talk for *ages!* Do you mind?" As Julia picked up the saucer, nodding, she spoke again. "Terry's out, Aunt Sally; but tell me how you are?"

Blessing the ancient aunt, Julia went across, under the vine trellis and into the farm-yard. There was no one about, but an outside staircase led up to what appeared to be the only dwelling, among the sheds and stalls; Julia climbed it, and tapped on the door. It was opened by a pretty dark-haired woman, with two or three children clinging to her skirts; Julia explained that she had brought the *medicamento,* as the Senhora was detained. The woman led her through into an inner room, where, on a large tumbled bed, Julia could just make out a small figure lying— the curtains were drawn and the light was very bad, but a deep gutteral cough from the bed told her that she was in the presence of the patient. Saying *"Con permiso?"* she went across and drew back one of the curtains; now she could see that the boy on the bed blinked at the light, and shifted his head on the pillow. She asked his mother how the pain was?—not much better, the woman said. Together they raised him up and popped the medicated grapes, one after the other, into his mouth; he made no trouble about taking them, but complained again of the pain in his head. Julia sat on the bed and tried to talk to him, but he only looked at her with a puzzled frown, turned away, and again gave that deep wheezing cough. She decided that with her bad Portuguese it would be useless to try to get anything out of him herself, and probably not much good questioning Carmen either; she just asked what he was eating?—milk and soaked bread, she was told. Then expressing sympathy and concern to the mother, she came away.

Back at the house, she could hear Penelope still on the telephone. "Yes, Aunt Sally, I will tell him, when he comes in. . . . No, I've no idea when. . . . He's taken Aglaia for a drive. . . . Yes, you *do* know Aglaia; I brought her to lunch only the week before last . . . look, I *must* go now—someone wants me. Goodbye!" She put down the receiver.

"God, what a scourge the old thing is!" she exclaimed. "Well, did he take them all right?" taking the saucer from Julia as she spoke.

"Yes, but the aspirin doesn't seem to be having much effect; he still complains of the pain."

"Well, if Fonseca can't do any better for him we shall have to get Dr. de Carvalho down from Funchal—he's young and much more up-to-date; he's worked abroad, I believe. Doctor F. is really not much more than a vet!" Penelope said, with her usual incisiveness.

In fact Dr. Fonseca, when he arrived shortly before lunch, and saw the boy again, was not able to suggest any fresh treatment, beyond trying Codeine instead of aspirin—"but with this, he must also take a purgative," and he produced some senna-pods in a screw of paper; Julia almost laughed. When he had gone Mrs. Armitage rang up Dr. de Carvalho in Funchal; he promised to come down sometime the following day.

Terence and Aglaia got back at tea-time, and Penelope at once poured out her anxiety about Marcusinho, her vexation with Dr. Fonseca's ineffectualness, and the fact that she had sent for Dr. de Carvalho. "Quite right" Terence commented quietly—"Everyone says he's excellent." Then he had to hear all about the telephone call from Aunt Sally—"Just at the wrong moment! Julia had to go and give Marcusinho his aspirin." Aglaia pricked up her ears at this.

"Well, how *was* the poor old Aunt?" Terence asked, with his usual patience.

"Oh, as silly as she always is. She'd quite forgotten who Aglaia was, and we lunched there only a fortnight ago!"

"Poor old dear" was all Terence said. However, after tea he found some pretext for taking Julia into the garden.

"Well, I think our friends the tourists must have come off that trawler" he began at once. "They came off 'a fishing boat' at Seixial a week ago last Wednesday, and got some men and a couple of mules to hump their stuff up from there to that junction of tracks near the far end of the tunnel. I spoke to one of the men who'd been along, and he confirmed about the brown cigarettes."

"Hold on. A week ago last Wednesday—and I arrived on the Tuesday, and saw her just off Funchal. Could she have got round to this place in the time?"

"Oh yes, easily. But what I don't quite understand is how they landed the two types who went up the day before to book the hammock-men, unless they had someone here on the island to help them."

"That's rather a horrid thought. But mightn't the two men have been put ashore—oh, anywhere—at night, and stayed somewhere? They must have Portuguese-speakers to do that sort of job, and people who know their way about here. Is there a pub at this Sisal place where they could have stayed?"

"Well, not much of one. There is at Calheta—they could have booked the men, and gone through the tunnel and down to Calheta to sleep, and then back again next day and down to Seixial to meet the others. Yes, that's quite possible" Terence said thoughtfully.

"Well, now we wait for the analyst's report on the water" Julia said. "And we still keep quiet about the trawler, I should say."

Terence hesitated a little.

"Yes—yes, I think so" he said after a moment. "You see, if you're right, and this, besides being most odd, turns out to be something rather nasty—well, if a lot of people know, it's almost impossible here to prevent some one of them talking. And if they have got local accomplices—well, obviously the less *they* know that we know, the better, till we get it cleared up."

"Of course. Talking of talking, did you have a go at Aglaia?" Julia asked.

"Yes, I did. I told her positively, as coming from you, that you had heard no hint of Colin being blamed in London in any way, or from any quarter."

"And what did she say?"

Terence gave his slow smile.

"I don't think she paid the smallest attention" he said. "She's positive that he *is,* and is indignant about it!"

"Well, did you rub it into her that she must keep her indignation to herself?" Julia pursued.

"I tried to. I don't think she paid much attention to that either."

"Oh really, she is the silliest little creature!" Julia exclaimed impatiently.

"I think you'll have to do anything more that is done on that front" Terence said, still smiling tolerantly. "She knows I know nothing about Intelligence, and she can't help realising that you know a great deal. I'm sorry not to have been of more use," he added, now unsmiling.

"Never mind. All right, I'll have a go at her" Julia said.

There was no difficulty about getting hold of Aglaia, who was longing to hear what Julia had thought of Marcusinho's symptoms; she pounced on her as soon as she got the chance, following her into her room for the purpose.

"Yes, I saw him; we went into the bedroom and I helped his mother to hold him up to swallow his grapes" Julia said, in reply to the girl's eager questions.

"And what did you think? Did you think it was like the sheep?"

"It's so hard to judge; people and animals are so different. He certainly had a wheezing sort of cough, and he did move his head about. I simply can't tell, Aglaia."

"Did you find out if he'd been up?"

"No, my Portuguese is so poor. Terence or someone will have to do that—if he will. He didn't seem to think there was much in the idea."

"Oh, did you talk to him about it?"

"Yes—but he wasn't much interested. If I were you I should wait till this new doctor has been, and the vet, before you talk to him. Now look, Aglaia, there's something else I want to talk to you about."

"D'you mean Colin?" Aglaia asked, a slightly mutinous look coming over her small face.

"Yes. I asked Terence to spell out to you, in so many words, that I hadn't heard the slightest whisper in London of Colin being blamed in any way for—for the failure of the last expedition" Julia said slowly; to her regret her voice, in her effort to steady it, came out very cold. "Did he tell you that?"

"Yes."

"And did he also tell you that it could really cause Colin to be blamed if you went on telling people that you thought he *was* being, and unjustly?"

"Well, yes." The mutinous expression was more marked than ever.

"And what did you say?"

"Nothing very much, I don't think."

"Well, I shall expect you to say something to me, when I've told you what I'm going to tell you now" Julia said firmly. "Listen, Aglaia—I've known Colin all my life, I love him dearly, and I don't propose to let you ruin his career out of ignorance, and lack of self-control. No!" she said, as the doll-like mouth opened in protest—"be quiet, and listen to me. You have married a man in Intelligence, and you have got to keep to the rules of that Service. You must *never* discuss him, or his work, or his prospects, with anyone who isn't either in that Service, or one of his close relations, so that they know all about him anyhow. Do you understand?"

"Well, you are his cousin" Aglaia said defensively—"and Terence is mine."

"Cousin-in-law isn't exactly what I mean by a close relation!" Julia said, repressing a strong inclination to shake her. "And how do you reckon that Mrs. Hathaway is related to him? You moaned to her about this, too."

Aglaia began to cry. Julia went on remorselessly.

"A man ought to be able to speak freely to his wife, and to trust her—"

"He *can* trust me!—he does trust me!" Aglaia interrupted angrily.

"He oughtn't to—you're not trustworthy" Julia said. "It's no good your fooling yourself, Aglaia—all this complaining to people is just the one thing that might get him thrown out of the Service, if the Office got to hear of it."

"But it wouldn't be *his* fault" the little creature said, staring at Julia, wide-eyed through her tears.

"They would think it was—his fault for marrying someone so unreliable in the first place, and for not keeping his mouth shut when he found that she couldn't be trusted."

"Then they're cruel brutes!"

"No, they're not—they just have to do their job, and maintain security; if a member of the Service has the misfortune to marry a foolish babbling wife, out he has to go" Julia said, implacably.

Aglaia's sobs became a storm. "Oh—oh—oh. What can I do?" she brought out at length.

"You can give me your solemn promise never to speak about Colin and his affairs to anyone but me" Julia said. "No, not now —you're too upset to think what you're doing. Go and wash your face, and get ready for dinner, and come to me last thing, and make a solemn promise."

"Oh, I will. Do you think they can have heard about Mrs. H.?"

"Not from her, certainly" Julia said, smiling—"and they won't from me, if you give me that promise, and keep it."

Julia's heart smote her rather when she saw Aglaia's small face at dinner, white under the make-up hurriedly and unskilfully applied, and with a sad and subdued expression. Had she been too harsh? No, she decided. Only a real drubbing would have made the feather-pated little creature realise the seriousness of the situation—a situation which would last as long as her marriage, with Colin's career continually at risk unless she learned a measure of discretion. It had had to be done. And when Aglaia crept softly into her room that night, and solemnly and penitently promised never to speak of Colin's work and prospects to anyone but her, Julia—"unless you say I may"—and went on to throw her arms round Julia's neck and thank her "for making me understand", she was more than ever satisfied with that evening's work.

6 THE SHERGOLDS and Julia left next morning. Terence went off earlier; he was going to drop the two thermoses with water from the pool, one on the analyst, one with the vet's assistant; "one or the other *ought* to be able to give a rational verdict" Penelope said, in her usual *cassant* fashion. She had been to see the boy, and reported him much the same—perhaps the Codeine had helped the headache a little, but very little. Pauline dropped Gerald off in Funchal, and did some shopping; then she and Julia drove on home. Mrs. Hathaway showed her usual lively interest in everything they had seen and done; naturally she was told all about the peculiar affliction that had smitten the sheep up on the Paúl da Serra—Pauline gave a particularly vivid description of their wheezing cough, the way in which they moved their heads from side to side, and their unnatural tameness—"as if they were doped" she said. "Gerald may be able to tell us tonight if the water up there really has been interfered with—Terence promised to let him know if he got the report in time."

Then Julia deliberately mentioned the boy's illness, and how it had completely stumped the local doctor; she described his symptoms minutely—the cough and wheezing, the frightful headache, which neither aspirin nor Codeine seemed to touch, and his dazed condition. It was with the utmost satisfaction that she heard the old lady ask—"Had he been up on this plateau place too?"

Pauline looked startled.

"Oh, I don't think there's any question of that" she said.

"Well actually, Pauline, Aglaia did think of it, you know, only

Penelope slapped her down—and when I'd seen the child I began to wonder too" Julia said.

"How long has he been ill?" Mrs. Hathaway wanted to know.

"Over a week—one would hardly expect an ordinary cold to last so long."

"I wonder if Nannie has ever met anything like it" Mrs. Hathaway said—and when Julia went up to the nursery to see the Philipino she described this peculiar ailment.

Nannie listened, looked wise. "And nothing much in his chest, according to this local doctor?" she asked.

"No—certainly not bronchitis, or anything like that, Nannie."

"Well, I hope they're keeping his bowels open; it's probably a stomach cough" Nannie Mack pronounced. "As to this pain in his head, it sounds like a mastoid, to me. That is a really shocking pain, aspirin and so on don't touch it—nothing but morphia is any good. Poor little fellow." Then she went on to her own concerns. "This crowd up here really are a set, Madam! What do you think they did yesterday? Put Master Philip in the goldfish pool —in his Sunday suit, and all!"

"Did Philip mind?"

"No—it was *lovely!*" the child said. "Can I be put in again, Mummie?" Nannie and Julia both laughed. Obviously everything was all right on the home ground, Julia thought, as she went to her room.

When Gerald Shergold got back that evening he brought some rather peculiar news.

"That water's all right" he began at once. "Both the analyst and the man in Pereira's lab could find exactly nothing in it but faint traces of coffee."

"Well, that's something" his wife said.

"I'm not so sure. It makes it look as though what the sheep have got must be some sort of infection, and that could spread all over the island—might be very serious."

"Is Pereira back? It's his opinion we need now" Pauline observed.

"Yes, he got back today—he's going down tomorrow."

"How is the little boy?" Mrs. Hathaway asked; she was more concerned about him than about the sheep.

"Manoel's child? Not so good. De Carvalho brought him back to Funchal in his car, and has put him into his clinic."

"Did he say what was wrong with him?" Julia asked.

"No, he's completely foxed—that's why he wants to have him under observation, and make tests. He went to see Terence at the office, and told him to make sure that he was rung up at once if anyone else showed the same sort of symptoms. I gather he gave Manoel and the whole family a tremendous going-over—and rather slated old Fonseca for having let it go on so long without asking for a second opinion."

"How did you hear all this?" Pauline asked. "Oh, from Terry, I suppose."

"Yes, I saw him in the Club. He said de Carvalho seemed rather bothered about it all, for some reason—he fairly grilled him about whether anyone else round about had had the same sort of cough and headache."

"And I suppose Terence told him only the sheep up on the plateau" Julia put in. Gerald Shergold stared at her.

"Yes, he did happen to tell him exactly that—what made you think so?"

"Oh, just an idea. And what did Dr. Carvalho say?"

"*De* Carvalho" he corrected her. "Oh, he was onto it like a knife! He wanted to know if the vet had seen the sheep, and what he said?—only of course he hadn't seen them yet. But Terence said he told him to find out if the boy had been up there at any point, and to let him know at once if so. Odd, that, isn't it?"

"No, Julia and Aglaia both had that idea" Pauline said.

"Then why on earth didn't you put it up to Terence?" Gerald asked, turning to Julia.

"I did, but he didn't think there was anything in it."

"Well, it looks as though you may have been smarter than the rest of us" Gerald remarked.

"There wouldn't be anything very new in *that*" Mrs. Hathaway observed, looking fondly at Julia.

"No, I daresay not."

"Well, thank goodness the vet is going down tomorrow. Be sure to see Terence and hear what he said" Pauline urged.

"I don't think Terence will be coming into Funchal—he'll wait to take Pereira up. But we can ring him in the evening, of course."

On the following morning Julia was sitting on the verandah, superintending Philip and Susan at play in the garden while Nannie did some washing—including the unfortunate Sunday suit, considerably the worse for its immersion in the goldfish pool—when she heard a car drive up. She was a little surprised; callers so early in the morning were unusual up at the Serra. She was still more surprised when Aglaia came running round the end of the house, darted up to her, and gave her a hug. "There you are—thank goodness! I simply must talk to you."

"Talk away" Julia said, returning her kiss. "But what on earth are you doing up here?"

"I had to see you—Terry let me have the small car."

"Well, tell me what's happened" Julia said comfortably. "Would you like some coffee?"

"Oh, I'd love some—no, I'd rather talk first."

"Well *do*—what on earth has happened?"

"Nothing—it's what he *said*" Aglaia stammered out.

Julia got up and rang the bell.

"I think you'd better have some coffee—help you to calm down" she remarked; when a maid came she ordered it. "Now, begin at the beginning, and tell me who said what."

"It was this doctor from Funchal. Penelope got Dr. Fonseca to come over to meet him, and when they'd seen Marcusinho together they came back to the house to talk it over, and to tell Penel that the boy must go into the clinic for tests."

"Yes, we heard about that last night" Julia said. So far there seemed to be nothing very earth-shaking in Aglaia's tidings. "Go on" she said.

"Well, then Penelope went across to get Marcusinho ready, and to cheer up Carmen, who was in a most frightful fuss, of course. And the two doctors went on talking to one another, and the one from Funchal—who is *much* brighter than old Fonseca,

I may say—said the only time he'd ever seen any symptoms in the least like Marcusinho's was when he was working in France. He said there was a factory there, and that the fumes from some process did bring on the same sort of thing when the workmen were careless and didn't wear their respirators!" She stopped and stared at Julia.

For a moment Julia simply stared back at her. At last, "Respirators?" she said, almost in a whisper.

"*Yes*. Well, *respiradori* was the word he used, of course; they were talking Portuguese. And Julia, Marcusinho *did* go up onto the plateau. After I'd heard that, when the doctors had gone off I went across and asked Carmen, and he had gone up one morning all by himself, they don't know why; and he came back late for their mid-day meal, and Carmen scolded him frightfully, and then she noticed that he was wheezing and coughing, and he had this fearful headache, and was sort of dopey."

"Good Heavens!" Julia said slowly. "Did you tell Dr. de Carvalho this?"

"No—he'd gone then, I said."

"Nor Terence?"

"No. But Julia, don't you *see?* If Marcusinho has really got the same thing as the sheep, he must have got it up on the plateau; and all those strangers going up there spending the night! *And* the symptoms being the same as people get from not using respirators! I think we ought to find out who those foreign tourists were."

Julia sat silent, frowning in thought. She and Terence Armitage had agreed not to talk about her guess at the nationality of the tourists who camped on the plateau, and their possible connection with the Russian trawler; but Aglaia's account of Dr. de Carvalho's words made her think that it would not be possible to stick to that line much longer. De Carvalho himself would have to be told, for one thing; it could give him a clue that might save the child's life. And the word "respirator" naturally led her mind back to the expedition to Central Asia—almost certainly onto Russian territory.

"Well?" Aglaia asked, rather impatiently.

"Let me think a minute. Ah, here's the coffee." She poured the girl out a cup and lit a cigarette. After a moment or two she reached her decision—Aglaia would have to be in on this.

"Listen, Aglaia; there's something I want to tell *you,* but you must promise me, if I do, not to speak of it to anyone unless I say you can. Will you?"

"Oh yes, I *will.* Like about Colin—I swear I won't say a word to a soul unless you say I may."

"Right—good. Well, Terence and I both think those men who camped up on the Paúl da Serra came off a Russian trawler, one of those spy-ships they use."

"No! Why does Terence think that?"

Julia told her why, and how all the dates fitted, except of Marcusinho's actual visit to the Paúl da Serra. Even that, she pointed out, was known near enough; the boy had been ill for over a week when she and the Shergolds went down to the *quinta,* and that fitted in fairly closely with when she had seen the trawler off Funchal, and when the strangers had landed at Seixial. "And now what the doctor said about fumes—well, it really does look at though it might tie in," she finished. "I think" —she paused. "Yes, I really do think, although it's all still so vague, that we shall have to let the Office know. They could send someone."

"*No!*" Aglaia exclaimed so loudly that Julia almost jumped. "No, Julia!—no, no, *no!*" She actually stamped her little foot.

"But why on earth not?"

"Colin!" the girl said. "It's he who must come and see about this."

"Could he get away?" Julia asked, practically.

"He'll have to! He *must* come" Aglaia said, with a determination Julia had never seen in her before. "If there is a connection between this and that job out in Asia, it's he who must handle it—they think he failed before, I know they do; but if he comes now, and succeeds, it will put him all right again! Oh, surely you can see that?" she said, clasping her hands and fixing her immense eyes compellingly on Julia's face.

"Yes, I do see what you mean." Julia spoke pacifically; she was far from sure that this was the right way to handle the matter, or that it would produce the results Aglaia so confidently expected, but she could not be indifferent to the girl's urgency. "Have you got an address for him in Spain?" she asked, remembering how in her own time of crisis in the Pyrenees Colin had failed to leave her one.

"Oh yes, at Pamplona—and a telephone number. But he says the telephone is pretty hopeless; it's better to telegraph—in Spanish, it has to be, if it isn't to get all muddled up."

"Well, there's no difficulty about telegraphing in Spanish" Julia said.

"Oh, *can* you? How marvellous!"

"Yes, of course; only one would have to think of a way of phrasing it that would give nothing away—even to his colleagues, if he's to get a head start of everyone else" Julia said. She was partly thinking aloud—undoubtedly, if Colin was off on one of his tours, the boy-friends would open any telegram that came for him in his absence.

"Oh, *would* you? I'm sure you could," Aglaia said eagerly.

"I expect so. Look, Aglaia, this wants some thinking about" Julia said slowly. "I don't think it would be at all easy to send a wire that would bring him off a job he's actually on, without giving too much away. I think he'll have to go to some place where I can talk to him."

"But where could that be? Come here, do you mean?"

"Not at first—that would blow the whole thing wide open. I think he'd better go to Gralheira and ring up from there. On the telephone he and I can talk in a way no one else would understand. Have you got his address on you?"

"Yes—in my diary." As she felt in her hand-bag—"Oh, what day of the month is it?" she asked suddenly.

"The thirty-first—why?"

"Then he'll be on his way to Madrid. He was going there for three or four days to report, arriving on the thirty-first or the first."

"Does that mean that you can only reach him through the Madrid office?" Julia asked, slightly taken aback.

"Oh no, he was going to borrow some friends' flat—the Twinings, I think he said—because they'll be at Santander. I've got the address." She began to look in her diary. "Oh, I *haven't!*" she exclaimed in dismay. "It's in his last letter, and I didn't bring it with me. Oh, what are we to do?"

"We'll draft the telegram, and you can send it when you've found the address" Julia said reassuringly.

"But it's no good *my* sending it" the girl objected. "He wouldn't come, or go anywhere, for a wire from *me*. You must send it. Oh, you will, won't you? He'd do anything you told him to."

"All right, I'll sign it" Julia said, thinking that a certain light was beginning to be thrown on Colin's relations with his wife, about which she had felt she knew next to nothing when Terence Armitage had first talked to her about Aglaia. She was also thinking that in any case there would be no point in alerting the Office in London until both the vet and Dr. de Carvalho had reported on their findings, so no great harm would be done, nor time wasted, by trying to get into touch with Colin first.

"Now keep quite quiet while I settle what to say" she said; she went through into the sitting-room and collected a pad and a pencil. "In English first; then I can put it into Spanish." She scribbled away for a minute or two, with a certain amount of crossing-out; at last—"I think this will do" Julia said. "By the way 'darling darling' is a sort of code between Colin and me, Aglaia; it just means something really serious is up—like the call-note a bird uses for danger."

"Oh yes—I remember he told me that once" Aglaia said readily. "He said it was so safe, because no one would guess. Well, what have you said?"

Julia read out: "Serious situation arisen darling darling essential we speak telephonewise urgentliest stop proceed immediately Luzia's home she has my number stop I believe very much the mixture as last time. Julia."

Aglaia began to giggle a little. "How shall you put 'telephonewise' and 'urgentliest' into Spanish?" she asked.

Julia laughed. "Well, I could, but as it's going to Madrid and not to Pamplona it can go in English—in fact I think that's probably as safe as Spanish there. In capital cities English is an international language for telegrams." She tore the top sheet off the pad and began to copy the telegram out in block capitals.

"Might I hear the last part again?" Aglaia asked—"about the mixture?"

Julia read it out.

"Will he know what that means?" the girl asked rather hesitantly.

"I think so. I want to warn him that it may be the same sort of thing as they were up against before" Julia said slowly.

"I thought perhaps you meant that" the girl said. Julia went on copying. "There" she said, handing the sheet over; "now you've only got to put the Madrid address, and hand it in. Where's the nearest post office at the *quinta?*"

"I'm not sure. Anyhow I think this had better go from Funchal; they might muddle it in a village office. D'you know, Julia, I think I'll go straight back now, and get the address, and run in with it—then it will go in good time."

"How are you off for petrol?" Julia asked.

"I filled up before I came out—anyhow I can get more in Funchal." She put the paper in her bag and got up. "I think I'll flash."

"Hold on a minute—if you're going to send that from Funchal you might as well take the other too" Julia said.

"What other?"

"To Luzia, giving the number for Colin to ring; I've no idea where the post office here is—if there is one! Just give me a minute." Again she bent her tawny-gold head over the pad and began to write and cross out, frowning a little. At length she read aloud—"Condesa Luzia Heriot Gralheira São Pedro do Sul. My dear cousin from Larège will shortly visit you stop please make him welcome and give him this number São Filipo da Serra 437 fondest love J. Probyn."

"Why Probyn?" Aglaia asked.

"My maiden name. Luzia always called me Miss Probyn when I was her governess—she still does sometimes, when I tick her off" Julia said, smiling, as she began to re-write the message in capitals.

"And will she know who you mean?"

"Yes indeed. She was with me at Larège when Colin was working that end of the Pyrenees before—she put him onto a red-hot clue at one point!" Julia replied, beginning to laugh a little. "There you are" she said, tearing off the sheet. "Oh bother—my purse is upstairs. I'll just get it."

"Don't bother—I've got heaps of money! I'd like to get off."

"Well, don't get too tired with all this dashing to and fro, Ag dear" Julia said, getting up and kissing the eager little face. "Bless you—drive carefully."

As she came back from seeing Aglaia off she encountered Mrs. Hathaway, accompained by Mme. Bonnecourt—the Frenchwoman was laden with *The Times,* two books, and a bag of knitting, which she disposed on a small table on the verandah beside Mrs. Hathaway's usual chair.

"Good morning, my dear" the old lady said. "I thought I heard a car drive off—has Pauline gone out?"

"No, it was Aglaia—she wanted to see me about something," Julia said. "She was sorry not to stay, but she was in a hurry."

"Nothing gone wrong, I hope?" Mrs. Hathaway asked.

"Oh no—this was a little private problem of hers; nothing serious" Julia said, for once almost regretting Mrs. H.'s habitual deep interest in everything that went on around her.

"Did she say how the poor little boy was?"

"No—he's in the clinic, you know, and I don't suppose she went there." Julia looked out over the garden. "Goodness, where *have* those children got to? I'd better go and see." She made her escape.

When Gerald Shergold returned in the evening Julia sat quietly by while his wife bombarded him with eager questions.

"Yes, I rang Terry before I left" he said. "He and Pereira had just got down. Pereira is completely puzzled—says he's never seen anything in the least like it. He's thoroughly worried, Terry says."

"Did he think the sheep will get over it?"

"Terry didn't say—I don't suppose Pereira aired any views on that, since he hasn't a clue as to what's wrong with them" Gerald said, with a cheerful grin. "But Terry said he's tremendously thorough; he insisted on going right to the far end, to satisfy himself that *all* the sheep were in the same state."

"And were they?"

"Yes, every helpless one of them!—all wheezing, and all tame and silly. I must say it is damned peculiar. However, Pereira took samples of their droppings, *and* of blood, so he may find out something from that, I suppose."

"How does one get a sample of a sheep's blood?" Pauline speculated. "You can't tie a finger and prick it, because sheep haven't got fingers!"

Gerald laughed. "No, they had rather a job over that. It seems you shave the animal's armpit, or what would be an armpit in us, and jab in a scalpel or something, and get the blood. Pereira had brought a razor and all the doings, Terry said."

"A good thing the sheep *are* so tame—when they're well you can't get near them" Pauline observed.

"No—and whatever their complaint is, it didn't make them relish being shaved! Terry said they kicked like anything."

"Poor creatures" Mrs. Hathaway said. "Did Mr. Armitage say how the little boy was?"

"No. Pereira was going to see de Carvalho when he gets back to Funchal; if they put their heads together I suppose they might come up with something, but I must say the whole thing is almighty queer."

Julia, listening to all this, again wondered whether she was doing right not to alert the Office in London as to what was going on. Of course it was Portugal's worry, not England's, this time, she told herself; but any form of Russian skulduggery was really a worry for the whole of the free world. The little she had seen of the workings of the Portuguese Security Police—at Gralheira, years before—had been efficient enough; but then Luzia and Nannie Brown had really handed the P.I.D.E. their principal victim on a plate, as one might say—in fact drugged into unconsciousness in a nursery armchair; all the detection and entrapping had been done by those two brilliant amateurs. And in a scientific matter London's resources, she imagined, must be greater than Lisbon's—wasn't there that place on Salisbury Plain where they investigated biological warfare, or whatever it was called? Or was it only the common cold? Julia was painfully vague about all branches of science, but she had a feeling that if it was a case of flying out exactly the right type of boffin, Major Hartley would probably do it faster than Colonel Marques. Rather uncomfortably, she nevertheless decided to allow Colin another forty-eight-hours' start.

As it turned out, she didn't have to give him so long. The very next day, as they were sitting at luncheon, the telephone rang; Pauline got up and went out into the hall to answer it. *"Sta? Sim, sim"* Julia and Mrs. Hathaway heard her say; there was a pause, and then she called out—"Julia, I think it's for you."

Julia hurried out into the hall.

"It's from Portugal, I think" Pauline said, holding out the receiver—"but the line isn't awfully good." Julia took the telephone from her—after a certain amount of buzzing, to her great relief she heard Luzia's voice: "Could I speak with Miss Probyn?"

"Yes, Luzia—here I am—Julia."

"Oh, excellent! He is here." And then Colin said "Darling?"

"Yes, I'm here. Can you hear me?"

"Yes, fairly well. Now can you give me rather more of an idea of what's in the wind?"

"Hold on a minute" Julia said. Pauline had left the dining-room door open, but she knew that there was an extension in Gerald's study; putting the receiver down on the table, she stepped softly across the hall and into the room, very gently closed the door after her, and took up the other telephone. "Now—can you still hear me?" she asked.

"Yes. Go ahead."

"Listen carefully, will you? I'm going to speak rather carefully."

"O.K."

"It's really in the message I've already sent you. I think you must come here at once, because you know more about this than anyone local. Can you come right away?"

"Not all that easily—I'm on a job, you know."

"Yes. Is your present job as important as your last? Because if not, I think you ought to come at once, darling darling."

There was silence at the other end of the line.

"Are you still there?" Julia asked.

"Yes—I'm thinking." A pause. "What I can't be sure of is if you are in a position to form a proper judgment on this—and *if* you are, *how*."

"Ah yes—and obviously I can't tell you. You'll just have to trust me. But listen—if you can't come right away, I shall let London know."

"As sure as that, are you?" She could hear the surprise in his tone.

"Yes. Only Ag wanted you to have the chance to come and clean this up."

"Good Lord, does Ag know? I say, do be careful! You really shouldn't have told her. It—it's—I mean, she doesn't understand this sort of thing very well."

"I didn't tell her. She found out herself, and told *me*. But look, darling darling, will you come?"

"Yes—yes, I think I must."

"How soon? The quicker the better or *les indigènes* may make a clanger, out of ignorance. So when can you get here? How did you get to Luzia's so fast, by the way?"

"Oh, the M.A. was coming this way anyhow, and I got him to take me on his plane and drop me off at the Red Stones. It's nearer than the other place, and I rang up Nick, and he came and fetched me. Look, I'd better ring off and find out about planes, and ring you when I know."

"Do that thing. I'll stay in for the call."

"And Julia, do you and Ag be careful about your*selves,* won't you? Promise?"

"Yes of course. But we're all right, darling. Good—ring as soon as you can. Bye."

On her way back to the dining-room Julia remembered to replace the receiver on the telephone in the hall, even while she was thinking rapidly what to say. Obviously she would have to mention that Colin was coming, since he would soon be in Madeira in the flesh; apart from that, she must play it off the cuff.

"I'm sorry about that" she said politely to Pauline as she re-seated herself. "It was Colin—he's coming over."

"Coming to Madeira?" Mrs. Hathaway asked in surprise. "I thought he was working in Spain."

"Yes he was, Mrs. H.—I suppose he's got some leave or some-thing" Julia said, with rather elaborate carelessness. The old lady took the hint instantly—"How very nice" she said, and nothing more. Pauline's curiosity was not so easily disposed of.

"When is he coming?" she asked.

"I don't know exactly—quite soon, I think."

"I wonder Ag didn't tell us—I suppose she knows?"

"I'm not sure" Julia said, still in that careless, near-drawling tone. "I rather think not."

"How funny of him to ring up you and not her," Pauline said.

"Not really, you know, Pauline" Mrs. Hathaway interposed, "if he wanted to talk about his work. Julia has helped him with that for years. Why, it was she who recovered all Aglaia's money for her, when it had been stolen from that bank in Switzerland."

"Did she really? I'd no idea. How on earth did you do it, Julia?"

"She tracked down the impersonators" Mrs. Hathaway an-swered for Julia, "and made friends with the poor little girl who had been made up to look like Aglaia; she was so silly that she gave the whole thing away. It was quite exciting—the police came to our hotel! *I* had Aglaia's whole fortune under my pillow for one night."

"Good Heavens!" Pauline's interest in this enthralling story temporarily swamped her curiosity about Colin's sudden arrival, and carried them safely through the meal.

After lunch Pauline suggested a walk up to the *levada;* Julia, with a heavy heart, excused herself on the grounds of having let-ters to write—now that the long one to her husband was no longer a daily pleasure she had, she felt, ample time for all the letters she cared to send, especially when she and Mrs. Hathaway were together. However, when Pauline had gone off, taking the twins, she sat in Gerald's study, by the telephone, and wrote to Edina Reeder, describing Aglaia's relations, and the *quinta,* and the Paúl da Serra; for good measure she put in Manoel's concern about the pigs being "crustato" and the unfortunate backwardness of the grapes—this would amuse the Spanish-speaking Philip Reeder, she knew.

When the telephone rang she lifted off the receiver instantly —there was some talking in Portuguese, asking for *"a menina Probeen"*, and then Colin's voice.

"Yes, it's me. Well?"

"I've managed to get on a flight tomorrow—I get to the airfield about six twenty-five. Can you meet me?"

"Yes, of course. Shall I let Ag know?"

"Well, don't let her be there at first" he said. "We must clear this up by ourselves."

"Yes, I meant that. But may I let her know that you are coming? She'll be so relieved."

"Well, if you must. But see that we have a good spell alone first. You fix it, darling darling—I'm sure you can."

7

JULIA HAD BECOME thoroughly accustomed, over the years, to being asked to "fix" something by her cousin Colin—or even to being suddenly faced with some situation of his creating, and left to fix it without even being asked; but as she sat in Gerald Shergold's study after Colin had rung off, she soon began to think that on this occasion fixing might be easier said than done. Six twenty-five was a most inconvenient time, too late for making shopping an excuse; and almost certainly Colin would have to spend the night in Funchal, if they were to have a reasonable amount of time together. And how was she to get down to meet him, just when Gerald would be coming home?—and where was he to stay? She cast round in her mind as to which, among all these near-strangers—after all, till a fortnight ago she had not seen even Pauline for seven years—would be most likely to help her without asking too many awkward questions, and unhesitatingly decided on Terence Armitage. He and she already shared one secret; she felt she could probably trust him to trust *her* over what was, after all, merely an extension of it. And after looking out the number of his firm in the telephone-book, she rang him up. When his voice came on the line, "Julia here," she said. "Are you in a room by yourself?"

"For the moment, yes."

"Good. Well look, I'm going to be most frightfully tiresome and mysterious, and I want you not to mind, and to help me all the same. Will you?"

She heard his low, slow laugh—a reassuring sound.

"I certainly shan't *mind,* and I'll help you in any way I can. What can I do for you?"

"Well, get me a car, in the first place. I shall want it up here, to drive myself about in."

"When?" was all he asked.

"Tomorrow, about lunch-time. Is there a car-hire place?"

"Not necessary, if the little Austin Aglaia borrowed yesterday would do. Can you drive an Austin?"

"Drive any make! How frightfully kind. But how shall I get it?"

"I'll send someone up with it—before lunch, or after?"

"Before, please. You *are* kind."

"A pleasure. Anything else?"

"Oh yes, lots more!" Again she heard that comforting laugh. "Now the mystery part begins" Julia pursued, more cheerfully —"And I'd like this kept quiet for about twenty-four hours. Colin's coming over."

"Oh, good. Ag will be pleased."

"Yes, but I don't want her to know—at least, I do, but not *when.* Do you think you can manage that?"

"Not if he comes to the *quinta.*" She could hear the chuckle in his voice, and began to gurgle with laughter a little herself.

"Well, I don't think he'll be able to get to the *quinta* tomorrow" she said; "the plane gets in so late. So I want two more things—somewhere where he and I can talk alone, as unnoticeably as may be; and somewhere for him to stay the night."

"Also unnoticeably?"

"That's less important—it would be preferable, of course, but I don't think it matters all that much."

"Can do!" Terence said. "I know exactly the place."

"Oh splendid! Where?"

"My aunt's house—the Quinta dos Arvores. She always goes to bed at seven, and doesn't show up again till eleven or twelve in the morning, so she need never see either of you. Anyhow she's over ninety, and getting a bit gaga."

"Is she the one who forgot that Aglaia had been to lunch?"

"Yes—Aunt Sally."

"She sounds ideal" Julia said, beginning to gurgle again. How helpful and *com*fortable dear Terence was being!

"Well, if you like to put it that way! Anyhow it's a most lovely place; I'm glad you'll see it. The trees are marvellous—some magnificent bombax, and a huge tulip-tree, nearly as big as the one Captain Cook planted in the Quinta do Val. I'll go round this evening and arrange it all with Porfirio; he's her butler, and nearly as old as she is, but not in the least gaga!—you'll get superb cocktails, and a smashing dinner."

"How perfect. You are *kind!*" Julia said again. "But how shall I find it?"

"I'll send a plan of the town up with the car; we've got plenty in the office—and I'll put a row of arrows in red ink to lead you to it."

"No, don't do that" Julia said, with an abrupt change of tone. "Put a ring round it in *pencil*—and send it in an envelope, sealed, if you don't mind."

"I don't mind anything—I keep telling you that! I'm getting a little curious, of course."

"Of course; and it's quite wonderful of you not to ask any questions! The very moment I can I'll put you in the picture— it's still only a sketch at present" she said, more lightly.

"Thank you. Anything else I can do, Moddom?"

"Yes. Put another pencil ring, quite faint, round the clinic."

"Oh, is that the idea?"

"It may be. How is the child, by the way?"

"Much the same. If you and your cousin could do anything to help there, it would be a mercy" he said, suddenly serious.

"I've no idea if he can. Does the doctor live over the shop?"

"Yes, as a rule. He's pretty booked up most of the time. Want his number?"

"Yes please."

He gave it. "And what do I say to Ag?"

"Ah yes—what do you? Oh, I think just tell her that I rang you up and asked you to tell her that C. *is* coming, quite soon, but that I don't know exactly when. Could you do that?"

"Yes—what is more, I don't mind!" he said, laughing again.

"Oh no, you needn't. It's my lie!" She paused. "I suppose Penelope can have him at the *quinta* later on?" she asked.

"Oh yes, she loves Colin. She mothers him!—she thinks he needs it."

"How right she is! Well, a million thanks, Terence." She hesitated a moment. "I think all this kindness of yours may ultimately prove to have been worth while" she ended.

"Isn't kindness always worth while?" he asked.

"Bless you, *yes!* Give Aglaia my love!" She rang off.

Well, that was all marvellous, she thought, lighting a cigarette. What a boon, a gift, Terence was!—why couldn't more people be like that? But though she had now secured a quiet meeting-place for herself and Colin, and harbourage for him for the night, she had still got to think up some excuse for her own absence tomorrow evening which would not excite Pauline Shergold's curiosity too much, and for this she decided to consult Mrs. Hathaway—who was, so blessedly, moulded from the same beneficent clay as Terence Armitage. She looked at her watch —four o'clock. By now the old lady would almost certainly have finished her nap; it would be better to see her in her room before she came down, when Pauline might be back, and about. She went upstairs and into the converted sitting-room; Mme. Bonnecourt was there, doing some embroidery. Julia asked if Madame still slept?

Mais non, Madame was awake, and having a *petite tisane.* Did Madame Jimmison wish to speak with Madame?

Julia said that she did, and a moment later was ushered into the room where Mrs. Hathaway lay on a large bed, a light shawl over her feet, sipping a small cup of some hot fluid.

"How nice to see you, my dear child. Would you like some *tisane?* This kind Madame Bonnecourt brews me a cup every afternoon—I find it easier to get up after a hot drink."

"What an excellent idea" Julia said, sitting down by the bed. "But I don't think I need it, thank you all the same—I'm up anyhow."

"*Pas pour Madame, merci bien*" Mrs. Hathaway said. Mme. Bonnecourt withdrew.

"Mrs. H., I want your advice" Julia began at once. "It's about Colin."

"Ah yes. I'm so glad he's coming; that will cheer Aglaia up. Did she send for him?"

"No, I did" Julia said. "You see, Mrs. H., I think he may really be able to be more useful here than doing that other job of his in Spain." She paused, wondering how to put what she had to say.

"Don't explain anything you don't want to" the old lady said at once. "If you think he ought to come here, that is quite enough for me. I expect it's enough for him too" she added smiling.

"Only *just*" Julia said, smiling too. "But the thing is, he wants to see me, and hear all about it, and perhaps make some plan, before he sees Aglaia."

"Naturally. After all, you've been working with him and his superiors for years—whereas I don't think that dear child understands much about it" Mrs. Hathaway said frankly.

"No—though she's sharper than one might think" Julia said loyally.

"So now you're wondering how to meet him quietly" the old lady went on.

"No, I've arranged all that with kind, *kind* Terence Armitage, or rather he's arranging it for me, *and* a place for Colin to spend tomorrow night—and he's sending up a car for me to use. It's how to explain my being away to Gerald and Pauline."

"I don't think you need worry much about Gerald" Mrs. Hathaway observed, with her usual candour. "Unless something is spread right out in front of him, with a magnifying glass, he leaves it alone! Pauline is rather different."

"And how!" Julia said, with a fervour which made her old friend laugh. "When does he come?" she asked then.

"Tomorrow evening—I get the car at lunch-time, and I want to go down to Funchal in the afternoon, and see to one or two things; but I don't know what to say to Pauline."

"I think you'd better let me tell her" Mrs. Hathaway said; "then I can make sure that she doesn't pester you with questions."

"That would be marvellous—though I can't think how" Julia said.

"I shall manage" the old lady said calmly. "Shall you be able to see the poor little boy?"

"I hope so—it's one of the things I want to do." She hesitated a moment. "You see, Mrs. H., I'm only guessing, and of course this is *quite* secret, but I think it's just possible that Colin may have some idea of the kind of thing that made the child ill, which might help the doctor to treat him." She paused again. "I don't know. I only saw Colin once in London, and—and the whole thing made him so wretched that we hardly talked about it at all. But it could be that Colin knows much more than anyone else."

"Of course, my dearest child." The old lady reached out and pressed Julia's hand. And later that afternoon, downstairs, she took her young hostess aside and told her that Julia was going down to Funchal next day to meet her cousin and spend the evening with him—"and of course they want to be alone. He was on that expedition when her husband was killed, and she has hardly seen him since. It will be very painful for her, and naturally she doesn't want to talk about it."

"No, of course. But how will she get down?—and get back? We're dining with the Frasers at the Golf Club, too; we can't very well lend the car. Oh dear—how awkward."

"She has got a car, Pauline" Mrs. Hathaway said repressively. "Just give her a latch-key, and *assume* everything. There is no need to discuss it."

When the car arrived next day Julia put the sealed envelope in her bag, unexamined; she yielded at once to Pauline's suggestion that she should have "a bite to eat" before she set out—her driver of course was fed in the kitchen. She drove down herself, to get accustomed to the car, dropped the man off at the Shipping Office with a tip, and then drove on to Reid's Hotel, which Pauline had pointed out to her on their way down to the *quinta*. To drive up to an hotel and order something to drink is one of the least noticeable of human actions; Julia left her car, sat down at a table on the terrace, and ordered an orange squash;

over this she studied the plan of the town. She worked out the route to Terence's faint circle with the initials "A. S." pencilled discreetly beside it. Precious Terence!—she had been wondering how she would know which circle indicated the clinic and which Aunt Sally's house.

This settled, she lit a cigarette and sat sipping her orange, and thinking about Colin. In a way this meeting, which she had so determinedly organised, was something she shrank from, now that it was close ahead of her, only two or three hours away. Their one or two encounters in London, on his return from Asia, had been torture to them both, brief and inexplicit; her own misery over the loss of her husband had combined with his distress to muffle their usual ease of communication. At the time she had even felt slightly resentful towards him. Surely he could have understood her overwhelming need to be told every possible detail, without her having to make the effort of asking questions?—and when she did ask them, to be met with stalling, with halting inadequate replies, and such evidence of his own unhappiness as practically to shut her up. Now, after that first painful talk with Aglaia, she understood at least partly what lay behind all that—not only the normal "security" caginess, which she had so much resented as between him and her, after their years of working together, but also his sense of failure; personal failure, however irrational the idea, towards her; official failure towards the Service, about which Aglaia had been so positive on her dash up to the Serra three days ago. Somehow, now, all this had got to be smoothed out and made easy for him—for them both.

Oh well—now to find her way to both places, so as to lose no time later on. She went first to the Quinta dos Arvores. Julia had already been startled by the steepness of Funchal's roads when Pauline first drove her up from the steamer, and Aunt Sally's house stood in a particularly steep one, with a most awkward entrance if approached from below; Julia did not drive in, but went on up the hill, and made a note of the name of the road above—good, with Colin she would drive down from the top. On a level space, when at last she found one, she pulled up, looked at the plan again, and then drove on to Dr. de Carvalho's clinic. This was in a lower part of the town, and the entrance presented no obstacles; moreover there was plenty of room to park. Julia left the car and went in. It was like any other clinic, bare and functional; she gave her name to a secretary at a desk, and asked if it would be possible to make an appointment with the doctor? The girl began to turn the pages of a diary for a fortnight ahead—"*Não não*" Julia said, slowly but firmly—"*Por favor, por esta tarda.*" There ensued a good deal of argument, and some consultation with a man, evidently a senior secretary: Julia mentioned that she was a friend of the Senhor Armitage, and at last she was given an appointment for twenty minutes past seven. This didn't allow much time—she must only hope that Colin's plane would be punctual.

Her appointment secured, she asked if it would be possible to see the little boy whom the doctor had brought back with him on Monday from the *quinta* of the Senhor Armitage? After some telephoning she was led upstairs, where a grey-haired nurse with a kind, intelligent face met her on the landing. No, no one was allowed to see the child; he was being kept in strict isolation. Was the pain any better, and the cough?—Julia asked earnestly. No, there was no improvement, the woman said; she looked worried and distressed. Was it the Senhora Armitage who was enquiring? No, only a friend, Julia said; but she had seen the child herself, down at the *quinta,* and was anxious on his account. "It seems strange that there is no remedy for the pain," she added.

"Ah, *Minha Senhora,* this whole malady is exceedingly strange," the nurse said, sad and puzzled. "But the Senhor Doutor has sent specimens to France and hopes to learn something from the results."

This brief interview somehow served to reinforce Julia's nascent determination to force Colin out of his normal caution and urge that if he had any knowledge, or even theory, that might help the doctor to cure Marcusinho, he must mention it at once. The Russians had got to be foiled, of course, whatever mischief they were up to, and the sheep relieved if possible, God help them; but here was a child, ill and in pain—there must be no stalling on Colin's part. Downstairs, she asked the secretary if she might telephone to the Senhor Armitage, and got Terence at the office.

"Oh good—I was afraid you might have left. Could you give Porfirio a message? You didn't give me that number. It's just to say that we may not get there till rather late—perhaps not till eight, or even later; I don't know for certain. Will that be all right?"

"I'm sure it will. I'll tell him. All going well?"

"So far. Thank you very much." She rang off.

Early as it still was, she drove out at once to the airport—along the road to São Gonçalo, over rising ground, and down to the coast again at Porto Novo; a few kilometres further on, beyond Santa Cruz, lay the new airport, built practically into the sea. Julia wanted to park in a position where she could not be boxed in by other cars, and in this, after some cajoling and a large tip to the attendant, she was successful. Then she sat and drank coffee in the lounge, and waited, and went on thinking about Colin. To spare his feelings she had given a lot of thought to what dress she should put on, at this first meeting on more or less neutral ground. At Gralheira, out of deference to Portuguese susceptibilities, she had of course had to wear mourning, but since it was summer she had supplied herself with a few half-mourning dresses: either white, or grey voiles with a black hair-line check; and, in particular, a sleeveless frock of dark charcoal-grey linen, which with a white belt and shoes hardly looked like mourning at all. This she had put on that morning, as the least likely to arouse his sensitive feelings on her account.

The plane was five minutes late. Julia had noted the time it took her to drive from the clinic to the airport—half an hour; if the Customs and Immigration people weren't *too* slow, they would just do it nicely. In fact the Maderense officials are not usually excessively troublesome about passengers on planes from Metropolitan Portugal, and they were not on this occasion; by a quarter to seven Colin's white face and black head appeared among the small crowd emerging from the Customs building; he was carrying a suitcase and a rather distended briefcase. He gave her a warm hug—"Got a car?"

"Yes, over here. Come on—we're a little late."

"Everything fixed up for this evening?"

"Yes—and tonight. You're staying with Terence's old Aunt Sally, and we're dining there."

"I say, I don't think that's a very good plan" Colin said, coming to a halt.

"Oh, I'm sure it's all right" Julia said reassuringly, tucking her arm in his and leading him gently forward. "The old lady will be in bed by the time we get there, and Porfirio won't let on. She's nearly gaga anyhow" she added, sliding into the driving seat.

He threw the suitcase into the back. "Isn't this Terence's car?" he asked, as they drove off.

"Yes, he lent it to me."

"I say, what have you told Terence?" he asked.

"Oh, dearest, only what he knows already. And Aglaia knows that you're coming, so she won't be fretting, only not *when*—I told Terence to tell her I'd said I didn't know for sure."

"You and Terence seem to be pretty thick already" he remarked, but now more cheerfully.

"Oh yes, we are! You see we've found out rather a lot together, that the others don't know about, except Aglaia—I had to let her know. Shall I begin from the beginning?"

"Yes, do, darling. I'm completely in the dark, so far."

Encouraged by his use of the word "darling", Julia told him briefly about the discovery of the sheep and their strange symptoms, then of the unidentified tourists who smoked *brown* cigarettes, and how their nocturnal visit to the plateau coincided with time of the Russian trawler's presence; then how the child had gone up, the onset of his illness, and how it had completely defeated Dr. de Carvalho—Colin listened intently.

"All that part about the sheep and the little boy, and the tourists, is common knowledge—to the Shergolds and Penelope, and the doctor and the vet" she went on, "so there's no secret about any of that. But only Terence and I know about the cigarettes and the trawler—and Aglaia. And why I sent for you is because of something Aglaia overheard the doctor say"—and she repeated his words to Dr. Fonseca about the factory in France, and the workmen there who were so careless about wearing their respirators, and then had symptoms rather similar to those of the child. "Naturally when I heard that, I thought it probably tied in with—well, with what happened to Philip" she ended, in a low voice.

"Oh darling!" the young man said, in a tone of unutterable sadness. Back in the town, as she swung the car sharply to the right—"Here, you're going wrong!" he exclaimed. "This isn't the way to Aunt Sally's."

"No, we're going somewhere else first."

"Where on earth?"

"To Dr. de Carvalho's clinic. That's where the child is. Before we do anything else, I felt sure you'd want to see De Carvalho, in case you might be able to give him some clue that would save it's life."

"That's a bit awkward" he said, uncomfortably. "Anyhow, if your guess is right, the child won't die anyhow."

"Won't?"

"No."

"How extraordinary! Well, anyhow he's in shocking pain, that nothing seems to touch—if you could help over that it would be such a mercy."

"It's frightfully awkward" Colin repeated.

"Well, I'm sure you'll manage somehow" she said with a cheerful certainty that she was not really feeling.

At the clinic they were shown into an obvious consulting-room; there was a couch, a desk with writing pads and huge books of reference, and a cabinet of instruments, one drawer of which was open. The elderly male secretary whom Julia had seen earlier explained that the Senhor Doutor was detained upstairs, but would they please be seated; he would be with them in a few minutes. For a moment or two Colin sat in silence, frowning a little; at last—

"Where are you staying tonight?" he asked.

"Oh, when we've talked all we want to I shall drive back to the Serra."

Colin opened his briefcase, which he had brought in with him, and took out a small white cardboard box with a Lisbon chemist's label, which he put on the corner of the desk.

"Well anyhow, you might as well have one of these now," he said. "I got them put up in Lisbon as I came through, for you and Ag and anyone else who might be exposed to this stuff—if it really is the same sort of thing." As he spoke he opened the box, slitting the paper round the lid with his thumb-nail; inside, each in a separate compartment, lay half a dozen syrettes, such as the R.A.F. were supplied with, containing morphia, in the last war —small disposable syringes, which can be used instantly and thrown away. Only each of these was labelled, not morphine, but atropine. Julia peered at them curiously.

"Atropine!" she said. "That's stuff for one's eyes, isn't it?"

"*Bonsoir! Je regrette de faire attendre Madame*" Dr. de Carvalho exclaimed, hurrying in; he checked at the sight of Colin. Julia introduced him—"My cousin, Monsieur Monro —the husband of the *cousine-germaine* of Monsieur Armitage."

Dr. de Carvalho was youngish, short and unusually thin for a Portuguese, with a sharp nose and chin, and an abrupt manner. He bowed rather perfunctorily to Colin, and turned to Julia. "Now, in what way can I be of service to Madame?" he asked, seating himself at his desk and waving his visitors to two chairs. Then he caught sight of the box of syrettes still lying open on the desk.

"What is this?" he exclaimed.

"Oh, pardon—it is just something I was about to give to Madame" Colin said, and made to retrieve the box. The doctor put his hand over it.

"*Momentinho!*" he said, in his excitement dropping into his native tongue; as he spoke he took up the box, examined it, and saw the label of the Lisbon chemist; peering intently at the small glass tubes he saw on each one a date in microscopic figures. "*Hoje!*" (Today) he exclaimed. "And now" he said, returning to French and speaking very gravely, "will Monsieur kindly explain why he had syrettes of atropine prepared *today* to bring to Madame, here, in Madeira?"

Colin looked desperately at Julia.

"Monsieur le Docteur, I think my cousin had them prepared as a precautionary measure" Julia said, in her slowest tones.

"Ah! And as a precaution against what, may one ask?" The little man flashed the question out.

"That, he has not had time as yet to explain to me" Julia replied, still slowly and calmly—though she was in fact stalling as desperately as Colin. It was clear that atropine had some particular significance for the doctor which was completely hidden from her; obviously this was also known to Colin, or he wouldn't have brought it. "Monsieur has only just arrived on the plane" she added, rather idiotically.

"Then how can Monsieur know that this remedy might be useful here?" the doctor asked impatiently. Then suddenly he smiled broadly, with a flash of white and gold-crowned teeth.

"Since Monsieur has brought this here, into my clinic, will he and Madame allow me to borrow one syrette? I should like to try it on a patient." He looked extraordinarily pleased with himself all of a sudden.

"If Monsieur le docteur wishes to use it for the little boy from the *quinta* of Monsieur Armitage, by all means" Julia said, smiling too.

"Ah, Madame knows more than she admits! *Excusez-moi.*" Taking a syrette from the box, he hurried out of the room.

"Well, that's torn it!" Colin said.

"Oh no—rather the opposite, I should have thought. He's just guessed for himself, and saved you the trouble of telling him anything. You've barely opened your mouth since you came into the room!" Julia said cheerfully. "Anyhow hadn't you better tell *me,* now, exactly what the atropine is for? When he comes back he's going to ask a whole lot of questions, and I might put my foot in it. What *is* behind all this? What were you looking for in Asia?"

"Well, we knew, more or less, that the Russians were developing a new type of nerve gas in Central Asia, and we were sent to try and get hold of some of the stuff; because if you know exactly what it is, you stand a better chance of developing an antidote."

"Oh, I *see*" Julia said, on a long breath. Then, in a voice as normal as she could make it—"Why did they want a new one? I thought there were a lot already invented."

"This was supposed to have special properties, for a special purpose" Colin said rather reluctantly.

"Oh. What special purpose?"

"For the invasion of Britain, actually; we did get onto that, from one of these scientific defectors, who came over to us, for a change. They've decided—quite sensibly, really—that the atom bomb is almost useless, because it destroys not only a hostile population, but the whole terrain as well; no form of life can carry on afterwards for ages. Conventional warfare is much better, because you only kill chaps; you leave the countryside and its potential, and even the factories and so on, more or less unharmed, with any luck."

"Go on" Julia said sombrely.

"Well, if you had a nerve gas that was ultimately non-lethal, but would completely incapacitate at least the armed forces, and perhaps the civilian population too, for three or four weeks, of course you could take over a country lock, stock and barrel, with the minimum of loss of life, and no material damage. By the time the people came to, you would be controlling everything. That was the idea, according to this defector type."

"It is very odd how it always seems to be scientists who defect" Julia said thoughtfully. "Fuchs and Pontecorvo going over to them, and now this one coming to us." She was trying to keep the conversation on a strictly practical note.

"I wouldn't know about that," Colin said. "Anyhow, that was what we were looking for, and why we were supposed to wear respirators when we were getting pretty warm. Well, we didn't get a sample—you know why" he added sadly. "But what I don't understand is why the Russians should be trying it out here, on sheep; and still less why this doctor man should want to use *my* atropine. It's stuff doctors always have by them."

"Why did you bring it for me and Aglaia? Is it an antidote?"

"Oh yes, I didn't tell you that. It is a complete antidote to most of the known forms of nerve gas, so of course we were all fitted out with these syrettes for the trip. And on what you told me on the telephone, I thought we might conceivably be the better of them here. But I still don't see why he's taken one of mine. As I say, he must have had plenty of it by him all the time."

"Mightn't he have been suspicious—faintly—about nerve gas all along, in view of what he said about the *ouvriers* in France getting similar symptoms from failing to wear their respirators? And when you suddenly turn up from the mainland with a whole box of the antidote, put up *today,* the penny drops. How quickly does it work, by the way."

"Quite fast, we were told—of course we never tried it out," Colin said hurriedly, his thumb beginning to jerk. "But look, Julia, supposing you're right, and he has guessed, what are we going to *do?* Even if it's only a guess, he's sure to feel bound to alert the authorities here."

"I don't see that there's an awful lot we can do" Julia said, frowning a little. "If the atropine relieves the child's symptoms, and the doctor really does know about nerve gases, he'll know what's the matter with the sheep, as well as with Marcusinho."

"But he'll want to know how *I* know, and who I am" Colin said wretchedly.

"Yes, it's a bit tricky. Let me think. And do stop your thumb!" she added, with an unwonted burst of impatience.

Colin sat in silence, holding one hand over the other, while she considered.

"Look" she said at last. "I think the only thing we can do is to try to strike some sort of bargain with him. The important thing now is to let the Office know as fast as possible, so that they can send an expert out from that place on Salisbury Plain; presumably he would be able to tell from the sheep's blood, or something, what the new features of this gas are. Or try to pounce on the trawler—at the Office they'll have their own ideas! And if de Carvalho would agree to keep quiet for a day or two, you could come clean to him and tell him all you know, and why you know it. He *might* agree—and then you would get all the credit in London, which is what Ag wants," she ended.

"I don't like it" said Colin glumly. "Anyhow, I don't deserve the credit—you and Ag have done all the putting two and two together."

"Well, what do you suggest?" Julia asked flatly.

"Nothing. I'm utterly stumped."

"Don't you agree that the Office ought to be told, at least?"

"Yes, of course. How do we set about informing them?"

"Who handled the Asia thing? Major Hartley?"

"Yes, it was, as a matter of fact."

"Oh good."

"Why?"

"Because he's so quick at the uptake on the telephone. Don't you remember how sharp he was about Bonnecourt when you were in Pau? Some people seem to lose the use of their wits when they get a receiver in their hand" Julia said. "Well, if we can come to some sort of an understanding with the doctor, we can ring Major Hartley up from Aunt Sally's." She looked at her watch. "It's after eight—I wish he'd hurry up. I'm getting hungry."

8 WHEN DR. DE CARVALHO came back into the consulting-room a few minutes later there was an indefinable change in his manner.

"Yes" he said in reply to Julia's enquiry, "he is better; there is a marked degree of relief already, I am thankful to say. I think this was not wholly unexpected by Madame," he added, but now unsmiling. Then he turned to Colin. "Monsieur will pardon me, but would he repeat his name? I am afraid I was not attending properly when Madame introduced us."

"Monro—Colin Monro" Colin said.

"Merci." Now the doctor looked Colin straight in the eye; he spoke with a new authority. "Monsieur is not, I think, himself a medical man; but should I be wrong in assuming that he has other, professional qualifications?" There was a certain stress on the word "professional". "If I am right" de Carvalho went on, "it would not of course be so surprising that Monsieur should visit Madeira just now, since he has connections here."

Colin barely hesitated—it was obvious that in his absence from the room the doctor had learned, or guessed, enough to make further concealment impossible. But he began with his usual caution.

"Monsieur le Docteur will of course comprehend that as regards my own status, I cannot enlarge on that. But it is the fact that the authorities in my own country, medical and otherwise, have been a good deal disturbed by recent reports of unexplained nervous affections. And when Madame my cousin informed me of these events here, it seemed to me to be my duty to come and verify the facts, in case they should have any connection with—*enfin,* with previous occurrences known to us."

The doctor nodded.

"I see we are beginning to understand one another" he said, in a satisfied tone. "I should be infinitely obliged if Monsieur could help me by throwing any light on those occurrences, out of his previous knowledge, which seems almost certainly to be greater than mine." He sat down at his desk, opened a box of cheroots, took one, and held the box out to Colin; he was evidently all set for a long, fruitful discussion. Julia, in desperation, intervened.

"Does Monsieur le Docteur never eat?" she asked. "I am famished, I!" She looked at him with beautiful, lamentable eyes. "We were about to go and dine—could we not persuade you to join us? Then we could talk at leisure."

De Carvalho gave a brief laugh.

"*Cette pauvre Madame!*" he said. "We must not starve her. Where were you proposing to dine?"

"Quite close by—at the house of an old aunt of Monsieur Armitage. But she will already be in bed" Julia added hastily.

"Ah, *la vieille Tante* Sally, at the Quinta dos Arvores! I know her. Yes, Madame—this would be a pleasure. If I may be excused for a few moments to arrange matters here, I shall be delighted to join you." He got up and left the room.

"That's going to be all right, I think" Julia said.

"Yes—for some reason I think he means to play, and that he's trustworthy" Colin said. "All the same, I wish we could check with the Office—they might know something about him, if he really was in on the gas racket in France."

"Why should he have been?" Julia asked, startled.

"I thought you said Ag overheard him talking about workmen at a French factory getting gassed."

"Fumes was all she said to me. I don't know what the factory was. Anyhow we can ask Hartley when we ring up."

"Ah, but that will be just too late—I'd sooner have known before we have this chat." He looked about him, and noticed for the first time that there was no telephone in the room. "That's funny—no telephone" he said.

"No, and we shouldn't have time here. I tell you what—when we get to the old lady's I'll say I must go and powder my nose, and try to get the Office then. If you don't mind leaving it to me," she added.

"Of course not—Hartley and Torrens both know you—in fact they all know *about* you" Colin said—and then bit his lip. "Yes, you'd better try that. How shall you let me know?"

"If they know anything *for* him, I shall nod as I sit down; if against, I shall just faintly shake my head."

"And if they know nothing?—which is more than likely?"

"I shall just sit down" Julia said—causing her cousin to laugh.

When the doctor came back they drove to the Quinta dos Arvores. It was now getting dark, and the street lamps were lit; but Julia remembered her way by the upper road, and went down on that awkward entrance from above; as they turned in at the gate she switched off her engine, and the car glided silently to a halt on the small nut-sized cobbles of the drive. The house was brightly lit, and as they drew up a small wizened figure in very smart livery—striped waist-coat, silver buttons—appeared at the open front door. Julia began to explain that they had brought an extra guest, but the little old man greeted the doctor with evident pleasure, and led them through a room which was a pure Victorian period piece, out onto a verandah festooned with bougainvillea, where a tray of drinks stood among wicker garden-chairs heaped with cushions and small tables with rose-shaded lamps; where the light caught a spray of bougainvillea here and there, the flowers were almost luminous against the shadowy darkness of the tulip-tree, a shapely mass of shapely leaves beyond a small lawn.

"Oh, what a lovely place!" Julia said. Old Porfirio held out a chair for her, but she asked to be taken to wash her hands first; with a bow he begged the Senhores to serve themselves with *as bebidas,* and led her away. Colin asked de Carvalho what he would like?—"There seems to be plenty of everything," he remarked, glancing at the huge and well-stocked tray.

"Let us see what the old one has in the cocktail-shaker" de Carvalho said. "If it is one of his champagne cocktails, they are not to be missed." He poured out, sipped, and nodded. "Yes—do try it."

Colin also poured himself out a glass. "Marvellous" he said, and sat down. But Colin had a use of his own to which he wished to put Julia's absence.

"Before we begin to talk, there is something I think Monsieur le Docteur should know about Madame" he began.

"Please tell me, since we have the opportunity" de Carvalho said politely.

"Madame is recently widowed" Colin said. "Her husband was a colleague of mine." He paused—the doctor nodded; a certain intensity appeared in his expression. *"Continuez"* he said.

"It was on an expedition connected with our researches into the cause of these nervous affections, of which I spoke before" Colin pursued, choosing his words carefully. "He—was affected, and in the event he was shot."

"Having of course temporarily lost the normal use of his faculties" the doctor said at once, nodding again. "But were you not supplied with respirators?"

"Yes, of course—and why he went out without his that day we shall never know. But the result was fatal."

"What a disaster!" De Carvalho said sombrely. "He was shot by *les indigènes?*—or by guards?"

"That also we do not know—he walked into some sort of ambush. We went out in strength, and recovered his body; whoever his assailants were, they made off. But the point is, I am not sure that Madame herself knows the *preliminary* cause of his death. I—we—we have not discussed it; until today I have hardly seen her since my return. She *may* have been told exactly what happened, by his superiors; from something she said just now at the clinic I suspect that she does know. But you see that the whole subject must be a painful one, to her."

"Evidemment. I am infinitely obliged to you for telling me this" de Carvalho said. He sat silent for a moment drumming with his fingers on a small bamboo table beside him. "Could we not talk about all this without Madame?" he asked. "No—I see that would not be so easy to arrange."

"No—and in fact she knows much more of the circumstances here, in Madeira, than I do. It was her discoveries and deductions which caused her to send for me" Colin said. "No"—he went on, "she will want to help you in any way that she can; she has great courage. But I wished you to be *au fait* with these circumstances."

"I am infinitely grateful to you" the doctor repeated.

Meanwhile Julia had run into an unexpected snag over her call to the Office. Out in the hall she asked Porfirio if she could first use the telephone? He led her to a very old-fashioned sort of box near the front door, and then asked, politely, if he could not get *o numero* for the Senhora? Julia was rather relieved—it was a personal call she wanted, she said, and to Londres. Porfirio's wizened face took on an expression of dismay. For Londres, he said, it would require at least uma hora to get a connection— "And then the Senhores will be at table, and the dinner will be interrupted! Already the *cozinheira* is troubled because of the delay to the repast."

Julia gently expressed her regret that they were so late, even while she was thinking what to do. She decided that she had better put the call in; the sooner they contacted the Office the better, though any information it might have about the doctor would probably come too late to be of much use in their conversation with him. She gave the number, and spelt out the name of the *Senhor Chefe* to the old man, asking him to make the call *muito urgente;* he wrote it all down on the pad in the box. While he was putting the call in she went and washed her hands at a downstairs lavatory, ran a comb through her golden tawny hair, and put a little powder on her face; then, still escorted by Porfirio, she went out onto the terrace again. Both men rose; Colin shifted his position a little as Porfirio drew forward a chair, so that he had a clear view of her; she sat down without making any movement of her head, and asked "What are you drinking?"

"The most wonderful champagne cocktail you ever tasted" Colin said cheerfully, in English. "We've saved some for you— rather reluctantly!" As he poured her out a glass—"Have plenty more" the old servant said in Portuguese; he took the empty shaker and hurried away.

"*Donc,* he understands English, does he?" Julia asked de Carvalho.

"A little. The old Madame Armitage usually speaks with him in French."

"*Tiens!* In that case we must have our conversation without him" Colin muttered.

"Then do let us have dinner first" Julia said, drinking her cocktail. "Yes, this is absolutely delicious, Colin." And when the ancient manservant returned she praised it warmly, but refused a second glass. "We wish to *jantar* now; it is late."

The dining-room was every bit as much in period as the drawing-room; the food, in spite of the delay, as delicious as Terence Armitage had predicted. But Julia was chiefly struck, during the meal, by the total absence of constraint between her two companions; on the contrary there was now a sense of ease, almost of mutual pleasure, in their conversation. De Carvalho talked well; he was interesting about Madeira's past, and amusing about its present—the sort of people who now came there, in contrast to the established families. He told wartime stories of the Americans in the Azores, and how amused the locals had been when the Germans, for the use of their distended Consulate-General during hostilities, had rented a large house called the Quinta Colonna! Julia was really happy, and enjoyed her meal; but her enjoyment was not only due to the perfect food, and the uncovenanted boon of all discussions being perforce postponed while Porfirio was waiting on them—she watched with increasing pleasure Colin's naturalness and composure, in circumstances where formerly he might well have shown nervousness.

Towards the end of dinner a faint distant tinkling came from the direction of the hall—Porfirio hurried out. When he returned—"The call of the Senhora to Londres" he announced.

Julia got up, and with a murmured excuse followed the old man into the hall. A moment or so later she put her head in at the dining-room door again—"Colin, could you come a minute?" When he went out and joined her—"I think you'll have to do the talking" she said. "Hartley isn't there, and the man on duty doesn't seem to want to get him."

"All right—I'll see to it. You go back to the nice doctor.

Where's the telephone?" She showed him the box; he went into it and shut the door.

"Monro here" he said abruptly.

"Monro? I thought they said the call came from Funchal," a surprised voice said.

"It does. Is that Daly? Look, I've got to speak to Hartley—*now*. Hold onto this line like grim death, and then get him and have us connected; put the operators onto it. Where is he? You must have his number."

"Yes, of course; he's at home. Only I didn't quite. . . ."

"Well, do now, *quite*" Colin interrupted him; "and do it fast. I'll hold on." And a few moments later he heard Major Hartley's familiar voice saying "Colin? Can it be you, where they say you are?"

"Yes; I fixed it up with Madrid before I came. Julia sent for me."

"Julia? You don't mean Philip's widow?"

"Yes. Look, this may be quite important; someone ought to come out at once. She thinks—and I'm inclined to agree with her—that she's stumbled here onto what we didn't find on Philip's last job."

"You don't say so!" The Major sounded genuinely startled. "The last thing I should have expected of our oldest ally!" he said.

"Oh, it's not them. They don't know about it yet. That's why there's the hurry; it would probably produce results much faster if we could start our own investigations before the local authorities get onto it, with their red tape."

"What is involved—if you can reasonably safely give me an idea?"

"A lot of animals; one human being—who is already reacting to the antidote."

"Did *you* give it him?"

"No—one of the local doctors."

"And you say the authorities know nothing yet?"

"Only about the epidemic, which is what they think it is—which stumps them completely."

"Then how on earth did poor Philip's wife—no, don't try to explain. She always was a wonder-girl!"

"Yes. In fact she spotted a boat of the same nationality as the inventors, and made the tie-in herself. No one else has bothered about the boat till now."

"But did she know about her husband?—that side, I mean? We didn't tell her. Did you?"

"No." Colin swallowed a little; he didn't want to give Aglaia away if he could help it. "But she *was* told—very fortunately."

There was a slight pause. Colin waited rather anxiously. But he knew the Major took his time on the telephone if he was thinking something over, and didn't interrupt him. At last "And this doctor man—what does he know, if he used the antidote?"

"That was a clanger of mine. I brought some over to the girls, and stupidly let him see it. I think he's probably guessed. I wanted to ask if you knew anything about him; we're with him now, as a matter of fact, and I'm inclined to think he'll play. But it would be useful to have anything you knew. He spent some time in France. Shall I give you his name?"

"You'll have to, I'm afraid. I haven't got the files by me, of course—I'm at home."

"De Carvalho" Colin said, with the usual reluctance of any Intelligence man to pronounce a name. Again there was silence from the Major's end of the line for a few moments.

"Yes, I think I remember the name" Major Hartley said at length. "There certainly was a Portuguese medico working at some point at the place where the French tinker away at this sort of thing. Thin fellow, is he?"

"Yes, noticeably so."

"Then I expect that's the chap. If so he was pretty smart. I'll ring Paris tonight—old Jean will know all about him. If it's the bloke I'm thinking of I should imagine he's quite reliable; I gathered the French employed him as being less likely to leak than one of their own compatriots. Do you think you can persuade him to put his professional conscience into neutral while we get going?"

"Yes, I'm beginning to think so. And can you send someone out?"

"Yes, I'll get onto that right away, and lay on a plane. I think old Mossy is probably the best person—he's senior enough to stand up to pretty well anyone."

"Is that his only name?" Colin asked. He heard the Major laugh.

"No—a recondite botanical joke. His name is the same as the Travellers' and the United Services, only with two B's!"

"Oh!" Colin was rather startled. Sir Percy Clubb was indeed senior, and an academic of great distinction.

"Yes, I'm sure he's the best person. And he likes a jaunt. I'll let you know when to expect him—sometime tomorrow, I imagine. Where can I get you?"

"Well, till ten thirty A.M. tomorrow, here—hold on, I must look out the number." In the dimness of the box he could not read it—he flicked his cigarette-lighter, peered at the dial, and gave the number.

"And after ten thirty?" Hartley asked.

"I simply don't know—I'm staying in a private house to-night, unbeknownst to the owner!" Colin said, with a small giggle.

"Can't the owner be persuaded to let you stay on?"

"I shouldn't think so—she's over ninety and slightly dotty! I'm sorry, but I only got in at six thirty this evening, and Julia had all this laid on."

"Well, get her to lay on something for Mossy—I should think he'd be with you by lunch-time—and for yourself too; I'm sure she can manage anything."

"All right to go to an hotel?"

"At a pinch, of course; a private house is always more convenient. See what you can do, and let me know tomorrow when I ring up. I'll ring our people in Lisbon and get them to arrange everything for the plane, so there's no trouble with the authorities about landing and so on. 'Night." The Major rang off.

Colin went back to the dining-room in a slightly worried frame of mind. A grandfather-clock in the hall rang a firm chime for a quarter to ten as he passed it. How, in little over twelve hours, Julia was to lay on hospitality for Sir Percy he didn't quite see. However, the first thing was to deal with de Carvalho.

The doctor and Julia were just finishing second helpings of *melon rafraîchie,* cubes of the pale-green flesh steeping in sugar and champagne in the darker-green bowl formed by the melon itself; Colin refused any, and asked for coffee, which was served almost at once on the verandah. As he sat down Julia watched him as he had watched her earlier; in seating himself he bent his whole body forward, and she could not be sure if he meant this as a nod or not. Porfirio hovered about offering brandy and liqueurs; de Carvalho, with friendly brusqueness, told him that they would serve themselves—"If we want anything, we will call you." When the old man had gone—"Does Madame wish to speak alone with her cousin about the results of the *coup de fil* to London?" he asked, with an amused and rather sly glance at her.

Colin answered.

"No, we wish to tell you of them" he said, without a moment's hesitation. "And we shall hope for your co-operation."

The Portuguese looked a little surprised. *"A la bonne heure!"* he said. "Of course I should wish to assist if it is in my power."

"I spoke with my superiors in London" Colin said. "They wish to send someone out here, at once, who is an expert in these matters."

"Someone from Porton? But this would be marvellous!" de Carvalho said, with such animation that Julia gave her slow warm laugh; the doctor looked at her now with pleasure.

"Yes" Colin said. "But it would be preferable if, at least at first, he could conduct his investigations with the maximum of privacy. Would you feel able to help over this?—for a short period?"

De Carvalho gave a brief laugh. "You mean, would I refrain from informing the authorities, here and in Lisbon, that quantities of sheep, and at least one human being, have been subjected to some form of nerve gas?"

Colin nodded.

"Yes, I think I could do that, for a short period, subject to one condition. You see, Monro, I am not a government employee at present; I have a private practice, and conduct my own clinic. But I must ask you one question first—is this gas ultimately lethal, unless treated with an antidote?"

"So far as our information goes, no; the effect is only supposed to last for three or four weeks."

"*Ah, c'est mieux, ça.* And how soon may we expect this expert to arrive?"

"Tomorrow—about lunch-time with any luck" Colin said calmly. This statement startled Julia as much as it did the doctor.

"But how? The Lisbon plane tomorrow only gets in at about the same time as that of today" he exclaimed. "*Paresce impossivel!*"

"Ah, but he won't be coming via Lisbon" Colin said, still calmly; he was beginning to enjoy himself a little. "He will fly direct from England."

"But the landing permission! A plane cannot just come in to land without authorisation" de Carvalho objected.

"Naturally not. Our people in Lisbon are arranging all that with the authorities."

The Portuguese eyed the pale young Englishman with a certain fresh respect.

"*Tiens!*" he said. Then he began to chuckle a little, showing his white and gold teeth. "I see, Monro, that your 'status', on which you did not wish to enlarge, is by no means negligible! But will our authorities not be informed of the purpose of this flight?"

"Oh, I shouldn't think so" Colin said cheerfully. "They'll probably just be told to expect a plane, and asked to be nice to the occupants—all very politely, of course. But there is one other thing I should be glad of your help about, de Carvalho."

"And what is that?"

"Could you recommend a nice, quiet pension where he could stay? I don't know anything about the hotels here, because I always go to the Armitages—and in any case we want to make this visit as unobtrusive as possible."

"I too, unfortunately, seldom stay in the Funchal hotels or *pensãos*" the doctor said, looking rather sardonic—then suddenly he slapped his hand on his knee, and began to laugh.

"What is it?" Colin asked.

"Let him stay in my clinic! I have two or three rooms vacant, as it happens; and what can be more unobtrusive than a patient in a clinic?"

"That's a marvellous idea!" Colin exclaimed—Julia, who of course had not yet heard anything of the conversation with Major Hartley, looked a little doubtful; Colin noticed her expression, and now gave a slight nod.

"Then he can see my other patient, if he wants to," de Carvalho pursued. He was obviously quite exhilarated by this notion of his; Colin guessed, rightly, that he was delighted at the prospect of himself being able to see something of the expert. "And you—where do you stay? Do you remain here?" the doctor went on.

"Only for tonight—I haven't settled about tomorrow."

"Then why not come to the clinic too? Then you and *ce monsieur* are together, without any complicated arrangements or plans. I assure you the food is quite good—all my patients say so!"

"Thank you very much—I accept that invitation" Colin said at once. "It will be most convenient."

"You will have transport for him, of course?"

"Madame will arrange that" Colin said confidently, with a smile at Julia.

Julia, still in the dark about both the expert, and the nature of Hartley's views on the doctor, had been feeling rather as if she were being swept off her feet; irrationally, she had had a swift movement almost of irritation with Colin's breezy assumptions —now, when he smiled at her so confidently, she suddenly smiled back, with a warm and happy glow which de Carvalho thought the most beautiful thing he had ever seen. Her face was lit from within by a sudden interior happiness: Colin was growing up!—he was taking decisions on his own, without nervousness or petulance or caginess. How it had come about, what inner happenings had led up to it, she might learn later; but it had happened, and it was a wonderful thing.

"Madame agrees with that?" de Carvalho asked, his eyes on her face.

"Most certainly" she said; she was radiant.

"That is settled, then" he said, still watching her, puzzled— there was something here he did not understand, but he let it go. "And now" he pursued, "there are certain matters which are still obscure to me, and on which I should much like enlightenment; as much as you feel it proper to vouchsafe, that is. But I am not sure to which of you I should address myself. You would appear to work as an *équipe.*"

"Oh yes; we have been partners for years" Julia said readily. "But address your questions to my cousin—he is the serious partner! I am only a freelance; I have no 'status' " she ended gaily.

Her cousin gave her an odd look, the doctor thought, at this utterance, but he said nothing.

"Nevertheless, your cousin himself told me that it was Madame who had sent for him to come to Madeira. What I am principally interested in is why she should have supposed that the trouble here was caused"—he paused for a moment— "*enfin,* was caused by something of which *he* had special experience?" he ended rather awkwardly.

"Oh, that was because of what you said to old Dr. Fonseca" Julia replied easily.

The doctor was taken aback.

"*What* did I say to Dr. Fonseca?"

"You told him the only symptoms you had ever seen that were in the least like the little boy's were those of some workmen at a factory in France who were careless about wearing their respirators."

"But—Madame was not present when I spoke with this old man!" de Carvalho objected.

"No, but Madame Monro was; and she put two and two together, and came up to the Serra and told me about it." The radiance had left Julia's face now. "So we decided to send for Monsieur Monro," she ended rather abruptly.

"So you see, de Carvalho, *you* are the ultimate cause of my being here!" Colin put in lightly.

"Yes, I see. One can never get ahead of the ladies!" the doctor replied, in the same tone; he was as quick at taking a hint as the next man. He glanced at his watch. "It is late" he said, getting up—"I ought to return to my patients."

"Shall I run you back?" Julia asked.

"I thank you—but I will just telephone for my car, if I may." He started towards the hall; Julia, to his surprise, went with him.

"Excuse me, but I think I left something in the telephone box" she said; she slipped quickly in, and stooped down, as if searching on the floor. When she re-appeared—"No, it isn't there" she said. "It doesn't matter. Goodnight, Monsieur le Docteur. You are being very good to us."

He bent over her hand and kissed it.

"*Au revoir,* I very much hope, Madame."

Julia went back to the verandah and waited while Colin and Porfirio saw the doctor off; Colin soon returned to her.

"I suppose you ought to be getting back too" he said.

"Oh, not for a little while. There are one or two things we ought to settle first. Is there any whisky on that tray?"

"Yes, and soda too. Have one?"

"Yes please."

"What did you dodge into that absurd box for?" Colin asked, as he poured out her drink.

"For the pad. The old fellow had written Hartley's name and the Office number on it." She put her hand down the front of her dress, drew out the pad, and tore off five or six of the top sheets. "There—now it can go back. I don't suppose it matters, since he's going to put up the person from Porton in his clinic—it was just habit" she said, tearing the thin leaves into small pieces. "Now, do tell me what goes on. Is Hartley really sending a boffin out tomorrow?"

"Well, rather a king boffin really" Colin said, grinning. He told her of the Major's dispositions, ending with—"Only he said *you* would have to lay on a quiet place for him to stay."

"What cheek! Well anyhow, you've saved me the bother of doing that."

"I'm not so sure. I think your *beaux yeux* may have had a good deal to do with it, as usual! But what about a car for Sir Percy? Can you keep the little Austin?"

"Not without asking Terence. Is it too late to ring him up now?"

Colin looked at his watch.

"Twenty to eleven—oh no, that's all right. Let's go and do it." He got up.

"No—half a minute. How much can I tell Terence of what I want it *for*? And what about Aglaia? He's sure to ask if you've come, and when she may expect you at the *quinta*."

Colin sat down again.

"Yes, we must plan something—I see that" he said slowly. "It's a bit dicey. Let me think."

While he thought, Julia sat silent, drinking whisky and watching the light-caught sprays of bougainvillea round the edge of the verandah. At last—"Can one get up to see these sheep without going past the *quinta,* do you remember?" he asked.

"I don't know, without looking at a map—I think so."

"Yes, of course!" he said. "I remember now. Only the turning off the main road is pretty close to the house."

"Will he want to see the sheep?"

"Yes indeed; and the place—and the whole lay-out. All that is frightfully important."

"Then Terence will have to be told, at once, that the King Boffin is coming."

"Why?"

"To lay on the hammock-men—unless he's a member of the Alpine Club! It's a fearful climb. And that will take some time, too."

Colin was silent again—and again Julia left him alone. Here he was facing his private problem, his relationship with his wife, she felt sure; and strongly, in her spirit, she held him to his newly born courage, his fresh resolution. She saw, with thankfulness, when his thumb began to jerk, that he grasped it firmly with his other hand, and so kept it still. After a longish pause he spoke.

"Yes, I think you'll have to let Terence know that the Office is sending out a big shot—I'd forgotten about the hammock-men. When I went up we all climbed. Don't say anything about Porton."

"Right."

"And ask if you can keep the small car, or get him to tell you where we can hire a bigger one."

"Right" Julia said again. "Do I tell him where you'll both be staying?"

She was reassured to hear his old boyish giggle.

"Yes, tell him that too—it'll amuse him!" He paused again. "As for Ag" he said then, "when you've fixed all that with Terence—and told him to keep quiet about it—I'll speak to her myself."

"Good-so" Julia said, getting up.

Of course Porfirio was lurking in the hall when they went out, and again volunteered to procure *o numero;* Julia asked him to get the Senhor Armitage at the *quinta*—*"el Senhor mesmo."* After a moment or two the old man stepped out and ushered her into the box. "Terence?" she asked.

"Yes indeed. *And* I'm in a room by myself! How are you doing?"

"Marvellously—we had a wonderful dinner. I adore Porfirio! But look, Terence—more help wanted."

"Ask away" was all he said.

"Well, can I keep the small car for another two or three days? If not, tell me a place where I can hire one."

"No, that's all right—keep it. Colin turn up all right?"

"Yes. He'll want to speak to Aglaia in a minute, but there's something else I want to fix with you first. Look, if it's at all possible I want you to keep this entirely to yourself for the moment. O.K.?"

"I'll try. More mysteries?"

"Not very—I mean not to you. The Office is sending some-one out tomorrow."

"What office?"

"No names, no pack-drill!" Julia countered smartly. "Colin's outfit, of course."

"Lawks!"

"Yes, and rather a big shot. So can you lay on those hammock-men again? He'll want to go up and see the sheep and all."

"I'm not sure that I can get them for tomorrow" Terence said. "Anyhow there won't be enough daylight after the plane gets in—it comes as late tomorrow as today."

"Ah, he won't be coming by that plane," Julia said.

"Cripes!—he must be a big shot! Does he want to stay at Aunt Sally's too?"

Julia laughed. "No, they're both going to stay at the clinic."

"Nonsense!—or are you serious?"

"Perfectly serious. The doctor has two rooms free, and has in-vited them both."

"Is he in on all this, then?"

"He more or less had to be—he's a good guesser!" Julia said gaily. "Hold on a second, Terence—I'd better ask if day after tomorrow will do for the hammocks?" She put her head out of the box and spoke briefly with her cousin. "Yes—at about ten thirty for three, please. You are a boon, Terence, being so kind; thanks a million. Now I'll put Colin on, if you can get Aglaia. Goodnight, and bless you."

"No, wait a moment. Will your top-brass worthy want to see Pereira?"

"Who? Oh, the vet. I don't know. But if he does, can't we get hold of him through the doctor?"

"Yes, I suppose you can. He seems to be more or less on the strength!"

"Or Colin and friend on his!" Julia said, gurgling. "All right —over to Colin." She put the receiver down on the shelf and left the box; Colin went in, and she went out to the verandah again. She sat smoking and sipping her whisky, in a rather un-wonted state of anxiety. She had often worried about Colin, over one aspect or another of his work; but this first encounter with Aglaia—when he was finding himself forced, quite definitely, to put that work first and her and her claims second, while she was actually on the spot—was, she felt, a sharper test than any he had yet encountered. And she herself now recognised, better than ever before, the core of quite ferocious toughness and ruthless determination which underlay Aglaia's innocently childish exterior.

When at last Colin came out onto the verandah again he was wiping his forehead with a handkerchief; he sat down, took a pull at his whisky, and lit a cigarette.

"What hell it all is!" he burst out, after a few moments. "Of *course* I'm longing to see her!—she must know that by this time. But this job has got to be done *now;* it can't be put off. And it can't be done with amateurs tagging along, either; the fewer people who are in on it the better." He paused, inhaled deeply, and blew out smoke; he looked at his cousin with distressful eyes.

"I'm so sorry" Julia said.

"But wouldn't you think anyone could *see* that? And that it's no good her having my telephone number? I've got to concentrate!—not be rung up all the time."

Julia listened, full of pity for them both, while he ran on for some time in this strain. It gradually became clear to her that Colin had stood firm; that was some comfort, however much he had hurt himself and Aglaia in the process.

"How much have you seen of her out here?" he asked at last.

"Quite a bit. They all came up and stayed at the Serra, and then we all went down and spent a long weekend at the *quinta;* that was when we found the sheep," Julia said neutrally. "We've talked quite a lot" she added.

"Well, perhaps I was unduly tough with her just now" he said then. "But sometimes"—he paused. "There was nothing else for it" he ended rather helplessly.

"To tell you the truth, I'm *thank*ful if you were a little tough with her" Julia said flatly.

"Oh really? Why?"

"Well, we may as well have this out now" Julia said. "Both

Terence and I have been worried because she is so frightfully indiscreet."

"Oh, have you? Indiscreet how?" he looked at once startled, and almost relieved.

"Talking about you and your job; complaining at your being sent to Spain; and quite openly suggesting that the Office was treating you unfairly over—well, over the Asia thing" Julia said, frowning a little in her effort to think how much to say, and how to say it, on this cruelly painful subject.

"You don't mean to say that she brought that up with *you?*" Colin asked; he looked horrified.

"Well, yes, in a way. She was upset" Julia said, reaching out a long white hand and laying it gently on his, "and she is very young, don't forget. Don't fret over that, dearest. What mattered much more was her moaning about how they were treating you to Terence, and even to Mrs. H."

"But that's simply frightful" the young man said. "It must be stopped."

"That's what I told Terence. He did have a go, but he's so gentle, he didn't do much good. But I think it has been stopped" Julia said, with a slow smile. "In the end I gave her a most frightful roughing-up myself, and she gave me her solemn promise *never* to talk about you and your work to anyone, except you and me. I really think she has got that much into her head."

He looked relieved. "Bless you" he said, squeezing her hand.

"Of course that's why she was so dead set on your coming here, as a sort of rehabilitation-course!" Julia went on. "And once she told me of the doctor's hint to Fonseca about the respirators, I saw that you ought to. How did you manage to get away so quickly?" she asked then.

"Oh, I had some leave in hand, and there was nothing much doing at Pamplona, so I rang Graham in Madrid from Gralheira and asked him to let me advance it a bit, so that I could flip over here and see my wife—I said there was illness here" he added, grinning.

Julia laughed. "How true!" She got up. "Well, there's lots more to talk about, but I think I'd better get back now."

"Shall you come down in the morning?"

"Have to, to bring the car for Sir What's-It! I'll be here at ten thirty sharp, to whisk you away before the old party surfaces." She began to laugh again. "*What* a card the doctor is! Oh, what did Hartley say about him, by the way?"

He told her.

"Well, let's hope it *is* all right. It sounds a bit vague, to me."

"Vague or not, it was inevitable" Colin said, calmly.

She stared at him—then smiled happily again.

"Yes. Bless you!" She gave him a quick kiss, went out to the car, and drove off. But all the way up to the Serra, driving fast through the dark along the now almost empty road, she was "singing and making melody in her heart to the Lord," as St. Paul so admirably puts it, for this new development in Colin. Something—perhaps the disastrous experience in Asia, which had cost her her Philip—had made him begin to grow up at last. She shrank from the thought of her husband, but the relief and thankfulness persisted. And when she had let herself in, crept upstairs, apologised to the watchful Pauline and refused a hot drink, and tumbled hastily into bed, she was aware of a peace and a sense of release that she had not known for a long time. This came in a sweet and curious contrast to her constant ache for Philip, and the buzzing immediate preoccupation with the business in hand—the arrival of Sir Percy, and what was to follow, all as yet unsettled. As she started to drift into sleep she was aware of the beginning of a sense of a load being lifted off her —her half-unconscious feeling of responsibility for Colin which, in its mixture of fondness and exasperation, had had a maternal element in it, unrecognised at the time. Now, from now on, she thought dreamily, the Philipino could be her *only* child.

That thought brought her broad awake again, oddly enough. She was suddenly consumed by such an urgent desire to see the little boy that she got out of bed and—barefoot and only in her nightdress, in the warm night—took her torch and crept along the passage, through the swing door, on and into the night-nursery. There, past Nannie Mack's stout, gently snoring form, she stood at the foot of the cot, shielding the light with her hand from the small sleeping face, and took a long look. Then she crept back to her room again and fell into a peaceful and profound sleep.

9 BY 9:30 the following morning Colin Monro had finished his packing as well as his breakfast, and was sitting on the verandah, with both doors through to the hall open, waiting for Major Hartley's call—the tulip-tree in early sunshine, and the vivid flower-beds, brilliant with dahlias, fuchsias, and geraniums round the small lawn, made him reluctant to sit indoors. Presently the bell rang: he hurried in, but old Porfirio of course beat him to it; he stood on the threshold of the telephone-box holding out the receiver, with a beaming smile, as Colin came up—"For the Senhor, from Londres."

"Good morning" Colin said cheerfully.

"Morning" Hartley's voice replied. "Well, the plane should touch down about twelve noon. Everything's laid on; you just hang about and meet him. He'll be wearing one of those Tyrolean felt hats with a chamois-tail sticking up at the back."

"Good. Dark or fair?"

"Dark—a small feller; *very* small."

"And what about the party who was in France?"

"Oh yes, that's your man all right. Old Jean knew all about him; he was in the French thing up to the ears. Now has that splendid girl fixed up accommodation for Mossy?"

"Well, it's *been* fixed. He's going to stay with that worthy who was in France—so am I."

"What, in his house?"

"No, as his patients."

Colin could hear the Major's "Ho-ho-ho!" loud and clear.

"That's first class! Couldn't be better. What's the number?"

"I got that for you last night—hold on a second." He pulled out his diary and read the number aloud.

"And when do you go there?"

"As soon as Mrs. Philip comes to collect me—any moment now."

"O.K. Well, the best of luck—you seem to be having plenty so far!" the Major said breezily, and rang off. As he stepped out of the box Colin saw the small car glide noiselessly up to the door; he went out to it.

"Perfect timing" he said to Julia, leaning in to give her a kiss. "I'm all ready—just tip the old fellow, and off we go." In fact Porfirio was close behind him with the luggage, which he placed in the back of the car; Colin gave him some notes, Julia again praised the dinner, and asked for her thanks to be passed on to the cook, and they drove off.

"What had Hartley got to say about the doctor? Did he get onto his pal in Paris?"

"Yes—and he is the Portuguese who was working on gas for the French. Sir Percy may know him too, for all I know. Anyhow Hartley is perfectly satisfied."

"Good. What luck we're having all round, between him and Terence."

"That's what Hartley said" Colin responded cheerfully.

He and Julia both felt that their luck was holding when de Carvalho showed them the quarters he had assigned to his new patients—two rooms at the end of a short corridor, both with balconies overlooking the garden, a bathroom between them; the rooms were not unduly small, and pleasantly furnished, with a couple of armchairs and a table in each; there were chaise-longues on the two balconies. While Julia was praising and ad-miring, a man in a white coat came in and plugged telephones into wall-plugs by each bed. "Oh yes, I often have businessmen as patients, and these cannot recover without a telephone in their room!" the doctor said, with a sardonic grin. "You will of course eat up here; you can ring and say on which balcony you would prefer your meals to be served. Will your scientist be here in time for luncheon?"

"I should think so—his plane is due in about noon."

"Your friends work fast!" De Carvalho exlaimed. "Then there should be time for drinks in the garden beforehand. Excellent! Now, if you will excuse me I must attend to my patients." He hurried away.

"Talking of drinks, hadn't you better have a small supply up here in your rooms?" Julia suggested. "I don't suppose Sir Percy will want to discuss *everything* with the doctor, *all* the time."

"No, I'm sure he won't. Good idea, darling. How do we get our supply?"

"Bother poor Terence, as usual" Julia said, going over to the telephone, which stood on the bed-table. "Oh good—that man's left a book." She looked out the number and dialled Terence's office. When he came to the telephone—"Me again" she announced.

"More mysteries?" Terence enquired.

"No—nothing could be more commonplace than this requirement! Where can I get a supply of drink for the big shot?"

"What does the big shot drink? Madeira?"

"We don't know" Julia said, beginning to laugh. "Only they'll be having all their meals in their rooms, so they'll want *vinho de mesa* at meals, as well as drinks before and after. I should play safe with gin and whisky, for a start, and some *vin ordinaire*. We've just got time to get it, if you tell me what shop."

"No, better let me have it sent in; then you'll get decent whisky, and won't be robbed. I'll have a couple of *garafãos* of wine sent in too, red and white; I'm sure the servants there can decant it. If you find he is a Madeira man, I can get you some really good stuff later on."

"Thank you very much indeed. Bill to Colin, please. Oh Terence, what a treasure you are!"

"Colin can give me a cheque—I won't let him and his Office off, don't you worry! That all? Oh, the hammocks will be all right tomorrow, by the way. And have you by any chance heard how Marcusinho is?"

"Not this morning, but he was as good as cured last night."

"Not really? But that's marvellous! How did it happen, d'you know?"

"The doctor had a bright idea, and tried a new drug" Julia answered readily. "Anyhow it stopped the pain."

"Thank goodness. I'll ring Penel, so that she can tell his parents."

"Yes, do do that. Bless you. Goodbye."

On their way out to the car Julia spoke to the elderly male secretary whom they had seen the evening before, and mentioned that a parcel would be coming for the Senhor Monro, and that it was to be put in his room. Then they drove out to the airport. As they topped the high ground and began to drop down towards Porto Novo they saw a small plane circling fairly low over the sea, preparatory to coming in to land.

"I bet you that's him" Colin said, accelerating.

"He's early, if so" Julia said, with a glance at her watch. "What makes you think it's him?"

"The plane—it's a Dominie. They have the range and the speed for this run, although they're rather small. Bother!—I hope he doesn't beat us to it."

"Well, don't drive *too* fast" Julia remarked. "It won't help at all if we don't live to tell him our tale." Colin laughed, but slackened speed slightly.

In fact it was a pretty close-run thing. They saw the plane touch down some moments before they reached the airport; as they drove into the small car-park a group of officials came out of the building and stood looking about—among them was a small dark-haired man wearing a Tyrolese hat with a chamois-tail in the back. Colin sprang out and went over.

"Good morning, sir. My name is Monro. Have you some luggage?"

"Morning" said the small man. "Yes, someone has my luggage." A porter at that moment brought out three largish suitcases. "Yes—and the camera?" Another man appeared with a bulky canvas case and what were evidently the legs of a tripod strapped together. "Ah, that's the lot—it *is* rather a lot, I'm afraid."

"Oh, we'll fit it in all right." Julia at this point drove the car up beside them. "My cousin, Mrs. Jamieson" Colin said; Julia said

"How do you do?" "Shall I drive, Colin?" she asked her cousin then.

"Yes, you'd better. Do get in, sir." With some trouble the luggage was all bestowed, the legs of the tripod sticking out over the back of the car, and Colin somehow squashed himself in as well. The small dark man took polite farewells in French of the airport officials, and shook hands with his plane's captain— "Thanks for a lovely ride." Then he got into the car and they drove away.

"Now, Monro," Sir Percy said, leaning over towards the back of the car, "will you begin at the beginning, and tell me exactly what has happened here?"

"Mrs. Jamieson will have to do that, sir; I only arrived last night."

"Oh." He turned to the woman beside him, and now appeared to notice her for the first time. Julia was again wearing the slate-grey linen dress; a broad white band held her remarkably coloured hair in place; she was smiling faintly. "That will be much more convenient" he said, smiling too. "Carry on, please, Mrs. Jamieson."

"Shall I begin at the *very* beginning?" Julia asked.

"Certainly."

"Well, as the boat on which I came from Lisbon was getting in to Funchal we saw a Russian trawler, with all those radar gadgets in the rigging" Julia began.

"How did you know she was Russian?" Sir Percy asked crisply.

"The Captain told me—I was on the bridge with him. He was rather cross; he said she was often hanging about. When we got into territorial water she sheered off. Then ten days later, down at Mr. Armitage's *quinta,* I saw her again."

"How did you know it was the same one?" he interjected.

"By her number—Mr. Armitage had his field-glasses, and I had seen it through the Captain's."

"And remembered it?"

"No, I jotted it down."

"Have you still got it?"

"Yes—as a matter of fact it was 0263, but it's in my diary."

"*Vairy* good." Sir Percy pronounced this phrase rather oddly. "Please go on."

"Next day we went up onto the Paúl da Serra, and found the sheep all sick. That's where you will be going tomorrow, to see them."

"Hold on—how long ago was all this?"

"We went up to the plateau exactly a week ago today."

"And you first saw the spy-boat ten days before that?"

"Yes."

"Please go on."

"Well, the sheep were coughing and wheezing frightfully, and seemed all dopey" Julia pursued. "Usually they are frightfully wild, according to the Armitages, but this time they took no notice of anyone till they were quite close to; and they were turning their heads about in an odd way."

"And what steps did Mr. Armitage take about this ailment in the sheep?"

"There was nothing much he *could* do, till Monday. Mrs. Armitage took a sample of the water in one of the pools on this plateau place, to have it analysed, and they sent for the vet—but he was in Lisbon, and only got back on Monday, so he couldn't get down till Tuesday. But Mr. Armitage asked the men who carry one up in hammocks if any other tourists had been there lately—in case someone had poisoned the water."

"And had they?"

"Not poisoned the water, no—it was absolutely normal."

"I expressed myself badly" Sir Percy said. "I meant, had any strangers been up to the plateau?"

"*Yes*" Julia said, with great emphasis. "*Ten* tourists had been up, and had spent the night, with lots of luggage and camping-gear, some days earlier."

"You are *sure* of that?—that they spent the night? That could be very important."

"The hammock-men were positive about it, because they were told to come again next day to carry everything down—an absolute gold-mine for them, of course; they'll remember it for years," Julia said, laughing a little. "They were vague about the exact day, as peasants often are, but we were able to settle that later, more or less."

"How?"

"Well, the men said they thought the tourists had come up from the other side of the island, so on the Sunday Mr. Armitage drove over to Seixial and made enquiries, and learned that a number of foreigners had landed there rather over a week earlier, and had hired mules to take their luggage up to the foot of the plateau, and down again next day."

"Was Mr. Armitage able to ascertain what boat they came off?"

"All the locals could say was 'a fishing-boat', but of course that is what these spy-trawlers are supposed to be."

"Quite so. Pray continue."

"Well, I had a sort of idea about the trawler, because I had met Russian trawlers before, engaged on illegal activities" Julia said.

"Indeed? What sort of activities?" Sir Percy asked in surprise.

"Planting satellite-detectors in remote spots in the Hebrides and the Scillies" she replied nonchalantly. "So I decided to ask the hammock-men one or two questions myself, and what they told me made me feel fairly certain that the people who had camped on the plateau were Russians."

"May one know what questions you did ask them?" Sir Percy enquired, bending a gaze half-admiring, half-quizzical, on the beautiful young woman beside him.

"Yes. I asked if they had smoked" she said, turning to him with an amused smile.

He gave a brief laugh. "I'll buy it! I'm no good at guessing. What did you learn?"

"That these tourists had smoked *brown* cigarettes, not white; that had created a great impression on the men. And of course Russians do smoke beige-coloured cigarettes. So I felt pretty sure those campers had come off the trawler."

"What did you do then? Send for Mr. Monro?"

"No, not then. I told Mr. Armitage, and we decided not to tell anyone else for the time being."

"May one know why?"

"Oh yes—to keep everything as quiet as possible till we know more. You see—or you will see when you look at a map—it seemed highly probable that local accomplices were involved. So it was much better not to alarm the authorities here too soon."

"*Vairy* good" Sir Percy said again. "Please go on."

"Well, then I saw the child" Julia said; "a boy of ten or eleven, who lives on the farm. He had been ill for a week—coughing and wheezing, and with terrible headaches; the village doctor could do nothing for him."

"Had he also been up to the plateau?"

"Yes—though we didn't know it then; Mrs. Monro found that out the next day, after the doctor from Funchal had been sent for to see him."

"Ah, the one human case that the good Major mentioned! Where is he now?"

"In a clinic in Funchal; the doctor took him straight back in his car, to keep him under observation."

"I shall need to see him" Sir Percy said, with a certain animation.

"Oh, you will!—you'll be staying in the same clinic" Julia said, laughing again. "But he's much better now—nearly well, the doctor told me this morning."

"How did this happen? Do you know at all?"

"Yes—the doctor saw some syrettes of atropine that my cousin had brought, just in case, and that gave him a new idea, and he dashed upstairs and gave the child an injection at once."

"When was this?"

"Last night, after my cousin arrived—we went straight to the clinic from the plane, because I was so worried about the child."

"By your cousin you mean Mr. Monro?"

"Yes—oh, sorry. We are cousins."

"Quite so. But you have not told me yet why you sent for him —from Spain, was it not?"

"Yes, I have been working in Spain" Colin put in, from the back of the car. "My wife comes in here, sir. She overheard a conversation between the village doctor and Dr. de Carvalho, which gave her a clue."

"Hold on a moment—the doctor who has the child in his

clinic now is Dr. de Carvalho? Who worked on gas research in France?"

"Yes sir, that is the man."

"Ah yes—Hartley mentioned him. He is quite reliable, it seems. And very helpful, since he is going to put me up! Where do you stay?" the scientist now asked Colin.

"Also in the clinic, sir."

"*Vairy* good. All right—now let us hear the clue."

"Here we are!" Julia said, swinging the car into the clinic's entrance; she pulled up at the front door. Two men in white coats at once appeared, took out the luggage, and led the way to one of those large lifts common in nursing-homes. "I'll wait down here" Julia called to Colin, as he and Sir Percy entered the lift.

In the small pleasant bedroom Sir Percy looked about him with approval. "Most pleasant! And you are where?"

"Next door, sir—through the bathroom; or I imagine this partition on the balcony has a door. Yes, it has. We eat up here —we are supposed to be patients."

"Are patients allowed to drink anything?"

"Yes—I ordered in a supply." He went along the balcony and into the next room—"Yes—it has come, but it hasn't been undone. I rather think the doctor is expecting us for drinks downstairs, though. But while I have the chance, will you just let me get this clue business over, without my cousin?"

"By all means." Sir Percy sat down on a chair on the balcony and lit a cigarette. "Does she not know about it?" he asked.

"Oh no—unhappily she knows only too much." He also sat down, and rapidly recounted the story of Philip Jamieson's death. Then he went on to tell of de Carvalho's reference to respirators in his talk with Dr. Fonseca, which Aglaia had overheard. "So my wife realised that quite probably it was some form of nerve gas that had affected both the sheep and the child, and got Mrs. Jamieson to send for me. But that was the clue—only I didn't want to explain it all to you in front of Mrs. Jamieson."

"I see. All the same she realises that I have come here expressly to try to ascertain what type of nerve gas is involved here, does she not?—if it *is* a nerve gas."

"Oh yes, sir. And she is as brave as a lion about that, and everything else! It's only that for her the word 'respirator' is like a thorn under a thumb-nail."

At this point one of the white-coated attendants appeared, and in rather halting French said that the Senhor Doutor desired their company downstairs; he led them out through a typical Funchal garden, a mixture of rampant flowers and neat beds of onions, lettuces and melons, in which avocado pear-trees stood here and there. At the upper end a vine trellis shaded a small paved space, open on all four sides and set with chairs and tables; here Julia was seated, drinking a cocktail. De Carvalho rose to greet his new guest; when Colin introduced him—"*Non!* Sir Percy comes himself? This is indeed an honour. Ah, now we shall resolve our problem!"

"*Espérons*" Sir Percy said briefly; he expressed polite gratitude for the doctor's hospitality. Then they got down to brass tacks. Julia, listening, was fascinated by the three different angles— the medical, the scientific, and the Intelligence—from which the three men approached their common problem. Almost at once Sir Percy asked for a map; one was coming, Julia said—she had just telephoned to Mr. Armitage's office for it. And indeed in a few moments an errand-boy brought a large-scale map of the island—a table was cleared, and the sheet spread out on it; the three men pored over it intently. Colin pointed out first the plateau itself, and then Seixial, down on the north-west coast—it was from there that the strangers had come up, he said.

"*Mais oui, mais oui*" Sir Percy said brusquely, brushing this aside; but what was the height of the plateau above sea-level?— and the temperature? The altitude was easily checked from the map, just under 5000 feet; but none of those present had any idea of the temperature up there in the early morning. At midday, Julia put in, it had been quite hot; "but when the mist came up, after lunch, it turned chilly." Sir Percy pounced on the mist— was it frequent? None of them could say. "Well, we must take temperature readings, and find out about the mist. Would your friend Mr. Armitage know?" he asked Julia.

"He might; he lives nearer the Paúl than anyone else."

"Show me, please." Julia indicated the *quinta* on the map.

"So you see, Monsieur le Professeur, the boy managed to walk all that distance, *after* encountering the gas" de Carvalho put in.

"Yes—most interesting. But one aspect at a time" Sir Percy said. "Mrs. Jamieson, how quickly do you think you could get hold of Mr. Armitage?" He was running his finger across the map from the *quinta* towards Funchal.

"Oh, if he's in his office, quite quickly; he was there ten minutes ago, when I sent for the map" she said.

"Then please try."

But here Colin intervened.

"You are quite sure you wish Mr. Armitage to know that you, yourself, are out here, sir?"

"I don't see how I can get very far without him" Sir Percy said. "He lives on the spot, he knows the terrain, he can talk to the locals; his help seems to me indispensable. And Mrs. Jamieson has told him of her suspicions about the trawler. Have you any reason for distrusting him?"

"Oh no—he's my wife's cousin."

"Then pray try to get hold of him, Mrs. Jamieson."

But when Julia telephoned to the office she was told that Mr. Armitage had gone out, and would not return till after lunch; she left a message asking him to ring up the doctor at the clinic as soon as he came in. When she went back to the garden no one was there but Colin.

"Where are the others?" she asked.

"Gone to look at the child. I seem to have floated slightly" Colin said.

"What about?"

"Oh, Terry. I mean, this Mossy person is so frightfully well-known." But he didn't look unduly troubled.

"All the same, I think he's right; he'll get on much better with Terence in on it. I wish I knew what he wants to know, exactly. What can the altitude have to do with it?—and the temperature?"

"They all come into the degree of efficacy, I believe. I'm not very well up in all that myself; I didn't get a lot of briefing on the scientific side."

Julia did not pursue that; she realised that the person who would have been most fully briefed was her husband. Just then Sir Percy and de Carvalho reappeared, talking hard in French. "So you took blood specimens on Tuesday morning, and sent them by air to Paris?"

"Via Lisbon."

"Then you should get a result any time now. *Très bien.* Certainly the symptoms as you have recorded them point to a strong nerve-agent; and his recovery with the atropine injections is almost conclusive, in that limited sense." The scientist turned to Julia. "Well, is your friend going to join us?"

Julia reported what had happened. "They could not say when Mr. Armitage would be free this afternoon."

"Oh well, we must get on with the ground-work by ourselves." He sat down by the table with the map.

"Sir Percy, may I ask you one thing, before you get going?" Julia asked, sitting down too.

"You may ask me more than one" he said, looking at her very benignly. "After all, we owe this opportunity mainly to your *astuce.*"

"Why should the Russians want to use this gas here, in Madeira?—and on sheep?" she asked.

"That is two questions" he said, smiling. "I will take the first first. You probably know, what the Major told me, that the defector who first reported the invention of this new agent to our authorities mentioned that it was intended for use against Britain."

"Yes, I did hear that."

"Then it was obviously essential to test it in a climate as like that of the British Isles as possible, what is called an 'oceanic' climate—fairly mild and fairly moist. There is nowhere within the bounds of the Soviet Union where such a climate is to be found; it lies entirely on the Euro-Asiatic land-mass, with the driest climates in the world, and great extremes of heat and cold. Where it does touch the ocean at all, it is either the Black Sea, much hotter than Britain, or the Arctic Ocean, much colder. Madeira is slightly milder than Britain in winter, but otherwise the climate is very similar."

Dr. de Carvalho had come over with the cocktail-shaker to fill up their glasses; at the mention of the Soviet Union he rounded on Colin.

"*Alors,* Monro, it is *les Russes* who do this thing? You did not tell me that."

"I assumed you would realise it must be them" Colin said.

"Have you any proof that the Russian Government is involved? This puts a more serious complexion on the matter." He looked worried, and rather cross. Julia decided to put her oar in.

"Doctor de Carvalho, it is only *my* theory that the Russians are responsible for this business, not my cousin's—he was not here. We have no actual proof, yet; it is an assumption, based on various clues. We hope, with Sir Percy's help, to learn much more—is not that your wish also?"

"Certainly" he said, but rather grumpily.

"Then should we not proceed on Madame Jamieson's assumption, which I do not reject—yet?" Sir Percy asked blandly.

"For the moment, yes." He now carried out his original intention, and refilled Julia's glass and Sir Percy's. That worthy thanked him, and then turned to Julia.

"As for your second question about the sheep, most mammals react to these agents in a way corresponding fairly closely with the reaction of human beings. Of course to carry out an experiment like this without the permission of the government concerned—which we must assume to be the case here—a certain degree of isolation is essential, and this plateau does seem to be very isolated." He studied the map again. "Yes, there appear to be no dwellings at all close to it. Tell me" he said, turning back to Julia, "is it fenced in any way?"

"Not that I saw; of course we only went half-way across."

"Where did you go up?—could you show me?"

Julia peered at the map.

"There's the end of the tunnel" she said. "Yes, and we went along this sort of faint track to where the hatching begins—that must be the cliffs."

"Where you were carried up in hammocks, I think you said?"

"Yes—and the people who went up and camped were carried

up at the same place. I imagine the cliffs are so steep that they don't need fences to keep the sheep on the top."

"I wonder how they get them up?—and down?" Sir Percy speculated.

"I believe I've heard that they are slung up in nets, as the sheep are slung ashore onto some of the Scottish islands" Colin put in.

"Yes—yes. Well, the whole set-up is of course a gift to our Tartar friends, for the purposes of this experiment" Sir Percy said. "A relatively confined space, and remote. Rather large though to get the concentration." He got out a small marked ruler, and laid it on the map. "H'm—between two and three miles each way, *vairy* roughly." He whipped round on Julia. "You say *ten* men camped up there? You are sure of that?"

"That was what the hammock-men said, and it's the sort of thing they would be dead accurate about, because of the money. Peasants are always as accurate about money as they are vague about dates, don't you find?"

"I know few peasants; no doubt you are right. *Ten* men" the scientist said again, thoughtfully. "It is very few for the space. I wonder—"

He was interrupted by a sudden disturbance in the garden. With loud shouts, which were echoed from neighbouring gardens, a man, a youth, and two little boys rushed in, and began frantically to adjust small wooden sluices, through which water now splashed and dashed over the melons, the lettuces, and the onions, and filled shallow trenches round the avocado pear-trees. "What on earth is going on?" Sir Percy asked.

"It is a water-day—I had forgotten" de Carvalho said. "I am sorry for the noise, but they must distribute the water." He explained about Madeira's irrigation system; Sir Percy listened with deep interest.

"I must say I would like to see one of these *levadas*" he said, watching the men and boys at work—their eagerness and enjoyment were so evident that involuntarily he smiled as he spoke.

"Oh you will, tomorrow" Julia assured him. "You'll go along one of the tunnels that brings the water through the mountains to the dry side of the island."

Of course this curious feature of Madeira had to be explained to the newcomer—with recourse to the map—the two climates, and the two different vegetations. "That's what's so splendid about the Paúl da Serra" Julia said with enthusiasm; "it's slap in the middle, so you can see both sides at once, where you first get up, the moist and the dry—two different worlds, really."

"H'm—yes. I hope Mr. Armitage will be able to tell us which climate prevails on the plateau itself" Sir Percy said, a little ruefully.

"Could I ask you one more thing?" Julia said earnestly.

"By all means."

"Why does the climate, or the temperature, matter so much?"

"Well, on the assumption—which for the moment I think we must make—that we are concerned with a highly volatile gas, which powerfully affects the nervous system of both humans and animals, we already know, from tests with previous, similar agents, that meteorological conditions—moisture and temperature—have a great bearing on the effectiveness of the agent on the people—or the animals—subjected to it."

"Half a minute—I expect I'm being dumb—is the gas the agent?"

"Yes" Sir Percy said smiling. "That is our normal jargon. I imagine you are more accustomed to think of agents in human terms?"

"I'm afraid so" Julia said, laughing a little. "Do carry on."

"Well, that being so, there is the question of getting a sufficient dosage, which brings one on to the means of distribution. There is what we call the C.T. factor: concentration multiplied by time. It is a little complicated" he said, half apologetically. "The evening is usually considered the most favourable time, as the gas hangs about for longer then. That will not do in this case, because of the boy—if it is certain that he went up in the morning, the release cannot have taken place overnight."

"Why not?" Colin asked, surprised.

"Because even with a really heavy concentration, and favourable climatic conditions, the gas will not normally continue to affect organisms after two hours, at the outside. The smell may remain much longer—it does with some of the agents commonly in use for riot control—but the activity is over by then."

"If this is a new agent, would the time factor necessarily be the same?" Colin enquired.

"I think so; or something very near it. It may be possible to produce variations in the effects—what parts of the nervous system are affected, duration and so on—but the *way* in which all gases disperse must be practically the same; this is simply a question of meteorology. And Dr. de Carvalho is satisfied that it *was* in the morning that the boy went up."

"That is what his mother told Mrs. Monro, undoubtedly" Julia put in.

"Yes, I am positive that this is the case" the doctor said. "Now that he has recovered, he talks quite lucidly."

"So the gas must have been distributed in the morning. The question is, *how?* A normal method, for destroying insects or vegetation, is to use an aeroplane. Is there any possibility of that having been done?" Sir Percy asked, looking at de Carvalho.

"Quite out of the question, I should say" the Portuguese answered. "Where could it operate from? Not from Santa Cruz— the authorities there would have noticed the attachments, which are unmistakable."

"Could the vessel you saw have carried a small plane?" Sir Percy asked, turning to Julia.

"No, not possibly, I shouldn't have thought" she said. "And if a plane was to do the spraying, why should *ten* men go up and spend the night?"

"An excellent question! Why indeed? No, I think they must have found some means of distributing it by hand."

"By aerosol sprays, such as one uses against insects?" Colin asked.

"Well, hardly those; they would have needed hundreds, if not thousands—the weight would have been colossal! No, more likely large knapsack sprayers, such as are used for insecticides on vegetation; in those the stuff could be carried in a very concentrated form."

"And the sprayers could of course have been wrapped up so as to pass for camping equipment—you said the hammock-men mentioned masses of that" Colin said, turning to Julia.

"Yes."

Sir Percy was using his little ruler again; then he did some sums on a small pad.

"All the same" he said at length, "it is a problem how even ten men could have covered the whole area in the time, to get a simultaneous distribution." He turned to Julia. "You say you only went half-way across—is it certain that all the sheep were affected?"

"Yes, they were." It was de Carvalho who replied. "The veterinary surgeon here, Pereira, went up last Tuesday, and walked to the extreme farther end of the plateau, and found the animals in the same condition all over it. Naturally he and I have been in touch."

"And he has presumably also taken blood samples from the sheep?"

"Yes. He has sent his to the laboratory in Lisbon."

"So we may expect to hear their findings shortly." Sir Percy drummed on the map with his fingers. "But even if both lots of blood show cholinesterase inhibition, it does not solve the problem of how the distribution can have been carried out."

"Might they conceivably have found some form of soluble container, which could have been placed in position during the night, and be dissolved by the action of sunlight?" the doctor asked, rather hesitantly.

"I suppose it is *just* possible—though I cannot think of such a substance off-hand" the scientist said. "And could they *count* on sunlight next day?"—he turned to Julia.

"The sun usually rises!" she said. "But I see what you mean— the mist. We shall have to ask Mr. Armitage about that— whether it often comes on first thing."

"Even so, is it the sort of ground one could plod over in the dark, methodically?" Sir Percy went on.

"Oh, not too bad—anyhow wasn't it full moon about a fortnight ago?" Colin said.

At this point a bell rang loudly from the direction of the house. De Carvalho got up.

"The *almoço*" he said. "Gentlemen, I am afraid I must ask you to go to your apartments and take your meal; I am very strict that all my patients should eat punctually!" he added, with his sardonic grin. "And I know that Madame easily gets hungry!"

"Yes, I'm quite ready for some nourishment" Julia said gaily.

"But you return this afternoon? And if possible bring Mr. Armitage?" Sir Percy said.

"I'll do my best. Thank you for the nice drinks" she said to de Carvalho.

"Where shall you eat?" Colin asked, catching her arm.

"Oh, Reid's, I should think. There's not time to get up to the Serra and back." She moved away with her light graceful step— the three men watched her as they followed.

10

IN FACT JULIA did not immediately go in search of nourishment. Instead she went to the Shipping Office to write and leave a note for Terence—it had occurred to her that her guarded telephone message, asking him to ring up Dr. de Carvalho, might worry him on Marcusinho's account. She sat in the big main hall at one of several tables which were furnished with writing-paper, writing away, when Terence himself suddenly stood over her. "Hullo! What are you doing here?"

"Writing to you!" she said, getting up, and smiling at him. "I tried to telephone you, but they said you were out."

"So I was—now I've come in again! What can I do for you next?"

"Oh dear dear Terence, what a pest you must find me! But this time it isn't for me, it's for the King Boffin."

"And what does *he* want next?"

"To talk to you. Could you possibly go to the clinic to see him this afternoon?"

"I might. What's he doing now?"

"Having lunch in his room—very strict, the clinic rules are!"

"Have *you* had lunch?" Terence asked suddenly.

"No."

"Well, come and have a bite with me; then perhaps you can tell me what he thinks *I* can tell him."

"Oh good—I am hungry. What about the car?—or do we go in it?"

"No, we go on foot. Where is the car?" he asked, as they emerged onto the steps.

"Just up there."

"Oh, that's all right." He spoke to the commissionaire, and then led her along the hot street, and into a small hotel; they passed through the hall, through the restaurant, and out into another of Funchal's amazingly flowery gardens, where tables stood under trees.

"What a nice place" Julia said, looking about her with satisfaction. "I never saw such heavenly gardens. I do love Madeira!"

"So do I. Let's settle what to eat, and then you can come clean about your boffin." They ordered a simple cold meal, and Terence, to save time, fetched drinks from the bar himself; over them—"Now, what does this type from Porton want to know?" he asked.

"About the climate up on the Paúl da Serra—whether the mist comes up in the early morning, and what the temperature is at night, and early—all that sort of thing."

"What on earth does he want to know that for?"

In the brief space of time since Terence had asked her to lunch, Julia had made up her mind that she would really have to "come clean" to him about Sir Percy's mission; that gentleman would almost certainly do so himself, but anyhow she was not going to wait on his initiative. She leant across the table towards her companion.

"Because the temperature and the moisture, and all that, make a difference as to how well nerve gas works" she said, with slow deliberation, in a low voice.

"*Nerve* gas!" But Terence also kept his voice down, in spite of his astonishment; he glanced round him. The nearest occupied table was some yards away; the two swarthy young men at it were talking in Spanish through mouthfuls of food, and laughing. "Is that what's wrong with the sheep?" he asked, in a low tone.

"Yes—and with Marcusinho too."

"But you said Marcusinho was better."

"Yes—it's him that makes it so certain" Julia said, ungrammatically but lucidly. "Colin brought over some of *the* antidote, in case any of us should get into it; de Carvalho happened to see the stuff, and tumbled to it at once; he gave Marcusinho a shot, and he was better in no time. Then he knew, of course."

"Did Colin bring enough for the sheep?" Terence asked. Julia gave her slow laugh.

"No, but Colin says they'll recover fairly soon."

"How on earth does he know that?"

The laughter died in Julia's face. She explained hastily about the defector's information concerning this new gas, its temporary effect, and its purpose for use against England. "That was what Colin and my husband went to look for in Central Asia" she said, holding her voice steady. "Well, they didn't manage to find out about it there, because Philip got killed; but it *looks* as if it was the same stuff that's been tried out here, what with that trawler and all—and I should rather like it to be identified this time. It—it would make it seem less of a waste" she ended, slowly.

The man looked at her with horrified pity—for a moment he said nothing.

"Well, of course I will help in any way I can" he said at last. "But I don't know about the temperature up there at night. The mist is rather apt to do what it did last week—come up in the middle of the day; one has a better chance of seeing the view if one goes up fairly early. I don't know what your man is to do about night temperatures."

"He said he was going to take temperature readings."

"Ah, then he's probably brought some form of recording thermometer. I wonder if he'll want stakes to put it on, so that the sheep don't trample it down?"

"No idea" Julia said.

"Well, I tell you what—I'll flip round and see him this afternoon, but I won't stay long; I think I'd better clear everything up at the office, and come up with you tomorrow. How would that be?"

"Excellent—I hoped you might be able to. He'll probably think of questions on the spot that mightn't occur to him down here." She paused. "What shall you say to Ag?" she asked then.

"Nothing! Poor little one, she was fearfully upset last night after she'd spoken to Colin on the telephone—I can't imagine what he said to her."

"He was trying to make her understand a little about being married to someone in Intelligence" Julia said in rather a chilly voice.

"Well, that wanted doing" Terence agreed.

They finished their lunch, still speculating about this curious mission; at one point Terence raised the same query as Julia had done—why Madeira?

"Oh, Sir Percy explained that to me" she began. "Because—"

"Hold on" Terence interrupted her. "Did you say Sir Percy? You don't mean that Sir Percy *Clubb* is your boffin?"

"Yes, he's the one. Why?"

"But he's a frightfully big shot—a Nobel Prize-winner, and an O.M., and all sorts! I thought you meant some little type in pebble-lenses."

"I did say he was a King Boffin, didn't I?" Julia said laughing.

"Yes, you did. But *him!* Oh well, never mind. What did he say about the Commies doing this in Madeira?"

Julia repeated the climatic explanation that Sir Percy had given her.

"Yes, that makes sense" Terence observed. "What are you looking at?" he asked suddenly.

"Those Spanish boys—they seem to be making a film."

Terence looked round. The two young men had propped a ciné-camera on a tripod, and one of them was turning the handle, making a whirring noise, while the other played the fool with a waitress at the door leading from the restaurant—taking a tray from her, and trying to make her sing. *"Mais forte"* he kept telling her; the girl giggled too much for her song to be very audible.

"They don't seem to be taking it very seriously" Terence said, after watching for a few minutes, "I think they must just be amateurs. They've got rather a good machine, though." He looked at his watch. "Goodness, it's later than I thought. I must get back."

"When shall you come to the clinic?" Julia asked.

"Do you know, I don't think I *will* come this afternoon" he said. "If I'm coming up with you tomorrow there's no point, really. Only find out from the great man whether he wants supports for his thermometer, and how many, and give me a ring before I go home, will you?"

"Yes, of course. Where do we meet you, by the way?"

"At the car-turn, I think. I'll be there at nine fifteen; it only takes about an hour, but we don't know how fast your *éminence grise* walks."

"The funny thing is, he isn't *gris* at all" Julia said. "His hair's jet black, practically, and yet he gives the impression of being quite elderly."

"Perhaps he dyes it" Terence said—Julia's laughter at this suggestion made heads turn as they passed through the small restaurant. As they walked back towards the car—"Shall you be in all this afternoon?" she asked.

"Bother—no, I shan't. And I don't know when I shall be in or out, because I must try and shift a couple of appointments I had for tomorrow."

"Oh well, I'll find out about the stakes, and drop a note at the office. Number and height is all you want to know, isn't it? I needn't say anthing else. All right, I'll go and settle that, and then go home."

"Up to the Serra?"

"Yes. I've rather neglected Mrs. H. this last day or two."

"Don't overdo it" he said. "Pity the doctor hasn't a room for you too."

"Oh, I'm all right. Thank you for everything, and for the lunch." She got into the car and drove off.

Julia polished off her business at the clinic very quickly. She sent up a message asking for Colin, and waited for him in the car; when he came down she explained that Terence Armitage was coming with them tomorrow, and was therefore too busy to get to the clinic that afternoon, and passed on his question about the stakes for the thermometer. Colin protested a little that Sir Percy was expecting him—Julia brushed that aside.

"He hasn't *bought* him!" she exclaimed. "Go and ask the old boy about those stakes, and let me get home. I want a shut-eye."

He looked at her with concern. "Are you tired? I wish you didn't have all this driving."

"Well, none of us had too *much* sleep last night!" she said. "And it will be an early start tomorrow—do you think you can have him ready and fed by a quarter past seven? We ought to leave here by then at latest, to get to the car-turn by nine fifteen."

"I'm sure I can. All right, I'll go and ask about the stakes." He went upstairs, and was back in a very short time.

"He wants a dozen, three feet six inches high, and *stout,* so that the sheep can't push them over. And then he wants some battens, four twelve-inch, four eighteen-inch, and four ten inch. And a hammer and nails."

Julia wrote all this down. "O.K.—I'll see to that," she said. "Goodbye, my dear." She started the car.

"No, half a second. What's Terry going to do about Ag?" Colin asked.

"Oh, he's not saying where he's going."

"Good. 'Bye, darling."

Back at the Shipping Office Julia went in and wrote the bare words that Colin had used, omitting the reference to the sheep, put the sheet in an envelope, stuck it down and sealed it with a stamp from her hand-bag—as she went out she gave the note to the commissionaire; he had seen her with Terence, and she felt he would certainly see that it reached its destination. Then she drove up to the Serra. A babel of the children's voices reached her from the garden as she parked the car—"Goodness, they *are* noisy!" she muttered. She went straight upstairs and tapped on the door of Mrs. Hathaway's sitting-room; as before Mme. Bonnecourt opened it. Yes, Madame was awake, and was taking her *tisane,* the Frenchwoman said; *"Entrez, Madame, s'il vous plaît."* Julia asked if she might have a cup of *tisane* too, and then went in to her old friend.

"My dearest child, I *am* glad to see you! Pauline said you only got in terribly late last night."

"Yes I know, Mrs. H. And I had to start rather early this morning. How are you?"

"Oh, very well. I put cotton-wool in my ears for my nap in the afternoon, if the children don't go for a walk; it works beautifully" the old lady said. "But how are *you?* You look a little tired."

"Just a little short on sleep" Julia said, sitting down. "I've asked Madame Bonnecourt for a cup of your *tilleul,* or whatever she gives you; then I thought I'd have a shut-eye till dinner."

"A very good idea. I hope you don't have to make another early start tomorrow?"

"Well, I do, as a matter of fact—even earlier; I've got to be off at six," Julia said. *"Ah, merci bien, Madame"* as the *tisane* was brought; she sipped it gratefully. Mrs. Hathaway looked at her.

"Dear child, do you really *have* to start so early tomorrow? I hope nothing has gone wrong."

"No, everything is going marvellously" Julia said. "It's just that rather a lot is happening, these few days. I'm quite all right, really—only sleepy. You know what a dormouse I am!"

"Couldn't Colin do some of this driving? How is he, by the way?"

"Better than I've ever seen him!" Julia said, with sudden energy, the glow coming into her face again. "Oh, and talking of being better, the child is nearly well."

"Oh, what good news! I am so thankful" the old lady said. "This doctor must be a very clever man."

"Yes, he is" Julia agreed, with secret amusement. "Mrs. H., dear, do you think you could fix something for me with Pauline? You're such a good fixer—and you ask no questions!" she added quickly.

"I expect I can. What is it?"

"Lunch for two, packed and ready in the hall, for me to take tomorrow" Julia said.

"Oh, so you and Colin are going on a picnic—how nice" Mrs. Hathaway said.

"Well, you could call it that." Again Julia smiled with secret mirth.

"But I should have thought Penelope would have wanted to do Colin's lunch herself" the old lady pursued—"and Aglaia's."

"Colin isn't *at* the Quinta—he's staying in Funchal; and Aglaia isn't coming tomorrow" Julia said. She reflected that though Mrs. H. might not ask questions, she could push one quite a bit by her cheerful assumptions. "This is an official picnic" she went on, "and Aglaia can't be in on it. I don't know when I shall be able to tell you all about it, if ever; if I can, it will make you laugh." She put down her cup and got up. "Bless you" she said, kissing the old lady. "I'm just going to see the Philipino, and then I'm for my bed."

"You'd better take some cotton-wool" Mrs. Hathaway said, handing her a small piece. "The children will be in the garden till their bed-time, because it's Marta's day out." Julia thanked her, laughing, and went off to see her son.

Colin saw, next morning, what Major Hartley had meant by saying that Sir Percy "liked a jaunt". The scientist was in tremendous spirits as they drove down the coast road in the bright early sunshine, full of interest in everything he saw, and of questions about it. Julia, refreshed by her pre-dinner sleep and a reasonably early night, played up to him excellently—she paused to show him the dragon-tree. "Ah, I wondered if we should see one of those" he said, delighted; on paper he was perfectly familiar with the peculiarities of Madeiran vegetation. "When we get up into the mountains, shall we see *Echium candicans?*" he asked hopefully. Julia could not tell him; Colin, however, said that they would not see this particular wonder that day, "unless we get through in time to go up towards the Grande Curral on the way back."

Terence was waiting at the car-turn when they reached it, accompanied by a peasant with a bundle of stakes and battens, a crowbar and a sledge-hammer; they both looked rather startled as the apparatus for Sir Percy's activities was unloaded from the car—the tripod for the camera, the camera itself, a knapsack, in fact containing the thermometer, and finally a wicker-work object looking more like a hamper in which one sends a cat on a journey than anything else. All this equipment was somehow distributed among the party. Sir Percy insisted on taking the camera himself; its tripod was tied to the bundle of stakes, which the peasant placed on his head, thus leaving his hands free for the hammer; Terence put on the knapsack—he, like Julia, already had a haversack of lunch slung round his shoulder; Colin carried the crowbar, and Julia was left to manage the wicker object. They set off up the ridge—Terence and Sir Percy were soon deep in talk; the cousins followed, the peasant brought up the rear.

"I say, this is a most hellish thing to carry" Julia said almost at once. "Have you got any string?"

"I think so—what for?"

"To tie it to my haversack. It won't go under one's arm, it's too big, and in the tunnel I shall want *one* hand for my torch."

"Damn! I forgot about the torches" Colin said, fumbling in the pockets of his shorts, from one of which he produced some lengths of string.

"I expect Terence has brought some."

"We'd better make sure" he said, and shouted. "Hi, Terry, did you bring torches?"

"Yes" Terence called back.

Even when the wicker object was attached to Julia's haversack, it proved a most awkward thing to walk with, the sharp corners bumping into her legs.

"What a brute it is! What on earth is it for?" she asked.

"To screen the thermometer. The air gets in, but not the sun. Look—" he tilted the piece of basketry up—"two layers, a couple of inches apart, and you see it's rather loosely woven; that's to let the air in; and made of the *split* cane. He was very insistent on that—he said the round cane might let some sun in. You must have seen those white wooden boxes with slats in them, standing on posts, at Kew and Wisley and that sort of place; this is the local substitute."

"Yes, I believe I have, but I never knew what was in them."

"Well, they're to hold recording thermometers—'Stevenson's screens', the old boy calls them. He didn't have time to collect one before his plane took off, so he counted on getting it here.

That wasn't too easy, so de Carvalho persuaded him to try wicker instead of wood, and we went round yesterday afternoon to one of those wicker-shops, and he showed them what he wanted, with a sketch, and they fixed this up in a couple of hours —two sizes of basket, held apart by little struts. He was as pleased as Punch."

"It was rather a bright idea" Julia said. "Our doctor is a bright boy."

When they reached the entrance to the tunnel Terence doled out torches, and they set off through that wet, noisy, echoing place. It enchanted Sir Percy—"So modestly simple, and *so* efficient" he pronounced; but when they reached the further end, and emerged into the lush, green, rich vegetation of the central range, his astonishment was extreme. He looked at his watch. "Barely half an hour's walk!—*quite* fantastic!" he exclaimed. At the foot of the rock wall he cast an appraising eye over it—"Yes, there is hardly need for a fence" he said to Julia. He was slightly taken aback by the hammocks, but when Julia lay down in one he followed suit, clutching his camera to his chest, and was borne and slung aloft, still repeating that it was fantastic. The stakes and other impedimenta occupied the third hammock, but Terence carried the knapsack with the thermometer; he, Colin, and the peasant climbed. At the top, released from his net, Sir Percy stood and gazed about him—at the stretch of grass and bracken ahead, then at the pale sunbaked landscape below to the east, and on the other side the mountains and valleys, moist, green with woods and ringing with waterfalls.

"You described it most exactly—it *is* between two climates" he said to Julia. He poked his stick into the short turf. "And would appear to enjoy a quite individual one of its own," he added to Terence.

"I think that is so, sir" Terence agreed.

"Well now, let us see if we can find some of these sheep" Sir Percy said. As before, they walked to the first pool; this time there were no sheep near it, but they deposited the heavier gear —the stakes, the haversacks, the rucksack with the thermometer, and, to Julia's relief, the awkward wicker screen—all in the care of the peasant, who was instructed by Terence to be sure not to let any sheep approach them. Sir Percy asked about the pool —were there springs in it? Terence could not tell him. The scientist went over to the water's edge and again poked the ground with his stick.

"Would it be a dew-pond?" he speculated.

"I should hardly think so—weren't they constructed by Neolithic man?" Terence said. "Madeira has no pre-history."

Sir Percy turned a startled gaze on him.

"Nor it has—barely mediaeval! I had forgotten for the moment. Oh well, never mind. Now the sheep." He picked up his camera, Colin shouldered the tripod, and they walked forward. Terence soon spotted a group of sheep away to their right, and they went across to them; the animals were obligingly coughing, wheezing, and turning their heads about. Sir Percy stood and watched them for some moments.

"Yes—*vairy* distinctive" he said at length. "Do you think we could get hold of one?" he asked Terence.

"Oh yes, easily—they're quite stupefied." Terence walked up to the sheep, who as on the previous occasion took no notice of him till he was within a yard or two; even then they only moved slowly, in a dazed fashion—he caught hold of one by the fleece and held it. Sir Percy handed his camera to Colin, went to the sheep, and examined its eyes.

"Yes, the pupils are markedly contracted. *Vairy* good!" he said in a tone of satisfaction. He pulled a small ophthalmoscope, such as oculists use, out of his pocket, and with it looked at the animal's eyes again. "Oh botheration!" he exclaimed. "I haven't used one of these things for years—I can make nothing of this contracted pupil!"

Julia was standing beside Colin, a few yards away, watching these proceedings; she was startled to hear him give a sort of moan, and turned to him—he was standing with a look of horror on his face. "What is it? Are you ill?" she asked anxiously. As he did not answer—"Colin, what is it?" she urged, shaking his arm.

"The whole people of England!" he said, under his breath, still staring at the bemused and helpless sheep.

"No!" she said firmly. "It shan't happen. We'll stop it! It *shall* be all right, darling." She was a good deal distressed by this sudden display of emotion in Colin. To distract him—"Here, let's set up the tripod" she said briskly; "he's sure to want to take a photograph."

Colin roused himself at that; he went across and asked the scientist if he wished to take a picture of the sheep?

"Oh no, thank you. This isn't a ciné-camera; a still would tell one nothing" Sir Percy said. "One ought really to have a reel of film and a tape-recording, to be of much use. But have you got any atropine with you?"

"No, sir—I'm sorry."

"I've got one syrette" Julia said; she unbuttoned the breast-pocket of her dress and drew the small object out.

"*Vairy* good" Sir Percy said, taking it. "Now, Mr. Armitage, can you—er—reverse this animal?"

Terence deftly turned the sheep onto its back, and held its head; Sir Percy lifted one foreleg, and plunged the needle in—the sheep kicked wildly.

"Shall I let it go?" Terence asked.

"No, please hold it for a moment or two." In fact the sheep soon stopped struggling, and lay passive; after a few minutes it ceased to cough and wheeze.

"Now you can release it" the scientist said. Terence did so, and set the creature on its feet. It stood still for a moment or two; then it shook itself vigorously, looked round at the group of humans, and suddenly galloped off at top speed. Terence burst out laughing.

"Fair enough!" he said.

Sir Percy looked pleased. "An excellent result" he said. "Well now, let us go on."

As they walked on across the plateau Julia, following the other two with Colin, muttered in his ear that she wondered what the old boy wanted the camera *for,* if he wasn't going to use it? However as they approached the farther end Sir Percy stopped, set up the tripod and took a series of photographs—back across the plateau by the way they had come, of the mountains to the east, and of the landscape to north and south of them; for these last he

fitted a telephoto lens. On the way they had seen plenty of the
doped sheep, and on the return walk they saw more still; at Sir
Percy's instance they took a route nearly a mile to the right of the
track, so as to see a different part of the plateau. He walked very
fast; he stopped twice to take more photographs, which would
show the place at a right-angle to the first pictures. Most of the
time he walked in silence—once he asked Terence when the
mist might be expected to come up?

"Any time now, if it's coming; there are days when it doesn't
happen at all" Terence told him.

It was nearly two when they got back to the pool, where the
peasant still sat, patient and contented, cutting slices off a raw
onion and a loaf of bread, and eating them. Terence produced a
thermos flask containing Martinis from his haversack, and a
leather-covered roll of tiny silver cups to drink them from.
"Goodness, I wanted that!" Julia said, as she sat on the grass and
sipped her drink.

Over their belated meal Sir Percy, in reply to a question from
Julia—who knew that Colin would have liked to ask it, but re-
frained out of an Intelligence notion of protocol—gave his
opinion on the sheep.

"I should say their condition is undoubtedly due to what you
suspected" he said, with a glance at the peasant, who sat within
earshot, taking swigs from a mug of red wine which Terence had
handed to him. "Our medical friend expects to get a report from
France any day now on the blood samples he sent which should
confirm it beyond any possibility of mistake, one way or another,
though seeing the behaviour of that sheep after the injection, I
have few doubts left myself. What still troubles me a little is the
means of distribution. I agree with you, Monro, that by bright
moonlight it would be perfectly possible for ten men to cover the
whole area, using knapsack sprayers; the terrain certainly per-
mits of that. But it still leaves the boy unaccounted for." He
turned to Terence. "Mr. Armitage, do you think it would be possible to establish at precisely what time the young boy left his
home?"

Terence considered.

"I should hardly think so" he said—"not precisely. You see he went off without his parents' knowledge, as he often does; they don't worry about him."

"Might he remember himself? He seemed an intelligent child."

"Oh, you saw him, did you? Yes, he's as bright as a button. But I doubt whether he would be very accurate about times; these people live by the sun, and by their hunger! Why—if you don't mind my asking—is it so important to know when he left home?"

"To learn the earliest time he could possibly have been on the plateau." Sir Percy explained again about the two-hour period of efficacy of nerve gases. "So if the gas was distributed during the hours of darkness, unless the boy was up here by sunrise, or an hour after it at latest, it is hard to understand how he could have been so seriously affected."

"Yes, I see. Well, he might possibly remember whether he got up here before sunrise. I should think it most improbable that he did."

"Why?"

"Because Manoel—his father, my steward—locks the door of the farm-house at night, and keeps the key under his pillow; he only opens it when he gets up in the morning."

"Which is at what hour?"

"Daybreak" Terence said briefly, "and it would take two hours, at the very least, to get here from the Quinta on foot."

"Could the child have climbed out?" Julia asked.

"I hardly think so."

"Might he at least remember if he had done this?" Sir Percy enquired, hopefully.

"He *might*—but it doesn't follow that he would admit it!" Terence said, with a faint grin.

"Not if you asked him yourself, Terence, and told him it was really important?" Julia urged.

"I could try—it would probably be better to lay on the priest, if it is absolutely vital to know. Even then, I shouldn't consider it hundred per cent certain" Terence stated firmly.

"Really?" Sir Percy looked startled.

"These people are rather like the Irish about trying to tell you what they imagine you want to hear" Terence said tolerantly. "However, when I get home I'll have another go at the parents, willingly. But I shouldn't like to base any firm conclusion on what we get either from the parents, or the priest, or the boy himself."

"H'm. That is unfortunate" Sir Percy said.

"Yes. But it's no good my raising false hopes, in a matter of this importance."

"No, I agree. Your personal knowledge of these people, and their characters, is of great value" Sir Percy said. He frowned. "In that case, we are thrown back on the possibility of some delayed-action means of distribution."

"Do you mean what Dr. de Carvalho suggested, some soluble form of container that would dissolve in sunlight and release the gas?" Colin asked.

"Something of the sort—though as I said, I cannot think off-hand of such a substance."

"Of course for the ultimate use of this gas, against a foreign country, that would have great advantages, wouldn't it?" Terence put in. "Distributed by night, but coming into action by daylight, when the maximum number of people would be about, and exposed to it."

"True enough. They might well be working at something on those lines, as well as on the new gas, with its temporary qualities" Sir Percy said thoughtfully. He was silent for a few moments, obviously pondering; the others said nothing. At last he roused himself.

"Well, we had better set up the thermograph" he said. "Where is that knapsack?"

Sir Percy took a good deal of trouble about siting his instrument. He walked round for some time, asking Terence about the direction of the prevailing wind, and using a compass to get the exact point on the horizon where the sun would rise at that season of the year; finally he chose a spot a considerable distance away from both the pool and the track, to lessen the likelihood of the machine's being noticed and interfered with. "One can't lock this basket contraption, as one can a Stevenson's screen" he said regretfully. The place chosen, the peasant brought over the bundle of stakes, and Terence, under the scientist's direction, made four holes in the ground with the crowbar, drove in four stakes, and then hammered battens across their tops, making a small oblong platform—this Sir Percy checked carefully with a spirit-level, which with the hammer and nails had come up in one of the outer pockets of the knapsack. "Hammer this one in a shade more, Armitage—gently. Now let us see—" he used the spirit-level again. "*Vairy* good!" he said at last. Then from the knapsack he drew out an object wrapped in a cloth.

His companions looked with curiosity at the thermograph, a word unfamiliar to all three of them. In fact it looked almost exactly like the familiar barograph, a copper box containing a cylinder covered with ruled paper, on which, Sir Percy explained, an inked point would record the temperature hour by hour— "This one runs for a week." He wound it up by a key, like a clock-key, at the top, tested the point to see that the ink was properly adjusted, and closed the lid. From a small leather toolcase he took out a gimlet, a screwdriver, and some screws, and screwed the whole gadget firmly on to the battens by lugs projecting from the base. Another check with the spirit-level proved satisfactory; then he placed Julia's enemy, the double basket-cover, over the whole.

"That should do" he said, contemplating the arrangement.

"Sir Percy, mightn't it be an idea to drive in two more stakes and fasten the cover to them? If the wind got up suddenly it could be blown away" Terence suggested.

"Yes, you are quite right." The two extra stakes were driven in, and the basket-cover lashed to them with string. Sir Percy regarded it with satisfaction.

"Marvellously clever these people are at wicker-work" he observed. "Lovely trays and baskets they had in that place where we went to get this—such fine delicate patterns. You never see anything like that at home."

"All the same, it was the English who introduced basket-making here" Terence said mildly.

"No—was it really?"

"Yes. Two old boys called James Taylor and William Hinton started it, a hundred years or more ago; they found the withies growing freely in some of the *ribeiras* here, and sent to Italy for patterns, and set the whole thing going. Now of course it brings in thousands of dollars a year. But they *are* good workers" Terence added; "neat-fingered, and very patient."

"That's most interesting. And what about the wine?—did the English start that too?"

"Well, only half" Terence said, with a slow chuckle.

"Pray explain" Sir Percy said, a little austerely.

"Prince Henry the Navigator started the wine, and the sugar-making too; he sent for Malvoisie vines from Crete, and sugar-canes from Sicily, as soon as he got reports of his new island having fertile volcanic soil and a warm climate. A *proper* coloniser, he was" Terence said cheerfully.

"Then what had the English to do with it? Surely he was the son of the Portuguese King?"

"Yes, but he was half-English; his mother, Queen Philippa, was John of Gaunt's daughter."

"John of Gaunt's grandson! That explains a lot" Sir Percy said approvingly. The party then set out homewards, pausing by the pool to collect the haversacks. At the foot of the rock face the hammock-men were paid off by Terence. "When shall you want them again?" he asked Sir Percy. "Tomorrow? The day after would be better, if it's all the same to you."

"For you? Could we not come without troubling you again, if it is inconvenient? You are being most good," Sir Percy said warmly.

"No, for them. Tomorrow is Sunday, and they'll want to get to Mass."

"Oh, then arrange for them to come on Monday, by all means," Sir Percy said. "Let us all keep the Sabbath!"

11 WHEN THEY RETURNED to the cars Sir Percy again raised the question of seeing *Echium candicans.* Julia looked furtively at her watch—the time was half past four. Terence Armitage noticed this, and intervened.

"Sir Percy, may I make a suggestion?"

"By all means."

"Let me come and pick you up tomorrow, immediately after lunch, and take you myself to see the *Echium.* I know exactly where to look for it, which I think is more than either Mrs. Jamieson or her cousin can say for themselves."

"Too right—I'd never even heard of it!" Julia said cheerfully, throwing Terence a grateful glance.

"That would be an excellent plan, if it is not putting you to too much trouble" Sir Percy said.

"Not at all—I always enjoy seeing it." He turned to Julia. "Come in my car as far as the turn" he said—"that will save you a little driving."

"Oh, I'd love to."

"All right—get in. Colin, you can see to stowing all the gear, can't you?"

"Of course."

As they drove off—"Remorseless old bastard, isn't he?" Terence said. "Let's assume, for the sake of charity, that he doesn't know you have an extra hour on the road before and after chauffeuring him. But even so—"

"Oh, I don't suppose he gives it a thought" Julia said. "He's fearfully tough himself, for a man of his age, isn't he?"

"I can't remember what his age is, but he's certainly no juvenile lead" Terence said. "Yes, he must be very strong."

"Terence, there's something I wanted to ask you—I'm glad to have this chance."

"Ask away" he said.

"That hotel where we had lunch yesterday—is it a respectable, clean place?"

"The Montefiore? Yes, perfectly respectable; and all Portuguese hotels are clean now. Why?"

"I was thinking I might stay there myself; I could shift down tomorrow, as there's nothing much doing. It would be more convenient in lots of ways."

"I think that's an admirable idea; it would be less tiring for you, if you really have to take the old boy everywhere. I was wondering, as a matter of fact, if Colin couldn't take him about by himself."

"Oh, I'm sure he could. It's just my natural curiosity that brings me along now." She began to laugh a little. "An old flame, years ago, used to call me Fatima."

He turned and glanced at her.

"No, I can't see that" he said. "I disagree with the old flame. I think they're probably the better of you, if you don't overdo it. I tell you what—when I get home I'll ring Da Silva, the landlord, and book you a room, and let you know at the Shergolds tonight. What time shall you get in?"

"About eight, I should think. That *is* kind of you. But supposing they haven't got a room?"

"They'll have one all right, if I tell them to; the office sends them more than half their guests. Shall you go before lunch, or after?"

"Oh, before, please. Then I can have a glorious sleep all the afternoon. How splendid! It will be more convenient for Pauline, too, not to have me coming and going at all hours," she added.

Terence duly rang up that evening to say that a room was booked for her at the Montefiore. Julia took the call in the hall; when she went back into the drawing-room—"What did

Terence want?" Pauline Shergold asked; she had answered the telephone.

"Oh, he was being angelic, as usual" Julia replied. She decided to get her announcement over at once. "While I have to be down in Funchal so much of the time, and keep such irregular hours, I thought it would save trouble all round, and especially for you, Pauline, if I stayed down there; so he has got me a room in an hotel. I do realise what a nuisance I must have been, although you've both been so kind about it—so this seemed the best plan."

"I don't think you've been any particular trouble, or nuisance" Gerald said bluntly, "but I think it's a much better idea for you—save all that extra driving at both ends of the day. Where are you going to stay?"

"At the Montefiore."

"Oh yes—that's a very decent little place. The food's nothing out of the way, but on the other hand their terms are very reasonable. And there are no evening dances to keep you awake. When do you go?"

"Tomorrow morning, I thought."

"What I don't understand is *why* you have to be down there so much" Pauline said.

"I expect she's helping Colin in some racket of his" Gerald said, cheerfully. "If so it's no good your living up to your name, Mrs. Parker, because she won't tell you!"

"Dear Pauline, you're so good" Julia said. "I'd much sooner be here. May I come back as soon as I can?"

"Yes, of course. I wish you didn't have to go" her hostess said, half-mollified. But only half, as her expression showed—they had all combined to frustrate her, Pauline Shergold felt.

Mrs. Hathaway always went to bed rather early, and Julia, pleading her six A.M. start, went upstairs with her. In the bedroom—"I do hope Pauline isn't really hurt at my going away" Julia said.

"She has no reason to be" the old lady said, rather tartly. "It is obviously the best plan. If only Pauline would learn to *accept* things, it would be so much more comfortable for her, and for everyone else." She unpinned a brooch from the front of her dress, and put it down on the dressing-table. "Have you any idea how long you shall be away?" she asked then, in a different tone.

"No, I don't know yet. I hope only for two or three days, at the outside" Julia said. "I'll ring you up now and then, when I get a minute—shall I?"

"Yes, do, my dearest child. And now you ought to get to bed. Try not to do too much tomorrow."

"Oh, tomorrow I shan't do anything at all!" Julia said gaily. "We shall keep the Sabbath, and I shall sleep the whole afternoon. Goodnight, precious Mrs. H. I'm so glad you've got Madame Bonnecourt."

"So am I. Really, she is a most charming person; so kind, and such good company," Mrs. Hathaway said. "Bless you, my dear child."

Julia reached the Montefiore next day a little before noon. She found that lock-up garages were provided for such guests as desired them, and took one for Terence's car, out of an ingrained habit of caution. Then she went up to her room. Terence had done her well—it was large and pleasant, and overlooked the garden; also it had a nice balcony with chairs and tables, and a telephone by the bed. She had told Colin the evening before, on their way back to Funchal, of her proposed move—"And if we need to talk, you ring *me* up, so that I'm not in any way linked with the clinic" she had said; now, when the telephone rang just as she was finishing her moderate unpacking, she assumed it would be Colin. But it was Terence's voice that spoke.

"Room all right?" he asked.

"Oh yes, perfect. Thank you *so* much; it couldn't be nicer."

"Good. Come down and have a drink."

"Oh goodness, I've put the car away!" Julia exclaimed, rather daunted by this suggestion.

"Well, you won't need the car to get out into the garden, will you?" he said, laughing at her.

"Terence, where *are* you?"

"Here, at your pub. I thought I'd see if you were all right."

"Oh, good—yes, I'll come at once." She snapped her suitcase

to, and went downstairs. Terence met her in the hall; he ordered drinks at the bar, and they went out and sat at the table under the trees where they had lunched two days earlier.

"Well, I've found out your old fellow's age, anyhow, and I think he must dye his hair" Terence said.

"How old *is* he?" Julia asked with interest.

"Seventy last week."

"Gracious, you didn't ask him?"

"Lord, no—I popped into the Club just now and looked him up in *Who's Who*. There's nearly a page of him—he's an Honorary M.D. of universities all over Europe, and an LL.D. all over the world, from Canada to the Antipodes. He's terrifically distinguished academically; been President of the Royal Society and head of the Medical Research Council, and I don't know what. So much for your boffin" Terence said, looking at her amusedly through his horn-rimmed glasses.

"Then I wonder why Colin's office got him to come out here" Julia speculated. "You'd have thought they'd have got someone who knows directly about nerve gases."

"Oh, he knows all right—no one better. He's on the Consultative Committee for Chemical and Biological Warfare, or whatever they call it, and advises about experiments at that Porton place."

"Goodness, do they put that in *Who's Who?*"

"No" Terence said, laughing a little—"he told me that himself. But he is primarily an academic." He got up. "I'd better be off—I'm going to have lunch with Aunt Sally."

"Give my love to Porfirio" Julia said. "And I hope you find Sir Percy's plant for him. We'd better settle now about meeting on Monday, if you're coming."

"Oh yes, I might as well. Same time, same place. It shouldn't be such a long day, though; he only wants to read his machine, I imagine. Have a good nap this afternoon."

When Terence had gone Julia went up to her room again and fetched a book; she ordered lunch in the garden, and sat there reading. Presently, to her surprise, Colin came out through the restaurant, and walked over to her. "Morning, darling" he said, giving her a kiss.

"Oh, are you coming to lunch? How nice."

"Yes please. I thought I could leave the old boy for a bit; he was going to look at the ceiling of some church this morning, and the doctor has got Pereira coming to lunch."

"Oh, are they going to tell Pereira? I wonder if that's wise" Julia said.

"I don't think they will tell him much—Sir Percy just wanted to hear his ideas about the complaint, in case he picked something up. But I'm getting slightly asphyxiated by so much science!" Colin said, grinning.

"Have you ordered your lunch?"

"No. I thought I'd ask first!"

"Silly!" Julia said. "Go and order it—my room number's eleven—and get yourself a drink at the same time."

When he came back with his drink Julia said—"If you've got the afternoon off, why don't you go down and see Aglaia? I shan't want the car; I'm going to snooze."

To her surprise Colin frowned and hesitated.

"No, I don't think I'd better" he said, after a pause. "I'd sooner finish this business first, before I get involved in all that again. I never was any good at doing two things at once."

"Yes, I see" Julia said slowly. In fact she didn't quite see, and wondered if he might not be making a mistake. But she left it alone—if Colin was growing up now, this might be part of it. To change the subject she told him what Terence had gleaned about Sir Percy's age from *Who's Who,* and his conjecture about his hair.

"Oh yes, I'm pretty sure he does dye it" Colin said. "I've been wondering why—because he's not in the least a vain man."

"No, I imagine anyone as learned and honoured as that has no need for vanity" Julia said. "It must be some funny quirk."

When they had nearly finished their lunch the two young Spaniards came out, and again sat down at the neighbouring table; they half-bowed to Julia as they did so.

"Who are your friends?" Colin asked.

"Oh, they were here when Terence brought me to lunch the day before yesterday" Julia said. "I suppose they're staying here too. They're Spanish."

"Not Portuguese?" Colin asked. "That's a Nazaré shirt he's wearing." One of the youths was indeed wearing a vivid red and green tartan shirt, such as the fishermen wear at Nazaré, near Lisbon.

"No, they talk Spanish."

She and Colin went on chatting idly; as soon as she had finished her coffee Julia said she was going to lie down—"Catch up with my sleep" she said. As she got up the two young Spaniards again rose and half-bowed.

"They seem rather anxious to scrape an acquaintance" Colin remarked.

"Oh, I expect it's just a Spanish habit" she replied carelessly. "In fact they might be quite useful acquaintances, because they've got just what Sir Percy wanted for the sheep, a ciné-camera."

"How do you know that?"

"They were playing with it the other day, taking pictures of the waitress."

"Oh well, scrape their acquaintance, by all means" Colin said laughing. "Goodbye, darling. See you tomorrow."

"Yes—at seven fifteen sharp."

"Right. Have a good sleep." He kissed her and left.

Julia went up to her room, but she did not at once lie down; first she finished her unpacking. As she was folding back the bed-spread and arranging the pillows for her rest she noticed that she had not got her book; she must have left it behind in the garden —bother! She decided to go and fetch it at once; she would want it to read with her tea. (Julia was one of the people who must have something to read during a solitary meal.) She started downstairs. In the otherwise empty hall, at the foot of the staircase, the two young Spaniards were standing beside the barometer, apparently engaged in an argument; the one in the Nazaré shirt tapped it irritably. "You *see?*—it falls!" he said. "If the weather turns bad we shall not be able to get pictures of the *ovejas.*"

The Spanish word for sheep brought Julia to a halt. She stood perfectly still, and listened.

"But Polunsky said to make the second record precisely at three weeks," his companion objected.

"Well, that is twenty-one days, and today it is seventeen. Is it not better to have a record a day or two early, than perhaps to get no record at all?" he of the loud shirt said, tapping the barometer again.

"Polunsky said we were to be most exact concerning the dates," his companion repeated.

"Well, if the weather stays fine we can go up again at twenty-one days precisely." Still arguing, they passed out towards the street.

Julia ran quickly downstairs, through the restaurant and out into the garden—yes, the book was on the seat of a chair, pushed in under the table, so that she had not noticed it when she left with Colin. But when she returned to her room, though she took off her dress and lay down on the bed, she made no attempt, at first, either to read or to sleep. Instead she lit a cigarette, got out her diary, and looked at various dates. It was a week yesterday—eight days—since they had first seen the sick sheep, and Marcusinho had been ill for at least a week before that, possibly longer; allowing for the peasantry vagueness of the hammock-men, give or take a day, it could well be just seventeen days since the ten "tourists" had gone up to the Paúl da Serra. It was exactly eighteen days since she had first seen the trawler, too, off Funchal —and Polunsky was surely a Russian-sounding name? Were these two Spaniards the "local accomplices", whose existence Terence had postulated as essential for laying on the mules from Seixial, and the hammocks? It all looked rather as though it tied in.

She looked at her watch—ten past three; Da Silva would still be having his siesta. Julia decided to have one too, drew down the Venetian blinds, settled comfortably on the bed, and was soon asleep.

She slept for over two hours, and awoke feeling fresh, cheerful and somehow determined. She rang for tea, and took it in bed; when she got up she put on a fresh white silk dress with a black belt, and black and white sandals, and went downstairs. The first thing to do was to learn anything that the landlord could tell her about the two Spaniards, but this must be done as casually as possible. She went into the bar and ordered a drink, and took it to a table by an open French window giving onto the garden, where a path led along to the door from the restaurant. As she had expected, Senhor da Silva presently appeared, checking on the laying of the tables in the garden, like the good landlord he was; he had greeted her on her arrival, and now, when he noticed her sitting there, he came over and asked very politely, in French, if her room was to her liking, and if she had everything that she required? Julia seldom had any difficulty about engaging a man in conversation, and she did not now; after praising her accommodation, the flowers in the garden, and the view, she went on to ask some very sensible questions about the length of the tourist season, and the relative profitability of the restaurant as compared with permanent guests. Oh, the restaurant by itself was not of much importance, Da Silva told her; few people knew of its existence except those, like the Senhor Armitage, who were connected with the tourist trade—"We cater principally for clients who make a prolonged stay, and like quiet."

And of what nationality, generally speaking, were most of his clients? Julia asked—English? American?

"Oh, a little of everything! The Senhor Armitage is very good about sending us English and Americans; often elderly people, who appreciate quiet and comfort."

Not all his guests seemed to be elderly, Julia pointed out, smiling, and referred to the two young men who sat at the table next to hers. "They are Spanish, *n'est-ce-pas?*"

To her great satisfaction, the landlord launched into a eulogy of his Spanish guests. They were wealthy, and though fond of a joke, as the Senhora had doubtless observed the other day, they were well-connected and well-behaved. This was their second visit—last year they had stayed for over a month. And this year? Julia asked. Oh, already they had been here for five weeks this year, Da Silva said. Julia expressed a little surprise at so long a stay, for young and healthy people—"How do they amuse themselves?" she asked. Oh, but the expeditions!—always they were making expeditions, visiting every part of the island, taking photographs of the architecture and making films of the peasants and their activities.

H'm—excellent cover, Julia thought. Aloud, she supposed they had a car?

No, they hired one from him; the hotel kept two or three cars for the convenience of guests who wished to go for drives.

With chauffeurs? Julia enquired.

"Oh, for the more elderly, I supply some excellent chauffeurs. But these young Senhores drive themselves; then they can come and go as they please. Often they drive to a place, and then walk or do their photography for hours; a chauffeur could be an embarrassment on such occasions."

"Quite so" Julia agreed heartily. In fact she agreed with all the landlord's propositions; if these two young men were really the local accomplices, such arrangements were ideal for their purpose.

When the landlord, excusing himself, presently returned to his avocations, Julia ordered another drink to be sent to her room, and went up there. This new possibility wanted some thinking about. She would have liked to discuss it with Colin, but decided to stick to their agreement that she would not telephone to the clinic—anyhow, she would be seeing him in under twelve hours, she thought, glancing at her watch. Terence, too, was probably still out of reach, plant-hunting with Sir Percy; she must settle her immediate course of action by herself. Colin, admittedly half-jokingly, had told her to "scrape an acquaintance" with the two Spaniards, in order to get a film of the sheep for Sir Percy; but if they were anyhow going to do precisely that for Polunsky, whoever he might be, Julia had an instinctive feeling that the less she saw of them, or they of her, the better. She took up the telephone by her bed, and asked to speak to Da Silva; when he came she asked if she could have a packed lunch and coffee and rolls in her room tomorrow at six A.M., and, in view of this early start, said that she would like a light dinner served in her room. These dispositions taken, she rang up Mrs. Hathaway and told her how comfortable she was at the Montefiore; then she undressed, had a bath and went to bed and quietly read her book.

On the drive down the following morning Sir Percy, who sat beside her, was full of the glories of *Echium candicans*—"a truly noble plant." This suited Julia, who had already decided only to mention her suspicions of the two Spaniards to Colin, in the first instance; plenty of time to tell the others when they had learned more—if they did learn any more. They passed through the last village, and up to the place on the ridge where cars were left, and turned; there was a car there, but it was not Terence's.

"Hullo, I wonder whose car that is?" Colin said.

"Are we to be observed? I should have preferred it otherwise" Sir Percy said.

A faint prickle of foreboding ran over Julia's nerves.

"Terry did say he was coming, Julia, didn't he?" Colin asked.

"Yes, definitely. We are a couple of minutes early" she said. And indeed at that moment a humming sound, coming up the road towards them, heralded the arrival of Terence on an outsize motor-cycle; the peasant, perched behind his great bulk, somehow reminded Julia of a monkey attached to a barrel-organ— the absurd idea made her smile.

"Morning. I hope we're not late" Terence Armitage said, getting off.

"No, we're early" Julia told him.

"Terence, do you know whose car that is?" Colin asked.

"No, no idea. It's a Funchal number-plate," Terence replied. He turned to Sir Percy. "I brought Tomás along, in case you wanted your gear brought down" he said.

"Oh, thank you; most obliging of you. I am not sure yet" Sir Percy replied.

As before, he walked with Terence, and the cousins followed. Julia at once told Colin what she had overheard in the hall of the hotel.

"Stone a crow!" Colin exclaimed. "What time was this?"

"About three. Why?"

"Why on earth didn't you tell me?"

"Because we'd settled that I wasn't going to ring the clinic from the hotel—don't you remember?"

"Yes, of course—but for something like *this!* Anyhow, couldn't you have come round and told me?"

"Yes, I suppose I could" Julia said, feeling considerably deflated. "But I didn't see that there was anything you could do, to make it all that urgent."

"So I suppose you just went to sleep!" Colin said indignantly.

"Yes, I did. But what could you have done about them?"

"Rung up Hartley, of course, and asked if the name Polunsky says anything to him—and if he has any lines on Spanish accomplices. What are their names, by the way?—at least, what names are they using?"

"Bother, I never asked Da Silva that," Julia said guiltily. "But you'd better let me finish telling you what Da Silva *did* tell me about them—that was what I waited for in the first place, for him to finish his siesta."

Colin laughed. "And you to get yours! You're slipping, Julia! All right, tell me."

He listened intently while Julia repeated the landlord's account of how his so desirable Spanish clients spent their time in Madeira—at one point he interrupted her recital to ask—"Do they do all these jaunts by car?"

"Yes—one of his. And they don't take a chauffeur."

Colin stopped, and glanced back down the ridge. "So that may actually be their car, down there at the turn" he said. "Murder! —I wish I'd known; I could have given it the once-over. I wonder if I'd better go back?"

"I shouldn't" Julia said. "If they were to spot you doing it from the top, they'd take alarm."

"Yes—probably." He started forward again. Any talk while they were passing through the tunnel was of course impossible, but when they emerged at the further end he said to Julia— "You can talk to these types with the hammocks, can't you?"

"Yes, well enough."

"Well, ask them if they've seen anyone go up today."

At the foot of the cliff, accordingly, Julia again spoke to the elderly man who had originally told her that the ten tourists had smoked brown cigarettes; she was beginning to regard the hammock-men quite as old friends, and they greeted her with beaming smiles. But no, no other tourists had come today; they chorused their agreement about this.

"Well, that's a let-off" Julia said, as she lay down in her fish-net hammock; she was becoming quite accustomed to this bizarre mode of transport. But when, at the top, she was released and stood up, all the same she looked a little anxiously across the stretch of grass and bracken in front of her. There, in the distance, were two figures; she was too shortsighted to see more than that.

"Terence, have you got your spy-glass?" she asked, as he came clambering up over the top.

"Yes. D'you want it?"

"Yes, please."

He pulled it out of his pocket and gave it to her; she adjusted it hurriedly, and then swept the green expanse, trying to pick up the distant figures—oh, why couldn't Terence carry field-glasses? At last she got them in the telescope's small field of vision; turning the screw of the lens, she got them properly in focus —they were standing beside a tripod, and one of them was wearing a green and red shirt; the enormous Nazaré tartan stood out plainly.

"Colin, come here!" she called, in a low tone; he was walking with Sir Percy towards the thermograph.

"What is it?" he called back—but then he too saw the little faraway group, and hurried back to her.

"It's them!" she said. "And I think they're using the film-camera."

He took the glasses from her, and also studied the men carefully.

"Yes, it's them all right, and that's precisely what they're doing!" he said excitedly. "Now what do *we* do?"

Julia had unslung her haversack and took out a very light fawn silk raincoat and a head-scarf; she tied the latter over her head, and put on the raincoat. "Oh, good girl!" the young man said approvingly.

"Yes—my hair's nearly as bad as his shirt!" she said. "Let's sit —then we shan't be nearly so visible. How on earth do you suppose they got up here without the men seeing them?"

"They must have climbed up further along; there are one or two routes. Or they may have got up before the hammock-types arrived. But we must go back at once—I must get onto Hartley."

"Can we wait while Sir Percy reads his machine?"

"No, not possibly—besides he may want to dismantle it and bring it down, which would take ages."

"So do I take you back to Funchal and come back for them?"

"No, that won't do either. Get hold of Terence—we must arrange something."

"Shall I tell him?"

"Yes of course—you'll have to."

Julia got up and walked quickly after the other two. As usual the scientist was walking very fast—she didn't want to be seen running, and presently called—"Terence! Could you come back for a moment?" She went on walking towards him, as he returned towards her; the moment they met she sat down on the ground.

"What's up?" he asked. "Aren't you feeling well?"

"No, I'm all right—only wanting to be inconspicuous! Sit, and I'll tell you."

He sat.

"Now, do you see those two men out there?" As she spoke she gave him back his pocket telescope. "No, perhaps you'd better not look with that now. But they're the two young Spaniards from the Montefiore; they're taking a film of the sheep."

"Well, why shouldn't they?" Terence asked reasonably.

"Because they're taking it for someone they refer to as Polunsky, who was very particular that they should make the *second* film recording at exactly three weeks" she said, opening her eyes at him.

"And is today exactly three weeks?" he asked.

"No, it's only eighteen days; but the one in the parti-coloured shirt was afraid the weather might break if they waited, so they've come up today. Terence, don't you *see*? Nine days today since we first saw the sheep; and Marcusinho had been ill fully a week before that, perhaps more—so it would be exactly eighteen days from the gassing. In fact it *must* be. Polunsky isn't a very *Spanish* name!" she ended.

"How do you know all this?"

"I overheard them yesterday, when they were looking at the barometer in the hotel."

"Were they talking French?"

"No, Spanish—like they were when we had lunch."

"Then how did you follow?"

"Oh, I've always talked Spanish—it's my second language. But the point is, Colin wants to get back to Funchal immediately to tell London—he can't wait while Sir Percy fiddles with his thermometer. Only what about the car, and him and you getting back?"

"I *see*" Terence said, thoughtfully. "Yes, there will be quite a lot of action wanted, and quite fast—and all possible inconspicuousness desirable! All right—you and Colin go off at once; look in at the Quinta on your way back and ask Penel to come up and fetch us—she's got the other car."

"Oh good—thank you *so* much."

"All right to tell *him* I suppose?" Terence asked.

"Not more than you can help; I mean, this isn't his side of the business."

"He'll be longing to get hold of their film, of course, if he knows they're making one" Terence said, with his slow grin.

"I don't doubt he'll get it!" Julia said, getting up. "Probably see it run off before they do, I shouldn't wonder. All right—'bye." She walked quickly back to Colin.

"That's all right" she said, taking his arm. "We're to tell Penelope to come up with the other car. Come on."

On the short walk between the foot of the cliff, where Julia was released from her hammock, and the entrance to the tunnel, Julia mentioned Terence's question about whether to tell Sir Percy what went on, and her reply. "Was that right?" she asked.

"Oh yes, I think so. I shall want to ask him if the name Polunsky says anything to him, but I can do that when he gets back."

They hurried through the tunnel and raced down the ridge to the two cars. Julia had turned the small Austin before she left it; she got in at once and started the engine.

"I say, do you think you could back that up the other side of their car?" Colin asked.

"There's not much room" Julia said—"Why?"

"To screen me, in case they should be on the look-out; I want to have a look at it."

"All right, I'll try."

The space was small, but she managed to edge the Austin up alongside the other car, between it and the mountains. "That do?" she asked.

"Yes, fine." He went round to the further side of the machine with the Funchal number-plate; it was an open sports-car, and the owners had not bothered to lock it. He got in and examined the glove-lockers—they produced nothing more interesting than a pencil, a packet of cigarettes, a slab of chocolate and a map of the island. This Colin examined minutely with a magnifying-glass; however it bore none of the giveaway pencil-marks for which he was looking. "They're more professional than de Lassalle and his poor chum in the Pyrenees" he remarked. "Do you remember the crazy marks they'd made all over their map?"

"Yes" said Julia briefly. When that map had been found Philip had been alive, happy and busy in the Near East, and she expecting his child. "Try the boot" she said.

"I'm going to." He got out and went round to the back of the car, saying gloomily "I bet you it's locked."

It wasn't locked—for the excellent reason, as he presently saw, that the lock was broken; the lid of the boot was roughly held in position by four broad straps of elastoplast. "Hell!" Colin exclaimed.

"What's the matter?" Julia asked, getting out; she came round and stood beside him.

"If I take that stuff off they'll see it's been tampered with" he said.

"Not if you're careful enough. Hold on a minute." From her

dress pocket she took out a small leather case which, besides her compact and powder-puff, contained a very small nailfile and a biro pen; these she laid on the ground on her handkerchief. Then, taking off her head-scarf, she first carefully wiped off all dust from the paintwork near the plaster—"The dust is the trouble" she said. Next, with the nailfile she very gently and carefully eased up the end of one strip. "I shall want something to roll the ends on" she said. "Have you got a pencil or anything on you?"

Colin had a pencil, and another biro; she rolled the end of the plaster strip onto this, and then, still gently, rolled the plaster back till the crack between the lid and the body of the boot was uncovered. "Now your hankie" she said, and laid the end back on it on the lid. She did the same to the other three strips; Colin brought the pencil he had seen in the glove-locker for the last one.

"Now, very slowly—we don't want a lot of dust to fly out" Julia said. "Up she goes." They raised the lid, and stood looking at the contents of the boot.

At first sight there seemed to be nothing very out of the ordinary. A large squashy rush basket with two handles, such as one finds all over Portugal, lay on its side in the centre; the rest of the space was filled with the gaily striped blankets which peasants use there.

"Their lunch, do you suppose?" Colin said.

"Well, let's see, anyhow." As she spoke Julia took the basket by the two handles, and made to lift it. "Gosh! What a weight! No, I don't think it's lunch" she said. "Give me a hand."

With Colin's help she raised the basket to an upright position, and they looked inside. An oblong metal box painted in battle-ship grey, some eighteen inches long and half as wide, met their eyes—on one long side they could just see a large dial and some smaller ones.

"Good grief!" Colin exclaimed. "Let's get it out—you pull at the basket—careful."

In a moment they had the object free of the basket; Colin set it down on the blankets.

"So that's what they use! The bastards!" he said.

"What is it?" Julia asked. "Wireless?"

"Yes, a transceiver; a transmitter and receiver. We use this sort of thing sometimes." He examined the machine with some care. "Yes—I expect it operates on the eighty-meter band," he said at length.

"What range will it have?"

"Two hundred miles minimum—possibly quite a bit more."

"Two hundred miles will be ample for the trawler, I should say; wouldn't you?"

"Yes. They must have an aerial, though" he said. "Let's find that."

They soon came on it, rolled into a fold of the blankets; it was a collapsible one, but when Colin extended it fully it was some eight feet in length; there were also some metal clips which fitted the base.

"Neat—mount it on the bumper" Colin remarked. "See?" He showed her. "I expect they dodge out of town to send their reports."

"And how would they get their instructions?—at fixed times?"

"Could do—more likely take the thing in their room and fix the aerial to the shutter, on the window-sill." He pushed the aerial together and replaced it in the fold of blanket.

"Wait a minute" Julia said; she took it out again, and holding it in a piece of her skirt, wiped it carefully with the bottom of her petticoat.

"Ah, that's right. This is a pretty sophisticated outfit—they might well be able to deal with finger-prints. We'd better wipe the machine too."

Julia took her head-scarf a yard or two away and shook it thoroughly; then with it she wiped the machine all over before replacing it in the rush basket. When this was back in its old position, well wedged among the blankets, they lowered the lid of the boot.

"Now, do you think you can make this infernal plaster stick again?" Colin asked rather anxiously.

"I think so." She knelt down on the dusty road behind the car, bent over the boot, and unrolling one strip of plaster she breathed on it hard, and holding it taut on the pencil, inch by inch pressed it down into place. It stuck, except at the very tip. "We'll have to cut that off" she said. "Give me my little *étui*— it's in my right-hand pocket." Colin pulled the small case out from the pocket of her dress—"Now the scissors" she said. He found a small pair of nail-scissors in the case, and while she held the pencil, he cut along the stretched material; as he cut, she pressed the newly formed edge down. "There you are!" she said with satisfaction.

"Perfect" Colin said. They treated the other three strips in the same way, and rubbed dust over the tiny marks left where the ends had been cut off; when they had finished, to all appearance the boot was just as they had found it.

12 COLIN WAS VERY silent as they drove down towards the Quinta. Julia was a little surprised; she had expected him to be rather exhilarated by their discoveries of the past twenty-four hours—settling both the identity of the local accomplices, and their means of communication with the trawler, at least. Warily, she threw a fly over him.

"I wonder if Polunsky's name will say anything to Major Hartley?" she remarked casually.

"We shan't know that for a day or two" he said. "That will have to go by letter; I see now. No—it's de Carvalho I'm worrying about."

"Oh—why him?"

"I can't see how much longer he *can* agree to keep quiet. Here we have what practically amounts to certainty that the Russians are using this place as a proving-ground, helped by Spanish thugs. You know how the Portuguese feel about Spanish Communists."

"*And* how! But must he be told yet?—about Polunsky, I mean?"

"That's what I can't make up my mind about. He's being such a help, I feel we ought to play *reasonably* fair with him!"

Still earnestly discussing this, they found themselves at the Quinta. "Cripes! I meant to wait on the main road" Colin exclaimed.

"Oh well, you wait in the car—I'll go in and find Penelope" Julia said. But even as she got out of the car, the front door opened, and Aglaia came flying down the steps, her face alight.

"*Darling!* You've come at last!" she cried, and ran to her husband with outstretched arms.

"Well, not really" he said, though returning her eager kisses fondly.

"What do you mean? Where's your luggage?"

"In Funchal—I'm still staying there. Where's Penel?"

Julia had gone up and rung the front door bell; she was vexed with herself for not having remembered to let Colin wait up on the road. Of the maid who answered it she asked if she could speak with the Senhora?—only to be told that the Senhora had gone out with friends, and would not return till the evening. No, she had not taken the large car; she had gone in the car of the friends. Reluctantly, Julia turned back to the other two— Aglaia, predictably, was already in tears.

"*Why* can't you do it from here? I could drive you—there's no need for Julia to drive all the time" she was saying.

"Aglaia, can you drive the big car?" Julia asked, in her slowest tones.

"Yes! Of course I can!" the little creature replied stormily, wheeling round on her.

"Then get it out right away—Terence wants you to fetch him back from the Paúl da Serra" Julia said. "Can you remember the way?"

"I—I think so." Aglaia faltered a little at being so suddenly taken up on her protestations of efficiency.

"Are the keys in it?"

"I'm not sure."

"Well, go and look—and check to see if it's full up with petrol at the same time, because you'll have to go all the way in to Funchal and back."

"Why on earth?" Aglaia asked, startled. "Isn't Terence coming here?"

"He has a friend with him who's got to be taken back to Funchal—and they're in rather a hurry." As Aglaia went off— "I suppose they keep petrol here?" Julia asked of Colin.

"Oh yes—but she won't know where to find it. I'd better go and help her" the young man said, and followed his wife across the fore-court and into the vine tunnel leading to the farm-yard. Julia sat in the car and lit a cigarette. How tiresome that Penelope should be out, just when she was wanted. She looked in the door-pocket of the Austin, hoping to find a map; yes, there was one, and getting out of the car again she spread it on the bonnet and got out her biro to mark the route to the car-turn below the Paúl da Serra. The biro was still faintly sticky from the Spaniards' elastoplast. Bother!—had Colin remembered to clean it off their pencil? She thought not. But even more she was worrying over the prospect of Aglaia meeting Sir Percy. Even her feathery brain might have registered something about him, and the sort of work he did. And someone ought to warn Terence about the ownership of the other car, but that wasn't a message that could be sent by poor Ag—whereas if she went herself she could do both things. And suppose the Spaniards came down before Terence? Julia had lived enough in Europe to recognise the effect of dazzling fairness like Aglaia's on Latins. No, it wasn't a good idea; but she must talk to Colin about it.

Folding up the map, she put it back, raised the bonnet of the car, and checked on the water and oil; then she leaned in and looked at the petrol-gauge. She would want some more, and she started the engine and drove into the yard. Manoel was filling up the big car from a jerrican; Colin and Aglaia were standing in the shade, talking—both wore rather unhappy expressions.

"Colin, here a minute" she called. He came over to her—to her dismay Aglaia followed.

"Colin, could I have some more petrol in this?"

"Yes, I'm sure you can, if you need it." He looked at the gauge. "That will take us back to Funchal all right" he said.

"Yes, but I've had another idea." She got out and stood between him and his wife. "I thought I might as well go and fetch Terence, and let Aglaia take you back to Funchal."

At this suggestion an absolutely agonised expression came over Colin's face—it was gone in an instant, but it filled Julia with dismay.

"The big car is faster" she said quickly, "and I know the way to the turn by heart."

"Come over here a moment" he said abruptly. As she went with him, Aglaia made to follow them.

"No, you wait there, darling" he said, gently but firmly. "Julia and I have business to discuss. We're on a job, you know." And he walked on to the vine tunnel. There Julia briefly explained her second thoughts.

"Yes, you're perfectly right" he said. "Terence ought to be told about the car, and if they do come down before him, you're pretty good at looking after yourself! Ag can drop me off at Terry's office—that won't give anything away."

"Shall you ring Major Hartley from Terry's office?"

"No, from the clinic. I shall see you when you drop Sir Percy. Take care of yourself." He went back to the other car, in which Aglaia was already sitting, and they drove off.

Julia told Manoel to fill up the small car with petrol; while he was doing this he asked her if she knew when Marcusinho would be coming home? Julia didn't, but said she would enquire. It had already occurred to her that both de Carvalho and Sir Percy would wish to keep the boy under observation, to establish the duration of the effects of the gas as precisely as possible; though how this could be done unless they stopped the atropine injections she couldn't see. Manoel next asked her if she would take the child some bantam eggs?—one of his bantam hens had started laying, and the eggs would give him pleasure. Julia of course agreed, the eggs were produced, carefully packed in hay in a small open basket, which she put in the glove compartment; thanking Manoel, she drove off.

As she turned out into the main road the thought struck her that she might well encounter the Spaniards in their car; she pulled up, and put on her head-scarf and a pair of dark glasses—that ought to do, she thought, if they just flashed past one another on the road.

In fact it didn't really do, because they didn't just flash past one another, owing to the presence of a herd of pigs. As Julia emerged from the last village onto the open stretch of road leading up to the ridge where they left the car she saw the Spaniards' car proceeding rapidly downhill towards her, and in front of it a dark, squealing mass of animals; they too were moving very fast, in fact galloping, but in a number of different directions, so that their progress, as a mass, was very slow—the barefooted boys who herded them with long rods and loud cries seemed mainly concerned to keep them together, and on the road. The Spaniards slowed down, and hooted; Julia accelerated, and hooted too. She moved faster than the Spaniards—it is always easier to pass through animals one is meeting than through those one is overtaking; but a point came when both cars drew level and almost halted, engulfed in the swirling mass of noisy animals. The Spaniards looked almost desperate, and swore loudly in their own tongue. Julia was almost free of the pigs, and shot on, looking about her for Terence and Sir Percy. The car-turn was empty except for the motor-cycle and Tomás, the peasant, sitting on the bundle of stakes and battens. She turned the car and got out, now beginning to feel a little anxious; then she saw the two men coming up onto the ridge from the further side. When they reached her—"Did they see you?" she asked at once.

"I expect so" Terence said. "We tried to melt into the landscape, but there isn't cover for a baby rabbit on this *lombo*." Indeed the brownish slopes of the ridge were completely bare.

"I see you've brought the thermometer down" Julia said.

"The thermograph" Sir Percy corrected her. "Yes. Someone had tampered with the screen—the string had been cut, and incompetently re-tied. It did not seem wise to leave it, and in any case I have got a perfectly good reading."

"Oh, good. Anyhow we now know pretty well everything, temperature or no temperature" Julia said thoughtlessly.

"How?" Terence asked.

"Colin gave their car the once-over when we came down, and they've got a wireless in the boot!"

"A transmitter?" Terence asked, rather sharply.

"*And* a receiver—a machine that does both. It has a collapsible aerial—we saw that too."

"Could Colin tell what range it had?" Terence asked.

"Two hundred miles plus, he said—ample to reach that trawler. He says his people use the same sort of machines sometimes."

"Where's Colin now?" Terence next enquired.

"Aglaia took him in to Funchal in the other car; Penelope was out, so we thought I'd better come up for you."

"Yes—well, we'd better be getting along," Terence said. He summoned Tomás, who placed the stakes and the other impedimenta in the back of the car; Terence got in along with them, and spoke to the man in Portuguese while Sir Percy and Julia seated themselves in front.

"Goodness, can he ride that thing?" Julia asked, as the peasant went over and started the motor-cycle.

"Lord yes—and it's his chief delight." Indeed Tomás now sprang onto the motor-bike and shot off down the road. As Julia started the car—"What did you do with the basket?" she asked Sir Percy.

"What basket?"

"What you put over the machine."

"Oh, the screen. Mr. Armitage, with great resource, put a large stone on it, and sank it in the pool."

"Did you see how those two Spanish boys came down? The same way as you did?" Julia asked of Terence over her shoulder.

"No. They must have used one of the two *couloirs* farther along. The hammock-men hadn't seen them."

To Julia's relief the pigs had been driven off down a side-road, so their progress was unimpeded. When they neared the turn to the Quinta Terence leant forward and said to Sir Percy—"If you don't need me any more today, sir, I think I'll go home."

"By all means. You have been most good."

"Shall you want these stakes and battens any more?" he pursued, as Julia slowed down. "If not, I might as well take them back."

"*Vairy* good."

Terence threw the bundle of wood out onto the roadside. As he got out—"Shall you have to carry that load yourself?" Sir Percy asked with concern. "I hope you have not far to go."

"Oh no, thank you—one of the men can come and get it later" Terence said easily. "No one will interfere with it."

As they drove on towards Funchal Sir Percy began one of his careful catechisings of Julia.

"Who exactly are those two young men in the other car? Mr. Armitage expressed considerable anxiety that they should not see us from close to, but he did not explain why."

"Did he not tell you anything about them?" Julia asked, startled.

"No—nothing definite. I think he suspected that it might have been they who had disturbed the screen of the thermograph, and he seemed quite anxious to have it removed as quickly as possible; and, as I say, that they should not see us. But why should they use a wireless transmitter? And in any case, what were they doing up on the plateau? They were too far off for me to see. Do *you* know?"

"Yes" said Julia crisply. "They were taking cinematic photographs of the sheep, with a very large machine that I *think* records sound as well."

"Dear me!" Sir Percy blinked a little at this information. "But such a record would be invaluable, if only we could get hold of it!"

"Well, I hope we may" Julia said, beginning to laugh. "That's what my cousin has hurried into Funchal to try to arrange with Major Hartley."

"But how does your cousin know that they are recording the movements of the sheep?"

"He and I saw them this morning, through Mr. Armitage's telescope. But they're staying in my hotel, and I saw them trying the machine out down there two or three days ago. Then, yesterday, I happened—by the greatest luck!—to overhear them talking about getting pictures of the sheep. They were worried about the weather perhaps breaking, so they came up today instead of three days later, when they ought to have gone. They were to make one recording at ten days—which they did—and another at twenty-one days after the gassing" Julia said, with emphasis.

"But that is exactly right! Did they actually mention the gas?" the scientist asked briskly.

"Not the gas, no—only the dates; but as those fitted in so closely with the little boy's being taken ill, I just assumed that someone wanted pictures of the sheep's reaction to the gas."

"A very reasonable deduction. But I thought you referred to these—er—cinemetograph operators as Spaniards?"

"Yes, they are Spanish right enough; that's what they talk to one another. But there are plenty of Spanish Communists about since the Civil War" Julia said.

"Who might be employed by the Russians, you mean?"

"Yes, Sir Percy. I think these two young men, who pose as wealthy tourists with a mania for taking amateur films of the peasants here, are in fact the local accomplices who arranged all the—the infra-structure—for the whole performance" Julia said flatly. "Getting the hammock-men to take the distributors, and the gas, up to the plateau, and so on. Total strangers off a boat couldn't do that; but these young men were here for a month last year—learning the lie of the land, and also establishing their cover-story, obviously."

"How did you learn that they were here last year?"

"Asked the hotelier. He thinks the world of them, as delightful clients!" Julia said ironically.

Sir Percy digested all this for some moments.

"Yes, I see" he said at length, slowly. "And a radio transceiver with a range of two hundred miles or more would of course enable them to keep in touch with the trawler, while she remains in these waters, and report progress. That would seem to indicate that some, at least, of the senior scientific staff who are responsible for this experiment are on board. I hope Mr. Monro will explain that to Major Hartley immediately."

"I should think the Major would jump to that conclusion on his own" Julia responded cheerfully.

"Yes, but my dear Mrs. Jamieson, it is essential to make certain that he *does* understand this." Sir Percy spoke quite agitatedly. "The Navy ought to apprehend the trawler at once! Do you not *see?* They might still have some of the agent on board!—if they had, we could analyse it and discover the exact formula, far more quickly and accurately than from laboratory results from blood specimens. This could be of the greatest importance."

"Yes, I see that" Julia said, thinking at the same time that the scientist had rather a naively one-track mind: she imagined that the Royal Navy might take some persuading to board the vessel of a foreign power, on the high seas, in peace-time. However, you never knew! But his remark about the possibility of some of the scientists who were directing the whole experiment being on board the trawler brought the name of Polunsky back into her mind, and once again—as when she had told Terence about the nerve gas without referring to Colin—she decided to jump the gun.

"Sir Percy, does the name Polunsky say anything to you?" she asked.

Seated close together as they were in the front of the small car, she could feel the start her companion gave.

"Certainly!" he exclaimed. "He is almost the top man in Russian chemical warfare research. Why? How did you hear of him? From London?"

"No, from those two young Spaniards. He seems to be the person they show up to; anyhow it was he who wanted them to take films of the sheep on the tenth and the twenty-first days."

"You are sure of the name?"

"Positive. They used it two or three times; and one of them said he—Polunsky—would be vexed if they made a film today, because it was three days too soon; and the other said it was better to get it three days early than not at all, if the weather broke."

"He was right, of course. But this is immensely important!" Sir Percy said. "Did they say if Polunsky was on the trawler?"

"No, they were only talking about the weather, and how precise his instructions had been."

"Yes, they would be. Well, let us hurry all we can—London must be told of this at once."

Julia had not been exactly dawdling during this conversation; however, she now drove as fast as she dared along that twisting road, and through Funchal. When they reached the clinic the scientist asked her to come in with him—"I may need you" he said abruptly. Upstairs they found Colin, sitting at a table on the balcony, writing a letter. He got up as they came in.

"Have you spoken to Major Hartley?" Sir Percy asked at once.

"Yes, sir. I told him that we have tracked down the local accomplices, and that they have that transceiver, so that they are able to keep in close touch with the trawler; and about their making film recordings of the sheep. He is going to contact our people in Lisbon."

"Did you tell him that it was Professor Polunsky who had given them the instructions to make these recordings?"

Colin stared at him.

"No." (How on earth had the old boy learnt about Polunsky?) "I didn't care to use that name over the telephone—I'm just writing it to the Major now, to go by air mail."

"It is too urgent for a letter! I can make the Major understand who it is. You had better ring up London at once." He began to explain to Colin how likely he thought it that Polunsky himself might be on board the trawler, or at least some fairly senior official who could conceivably have some of the actual substance which produced the gas with him; Colin, after asking the secretary downstairs to put the call in, and replacing the receiver by the bedside, tried to get the protesting scientist to understand about the inevitability of an hour's delay on all calls between Funchal and London. Julia, laughing a little to herself, decided to take his bantam eggs to Marcusinho, and slipped out, leaving them to it.

She went downstairs and spoke to the elderly male secretary, who took her up to the landing, in another part of the building, where she had gone to enquire for the child on the day of Colin's arrival. The same grey-haired nurse, who had then shown such distress, now greeted her full of smiles, and took her in to a small bright room where the little boy was sitting up in bed doing a jigsaw puzzle; Julia gave him the basket of eggs and told him that his father had asked her to bring them. Marcusinho, who looked perfectly well, asked eagerly how many of the bantam hens were laying, and of the nurse, whether he could have two of the eggs cooked for his supper that evening?—as an afterthought, he enquired if his parents were well, and when he was going home? The Senhor Doutor would have to settle that, Julia and the nurse both told him. Then the child asked Julia, most earnestly, if she could bring him his *cofrezinho* from the Quinta? Julia looked enquiringly at the nurse.

"*Minha Senhora,* it would be a real kindness if you could do this" the woman said. "He begs for it all the time."

Julia, sitting down by the bed, promised to try, and asked what the *cofrezinho* was like?—she was puzzled by the unfamiliar word. It was small, long and also round, Marcusinho explained —his little brown hands vividly shaped a small cylinder; it was of metal, and shining, he said eagerly. And then he added words which startled Julia—"I found it on the mountain where the sheep are." Concealing her excitement, she asked where he had put it, so that she could be sure of finding it. The child's small face crumpled with distress.

"Ah, *Minha Senhora,* this I *can't* remember. The pain in my head got so bad! But I am *sure* I brought it home. My mother would know."

Julia promised to try to find it the next time she went to the Quinta; she kissed the child, and left. As she went downstairs she heard the luncheon-bell ringing; she had sandwiches in her haversack, but thought she would see if she could get some soup along with Colin and Sir Percy—tempted as she was to go straight to the Quinta, she realised that the sensible thing would be to eat; she had had no food since 7 A.M. She was touched, when she reached their quarters, to find a place laid for her at the table on the balcony.

"Ah, *vairy* good!—I hoped you would eat with us, and be-spoke some food for you" Sir Percy said. "You have had a long morning."

Julia thanked him, and tucked gratefully into the excellent meal provided; the doctor had not overpraised his food, she thought, and on an impulse she asked if they had seen him that day.

"Only for a moment—I'm rather holding off him at present, till London have made up their minds how much they want to tell the Ports" Colin said. He spoke rather worriedly. "Hartley says they'll have to talk to the Foreign Office about it all." He crumbled his roll nervously. "I wish those Spaniards hadn't seen the thermograph—it's bound to make them suspect that something is going on."

"We don't know for sure that they did see it" Julia said, "if they climbed up further along."

"They could hardly miss it, surely? And if it's they who originally prospected and found the place, and have been up there several times, photographing and all that, they must know that there's never anything there but sheep and mist! To find a scientific instrument, carefully fixed on a stand, and elaborately screened, can only make them suppose that someone besides themselves is taking an interest in the climate, and probably in the sheep too—and what is more, someone who knows what he's about" Colin said gloomily. "I wouldn't mind betting they're reporting it to the trawler at this moment."

"I don't see what the trawler can do, even if they do report it" Julia said. "Madeira is part of a sovereign state; they're not even supposed to enter its territorial waters, though obviously they often do."

"Why do you say that?" Colin asked quickly.

"Well, for one thing, when Terence and I saw the trawler, the first evening I was down at the Quinta the week before last, she certainly wasn't three miles off shore; I doubt if she was a mile out" Julia said calmly. "And when they put those ten men, with the gas and all the doings, ashore at Seixial, either she has a biggish launch, or she *came* in herself. Did you ever ask Terence about that?"

"No, I didn't."

"Might they have been given permission, for what purported to be an innocent landing for a harmless recreational expedition?" Sir Percy asked.

"I suppose it's possible" Colin said, more worriedly than ever. "Our people in Lisbon could find out about that, I suppose. Look, sir, when you get that call to London, let me have a word with the Major too, will you? We ought to get that enquiry put in at once."

"Certainly—of course you must. Do calls from London to

Lisbon also take an hour to make?" the scientist enquired, with a hint of sarcasm.

"No, more like two minutes!" Julia said, laughing. "And from here to Portugal isn't too bad. It's just something about *here,* to and from London."

Sir Percy looked at his watch.

"We should be getting the call in a quarter of an hour" he said.

Julia decided not to wait for coffee, though Sir Percy pressed her to stay and have some; the sooner she could lay her hands on the *cofrezinho* the better for everyone, she felt. Colin asked where she was going?

"Down to the Quinta, to get something Marcusinho wants" she said.

"Well, just have a word with Ag if you can" he muttered in her ear. "She's a bit upset, but I *couldn't* wait to sort her."

"Will do" she replied, and went off.

When she had gone and Colin returned to the table, Sir Percy addressed him rather solemnly.

"Could not some other accommodation be arranged for Mrs. Jamieson, instead of that hotel?" he asked.

"Oh, I suppose so" Colin said carelessly—he was trying to plan in his head exactly how to phrase his question to Major Hartley about whether the trawler had had permission to put in at Seixial. "But why? She says it's quite comfortable."

"Did she not tell you that those two Spanish accomplices are staying there? If their suspicions are aroused, ought she to stay under the same roof with them, unguarded? I should have thought it extremely unwise."

Now at last Colin began to pay attention; he frowned, and his thumb began to jerk.

"Perhaps you are right" he said. "It hadn't occurred to me that they would be likely to tie her in with the thermograph; after all, you and Terence are the only people they have seen, and she wasn't with you then." He paused, and then gave a sudden exclamation—"Damn!"

"Damn what?" Sir Percy asked.

"Terence *was* having lunch with her at the hotel, the day they were trying out the ciné-camera—that's how she knew they had one. No, that isn't so good."

"I should, on the contrary, call it very bad indeed" Sir Percy said, in his precise manner. "In my opinion, she should go to another hotel—unless our good friend the doctor could give her a room here."

"No, I think that would be imposing on him too much" Colin said decidedly. "I'll ring up and get her a room at Reid's, if I can." He went in to the bedroom; as he did so the telephone rang —it was, the operator said, the Senhor's call to London. Sir Percy went over and took the receiver.

Julia, spinning along the sunny coast road for the third time that day, but for once alone, was aware of a curious mixture of feelings. There was the familiar surge of excitement as one approached what might be the end of the trail, coupled with a determination to let *nothing* come between oneself and the goal; but in the past this excitement had usually had a gay, almost a gleeful tinge about it. This time there was no gaiety, no glee— only a cold, sad resolution. That she must be nearing the end of the trail she had little doubt. A metal cylinder, picked up on the Paúl da Serra on the very day that the gas was distributed, could hardly be anything but one of the containers holding what Sir Percy so irrationally wished the Navy to snatch off the trawler— or could it be just an unopened soup-tin? A chill of doubt crept over her. Surely Polunsky's men would have kept an exact tally of the number of their containers, and if one empty one was missing, would have laid on the two Spanish boys to seek diligently, like the woman in the New Testament, until they found it?— they would be in touch by wireless, with the efficient machine which she and Colin had seen in the boot of the car only that morning. Ah, but if Marcusinho had carried the thing off, however diligently the Spaniards searched, they could not have found it—and then what could the people on the trawler do? Really nothing.

Oh well, she would soon know now, she thought, stepping on the accelerator as the road, swinging inland onto the open country, became less twisting and therefore faster. But soon she slowed down again. Just short of the turn-off to the Quinta, on the left, stood a grove of Terence's banana-trees, which masked the turn itself till one was fairly close to; as it came in sight she saw the two young Spaniards bending intently over something on the bank just beyond it—the Nazaré shirt of the one was unmistakable, and as she decelerated she saw that the bundle of stakes which Terence had thrown out of the car onto the roadside had been undone, and the white pieces of wood scattered about. With her shortsighted eyes Julia peered desperately at the bank, to see what the two youths were examining with such interest—all she could see was two or three more pieces of the newly sawn wood. As she swung into the side-road and shot down it, thinking hard, it came to her—the battens with the screw-holes! If it was the two youths who had disarranged the basket screen, and so seen the thermograph, these might interest them as evidence. Well, she would tell Terence, of course—but the first thing was to find the *cofrezinho*.

She drove straight into the farm-yard; the big car was back, so Aglaia must have returned. Julia went up the outside stairs and tapped on the open door of the farm-house; Carmen came at once, greeted her warmly, led her into the kitchen, and asked if Marcusinho had been pleased with his eggs? Delighted, Julia told her, and he was going to have two of them cooked for his supper. Then she put her own question. The child kept begging for something he said he had brought down from the mountain the day he was taken ill; he called it his *cofrezinho*. Had she, his mother, any idea what it was?

But yes—here on the window-sill! And there sure enough it was, sitting demurely between a flower-pot and the coffee-tin— a small bright metal cylinder; Julia almost gasped as the woman handed it to her, and she saw the Russian lettering stamped on it. And it was curiously heavy, she noticed, as she stowed it in her hand-bag; and tightly sealed, so that it could only be opened with a stout instrument. She thanked Carmen, got into the car again, and drove round to the front door. This stood open, but Julia was rather a stickler for ringing other people's front door bells; she did so now. Terence, in his shirt-sleeves, came wandering through the hall from the back of the house; a sound of voices came with him.

"Oh hullo—back again! Come in and have some tea; Penel's just come in with Pauline Shergold—earlier than she expected."

"Look, do you mind if I don't?" Julia said, rather taken aback. "I'm in a bit of a hurry, but I promised Colin I'd see Aglaia for a minute."

"Come in here" Terence said, and led her into his study, which to Julia's relief looked out over the drive; she didn't want to be involved with Penelope, let alone with Pauline, at this precise juncture. "Sit a minute, and have a cigarette" he said comfortably—as he lit one for her—"I'm not sure about seeing Ag" he went on. "She came back from Funchal in a frightful stew; she wouldn't have any lunch, and slammed into her bedroom and locked the door."

"Oh dear!" Julia said. "I'm sorry about that, but I suppose it must wait. Anyhow I wanted to see you, too."

"Look away!" he said, with his calm grin. "Anything I can do?"

"I'm not sure—but there's something you ought to know, anyhow." She told him about the two young Spaniards up on the main road, examining something from the loosened bundle of stakes. "I'm pretty sure they *had* noticed Sir Percy's machine, and were checking for the screw-holes in the battens."

"Cheek!" Terence commented coolly. "How long ago was this?"

"Five—ten minutes perhaps." Then as the man got up— "No, don't do anything!" she said urgently. "It's much better they shouldn't realise that we know what they're up to, and *what* they know."

"Why?"

"Oh, it's always better that way! I expect they've been reporting to their bosses on the trawler about someone using a thermograph up there, and being worried over it; but it's much better not to underline it. It's tiresome enough that they should connect you, and this house, with the thermograph anyhow" she added rather worriedly.

"Why?" he asked again.

"Oh, they might start hanging around, and snooping. Tell all your people not to talk to any strangers—especially Tomás, who was up there with you."

"Tomás is a perishing nuisance" Terence said, without heat. "If he'd gone up at once, as I told him to, and fetched those stakes down, the Spaniards wouldn't have been able to examine them."

"Well, do tell everyone, now that they have, that they're not to be talked to."

"I'll try. D'you know if they speak Portuguese?"

"They *must* do, to have arranged all this." She paused. "Do you think there's any chance of my seeing Aglaia? Because if not I think I'd better be off."

"To tell you the truth, I don't think it would be the slightest use your seeing her, even if she would let you in" Terence said, with a sort of calm bluntness. "It's you she's so upset about."

"What, my driving Colin and Sir Percy, and not her?"

"Yes—why, has she been on to you about it, too?"

"Well yes, when Colin and I came down to get the car—more to him" Julia said. "Oh dear, *how* silly!"

"Unfortunately she is a very silly girl, if she is my cousin" Terence said. "She knows it, too, up to a point, which is what makes her so wildly jealous of people who aren't silly."

"But I thought I'd made her see, when I was down here the first time, that she couldn't be told about all his things" Julia said distressfully.

"Well, if she saw it then, she's forgotten it now—she was quite wild at lunch-time. I'm sure you'd better not try to see her."

"No, I won't, of course." She got up. "Oh, if only she could get away!—it's so dangerous to have anyone wild and reckless about, just now."

"I was thinking about that" Terence said, getting up too. "How would it be if Pauline were to take her up to the Serra for a bit?"

"When? Today?"

"That's what I thought. Penel is quite prepared to be tough with her; she's pretty fed up with having a door locked against her in her own house."

"Oh, if you *could* arrange that, it would be perfect" Julia said. "It won't be much longer now" she added, relief making her a little reckless.

"Oh, won't it? I'm glad of that" Terence said, beginning to grin again. "Are you laying on the Royal Navy to sink the trawler?"

"That's what Sir Percy would like!" Julia said, laughing too. "But, no—I don't think so."

"Oh well, hurry up and produce a *deus ex machina* from somewhere!" Terence said, as he saw her out.

13 THE DISCUSSION WITH Terence on what to do about Aglaia had for the moment almost made Julia lose sight of her main preoccupation—to get the *cofrezinho* into Sir Percy's hands as soon as possible. Now, as she drove off, this returned in full force; she slowed down and actually opened her bag, on the seat beside her, to make sure that the metal object was still there. It was, bright and shining; in a sudden panic she wrapped it in her handkerchief, to make it less conspicuous. Then she began to wonder if the Spanish boys would still be at the turn onto the main road; they could have no earthly reason for suspecting that she had got the thing that her bag contained, but she was immensely relieved, as she swung out onto the road, to see no sign of them. She slowed down to check if they had carried off the stakes? No, these had been roughly bundled together and re-tied—"incompetently", as Sir Percy had said of their re-attaching the basket screen. Then they weren't all that efficient!—careless about small details. Now for the first time she wondered what they had done with their car? —they would surely not go any great distance from it, seeing what the boot contained. The only cover near at hand was the banana-grove, now on her right; she looked carefully as she drove past to see if there was any way into it. Yes—at the farther end a cultivation track, quite wide enough for a car, led in; no doubt they had parked there, safely screened, to make their report to the trawler about the thermograph. Well, let them get on with it while they had the chance, she thought rather grimly.

But as she drove back towards Funchal her thoughts turned, inevitably, to her husband. That expedition to Central Asia had been mounted, presumably at great expense, to try to get hold of some of the actual substance which produced the new Russian nerve gas, and it had cost Philip's life; now, if her guess was correct, at least a small quantity of that very substance lay here, under her hand—picked up quite casually, by an inquisitive Madeiran peasant boy on a mountain plateau, and equally casually handed to her off a window-sill in a Madeiran farm-house kitchen. The thought struck her—it must have been standing there when she first went to see Carmen, to take the aspirin-filled grapes for the child!—before they even sent for Colin, let alone before Sir Percy flew out in his executive jet from England. How strange!—no one had missed it, no one had paid any attention; if Marcusinho's bantams had not begun to lay, just then, and his father had not asked her to take some eggs to him, it might never have come to Sir Percy's knowledge at all. Well, it should now, she thought, her face set; resisting a strong impulse to speed, she drove steadily on into Funchal.

At the clinic she ran into Dr. de Carvalho in the hall.

"Ah, *bonjour,* Madame. Do you come to visit my patients? *À la bonne heure!*—I will come up with you; I have some news for Sir Paircy."

For a moment Julia stared at him almost with dismay. Then pulling herself together, she made some suitable response, and went up with him in the lift; it would only be a few minutes extra delay, anyhow.

On the balcony of Colin's room, which they had all come to treat as a common sitting-room, they found only Colin himself; Sir Percy, he explained, was having a nap, after his early start.

"Can he not be awakened? I have some important news for him" the doctor said. Colin looked a little dubious.

"He did say he didn't wish to be called till five thirty" he said, rather hesitantly.

"But I have the results! From Paris!" the Portuguese exclaimed urgently. "They are excellent—I would say conclusive! I am sure he would wish to have them at once."

"I think you ought to wake him, darling darling" Julia said, slowly. The doctor looked at her, in slight surprise at her last words; Colin looked at her too—still slowly, she nodded her head. He went through to the next balcony, where they heard him tap gently on the French window. There was a long pause. At last Colin re-appeared, followed by Sir Percy, wearing a towelling bathrobe; his hair appeared to be wet—Julia wondered, with ill-timed frivolity, if he had been applying whatever "rinse" he might use to keep it so black.

De Carvalho, seating himself at the table, pulled a typed letter out of his pocket and spread it out in front of the scientist.

"Where is this from?" Sir Percy asked.

"But from the laboratory in Paris!—results of the analysis of the specimens of blood that I sent. De Boisson signs it himself! See—in both cases it is positive."

"Why 'A' and 'B'?" Sir Percy asked, rather unhelpfully— Julia felt increasingly sure that he had been interrupted in giving himself a shampoo.

" 'A' was the blood of the sheep; 'B', that of the child. But you see, both cases show positive cholinesterase inhibition."

Sir Percy now began to pay a little more attention, to Julia's relief; she couldn't bear to see the doctor's enthusiasm damped down. But everything to do with cholinesterase was Greek to her, and when the two men got down to discussing dates and times, and probable density of distribution, she slipped through into Colin's bedroom, took up the telephone, and put through yet another call to the Office in London—Sir Percy would want to talk to Major Hartley again, she felt sure, when he had seen what she was about to show him, and this would save delay; then she went out into the corridor and stood by the window at the end of it, looking out over the sunny, flowery, fruitful garden, thinking how inappropriate it was that it should have been the scene of so many discussions on horrors like the distribution of nerve gas.

Presently she heard the door open, and Colin and de Carvalho came out.

"Then you will send me up two copies of that, as quickly as possible" she heard Sir Percy's voice say. "I am very much obliged to you." As the two men hurried off, she slipped quickly back into the bedroom, and out onto the balcony.

"Sir Percy! Could you spare just a minute?" she called, as the scientist started towards his own room.

He turned back with evident reluctance.

"Could it wait till I am dressed?" he asked.

"I suppose it *can* wait almost indefinitely" Julia said coolly, opening her hand-bag. "It seems to be well sealed." As she spoke she put the metal cylinder down on the table; Sir Percy came over towards it. "Is that Russian lettering? It looks like it to me" she said.

The scientist's reaction was all Julia could have wished. He took the cylinder up off the table, peered at it, turned it about, and weighed it in his hand. "Lead-lined" he muttered. "Where did you get this?" he asked sharply.

"I've just been back to the Armitages' Quinta to fetch it. The little boy picked it up on the plateau the day he was gassed."

"Where has it been since?" Sir Percy enquired, putting the thing down again on the table, and eyeing it as one might a venomous reptile.

"In his mother's kitchen, on the window-sill."

"Why was it not shown to anyone before?"

"No one knew anything about it, nor what it was. Come to that, I don't really know what it is" Julia said, with her slow smile. "I'm just guessing that it contains gas, in some concentrated form. What do *you* say?" she asked the scientist.

"It must be that—it *is* that" he said. "But why did you go to look for it?" he asked now.

"When the child got better he remembered about the tin, but not where he had put it; he calls it his little coffer" she said. "And when he told me this morning that he had picked it up on the mountain where the sheep were, I thought I had better see if I could get hold of it for you."

"You did perfectly rightly. This makes all our other endeavours needless, or nearly so." He paused. "This must be got to England at once" he said, with sudden emphasis. "I will get dressed. No—this infernal telephone! I had better put in a call to London first."

"If it's Major Hartley you want, I put in a call to him while you were talking to Dr. de Carvalho" Julia said. "I thought you might want a word with him."

"I do—and I want a plane! *Vairy* good—I will go and dress." He went rapidly through to his room. Julia picked up the cylinder and put it back in her hand-bag.

A few minutes later Colin returned, with two sheets of typescript. "Where's Sir Percy?" he asked.

"Gone to dress. How did you get on with the doctor? Is he getting curious?"

"Not for the moment—he's too pleased with his lab results," Colin said, putting the typed sheets down on the table, and weighting them with an orange off a bowl of fruit on a side-table. "What did Ag say?"

"I couldn't see her—she'd gone to lie down" Julia said; for the moment she decided to suppress the fresh plans for Aglaia— she wanted Colin to concentrate on the job in hand.

"Surely you could have popped up to her room and had just a word with her?" the young man protested.

"No, I couldn't—I was in too much of a hurry" his cousin said firmly.

"What on earth were you in such a hurry about?"

"This—I thought you and Sir Percy ought to see it at once" she said, and again took the cylinder out of her hand-bag, and handed it to him. "Feel the weight" she said.

"Good God!" For a moment, staring at the lettering, he looked almost aghast. "But—but this it IT" he stammered. "How on earth did you get hold of it?"

She told him of her visit to the child before lunch, and how he had begged for his *cofrezinho*. "So I thought I'd better nip down and see if I could find it. And there it was, sitting in Carmen's kitchen!—been there all this time."

Colin got up hastily and started towards the bedroom.

"If you're wanting to ring up the Major, I put the call through twenty-five minutes ago" Julia called after him. He came back, laughing.

"Oh darling, you're running *absolutely* true to form!" He gave her a tremendous thump on the back.

"Ouch! Steady on!" Julia protested. "I'm not wearing riot-control protective clothing!"

"Sorry, sweet. But this is so marvellous!"

"Yes, isn't it a piece of luck? Now tell me what the Major said about the Spanishes and their radio?"

"Oh, he'd assumed their existence, of course. He was going to get on to Lisbon and Madrid and see if any more was known about them."

"What about the trawler being given permission to land at Seixial?"

"Well, Hartley said he'd have to ponder a bit about that—he seemed to think it might be difficult to find out without alerting the locals, and Sir P. is rather against that still."

"I should think he'd be more than ever against it now," Julia said. "But look, even now we've got this, I hope the Major is going to take steps at *some* point to get hold of those boys' tapes and films of the sheep? If Polunsky wants them so much, they ought to be useful to Sir Percy too."

"Who is taking my name in vain?" that gentleman said, suddenly re-appearing from beyond the bamboo screen that divided the two balconies. He was now sprucely dressed; his hair, still damp, neatly brushed close against his head; he looked uncommonly brisk and cheerful.

"I was—I was just saying I thought you would probably want to have the film and the tape-recordings that those two boys have taken of the sheep."

"Yes—most certainly. But that can wait, can it not? The essential thing is to get that sample back to England."

"Well, *can* it wait? They may put them in a sponge-bag and row them out to the trawler tonight, for aught we know" Julia said.

"Oh, do they use a rowing-boat?" Sir Percy asked, quite seriously.

"I've no idea *what* they use, or even if they are having any physical contact with the trawler at all" Julia said. "All I mean is that as things are, we have no knowledge of their movements, and no control over them; so that we can't prevent their disposing of these recordings that your chum Polunsky is so keen on having. They could do them up in a parcel and post them quite openly, here in Funchal, come to that."

"Then what is your idea?" Sir Percy asked.

"I can't see anything for it, if you really want this stuff, but to ask London to get Lisbon to lay on the local authorities here to pounce on the Spaniards at once, search their rooms and their car, and impound anything that could be of use to us."

Sir Percy frowned, and was silent.

"Do you know, sir, I believe she's right" Colin said. "It would be much better if those boys were taken into protective custody, or whatever they call it—or at least tailed, so that their movements would be known."

"How long would that take to organise?"

"A very short time, I should think. The Portuguese Security Police could fly some of their own people out here in a couple of hours, or less."

"But would not these Security Police have to be told the reason for taking this action?—what has been going on here?"

"Well, some of it, I suppose," Colin said.

"No!" Sir Percy suddenly pronounced. "Police are always busy-bodies; they might wish to interview everybody concerned —*me!*" he said with an indignant stress that amused Julia— "and that would hold everything up. I do not wish *any* of the Portuguese authorities to know anything about this affair until that sample is safely in England." He looked about him. "Where is it now?" he asked sharply.

"Here, in my hand-bag" Julia said. "I didn't want to leave it standing about, in case the doctor or anyone else came in."

"Quite right. May I take it now?" When she produced the cylinder he buttoned it into an inside pocket, and patted his jacket with a satisfied air.

"Do you propose to take it to England yourself, sir?" Colin asked.

"Most certainly. And once it is airborne, you can collogue to your heart's content with your Portuguese colleagues in Intelligence, and the good doctor, and the local police," he said cheerfully.

"What about the boy? I thought you wanted to check on when the effects of the gas pass off with him?" Colin persisted.

"The doctor can see to that. He will arrange temporary pauses in the atropine injections, to make that clear; he is after all perfectly competent in such matters" the scientist said airily.

"I don't much like that—will the child have to have that fearful pain again?" Julia asked.

"Only for a few moments—as soon as the symptoms recur he will be given another injection. The doctor will be in touch with the vet, of course, who will make periodic inspections of the sheep, as a double check."

At that moment the telephone rang. Sir Percy darted towards the bedroom door; Colin, courteously but firmly, took his arm. "Just one moment, sir; when I am sure that we have the proper connection, you shall speak if you wish to." Julia looked on with deep pleasure—here was the Intelligence man on the spot, in charge; Colin really was growing up. She stood by Sir Percy as Colin lifted the receiver; both listened intently.

"Daly? Yes, I do want him again, personally—as quickly as you can." A pause. "Hullo—yes, here we are again! First, can you send the little machine back at once, same place as before? Right; the sooner the better. Yes, our learned friend is returning at once—you might almost say mission completed."

At this point Julia did a rather unwonted thing; she went quickly back onto the balcony and through into Sir Percy's bedroom, where she noiselessly lifted the receiver of the other telephone. Now she could hear both parts of the conversation—Colin was speaking.

"Yes; in fact we have got a small sample of the thing itself."

"*No!*—how on earth?" Hartley said. "No—don't tell me—the wonder-girl, I suppose?"

"It was, as a matter of fact." Colin laughed a little. "Now, how soon can the machine be with us?"

"Say seven A.M. tomorrow—that all right?"

"Yes, fine. And look, there's another thing, that you might be laying lines for in advances. You remember the two worthies I mentioned earlier today, with the very up-to-date equipment?"

"Yes."

"You were going to ask about them. Well, I think it might be advisable to get on to our people in the metropolitan capital, and ask them to contact their *chers collègues* there—"

"Hold on—*what* capital?"

"*Metropolitan;* that régime has a number of overseas provinces" Colin said smartly.

"Oh ah—I get you. Sorry—go on."

"Contact their *chers collègues* there and let them prepare to act promptly," Colin continued. "It will probably be necessary for them to send some of their own people over to collect that other, also very valuable material, which can only be secured by official action. In fact they may well want to take action against certain individuals."

"The 'worthies' you spoke of just now?"

"Yes."

"All necessary information to be supplied by you, on the spot, I take it?"

"Yes, when they arrive. I shall stay at this same number, and will meet them when I'm told what time. But the point is, they ought to be ready to start the moment you tell them the sample is airborne, and none of the inhabitants of that part of the world are noticeably quick off the mark, in my experience!—they take a lot of persuasion and prodding. I think our people ought to get cracking tonight."

"Will it be easy to prod and persuade without any facts?"

"They'll have to get along with hints and insinuations!—you can provide them with material for plenty of those, so long as no inkling reaches anyone *here* that anything is happening, or going to happen."

"All right. I don't envy Henry his job, but I'll tell him to try."

"I'd like them here by eight A.M." Colin said firmly. "Hold on a moment—now sir, do you want a word?"

Julia couldn't hear Sir Percy's reply, but it was evidently a negative one. "No—that's the lot" Colin said. "Thanks—'bye."

Julia hurried out into the corridor, not wishing to be caught in Sir Percy's room; in a moment Colin came out.

"Well, that's all laid on" he said. "Where did you vanish to?"

"His room—I wanted to hear what Hartley was saying."

"Well, you came off better than listeners are supposed to do, if you came in time" he said, grinning.

"Why did you do all the talking?" she asked.

"Oh, the old boy's *frighteningly* bad on the telephone; you should have heard him this afternoon!—shooting out all sorts of facts without any attempt at disguise."

"That's odd, because he's not stupid."

"No, it's just that he isn't accustomed to our sort of work. After all, we're not much good at science" Colin said tolerantly.

"Did he ask the Major to have the trawler seized?" Julia asked, beginning to giggle.

"Practically! And I almost had to clap my hand over his mouth to prevent him from using Polunsky's name. He was a bit miffed altogether; I think that's why he didn't want to talk just now."

"Poor old thing! Well anyhow, there's nothing much more we can do till his plane comes tomorrow morning" Julia said. "Only another twelve hours, thank goodness."

"There is one thing—I think you ought to shift from that hotel."

"Why?"

"I don't like your being there with those two boys, and nor does he."

"Who, Hartley?" Julia asked in surprise.

"No, Sir Percy. He said they must have seen him and Terence quite close enough to recognise when they were waiting for the car; and you and Terry were lunching together the day you saw their camera, so they might tie you in with him."

"They'd probably do that anyhow, because of the pigs" Julia said.

"The pigs? What on earth do you mean?"

She told him about her encounter on the road on her way to collect Terence and Sir Percy.

"Yes, well there you are—you could only have been going to

fetch them. And if they did see that thermometer thing, it would be bound to make them suspicious."

"I think they did see it, and *were* suspicious" Julia said thoughtfully—she reported how she had seen the two young men poring over some pieces from the bundle of stakes by the turn down to the Quinta, "checking for the screw-holes, I thought, though I couldn't actually see."

"I bet that was it. Well then, darling, don't you *see?* It really doesn't make sense for you to stay there, alone" he said urgently. "They've seen the thermograph, and probably guessed why it was used up there; they've seen Terence, if not *at* it, on his way from fetching it; they've seen you *with* Terence, and on your way to fetch him. And presumably they know that the types from the trawler are short of one gas-cylinder. It's madness! I shall ring up Reid's for a room at once."

"No, wait a moment—let's think." As Colin stood waiting, holding the door-handle—"I could go back to the Serra" she said. "Oh no, perhaps they won't have room."

"Why not? They had room before."

Julia regretted her thoughtless words; but Colin would have to be told sometime, and as more or less everything was settled, it might as well be now.

"Come into your room," she said—"we've got to talk." They went in; there was no sign of Sir Percy; Julia went over and shut the French windows onto the balcony. "Did Terence send in that whisky? If so I could do with some," she said, sitting down in an armchair.

"I'll fetch it—the cellar is outside!" he said. He returned in a moment with two brimming glasses, and gave one to her.

"Oh good—thank you" she said, taking a long pull.

"What have we got to talk about?" Colin asked, doing likewise, and seating himself on the bed.

"Aglaia again, I'm afraid."

"What's happened?" he asked, anxiously.

"Nothing much—but she's going up to the Serra; that's why they may not have room for me."

"Has she had a row with Penel?"

"She hadn't when I was there. Look, just let me tell you quietly what happened. She came back from dropping you in Funchal in rather a bad state—I suppose she'd been stewing over everything all the way, alone in the car. Anyhow she wouldn't have any lunch, and locked herself into her room; Terence could do nothing with her—he said she was quite wild. That's why I couldn't see her, even if I had more time."

"She gets like that, sometimes" Colin said worriedly, rubbing his hands through his black hair. "Go on."

"Well, when I told Terence about those Spanish boys snooping over the stakes by the turn, he got a bit worried; if they snoop there, they might come down and hang about the place and talk to anyone they could get hold of—he was going to warn all his staff not to talk to strangers. And he just didn't think it very wise to have anyone who was *un*-warnable about the place. So he was going to ask Pauline Shergold to take her back with her."

"Why, was she there?"

"Yes. Penelope had been out with her all day—wild-flowering, I suppose. I didn't see them. But I thought Terence was right," Julia said sadly.

"Oh God yes, of course he is!" Colin groaned. For a moment he sank his head in his hands; then he raised it and looked steadily across at Julia.

"What do you think I ought to do?" he asked. "Resign? You must see that it can't go on like this."

"I shouldn't do anything in a hurry" Julia said. "She's very young still, and she has had this knock over losing the baby." She paused. "When she gets into one of these bad fits, have you ever tried actually slapping her face?"

"No." He looked horrified.

"It's what they do when people have hysteria, and I get the impression that this—this indiscipline of hers is somehow related to hysteria. I should talk to Mrs. H. about it. She knows more than most people what is the wisest thing to do."

"Yes, but *when?*"

"Oh, when all this is cleared up—it won't be long now. Anyhow if she's up at the Serra she's out of harm's way for the moment."

"Let's find out if she is there" he said, moving to the telephone. As he lifted the receiver—"Would *you* ask?" he said.

"Yes of course—I'd better." When he had asked for the number she took the receiver.

It was Gerald who answered.

"Hul*lo*, Julia! I thought you'd forgotten us, or left the Island."

"Not a bit of it! Is Pauline back?"

"Yes. D' you want her? She's upstairs."

"With Aglaia?" Julia asked.

"Yes. She's seedy or something. But I can yell for Pauline."

"No, don't bother her. Is Mrs. H. about?"

"Yes, I don't think she's gone up to dress yet. Hold on."

"Yes, she's there all right—Pauline's upstairs with her" Julia said to Colin, putting her hand over the mouthpiece. "I'm trying to get Mrs. H."

"Well, ask about a room for you" he said urgently.

"My dearest child, I was *hoping* you might ring up." Mrs. Hathaway's voice, warm and happy, came down the line. "How are you? I rang up your hotel, but they said you were out."

"Yes, I've been out all day, or I would have rung. Have you seen Aglaia?"

"Yes, just for a few minutes. Pauline is getting the doctor for her; she thinks she really needs treatment."

"Goodness!" Julia was startled. "Who's she getting?" she asked then.

"Oh, there's a very nice old Scotch doctor, retired, who lives up here; he treats the casualties at the Golf Club!" Mrs. Hathaway said. "He's been in once or twice to keep an eye on my chest. I should have much more confidence in him over a thing like this than any modern person, especially a foreigner; I'm sure he would never go in for any clap-trap about psychology!" Julia laughed. "And now, when do you come back, dear child?"

"Well actually, Mrs. H., I was wondering if I could come up tonight. Do you suppose that would be all right, or is Aglaia in my room?"

"No, Pauline has bundled the children up somehow, and put

her along next to Nannie Mack, so that she can keep an eye on her tonight. I'm sure you can come back to your little room by me. Shall I ask? Madame Bonnecourt is here—she can run up."

"Yes, do, Mrs. H.—I'll hold on."

"What was all that about Ag?" Colin asked, rather anxiously.

"Only Pauline is getting a Scotch doctor they know up there to see her—I expect she thinks Aglaia would be the better of sedation" Julia said, in as comfortable a voice as she could.

"Oh, I know—old Dr. Urquhart. Yes, he's a splendid old boy; I'm very glad. I'd been wondering whether I ought to get de Carvalho to go up; but this is really better."

"Hullo" Julia said, as Mrs. Hathaway came back on the line. "She can have me?—oh good. Say I shan't get up till after dinner; I haven't packed yet. All right—see you tonight." She rang off.

"Well, that's all right. Now I suppose I'd better go and get packed. I'll just say goodnight to Sir Percy, if he's about."

In fact Sir Percy was on the balcony pouring himself out a whisky and soda.

"Have you got a room, Mrs. Jamieson?" he asked her at once.

"Yes, thank you, Sir Percy; I'm going back to my friends up at the Serra. Oh, I shall be down tomorrow morning to drive you over to the airport" she said, seeing a slightly worried expression come over his face.

"I'm very glad that you are leaving; that is much more prudent."

"Yes, I'm going round to pack now."

"But you ought not to go alone!" the scientist said.

"Oh, surely that can't matter! I shall only be half an hour."

"No—you ought not. Can your cousin not go with you?" He looked rather severely at Colin.

"Oh Sir Percy, you must be crazy!" Julia exclaimed. "Those boys know him by sight far better than either you or Mr. Armitage—he and I were lunching at the next table to theirs only yesterday."

"Ah—I did not know this. All the same, someone should go with you" Sir Percy persisted.

"Could we borrow a nurse or an orderly from here?" Colin suggested.

"I don't see how, without quite a bit of explaining to the doctor" Julia said.

"This must be avoided" Sir Percy said with great emphasis. They stood in baffled silence for a few moments, looking at one another.

Suddenly Julia looked at her watch. "I know!" she exclaimed.

"Who?" both men asked.

"Porfirio" she said. "Aunt Sally will be in bed by now; it's half past seven. Porfirio is a wonderful old Portuguese servant of Mr. Armitage's aunt; he's as good as a division!" she said gaily to the scientist. "I'll ring him up at once." She went through into the bedroom, where presently they heard her talking away in Portuguese. *"Pode ser, Porfirio? Muito bem. In tres minutos."*

"That's all right" she said, coming back. I'll be off. See you tomorrow."

When she let the car slide into the drive at the Quinta dos Arvores Porfirio, as before, was standing waiting for her; but this time he had closed the front door behind him, and had exchanged his rather grand livery for a plain dark suit. Julia made him get in beside her, much against his will, and as they drove off explained her errand. She had remembered by now that he spoke French, and told him what she thought fit—that she was going to her hotel to *faire ses malles,* in a hurry, and that she might want help with her luggage, as it was near the hour of dinner.

At which hotel was Madame staying? Porfirio enquired politely—the Montefiore, she told him. The old man was delighted. "An excellent establishment!" he exclaimed. "One of my nieces is *femme de chambre* there, since six years; the Senhor da Silva is an admirable employer; his staff remain with him."

This piece of information gave Julia a new idea—it was only a chance, but it was just a chance. "I shall require you to remain with me all the time, to help me" she told him; "but I hope you may have the opportunity of seeing your niece." At the Montefiore she went straight to the reception desk and asked for her key; but instead of going upstairs she first looked at the hotel register. Turning back to five weeks earlier, she studied the names. Yes, there was what she was looking for—Cristofero and Domingo de Calderón, and an address in Madrid; the room number was 17. Now she asked for the Senhor da Silva, and when he came out of his office told him, with many regrets and apologies, that she was obliged to leave at once, a sudden emergency. She was going up now to pack—could her bill be ready for her when she came down? Senhor da Silva was all regrets too, but he was not going to make any difficulties for a client brought to him by the Senhor Armitage; he asked if the Senhora had dined?—if not, might he not have something sent to her room? This struck Julia as a good idea, and she indented for a bowl of soup and some toast; she suggested that it might be brought by the chambermaid who was related to her attendant—indicating Porfirio, who stood, smiling and silent, in the background. Da Silva of course knew the old man, and greeted him amicably; certainly Speranza should bring the Senhora's soup, and see her uncle; she might also be of service to the Senhora.

At this point Julia had to make a choice. What she wanted, desperately and immediately, to know was whether the Spaniards were in or out—and if out, when they were likely to return; the question was whether to risk making a direct enquiry of Da Silva, or hope to learn about their movements from Porfirio's niece. The niece was an unknown quantity, whereas Da Silva she knew up to a point, and felt him to be reliable; besides, she might have another use for the niece, if her gamble came off. With elaborate calmness she made a playful remark about *ces jeunes Messieurs Espagnols,* and asked if they had been making any more films of the pretty waitress? Da Silva laughed and said no, and he had asked them to refrain; he did not want the girl's head turned! Then in his turn he asked if Madame wished to see them before she left? Oh no, Julia said; she was not really acquainted with them, and besides they were probably at dinner. No, that they certainly were not; they never dined before nine or nine-thirty, the landlord said. He turned to the receptionist and asked if the Senhores de Calderón were dining in or out? Out, the receptionist thought; they had said they were going

over to Santa Ana, and would eat on the way home. H'm—
probably going to unload their tapes and films on the trawler,
somewhere in the seclusion of the north side of the island, Julia
thought grimly to herself—aloud, she expressed a laughing
hope that there was another pretty waitress at the hotel at Santa
Ana, and, accompanied by Porfirio, went up to her room.

There she first caused the old man to lift her two suitcases
down off the top of the wardrobe, and put them on the bed; she
spread the bath-towel over the quilt to protect it, which brought
an approving *"Muito bem"* from the well-trained old servant.
Rapidly she took down and folded several dresses and put them
in one case, leaving it open. Then she turned to him and spoke
low and earnestly, in French.

"O Porfirio, is your niece discreet?—reliable? Can she keep
silence if required?"

Looking rather startled, as well he might, at this unusual question, Porfirio nevertheless replied that if Speranza was told to be
silent, she would *be* silent.

"Très bien. Now listen carefully. She has of course a pass-key
to all the rooms in the hotel?"

But evidently, the old man said—otherwise how could she
arrange the rooms of the guests?

"Precisely. Now there is one room in this hotel that I wish to
search" Julia said firmly. "It is occupied by spies, enemies of your
country and of mine—oh, not by any fault of the *patron!* He is a
good man, but he has been deceived. And when she brings my
soup, you will tell her to take us to this room, and we will all
three enter, and I will make the search. But she must not speak of
it to the *patron,* or to anyone, or it would bring danger. Can you
arrange this?"

"Anything *I* tell her, she will do" the old man said quietly.

"Très bien. Now we will pack." Julia showed him how to wrap
her shoes and sandals in squares of coloured linen; while he did
this she hastily stowed the rest of her belongings, and the shoes,
in the second case. They had nearly finished when there was a tap
on the door. Porfirio opened it, and bearing a small tray Speranza, his niece, walked in.

14 JULIA WATCHED WITH interest as Porfirio took the tray from the maid, set it on a small table and then, after greeting, led her aside and began to talk to her in a low voice. The woman was middle-aged, with a square cheerful face over which a look of concern gradually spread as her uncle unfolded his wishes—or rather, what were, as presently became evident, his instructions; she looked doubtfully at Julia, who had started taking her soup, fingered her keys nervously, and talked rapidly, clearly uneasy at what she was being asked to do. Porfirio spoke more and more vigorously; the maid looked more and more unhappy—Julia began to wonder if he would succeed. Buttering a piece of Melba toast—"O Porfirio" she said, speaking in Portuguese, slowly and clearly, "does your niece understand that this so short visit to the room of the Senhores is being made at the wish of the Senhor Armitage, from the Shipping Office, who sends so many guests to the hotel?" In her hurried briefing of the old man she had not said that; it occurred to her that this information, though not strictly true, might conceivably reassure Speranza, if indeed she had ever heard of the Shipping Office. Evidently she had; her expression relaxed a little, and after some further exhortation on Porfirio's part, she at last nodded, and asked when the Senhora wished to see the room.

"Now" Julia said, still slowly and coolly; she took another spoonful of soup, and then got up and moved towards the door.

Number 17 was on the same floor as Julia's room, but at the opposite side of the building; looking rather anxiously about her to see if the corridor was empty, the maid unlocked the door and ushered Julia and Porfirio in, and slipped in herself, bolting the door after her. "But with all possible speed!" she muttered urgently.

Julia lost no time. She glanced about first to see what luggage there was—several suitcases, but all were unlocked, and empty. Bother!—then perhaps the Spaniards had already disposed of what she was looking for, or were keeping it with them. However, quickly and methodically, she opened drawer after drawer, feeling among scarves and handkerchiefs with deft hands, but replacing everything exactly as she found it. Julia knew well enough what tapes looked like, and how they were packed, in very thin flat round boxes, but film she had never seen. Next the lower drawers, with the shirts and pyjamas; one held several of the gaudy Nazaré tartan shirts which had made it so easy to recognise that Spaniard at a distance—and here her hand came on something hard, folded into a shirt in the middle of a pile. With quickened breath she used both hands to draw it out. It was a flat round metal box, some six inches in diameter and an inch or more deep, sealed with insulating tape; it felt rather heavy, and when she lifted it she could hear and feel something solid move slightly inside. Quickly she put it in her hand-bag, rearranged that drawer, and went through all the others—she found nothing else.

At this point Speranza came over to her, and rather to her surprise tapped the hand-bag—"Could it be opened?" she asked, still in that low voice. Julia opened it; the woman took out the round box, examined it, and put it back—then muttering *"Mais tres!"* she led Julia across the room to where an old-fashioned painted wicker clothes-basket stood by the bathroom door. Out of this, from under a heap of soiled socks and shirts, she drew out a round bundle tied up in a scarf, and undid it; it did indeed contain three more of the metal boxes.

Julia sought no farther; she glanced round for the camera, but it was not there. She thanked the maid warmly, and gave Porfirio the boxes to carry—"in your pockets, *por favor.*" Speranza unbolted the door, and they returned to Number 11; the whole operation had taken less than ten minutes, and so far as Julia could see had passed entirely unobserved. Back in her room she first thanked the maid again, and dismissed her with a small tip; then she quickly finished her supper and her packing. She threw out her unused sandwiches, and managed to squeeze all four tins into her capacious haversack; then she went downstairs and settled her bill, leaving Porfirio to follow with the luggage.

Back in the car—"Has the Senhora found what she required, to defeat our enemies?" the old man asked earnestly, as they drove off.

"Thanks to Speranza, I am confident that I have," Julia said —"And I am most obliged to you for your help." When they reached old Mrs. Armitage's Quinta she did not drive in, but pulled up in the road; she took two very large notes out of her purse and handed them to the old man. "One is for you, the other for Speranza—but do not give it to her till *next week*" she said. "Be sure to remember this—it is very important. *Boa noite.*" And drove quickly away.

However, in a quiet street she pulled up and reflected for a little. Yes—though it was getting late, she had better unload her haul onto Sir Percy tonight; he would have to fit it into his luggage somehow. She drove back to the clinic, asked the doorman to keep an eye on her car and luggage, and went upstairs.

Sir Percy and Colin were sitting on the balcony, drinking Madeira in the warm dark. Sir Percy, as it turned out, had proved to be what Terence called "a Madeira man," and Mr. Armitage had found time to arrange by telephone for a bottle of something really good to be sent in—they got up in surprise when Julia appeared.

"Goodness, haven't you gone yet?" Colin asked.

"I'm on my way. I just brought a little present for Sir Percy."

"I have already received a magnificent gift from good Mr. Armitage" the scientist said, beaming. "What can you have brought for me?"

"Something I thought you might be glad of" Julia said, "but I'd rather give it to you indoors, if you don't mind." She went back into Colin's room and bolted the door; when the two men followed she emptied the contents of her haversack onto the bed.

"Good God!" Colin exclaimed, as the four round tins rolled out onto the coverlet—he knew at once what they must be. "How on earth did you get those?"

"From their bedroom. The Hidalgos, most tactfully, were out for the evening, so Porfirio and I went and had a look" Julia said, beginning to laugh a little.

"Are you sure they're the right ones?"

"No, not dead sure, but I think at least three are, because they were so carefully hidden."

"Where?" Colin asked.

"In the dirty-clothes-basket. I should never have found them but for Porfirio's niece."

"What was she doing there?" Colin asked, looking slightly bewildered.

"She's the chambermaid; she let us in with her pass-key."

"Well, I'm damned!" For the second time that day Colin thumped his cousin on the back. "How marvellous!"

"Well, mostly luck, really" Julia said.

Sir Percy, during this interchange, had stood by the bed, rather doubtfully fingering the round boxes. "Could you explain to me what these—er—presents of yours contain?" he asked Julia.

"I think they are rolls of film" Julia said—"and I *hope* they are of the sheep up on the Paúl da Serra. I told my cousin that with any luck you might see them before Polunsky did!" she added gaily.

"As a matter of fact I fancy that these must be film and sound-track combined" Colin put in. "The boxes are a bit thicker than for straight film."

"Could be—I remember when they were filming the waitress at the hotel that day they were trying to make her sing," Julia said.

Sir Percy looked from one cousin to the other, slightly incredulous.

"And you actually took these things from the bedroom of these young criminals? Surely that was most imprudent?"

"I don't think so—the receptionist was positive that the boys were going to be out late tonight" Julia said. "Anyhow it's all your fault, Sir Percy, that I did it!" she added laughing.

"How so?" He looked almost indignant.

"Because you insisted that I mustn't go back and pack without an escort, so I took Porfirio; when he told me in the car on the way that his niece was a chambermaid at the Montefiore, it put the idea into my head!—and it all worked out. Now, you can stow these in your luggage, can't you?—and what with those, and the child's little tin, you've got most of what you need, haven't you?"

"Indeed *yes*—and more than I ever expected! *Two* unconvenanted boons—and both owed to you."

"Good—I'm so glad. See you in the morning. Now I must go." While Colin unbolted and opened the door, to her immense surprise the scientist bent over her hand and kissed it as she went out.

It was after ten when Julia got back to the Shergolds; Mrs. Hathaway had already gone up to bed. Gerald greeted her boisterously, as usual. "Glad to see you back, Julia! Does this mean that your espionage activities are over?"

"Not quite, Gerald. It's lovely to be back, though."

"I hope you haven't got another early start tomorrow" Pauline said.

"As a matter of fact I have—but I shan't need any breakfast, or lunch, Pauline."

"Hungry work, espionage!" her host said.

"Mine is really counter-espionage, you know, Gerald" Julia said cheerfully—"and I think it's the hungrier of the two! Pauline, I think I'll go up, and flop into bed; it is good of you to have me as well as Aglaia."

"Oh, *you're* no trouble!" her hostess said, with her usual candour. "Goodnight, Julia."

Up in her room, where her luggage had been sent, Julia found Nannie Mack at work—her unpacking was almost done, her night-things laid neatly on the bed, her effects spread on the dressing-table.

"Oh bless you, Nannie! How perfect."

"Shall you want a bath, Madam?"

"No, not tonight, Nannie, thank you. How is Philip?"

"Very well indeed. I wish I could say the same about that young lady" Nannie observed portentously. "I don't like the look of her at all."

"Oh dear. Is she asleep?"

"Nearer unconscious, to my mind" Nannie said. "I don't know what was in that injection the doctor gave her, but it felled her like an ox!" Julia was startled by this verbal flight on Nannie Mack's part. "Still, she needed something," the Scotswoman went on. "She was verra hysterical when she got here. And I trust Dr. Urquhart; he was in practice in Edinburgh for years." She put her hand in her open pocket and took out a small round white box. "I don't know if you would recognise what these are, Madam? I'm to give her two if she starts creating again when she wakes up."

Julia looked at the small tablets which the box contained; they were pale yellow, with an E stamped on one side—she recognised them as a fairly usual tranquilliser.

"Oh yes, Nannie; it's one of those sedative things."

"Oh well. Now I'll go and fill your bottle, Madam. Would you like a glass of hot milk?"

"Love one. I think I'll just go and say goodnight to Mrs. Hathaway. Goodnight, Nannie."

Madame Bonnecourt was still tidying up in Mrs. Hathaway's sitting-room when she went across the passage; yes, Madame was awake, she said. Julia tapped on the bedroom door and went in.

"Oh, there you are at last, dear child. I'm so glad you're back."

"Yes—I'm sorry to be so late" Julia said. "There were some last-minute things to see to."

"Does that mean that your work with Colin is over?" the old lady asked.

"Well, very nearly, Mrs. H. One more early start tomorrow, and after that it will be only mopping-up, which won't involve me much, I don't suppose."

"I'm glad—you'll get some peace and quiet then. And I'm glad you've been able to help Colin, of course; this must have been a trying time for him."

"Oh, not much worse than usual, only rather important" Julia said. "Mrs. H., you said you only saw Aglaia for a few minutes—what did you think of her?"

"Completely hysterical" the old lady said decidedly. "Pauline was quite right to get Dr. Urquhart."

"Nannie said he'd given her a terrific injection—she said it 'felled her like an ox' " Julia said.

"Did she really? Nannie Mackenzie is full of surprises" the old lady said smiling. "But he is rather troubled about that poor child, and so am I."

"Oh, did you see him?"

"Yes, as he was here he just came in to listen to my chest—which is in perfect order! But he is anxious to get to the bottom of what has caused her to get into such a state."

"Well, I hope he'll keep her under sedation for a day or two, and then manage to put her right" Julia said, worriedly. She got up. "Goodnight, Mrs. H.—sleep well."

When Julia drove up to the clinic at a quarter past six the following morning, Sir Percy and Colin were already standing at the door. Colin quickly put the luggage into the car and got into the back, while Sir Percy got in beside her. "That's right—on you go" Colin said, rather urgently.

"Why? Surely we're all right for time?" Julia said, glancing at her watch as she started the engine.

"Sir Percy's making the equivalent of a moonlight flit!" Colin said, giggling.

"Gracious! You don't mean to say the doctor doesn't know you're going?" Julia asked in surprise, as she turned out into the road. "Didn't you say goodbye to him, or anything?" she said, in rather shocked tones.

"Mrs. Jamieson, in these quite exceptional circumstances I thought it more prudent to omit the usual courtesies" the scientist said, looking a little guilty. "I have written Dr. de Carvalho a letter, thanking him for his *great* kindness and invaluable help, which I hope you will give him yourself, once I have left. And I deposited a week's fees in the office."

"Good gracious!" Julia repeated.

On this occasion they arrived before the plane—sky and sea

were alike empty, in the cold pale light before sunrise, as they topped the hill and dropped down to Porto Novo; and there was still no sign of the little jet when Julia drew up at the airport building. Sir Percy got out, and consulted his watch with a worried expression; Julia got out too.

"It's not ten to seven yet" she said, glancing at the clock on the front of the building. "Sir Percy, can I have a word with you? Colin can see to the luggage."

Rather reluctantly, he followed her, glancing back doubtfully towards his suitcases. "Colin *is* in Intelligence, you know—he's quite accustomed to security" she added, laughing.

At that he laughed a little too. "Was there something you wished to say to me?" he asked.

"Yes. Shall you be seeing Major Hartley and the people at the Office when you get home?"

"Certainly." He looked surprised.

"Well, will you make it clear to them that they owe the successful outcome of this enterprise to my cousin?"

"To Mr. Monro? *You* ask me to say this?"

"Yes, I do. If he hadn't come, none of this would have happened. I want you to rub it into them, hard, that this was *his* job, and *his* success. It's true about everything that wasn't pure luck, and it is more important than you can know."

He looked at her in silence for a moment. At last—"Anything you ask me to do, I will do" he said slowly.

"Thank you. I rely on you" she said. "Oh, there is one other thing."

"What is that?"

"When you've emptied that lead-lined tin, do you think you could have it sealed up again and sent back to me?"

He looked doubtful. "This might be difficult" he said. "Of course my—er—people will deal with the contents, but I imagine Intelligence will want the container itself as—well, as Exhibit A in the documentation of this particular Russian performance. May I ask why you want it?"

"Oh yes—for the little boy who picked it up; he's longing for it, and I promised to get it for him. His mother will tell him she gave it to me, and I shall feel such a traitor! After all, Intelligence owes quite a bit to him."

"They do indeed!" he said, with a smile suddenly warm and charming. "Our youngest ally! Yes, I will certainly do what I can. Would a replica do?"

"Perfectly—if it's a fairly *exact* replica. It's for a child, remember, and a peasant child at that; they notice everything."

"I will do my best" he said.

As they walked back towards the building a hum suddenly filled the air, and grew into a roar as the small jet made a couple of turns over the sea, and then came in to land. "Oh, the letter for the doctor!" Julia said, as the machine taxied to a halt.

"Ah yes!" He gave it to her. "And please make my profound apologies to the good doctor; I am truly grateful to him."

The pilot got out and chatted with the airport officials, while two small tank-wagons were moved out to re-fuel the machine. Sir Percy went over to him.

"Oh, good morning, Captain. Can I go on board?"

"Not till we've filled her up, sir. Have you had a good time?"

"Yes, most agreeable, thank you. Can my luggage be put on board?"

"When we've filled her up" the pilot said equably. Julia watched with amusement poor Sir Percy fretting and fussing for the next twenty minutes; but at last the bowsers were moved away, the luggage was put on board, the pilot and the co-pilot took their seats, Sir Percy got in and waved, and the plane rose, made two turns, and skimmed away.

"Good!" Colin said. "Now for Hartley. Come along—it's just about time."

"Time for what?" Julia asked, as she followed him into the building.

"My call. I put in a fixed-time one last night." He led her into an office, where he asked one of the airport officials for his call to London; in less than two minutes the man handed him the receiver—Julia, standing at his side, could actually hear the Major's resonant "Colin?"

"Yes. All airborne. So you can give them the green light at the place I spoke of at once. Has Henry got everything laid on?"

"Yes, they're all standing by at the airport; they're sending some of their own people—top ones, I gather."

"Good. Well, tell Henry I shall wait for them at the airport here—oh, and he'd better get them to ring up and have a police car sent out to take us where we want to go."

"What's happened to your own transport?" Hartley asked.

"I'm using it for another purpose" Colin said blandly. "It's borrowed, anyhow, and not nearly big enough. Make Henry do that thing—we don't want to waste any time."

"O.K." Hartley said cheerfully. " 'Bye."

"Now what?" Julia asked; she was feeling pleased at Colin's firm words to the Major.

"Come outside" he said; he thanked the official, paid for his call, and saying—"I return in two instants," went out with Julia onto the tarmac. They sat in the car. Colin lit a cigarette for her, but refused one himself.

"The next thing is de Carvalho" he said. "As you heard, I'm waiting here to meet the Lisbon people, but he must be put in the picture before these P.I.D.E. types arrive. Most tactless of Sir Percy, rushing off without even saying goodbye or thank you!— silly old puffin, I can't think why he wanted to make such a cloak-and-dagger performance over leaving."

"Just being inexperienced, and therefore bad, about our sort of work" Julia said tolerantly. "But it was very rude and silly of him, I agree."

"Yes. Well, you'll just have to do the best you can with the doctor," Colin said gloomily. "I'm sorry to put this onto you, but it's the only way, and he'll probably take it better from you than from me, even if there was time."

"How much can I tell him?"

"The lot!—he deserves it. And it will all have to come out now; he must know where he stands when he meets the crowd from Lisbon."

"Oh, is he to meet them? What do you actually do first? Pounce on the Spaniards?"

"That's up to Portuguese Security now—thank goodness

Hartley arranged for them to come right away! But I imagine they'll want to see the doctor."

"Will he want to see them? Isn't that rather the point, when he's done so much, and been so nice? I mean, he's got nothing to contribute in the way of evidence except the report on the sheep's blood, and about the boy's condition; the actual witnesses to the crime are—"

"Well, who are they?" Colin interrupted.

"You and I, and of course Terence. I'd better let him know what goes on too, hadn't I?"

"Yes, you must. In fact you'd better get cracking, darling." He kissed her, and got out of the car. "Breeze off! Good luck with the doctor. Oh, find out if he does want to see the P.I.D.E. people; I'll look in, or ring up, and ask."

"Right." She started the engine and drove off.

Oh her way back to Funchal Julia wondered a little about getting hold of Dr. de Carvalho; if he was busy with his patients, how was she to extract him from his morning routine? She need not have worried. After parking the car, even as she entered the clinic she could hear his voice, raised in loud reproof to his wretched orderlies—"You allow one of my patients to leave, *with* his luggage, without informing me? Are those your orders? Is this in accordance with my rules?"

She hurried in. De Carvalho was standing in the door of his office; the two orderlies stood by, cringing.

"Dear Doctor, may I see you for a moment?" she said, going up to him. He rounded on her.

"Indeed you *may*! I am told that it was you who drove Sir Paircy away. Is this the famous *polidez Inglesa?*" the doctor asked angrily.

"No—it was an inexcusable rudeness" she said calmly, "on the part of a nervous old man. I bring you his apologies—and also some quite important news. But this I can only tell you when we are alone."

"Very well—come in." He waved the orderlies off with a gesture, and shut the door. "Now, what is the explanation of this extraordinary behaviour?" he asked. "Pray be seated" he added.

"Thank you." Julia sat down. "Sir Percy has hurried back to

England because he wanted to take a sample of the gas which he had received to Porton immediately" she said.

"A sample of the gas! How came he by this?"

"I brought it to him" Julia said, smiling. "The little boy picked it up on the plateau the day he was gassed, and took it home; when I went to see him yesterday he asked me to get it from his mother—he called it his *cofrezinho*."

"Ah, this famous *cofrezinho!*—yes, I have heard him asking the Sister for it. But how do you know that it contained a concentrate of the gas?"

"I didn't know—but when the child told me where he found it, and *when,* I guessed that it might. So I drove down and asked his mother for it. Of course when my cousin and Sir Percy saw the container they knew at once what it was."

"How?"

"There was some Russian lettering on it; and it was so heavy for its size that they realised it must be lined with lead."

"Yes, naturally." He seemed to reflect for a moment. "When did you give this to Sir Paircy?" he asked sharply.

"Yesterday evening—*after* you had shown him the reports from Paris" Julia said carefully.

"Nevertheless, I was available! He could have let me see it at any time last night. He concealed it from me!—deliberately" the Portuguese said, quite indignantly.

"Doctor de Carvalho, my cousin at least thought that it might be embarrassing for you to know too much about this discovery, too soon" she said soothingly. "You have shown us so much consideration, and kindness, that he wished to avoid that."

"But why leave so early?—and without a word of farewell?"

"That, as I have said, was inexcusable—and I had no idea that he meant to do so."

"Not that he was leaving? But you come to fetch him!"

"To take him to his plane—yes. But I did not know till we were on the road that he had failed to bid you goodbye, and thank you, himself. This shocked me. By the way, he asked me to give you this letter, as well as his apologies and his warm thanks" —and she handed over Sir Percy's missive.

With an abrupt *"Vous permettez?"* the doctor opened it, and read it rapidly through. At the end—"Well, he writes a good letter; very persuasive, and very discreet!" he said, with a return to something of his old cheerful irony. "He hints that I might not have felt able to preserve what he calls 'my tactful silence' in the face of such concrete evidence!" his white and gold teeth flashed at her in a grin—"though he is careful to give no indication of what this evidence was."

"No, he was terrified of possibly getting involved with the police, or any form of officialdom" Julia said, relieved. "And when you have heard the rest, you may feel that it would have been difficult for you not to inform the police."

"The rest? What more has he discovered?"

Julia told him, then, about overhearing the two Spaniards at her hotel, their filming activities on the plateau, and Colin's discovery of the radio transceiver in their car. De Carvalho became very excited.

"For this, the police *must* be called in!" he exclaimed. "These recordings should be secured at all costs."

"Oh, I got those last night" Julia said.

"*You* got them? How?"

"I went with old Porfirio and searched their room while the Spanish boys were out."

"But how did you get into their room? Ah, the niece, of course!" He began to grin again. "The old Porfirio shall have enjoyed this expedition!" he said. "And where are the films now?"

"On their way to London, with Sir Percy."

"*Pena!* I should have liked to see them." He paused. "But these two Spaniards must be arrested too, before they have a chance to escape—I should alert the police!" He got up hastily.

"The P.I.D.E. are on their way from Lisbon; they should be at Santa Cruz any minute now" Julia said, looking at her watch. "My cousin is waiting at the airport to meet them, and tell them what has been going on."

"But why do they come, if they do not yet know?"

"Oh, that was arranged through London. They've been told enough to bring them! By the way, would you like to see them when they come?"

"Of course I should like to see them! And they should see the child."

"All right. Mr. Monro said he would ring you up and ask. They may go to the hotel first, to pounce on those Spaniards" Julia said, as the doctor showed signs of getting up again.

"But how will they get here from the airport? They have no car."

"Lisbon was being told to send a police car out from Funchal to meet them."

De Carvalho sank back into his chair with a brief harsh laugh.

"Your English organisation is very efficient! You leave nothing to chance" he said, rather wryly.

"If one leaves nothing to chance, chance sometimes favours one" she said. *"Look* at the luck we have had here!—your knowing all about nerve gases, and then being so kind and putting up my cousin and Sir Percy; my happening to overhear what those Spanish accomplices were up to—to say nothing of the child bringing down a tin of gas!"

"Yes—you have been greatly favoured by fortune. On the other hand you have made very prompt use of the favours she gave you! But it occurs to me that as regards our Security Police, you—or rather Sir Percy—may have been almost too prompt. Will they not wish to see Sir Percy, and hear his evidence?—and see the container of the gas concentrate? And also the film?"

"If wishes were horses, beggars would ride!" Julia said, making a rapid translation of that homely, and so English, proverb into French—the doctor laughed.

"No, but since all these things are now out of their reach," De Carvalho pursued, "might it not be wiser to direct their attention principally to those matters with which they can concern themselves—the sheep, the child, the presence of the Spanish spies and the trawler, all of which are available?"

"Do you mean suppress all mention of Sir Percy and the rest of it?" Julia looked startled.

"Well, at least not bring him into the foreground. They can be a little—sensitive—about their prerogatives."

"Oh well, they're your fellow-countrymen!" Julia said. "But in that case I'd better have a word with my cousin, if I can catch him in time, and tell him to keep Sir Percy and all that part dark. May I use the telephone?"

"I have one in here" the doctor said; he opened a door in some bookshelves, and led her into a very small room with a telephone in it. He got the number for her, asked for the officer in charge, and handed her the receiver. Julia asked for the Senhor Monro, and gave her name—in a moment Colin answered.

"Yes, what is it? They're just coming in to land."

"Oh well, the doctor has had an idea—to pipe down about Sir P. and everything he's taken with him, till he's seen the people you're expecting himself. . . . Yes, he *would* like to see them. . . . Well, he thinks it would be better that way; they might be *froissés* by the removal of Exhibits A and B. I should leave it till you come in here. . . . No, I haven't spoken to him yet; I'm going to now. . . . Yes, all going fine. . . . No, no trouble with him. 'Bye."

After ringing off Julia put her head out of the door, but the doctor's study was empty; she closed it again and rang up the Quinta. Penelope answered.

"Oh, is Terence there?" Julia asked.

"No, he's gone to the office early—he wanted to make up for lost time!" Penelope said, but quite amiably.

"I'm not surprised!" Julia said. "Oh well, never mind."

"How's Ag?" Mrs. Armitage asked.

"Under sedation—and in Nannie Mack's care."

"*I* think she ought to see a doctor" Penelope said, decidedly.

"Oh, she has. Pauline got him in last night."

"What, de Carvalho?"

"No, the old Scotch one close by."

"Oh, old Urquhart! Well, he's not very up-to-date, but I expect he's better than nothing. What does he say?"

"I haven't seen him" Julia said. "But I know he gave her a strongish sedative. Goodbye, Penelope." She rang off rather abruptly; she didn't want to waste too much energy on parrying Mrs. Armitage's rather *cassant* questions. She rang the Shipping Office and asked for the Senhor Armitage—he had not yet arrived. Julia decided to go down and try to see him; that would be better than guarded hints on the telephone. She went out and spoke to the elderly male secretary, asking him to tell the Senhor Doctor that she had gone out for a short time, but would return.

The Shipping Office was so close that as before she left her car in the care of the doorman, and set off on foot, in the bright early sunshine, through quiet streets where flowering trees and creepers showed over the walls. But charming as Funchal's streets are, they have their dangers; the small nut-sized cobbles of the steep pavements are exceedingly slippery, especially when walking downhill—the prudent wear rubber-soled shoes if they are going to walk any distance. Julia was not wearing rubber soles, and presently her feet went out from under her, and down she came, hitting her right elbow hard—the pain was so sharp and sickening that she had to sit on a step till it passed off; then she pushed on, hoping she had broken nothing. At the office Terence had arrived, and she was promptly shown up to his office.

"Hullo, what's the matter?" he asked as she came in. "You look awfully ill."

"Oh, it's nothing—I fell and hit my elbow."

"Have you had anything to eat?" he asked, with concern.

"Come to think of it, I haven't yet" she said.

"Julia, you are *mad!*" He telephoned and ordered coffee; then he sat down opposite her. "What on earth are you doing, out at this hour? and breakfastless?"

"Well, first I was taking Sir Percy to the airport, and then I came back to soothe de Carvalho's troubled breast" Julia said.

"Goodness me, has Sir Percy cleared off? Why on earth?"

"He's got what he came for" Julia said.

"What, those thermometer recordings?"

"Plus a good bit more. The reports on the sheep's blood came in yesterday, and the doctor gave him copies of those; and I managed to collect what I *think* are the films those boys were taking of the sheep—and best of all, he's got a sample of the actual stuff they used to make the gas."

"It's not possible!" Terence said, incredulously. Then, as she nodded—"Where on earth did he find that?"

"It was in Carmen's kitchen!" Julia said; she began to laugh at his astonished expression, and told him, then, of the little boy's begging her to bring him his *cofrezinho,* and how she had collected it the previous afternoon.

"So when I told you to produce a *deus ex machina,* you'd got it all the time!" Terence said.

"Well, the machine part, yes. But that put Sir Percy into a fearful tizzy; he was determined to get it back to England at once, and rang for a plane, and left this morning, gas and films and all, just after seven."

At this point the coffee was brought; Terence poured her out a cup—"Yes, masses of sugar, please" Julia said; she took several sips, thankfully. "That's marvellous" she said.

"Go on, when you're ready, and tell me why the doctor's breast needed soothing" Terence said.

"Oh well, that silly old puff was so petrified of getting held up in any way that he wouldn't let de Carvalho know about any of this till he was airborne; he even slipped away this morning without saying goodbye," Julia said.

"Really? That was rather crass—I shouldn't have expected it of him" Terence remarked thoughtfully. "But why did the doctor have to be told at once, before you got some breakfast?"

"Because he's been so frightfully decent and kind, for one thing" Julia said warmly—"putting them up, and keeping quiet to his local authorities while Sir Percy made all his recordings. Now he simply *had* to know what's going on because of the Special Police coming."

"The Special Police? D'you mean from Lisbon? When are they coming?"

"They must be on their way in from Santa Cruz now. Colin told London to get our Lisbon people to lay them on last night, and they were standing by over there till they got word. He rang London from the airport as soon as Sir Percy and his precious specimens were airborne—he'd put in a fixed-time call overnight."

Terence began to laugh; and went on laughing for some time.

"What's so funny?" Julia asked, almost laughing herself.

"Only the way you and your crowd go about things! I can't

think why spy-books are called 'cloak-and-dagger' stuff—'plane and telephone' would be much nearer the mark" Terence said. "But did you say Sir Percy had got the films the Spaniards had taken of the sheep? How in the world did he—or you—get hold of those?"

"Oh, that was heaven Porfirio! Sir Percy and Colin said I mustn't stay on at the Montefiore with them there, and then Sir Percy said I mustn't even go back alone—so I fetched Porfirio as an escort. Of course it was no good either Sir Percy or Colin coming, because that might have roused the boys' suspicions, as they know them both by sight. And then on the way Porfirio told me. . . ."

"His niece!" Terence interrupted her. "Don't tell me she let you go and raid their room?"

"She didn't want to—the old fellow *made* her. But when she saw what I'd found among their clothes she led me to the main haul, hidden in the clothes-basket."

"All this while the thugs were having dinner, of course."

"No—I'm not sure I'd have risked that. They'd gone out for the evening, luckily. So I just dropped the stuff on Sir Percy, and that was that."

"And where did *you* sleep" Terence asked merrily—he seemed to find all this a huge joke.

"Up at the Serra."

"Oh." The man's expression changed. "Did you see Ag?" he asked.

"No. Pauline got that old Dr. Urquhart in, and he gave her some terrific sedative injection, which knocked her out flat."

"Poor child" he said sombrely.

"Yes. But that can wait" Julia said briskly. "The thing now is to do something about da Silva."

"What are we to do about him?"

"That's what I want to ask you. It wasn't very nice for him, my clearing out in the middle of the night, with no notice, though he was perfectly polite about it; but it will be even less nice if the P.I.D.E. come and arrest his two favourite clients!" Julia said urgently.

"*Are* they going to arrest them?"

"I've no idea. I suppose they might have them tailed for a day or two, and try to pick up their wireless messages to the trawler; I suppose it depends on what they make of what Colin, and de Carvalho, and you and I tell them."

"Why should I have to tell them anything?" Terence asked, looking rather startled.

"Well, you found the sheep, didn't you? Anyhow you can vouch for da Silva, can't you? I'm positive he hasn't a clue about the Spanishes not being what they seemed."

"Yes, I can do that," Terence said.

"Right." Julia got up.

"Where are you going now?" he asked.

"Back to the clinic. Oh, one other thing—de Carvalho thinks it might be as well to play Sir Percy down as far as possible, not to hurt local susceptibilities" Julia said.

"Yes, I can see he might prefer that!" Terence said. "I'm not sure that it will be possible. All right—thank you for coming."

"Thank you for the coffee" Julia said.

15

WHEN JULIA GOT back to the clinic Colin was in the telephone-box in the hall; she waved to him, whereupon he slammed down the receiver and came out.

"*There* you are! Where on earth had you got to?"

"Been to wise-up Terence" Julia said.

"Well, come along and wise-up the Lisbon party!" Colin said. "They want you."

"Where are they?" Julia asked—"and what do they want me for?"

"Up in that summer-house place" he said, leading her out into the garden. "They want to know about the trawler, and the Spanishes—I can't follow it all, but I get the impression that they're being a bit tiresome to the Doctor."

"Could be, I suppose" Julia said, obediently following him up the path through the beds of vegetables and the avocado pear-trees. "Is that their car in the drive, with the two policemen in it?"

"Yes."

In the open-sided garden-house sat four men—a short stout Portuguese, a tall, sandy, quite obvious Englishman, whom Julia guessed to be Henry Hamilton, and Dr. de Carvalho in vigorous and declamatory argument with a man who was seated with his back to her—when Colin announced *"Voici Madame Jamieson"* they all rose, and this individual turned round. Then he fairly ran at her with outstretched hands—*"A Menina Probeen! Che prazer!"* Though he was a little greyer, and even stouter than when she had last seen him at Gralheira some years before,

Julia at once recognised Colonel Marques, the head of the Portuguese Security Police.

"Oh, hullo, Colonel—how nice to see you again" she said; one of the amusing and unexpected things about Colonel Marques had always been that he spoke such excellent English. The others stood by in surprise while they chatted for a few moments as old friends, deploring the death of the Duke of Ericeira, discussing Luzia Ericeira's recent marriage to Nicholas Heriot. "And imagine, Nannie Brown is back at Gralheira, to look after Luzia's baby when it comes! That will be her third Ericeira baby!" Julia said happily. Then Colin, a little impatiently, introduced Major Hamilton, and Marques his number two, also a Major, and they all sat down.

"*Alors,* Monsieur le Colonel" Julia began, switching to French—she knew that de Carvalho's English was limited— "Monsieur Monro said you wished to speak with me. What can I tell you?"

"But everything!" the Colonel exclaimed. "We seem to have been told remarkably little so far" he said, with a slightly unamiable glance in the doctor's direction.

"There was very little to tell but suppositions and guesses, till yesterday" Julia observed calmly—"and I know that Monsieur le Colonel prefers hard facts to those."

"Yet Monsieur Monro is here, from British Intelligence, since some time" Colonel Marques countered.

"No, *not* from British Intelligence" Julia stated firmly. "He came from Spain, on leave, to see Madame his wife, who is staying here; though in fact I asked him to come, on account of those suppositions and guesses which I have referred to."

"You sent for him without informing London?" Marques asked, surprised.

"Certainly—can a lady not invite her cousin, if she wishes to seek his advice?" Julia said, smiling a little. "We only informed London after Monsieur Monro was already here."

During this interchange the doctor sat watching Julia, relief and satisfaction gradually spreading over his dark face. "But now" Julia pursued, in her slow, measured tones, "would Monsieur le Colonel care to hear the sequence of events from the beginning, as far as I know them? It might help him to a clearer appreciation of a situation that for some time remained excessively confused."

"Certainly" Colonel Marques said; after their warm-hearted meeting he was ever so slightly deflated by this formal manner.

Julia held forth at some length: her two encounters with the Russian trawler, finding the stricken sheep, the hammock-men's account of the ten nocturnal tourists, and their smoking pale-brown cigarettes with cardboard mouthpieces—"which to me suggested that they were Russians"—the mysterious illness of the child, and his being taken to the clinic for observation. "Then Madame Monro had a fortunate connection of ideas— one might say a guess. We owe much to her feminine intuition!" Julia said gaily, though in fact she was choosing her words with considerable care. She slid lightly over the fact that Mme. Monro of course knew that her husband had recently been in Central Asia in search of a new Russian nerve gas, whose existence had been revealed by a defector, and suggested that he should come to investigate—"but since this was all still a matter of guesses and suppositions, we did not inform London at that stage."

At this point de Carvalho began to look slightly nervous. Julia flowed on.

However, Dr. de Carvalho had at once taken the precaution of sending specimens of the child's and the sheep's blood to laboratories on the mainland, and their reports, which he received yesterday, confirmed Madame Monro's guess. *"Madame a une très jolie façon de sauter"* Julia observed, smiling again. De Carvalho looked relieved; Colonel Marques asked if he could see Madame Monro?

Alas, not for the moment, Julia told him; Madame was confined to her bed with a feverish complaint; her doctor would not allow her to be disturbed. "But now we come to the matter which is, I assume, of most immediate concern to Monsieur le Colonel" Julia pursued blandly—"the local accomplices, about whom my cousin has already told you."

"Ah yes—how were these discovered?" the Portuguese Major

asked, speaking for the first time; he had been making notes on a pad.

"By pure good fortune!" Julia said. Their existence, she went on, had of course been assumed from the outset, but it was just an unheard-of stroke of luck that she should have been staying in the same hotel, and have overheard them discussing the question of photographing the sheep on behalf of someone called Polunsky. At this point Marques held up his hand.

"One moment, Madame, *je vous prie*." He turned to Colin. "Was this name already familiar to you?"

"No" Colin said.

"To you?" Marques asked, turning to de Carvalho.

"Certainly—he is one of the principal Russian experts on nerve gases" the doctor said. "But . . ."

Marques interrupted him. "Yet you did not inform the local authorities that there were people here, in Funchal, acting on this person's behalf? An employee of a foreign country?"

Julia leaned over and put a long white hand on Marques' sleeve.

"Monsieur le Colonel is trying to go too fast" she said quietly. "Dr. de Carvalho only heard Polunsky's name this morning, less than an hour ago. I told him myself. I only told Monsieur Monro of his existence yesterday, and I think your office was given this information yesterday evening, quite early, was it not?"

The Colonel grunted. "That is so" he admitted.

"Then I do not think there was any unreasonable delay in the information being passed to you" Julia said firmly, causing the Portuguese Major to stare at her. "Mr. Monro informed London as soon as he got within reach of a telephone, and British Intelligence decided that in a matter of this importance it was better to inform your office rather than the local police. If Monsieur le Colonel has any complaints on that score, he should address himself to London" she added quite stiffly—"not to Dr. de Carvalho, who in any case was unaware of any of the facts; nor to my cousin."

Marques grunted again—the Portuguese Major stared harder than ever at this young Englishwoman who so hardily rebuked his chief.

"Why was Monsieur Monro not within reach of a telephone?" the Colonel asked now, but less disagreeably.

"Because when I told him, we were already on our way to the plateau again, to see how the sheep were getting on" Julia said easily—"and there we got confirmation of what I had heard about the photography, for the two young Spaniards were up there with their machine, taking ciné-pictures of the sheep!"

"And it was on the way down that you examined their car, and found the radio-apparatus?" Marques asked, of Colin this time.

"Yes, sir."

The Colonel was silent for a moment or two; he appeared to reflect.

"Monsieur le Docteur, I ask your pardon" he said at length. "Mademoiselle is right—I was going too fast!" he added, turning to Julia with a smile.

"Well, now I suppose you go and apprehend them?" Julia said.

"Assuredly. Do you know what names they are using?"

"Yes—Cristofero and Domingo de Calderón" Julia replied. "And their room number is seventeen—I looked them up in the hotel register."

"*Merci,* Mademoiselle. Your assistance has been of the greatest value" the Colonel said—"*Sous tous les aspects!*"

"Thank you, Colonel" Julia said, now again in English; she smiled at him, pleased that his usual urbanity had been restored.

"Then let us be on our way" Colonel Marques said, getting up. "Monro, do you know these men by sight?"

"Certainly, sir."

"Then we need not trouble Mademoiselle" the Colonel said. He turned to de Carvalho. "You will be able to furnish us with these reports from the laboratories later" he added. "They will be valuable as evidence."

"You do not wish to see the boy?" the doctor asked.

"Not at this moment. He will assuredly not attempt to escape!" Marques replied cheerfully.

As they started down the garden Colin drew Julia aside.

"Well, you pulled that off all right" he said. "Why are you and he such chums?"

"Oh, we met at Gralheira, when Luzia and Nannie Brown

snaffled a rather important Communist for him. But I wish I'd asked you on the way up whether you'd told him about Sir Percy —as it was I had to take a chance on that."

"No, I hadn't—I thought we'd agreed I wasn't to."

"Oh well, it worked. But I should try and get word to the people at the airport to keep their mouths shut about Sir Percy's plane, if I were you."

"I dare say if he gets his Spaniards he won't worry too much about that" Colin said easily. "It's bound to come out in the end, of course; but let's hope at governmental level. After all this whole operation is directed against us, not the Portuguese. What are you going to do now?"

"Go up to the Serra and get some breakfast."

"Goodness, haven't you had any? Well, if you get the chance, you might have a word with old Dr. Urquhart about Ag."

Julia in fact intended to do that very thing; but after the police cars had driven off—a second one had appeared—she was intercepted by Dr. de Carvalho, who thanked her warmly for her defence of him—Colonel Marques, he said, was not a person in whose bad books it was at all comfortable to be! He, too, wanted to know how she came to be on such familiar terms with that remote and dreaded figure; Julia again explained. "But I'm only sorry I couldn't tell Colonel Marques just how much you have in fact really helped us" she ended. "I may get the chance later."

"Do not trouble; you have done all that was necessary!" the doctor said, showing his white and gold teeth in a cheerful grin. *"Au revoir,* Madame."

It was after half-past nine when Julia reached the Shergolds, and she was very hungry indeed. She hurried into the dining-room—it was empty of occupants, but coffee still stood on the hot-plate, and a place had been laid for her—she tucked into rolls and bilberry jam thankfully. What a lot had happened since that bilberry-picking with the children, she thought—how little, on that quiet and innocent afternoon, she had guessed what strange doings lay ahead. Well, all that was nearly over now; what remained, as unfinished business, was how to sort out Colin and Aglaia.

During her meal she occasionally cautiously felt her elbow with her other hand; driving, especially on bends, it had been rather painful; she decided to let Dr. Urquhart see it when he came; it would be a good excuse to meet him, and hear his views on Colin's wife. She rang the bell when she had finished, and asked the maid where her hostess was?—out with the children, she was told. Julia went up to see Nannie, whom she found doing some ironing; Philip had gone out with the others. "How is little Mrs. Armitage?" Julia asked.

"Still under" Nannie said. "Not a sound out of her all night."

"Oh good. Nannie, I want to see the doctor when he's seen her; I've hurt my elbow, and I'd like him to look at it. Will you tell him so? I expect I shall be with Mrs. Hathaway."

Nannie of course wanted to see the elbow herself. "That's a nasty bruise, Madam—you'd better let me put on some Pomade Divine." She did so, and wrapped it in gauze—"Now you won't greasy your dress."

Mrs. Hathaway was still in bed, and Julia sat with her. "Oh yes, Colin's job here is nearly finished" she told the old lady; "I should think he'd be free any day now."

"And then what will he do? Take that child home and look after her?"

"I don't know" Julia said sadly. "I expect it depends partly on what the doctor says."

"Well, I am sure you ought to see him" Mrs. Hathaway said. "He asked me and Pauline all sorts of questions about her, and about Colin, that of course we couldn't answer—you might be able to."

"Yes, I will see him" Julia said.

Her interview with Doctor Urquhart took place half an hour later, after he had seen both his other patients, in her own room. While he examined her elbow she studied him—except for his grey hair he gave little impression of age, but a strong one of competence and kindness. Nothing was broken, he pronounced, washing his hands, and no treatment better than Nannie's prescription. "Get her to put some more on. And lie on your bed for a while; it was a bit of a shock, yon fall." Julia obediently lay down; he drew up a chair and sat beside her.

"Mistress Hathaway tells me you know young Mrs. Monro and her husband well" he began.

"Him, very well; he's my cousin, and we've seen a lot of one another ever since we were children. Her, no; I've seen very little of her till we came out here, and to tell you the truth, we all found her rather difficult to get to know" Julia said.

"The truth is what I want!" Dr. Urquhart remarked with a rather quizzical smile. "First, who are 'we all'?"

"Mr. Monro's sister Edina, Mrs. Reeder; Philip Reeder, her husband, and me and Mrs. Hathaway," Julia replied readily.

"A close-knit group, would you say?—a little difficult for a newcomer to settle into?"

"Philip Reeder didn't find it so! But he's a very mature and confident person" Julia said, smiling at his shrewdness.

"Quite so. When she is in normal health is Mrs. Monro confident? She doesn't seem very mature."

"No, confident isn't a word one would use for her—at least not superficially" Julia said slowly.

"Just what do you mean by superficially? Can you say?"

"I'm trying to think how to put it" Julia said. "She's timid with people, I think because she realises that she is rather silly—or perhaps I mean rather *less* of a person than many people are; but inside she has a quite ruthless determination, and an intense conviction that her own ideas are right, and everyone else's wrong!"

"How did you discover this—since you found her so hard to get to know?"

"Well, I'd better tell you something of her recent circumstances, and give you an example" Julia proceeded. "Colin Monro is in the British Intelligence Service, and was number two to my husband on an expedition to Asia some months ago—my husband was killed, and Colin brought the expedition back—unsuccessful. Aglaia got it into her head that Colin was being blamed for the failure—unjustly, she thought; especially as he was sent to do a rather dull job in Spain."

"*Is* he being blamed, in fact?" Dr. Urquhart interjected.

"I don't know. I heard nothing of it, but then I might well not have done. Well, something has happened here recently—I can't tell you what—that made both her and me suspicious; and she was very sharp about that, and gave me an invaluable clue! Now the normal thing would have been to inform Mr. Monro's Office in London; but she was absolutely adamant that he should come here and go into it, to have a success to counterbalance his imagined failure—she was so set on this, and so distressed, that I did as she wished, and sent for him."

"Are you in British Intelligence?" the doctor asked.

"No" Julia replied smiling. "But one way and another I have worked in with them for years—through my husband, and Colin, and other people. Let me tell you one rather key thing: when she was pressing me to send for him she said—'He'll come if you tell him to; he wouldn't for me.' A sense of inferiority, you see, even about her own relation with her husband."

"H'm" Dr. Urquhart said thoughtfully. "Thank you—that is a useful pointer. Is he—your cousin—a very dominant person?"

"Far from it! He has always been almost as lacking in self-confidence as she, till just lately—it's been a constant worry."

"To whom?—his mother?"

Julia laughed out.

"Poor Aunt Ellen! No; she's much too vague to notice anything of that sort! No; Edina—his sister—and I have done the worrying mostly, I think."

"Not his wife?"

"I don't know" Julia said, not laughing now. "My impression is that she would be thinking more about herself. But look, Dr. Urquhart, this business with Aglaia is really serious."

"To whom, Mrs. Jamieson?—and serious in what way?"

"To her husband, primarily—and as it affects his career" Julia said sombrely. "She cannot seem to understand that when one is married to someone in Intelligence one just *can't* be told everything that they are doing, let alone share in it; and that one must never talk about them, and whether they are successful or not, to other people—in fact one should practically never talk about them at all!"

"Has he pointed this out to her?"

"I don't know. Mr. Armitage—the cousin she's been staying with here—has tried to, and so have I; but even when she is well, and normal, she is terribly impulsive and uncontrolled. Unless she *can* realise the position, he may have to resign; he told me so yesterday."

"Is he a good Intelligence officer?"

"He's getting to be" Julia said slowly. "My husband, and some of his other superiors, thought he had it in him to be a very good one indeed: he had a remarkable gift for languages, and great adaptability; the one thing he has lacked was self-confidence, and now, just when he was getting that—" she broke off, suddenly uncertain of her voice.

Dr. Urquhart tried a fresh tack.

"Have you any idea what brought on this attack of hysteria in Mrs. Monro? You realise that it is quite a serious one?"

"I assumed so, because you felt it necessary to knock her out" Julia replied frankly. "I think this has been building up for some time. First, of course, he had to be away from home a lot—I imagine much more than she had bargained for. Then just a short time ago she was in a car smash, and lost the baby she was expecting—utterly miserable for her, of course; and on top of that he had to go off to this job in Spain, which she felt, rightly or wrongly, was a sort of demotion for him. So she has been stewing and fretting over that, as well as all the rest—quite a plateful for a very young and not very disciplined person, wouldn't you say?"

"Certainly. Most trying, not to say painful, for any young married woman" Dr. Urquhart said.

"But I think the immediate thing that has tipped her over the edge—" Julia began, and then paused.

"Yes—what was that? Take your time" the old Scotsman added kindly.

"I think she expected, when she was so insistent on his coming here, that as well as bringing off an important job successfully—which she did desperately want him to do—that he would be staying in the same house with her, and that she would be—well, be in on everything he was doing" Julia said thoughtfully.

"And did he not stay there?"

"No, he stayed in Funchal. He had to see me first, of course, and hear what was going on, so Mr. Armitage got him a room there for the first night; and in the course of that evening we stumbled, accidentally, on some quite fresh information which practically confirmed our suspicions. When he reported this on the telephone to London, that same night, they sent out someone very high-powered indeed, who got here the next morning."

"How?" Dr. Urquhart interjected.

"Oh, on a special plane. But this person was so very well-known that his visit had to be kept secret, if possible; we were lucky in being able to arrange a hide-out for him in Funchal, and my cousin stayed there with him while he made his enquiries. And the most unobtrusive form of transport was for me to drive the two of them about in the little private car I was using anyhow."

"Clearly. When did this high-powered person arrive?"

"Last Friday. And my cousin—I'm afraid quite rightly" Julia said sadly—"would not let his wife know where he was staying, nor even his telephone number."

"You agree that these were necessary precautions, in her case?"

"Yes" Julia said—"and in his. He was really *afraid* of being in touch with her until the job was done, because of the distraction and—well, the general botheration."

"That doesn't sound as if he were very mature either" Dr. Urquhart said, but with a quite benevolent smile.

"No, he isn't. He's only just growing up," Julia agreed readily. "Look, Dr. Urquhart, this job my cousin is on is really very important indeed; I'm not exaggerating. And I can't help being tiresome and mysterious about it, because I really can't tell you what is going on."

"Don't apologise—I don't even suspect you of exaggerating. I can see that it is a very difficult situation for all three of you."

"Good—I'm glad. And you see this has really rather rubbed her nose in that situation" Julia said. "It was one thing to know in theory that Colin and I often worked together, but quite another to have us doing it close by, and she being excluded."

"Has she in fact seen him?"

"Yes—that was what finally did it." She told the doctor then of their encounter with Aglaia at the Quinta the previous day, and how Colin had had to be taken in to Funchal by his wife—"I had to collect the big shot from somewhere else"—and how Aglaia had returned to the Quinta already in a state of hysteria, and locked herself into her room. "Her husband was in too much of a hurry to be able to straighten her out or soothe her down, because he had to telephone some fresh information to London at once" Julia explained. "That's just an instance of how difficult it all is for him."

Dr. Urquhart was silent for a few moments, reflecting on what he had heard. Presently—"Since her husband is anyhow not staying at the Quinta, do you know why it was considered necessary to send her up here?" he asked. "Mrs. Shergold only said that she had been asked to put her up for a few days, and had agreed."

"Yes, I do know" Julia said at once, "but I'm afraid you will think as much of the reason as I am able to give you absurdly melodramatic."

"Give it to me all the same" he said, again with that benevolent smile.

"Dr. Urquhart, there have been some very unsavoury characters about on the island for some time past" Julia said carefully, "and my cousin, and Mr. Armitage, and the big shot from London have been working against them. They know us all by sight but, except in my case, not where we live. They picked up a clue yesterday that would lead them directly to Mr. Armitage's Quinta—in fact I saw them doing it. So I told Mr. Armitage this, and asked him to warn all the people on the place not to talk to strangers. Then he remembered Mrs. Monro, and decided that it would be safer if she could be got away at once—and as Mrs. Shergold happened to be down there for the day, he asked her to bring Aglaia up here."

Dr. Urquhart listened gravely.

"This was Mr. Terence Armitage, of the Shipping Office, who wished to have Mrs. Monro removed?" he asked at length.

"Yes—she's his cousin."

"H'm. He is not an alarmist—he has very sound judgment" the Scotsman said. "Yes—it is an impossible situation for young Monro."

"Is there anything one can *do* about people like that? Cure them, I mean?" Julia asked, rather desperately.

"Sometimes. When she is more herself I will talk to her" the doctor said. He got up.

"Thank you, Mrs. Jamieson. What you have told me has been very useful" he said. "When your cousin, young Mr. Monro, is free, I should like to see *him*. One always needs to see all concerned, in a case like this. Goodbye."

16 WHEN THE POLICE CAR drove away from the clinic it was rather crowded. A uniformed policeman drove, with Colin, at Colonel Marques' instance, beside him; Marques and the Major sat in the back, with two plain-clothes men on the tip-up seats. A second car with several more uniformed police followed. They reached the hotel a little before nine—"I don't suppose the *patron* is up yet" Colin remarked to the Colonel, "but I suppose you'll want to see him?"

"Certainly. We want to do everything quietly and correctly" Marques said, getting out.

"Well, the guests' cars are all in lock-up garages round at the back; it mightn't be a bad idea if this other car with the local men waited round there" Colin said. "More unobtrusive, and then they can keep an eye on all cars."

"A good idea—show me, please." Colin led him round the corner of the building to where a row of garage doors fronted onto a long yard; all were closed except one, outside which a chauffeur in his shirt-sleeves was polishing a black saloon.

"That their car?" Marques asked.

"No—they use a sports convertible."

"Right." They went back to the front of the hotel, where Marques told the other car where to wait; then he rang the bell. The door was in fact open, and a valet in a green baize apron was polishing the parquet with a weighted felt on a broom-handle; he came over to the door and asked what he could do for them? Marques asked for the receptionist, and stepped into the hall; the Major, Colin, and the two plain-clothes men followed; there was no one at the desk. The valet disappeared.

"What did you say the landlord's name is?" Marques asked Colin.

"Da Silva."

After a moment a young receptionist appeared, struggling into his jacket; Marques told him, very politely, that he wished to see the Senhor da Silva. This flustered the receptionist slightly —he was not sure if the Senhor was about. "Please fetch him" Marques said, still politely. "My name is Marques." The receptionist vanished; the valet re-appeared, and went on polishing the floor. Colin walked over to the barometer and looked at it with interest; then he glanced across towards the staircase. "What have you found there?" the Colonel, bored, asked, coming over to him.

"This is the barometer the two boys were tapping when my cousin overheard them talking about photographing the sheep for the Russian."

"Where was she?"

"Coming downstairs."

The Colonel also measured the distance to the staircase with his eye.

"Miss Probeen must have good hearing" he said.

"Just what I was thinking. Her ears are as good as her eyes are bad. But look, sir—I wanted to tell you this sooner—my cousin is not Miss Probyn any more; she is Mrs. Jamieson now."

"She is married? I hope to someone worthy of her?"

"She's a widow now; he died a few months ago. He was in my Service—a splendid chap" Colin said briefly. "I didn't realise that you and she had met before, or I would have made this clear sooner."

"Ah yes—you said 'My cousin', but I did not know of whom you were speaking" the Colonel said. "My apologies."

At this point da Silva appeared; he was fully dressed, but evidently had not shaved. Marques went over to him.

"The Senhor da Silva? My name is Marques. I am sorry to disturb you so early—could perhaps speak in your office?"

Da Silva, looking slightly surprised, led the way into his office, a large tidy room behind the reception-desk; the Major and Colin followed, the two plain-clothes men remained in the hall. Marques shut the door after him; then he drew out a small leather case with a card in it and showed it to the landlord—da Silva took it, read it, and looked aghast.

"From the P.I.D.E.!" he said, under his breath.

"Yes, Senhor. I wish to speak with two of your guests, to check that their papers are in order."

"Which guests?" the unhappy da Silva stammered.

"The Senhores de Calderón, in Number seventeen."

"But these are most excellent clients! This is their second visit, and they never give any trouble."

"I am sure they would not, to you, Senhor" Marques said, with a small cold smile. "Tell me, on which side does their room look out?"

"Over the yard where the garages are. They say that they see so much scenery on their expeditions that they do not require a room with a view" the wretched hotelier said, still eagerly defending his guests.

"Quite so. *Muito bem*" the police chief said.

"But I assure the Senhor Chefe that their papers are in perfect order—I sent them, as with those of all my guests, to the Policia, and they were perfectly satisfied" da Silva persisted.

"No one is blaming you, Senhor; all the same I wish to see these gentlemen. Please be good enough to take us up to their room."

Plainly uncomfortable, da Silva opened the door and led the way upstairs; Marques indicated to the Major with a gesture that he should remain below—"Come with me" he said to Colin, and nodded a summons to the two plain-clothes men, who followed them up, but remained in the corridor, one on each side of the door. da Silva knocked; there was no reply. He knocked again—this time a sleepy voice said *"Entre,"* and the landlord opened the door, saying—"Some gentlemen to see the Senhores."

Two sleepy figures with tousled heads sat up in bed as Colin, Marques and da Silva walked into the room, and gaped in astonishment. Marques walked over and stood by the window.

"Good morning, gentlemen. I am sorry to disturb you so early, but I must ask you to dress and come to the Policia" he said. "Bringing your papers, please; I wish to see whether they are in order." He turned to Colin, and asked in English—"These they?"

"Yes."

"Right. Just look in the bathroom—is there a window?"

Colin walked over and opened the bathroom door—"No" he said.

"Thanks." He turned to the two Spaniards and said, now in Portuguese—"You can go into the bathroom, one at a time, and dress there, leaving the door open."

At this point one of the young men sprang up and darted towards the door, knocking da Silva, who stood near it, aside; Marques called a monosyllabic order, and the youth was promptly seized by the two waiting plain-clothes men and brought back into the room.

"You see that resistance is of no use" Marques said calmly. "Please get dressed quietly." He turned to da Silva. "Senhor, are you hurt?"

"No, I—I do not think so" the landlord said uncertainly.

"Good. You need not remain; I am sure this is trying for you" Marques said pleasantly. "Let the Senhor out" he said to Colin, "and then lock the door." Colin did as he was told; the other Spaniard, apparently seeing that the game was up, got out of bed, picked up an armful of clothes off a chair, and went towards the bathroom.

"Stand by the door and hold it open" the Colonel said to Colin, again in English. "See that he doesn't take anything— you'd better just give his clothes the once-over before he puts them on."

This was a routine that Colin was quite familiar with. He took his shorts and Nazaré shirt from the Spaniard, and felt with a practised hand in the shirt pockets, round the bottoms of the sleeves, and the hems of the shorts. "Ah, here we are" he said— "Oh no you don't!" as the youth tried to snatch the garment from him; he unpinned a small piece of muslin, opened it, and after a glance at the contents handed it to the Colonel.

"Ah, the usual thing!" Marques said.

"I think so—it looks like a cyanide capsule to me."

"Well, go back to that door." Marques spoke in Portuguese to one of the plain-clothes men, who left the job of holding the other Spaniard to his colleague, and searched a second pile of clothes lying on another chair—this time without result.

"Where is your pill?" Marques asked the youth who had tried to make a dash for it.

"I think it may be in a shirt that I wore yesterday—in the clothes-basket" the young man said.

"Let him look" Marques told the plain-clothes man, who led his captive over to the basket, still holding him by one arm. With the other hand the young man felt down among the dirty clothes —he straightened up with a cry of dismay. "Domingo! They are gone!"

The other youth, half-dressed, dashed out of the bathroom. "Impossible!" he exclaimed; he turned the basket upside down —a heap of dirty clothes fell out onto the floor, which he turned over with feverish haste. "*Carajo!* Who can have moved them?" he said. He fairly ran across to the chest of drawers, pulled out the middle one, and looked in that, tossing out shirts in a parti-coloured shower; then the bottom drawer, hurling pyjamas about. "Nothing!" he said. "Who can have done this?"

"Go and finish dressing" Marques told him; as the young man obeyed, "What is all this, do you suppose?" Marques asked of Colin in English.

Colin knew well enough what the wretched boys were looking for—the rolls of film which Julia had removed from this very room the night before; but since they were now on their way to England in Sir Percy's plane, and it had been agreed that the Colonel was not to be told about Sir Percy and his activities as yet, he stalled. "Could it be more of the suicide pills?" he suggested.

"They would hardly have more than one each" Marques said.

"By the way, Colonel, while we're up here should we see if they've got their radio installed?" Colin asked.

"Might as well." Marques was standing by the window; he now

opened it, and looked right and left. Sure enough, clipped to the hinge of the shutter was the radio aerial, in a fairly inconspicuous position. "Yes, that is it all right. Fernandez can collect it when he comes to bring down their gear" he said easily. He leaned out of the window and called down to the driver of the police car to come round to the front door.

By this time the second young man was in process of getting dressed in the bathroom; the first sat dejectedly on a chair. "Now get your papers," Marques told him—"Ah, you have them—good. My people will pack all your effects and bring them to the Policia."

"Do we not return here?" the Spaniard asked gloomily.

"No, you do not."

In a few moments the two young men, now dressed, and each handcuffed to a plain-clothes man, were led downstairs and out to one of the waiting cars; inside it a switch was made, and the men were re-handcuffed to two uniformed policemen; the plain-clothes men rejoined Marques and Major Fernandez in the hotel. The whole business had taken less than twenty minutes. Da Silva stood in the door of his office, looking on dismally; now he approached Colonel Marques.

"Do the Spanish Senhores not return?" he asked.

"No, Senhor; I am taking them to Lisbon."

"But their bill! Do they not pay their bill?"

"If they have sufficient money with them, it shall certainly be paid" Marques said. "Make the bill out, Senhor, if you please." He turned to Fernandez. "Major, will you go upstairs now and clear everything; bring it with you—if there is any money among their effects, pay the bill." He turned back to the landlord.

"Senhor, I regret this on your account," he said. "Do not distress yourself; it was not your fault. These individuals were sailing under false colours. Just one more thing—their car."

"But the car is mine!—they hired it from me" Da Silva exclaimed.

"Nevertheless I wish to see it" Marques said, smiling a little, but not unkindly. "Let us go to the garage now."

The landlord stepped back into his office and fetched a bunch of keys; then he went out, followed by Colin and the Colonel. Both police cars were still standing in the drive—Marques spoke to the driver of the one in which the Spaniards were, and it drove off.

"They can wait at the police station" he said to Colin; "the car will come back for the Major and his men."

Out in the yard da Silva unlocked the door of one of the garages, revealing the car which Julia and Colin had searched to such purpose the previous day; the key was not in it.

"They have taken the key!" the unhappy landlord exclaimed.

"No matter—it will be returned to you; we shall find it" the Colonel said reassuringly. "Let us shove it out" he said to Colin; "we can see nothing in here." The car was not locked, and they pushed it out into the sunshine; but there was nothing in it of any interest—only the blankets in the boot, and the map, which Marques took, in the locker. They went back to da Silva's office, where Marques jotted down the dates of the Spaniards' visit the year before, and the address in Madrid which they had given— "It's probably false, and the names they are using too" he said to Colin; "but the times of their absences may help my Spanish colleagues to get a line on them." He asked the landlord, as Julia had done, how his two clients had appeared to occupy themselves. "Yes, perfect cover for the job, of course," Marques said to Colin, as they drove off in the second police car. "They would have all the locals eating out of their hand, with this filming caper." The phrase startled Colin, who was not accustomed to the head of Portugal's Security Police's addiction to English slang.

"Where do you want to go now?" Colin asked.

"Back to the clinic; I must pick up Major Hamilton, and those reports on the blood that Dr. de Carvalho says he's got."

"Do you wish to make any more enquiries here?"

Marques was silent for a moment.

"I'm not sure. This is all a bit tricky, Monro. You see I've just picked up two foreign nationals on what is mostly suspicion that they have been acting as agents of another foreign power; and I would rather keep the local police out of it as far as possible. On the other hand, I do need to find out whether any of the people here in Madeira were knowing accomplices, or innocent ones."

"What sort of people?"

"Well, this fellow at the hotel, for a start; he seemed genuinely upset, but he may just be a very good actor."

"What others?"

"All those men who carried the types who actually distributed the gas up onto this plateau place—and the harbour-master, if there is such a thing, at that port where they were allowed to land. I don't mind the local Chief of Police getting reports on the trawler's movements from our coastal officers—though they seem to have been much less observant than your cousin! But the other thing is more difficult."

"There is someone who I believe could help you about all that," Colin said.

"Who's that?"

"Terence Armitage, my wife's cousin. He was born here, and has lived here all his life—he works in the Shipping Office, who of course knows everything there is to be known about all the hoteliers. He could certainly give you a line on da Silva, and I think on the people over at Seixial too."

"Where's that?"

"On the far side of the island, where the gas-merchants came ashore. He went over and made enquiries there about the trawler the very day after they first found the gassed sheep."

"Why did he do that?" Marques asked, suddenly very alert.

"Because he'd seen the trawler about several times, and when my cousin told him that she'd established from the hammock-men that the supposed tourists had smoked Russian cigarettes, he decided to go and find out all he could."

"How can I get hold of him?" Marques asked briskly.

"Ring him up from the clinic—his office is only five minutes' walk away."

"Do that, there's a good chap, as soon as we get there" Marques said. "He sounds just what I want. And what are your plans?" he asked then.

"I shall have to go back to London and report—I'm not sure how soon. I'd rather not leave till my wife is better."

"Ah yes, of course—I'm so sorry she is ill. Is it serious?"

"We don't know yet" Colin said, truthfully. "Now that this business is finished I may get a chance to see her doctor—I haven't so far."

"Hard luck" the Colonel said—but with genuine sympathy. "And what about your cousin? Do you know when she is thinking of coming to Lisbon?"

"I don't think she has any idea of going—she's only just come from Gralheira."

"I presume she could come at a pinch, though" Marques said. "She is rather a key witness. You realise of course that this will all have to be discussed at the highest level, before it is decided what action to take."

"I 'spose so" Colin said dully.

When Terence, on the heels of a telephone call, reached the clinic Marques and Major Hamilton were again sitting in the garden-house; to Colin's surprise Terence greeted Hamilton with "Hullo, Henry! What are *you* doing here?"

"Oh, the usual thing!—I came with the Colonel here. Marques, this is Terence Armitage."

Marques at once got down to business with some questions about the landlord of the Montefiore—Terence answered them fully, and with complete confidence. The hotel had been started some forty years ago by da Silva's father; when he died the son had taken it over from him. It was an ultra-respectable, rather stodgy place, which the Shipping Office constantly recommended to clients, mostly English and Americans, who wanted to make a long stay in peace and quiet. Had the hotel a regular Spanish connection?—Marques wanted to know. Definitely *not;* "So far as I know your two thugs are the first Spanish clients da Silva has ever had" Terence said, with his slow grin.

"He expressed great dismay at any of his guests falling under suspicion—should you think that was genuine?"

"Oh, have a heart, Colonel!" Terence said, cheerfully. "*No* pub likes having the P.I.D.E. nosing about! But if you're asking me whether da Silva is an honest, law-abiding citizen, and a good patriot, the answer is yes, every time, to all three questions."

"Thank you" Marques said, smiling himself. Then he asked about the harbour officials at Seixial, and the hammock-men. Terence was equally positive about the latter.

"They're just the simplest of peasants; I've known most of them all my life. All they care about is to earn a little extra money by doing a most exhausting job—they ask no questions, and they wouldn't know what questions to ask! One *toristo* is just like another to them, so long as he pays."

"And the officials at the port?"

"Actually I didn't see any official; it was a Sunday, and they were probably at Mass—anyhow I didn't want to make a thing about it, at that stage. I just spoke to some of the usual loungers on the quay, and established that ten men, with a huge lot of luggage, had come off a fishing-boat, and had gone up with a mule-train to the foot of the plateau."

"You didn't ask who had hired the mules?"

"No" Terence said, again with his calm grin—"And obviously it doesn't matter, since now we know!"

"We shall know very definitely in another forty-eight hours!" the Colonel said, rather grimly. He wrote down the name "Seixial" in a note-book, and got up. "Well, thank you very much, Mr. Armitage; you have been very helpful. I suppose you could pop over to Lisbon at any time if we need you?"

"Ah, that might not be so easy" Terence said. "I've used up a lot of time already over your thugs, and we're getting on to the busy season. Anyhow, what would you need me for?"

"To give evidence—tell our people what you have just told me."

"Oh, I should think they'd take your word for it" Terence said easily. "Anyhow we can cross that bridge when we come to it. Goodbye, Colonel."

" 'Bye, Terence. Stay with me if you do come over—it's time I repaid some of your hospitality here. Give Penelope my love" Major Hamilton said.

"I will." He went off down the garden.

"Now, let us just get those reports on the sheep's blood from the doctor, and then we'll be on our way" Marques said.

"Aren't you going to see the boy?" Colin asked, as they too walked down towards the house. "The doctor will be a bit disappointed if you don't."

"All right. Get hold of him, do, Monro."

Dr. de Carvalho was produced, the laboratory reports on the blood were handed over, and Marcusinho duly exhibited; he was still at work on his jigsaw but asked the doctor at once when the Senhora was going to bring his *cofrezinho?* "She promised—she was going to get it from my mother" the child said urgently.

"What's he talking about?" Marques asked.

"Oh, some toy of his that a lady was going to bring him" de Carvalho said, with a glance at Colin. "I'll remind her" he told the boy, and hustled his guests out. Marques thanked him for his help, adding, "The government will probably be sending an expert over in a day or two, to examine the sheep."

"He will not be able to tell them any more than they will find in those reports" the doctor said curtly. "But let him come, by all means. You will excuse me—I have not yet finished seeing my patients" he said, and hurried away.

"Rather a brusque customer, isn't he?" Marques observed to Colin. "I thought he could have arranged for the expert to see the sheep."

"Mr. Armitage can do that" Colin said, "or I can. He will have to get the hammock-men for him, anyhow."

"Where do I get hold of you?" Marques asked, pulling out his note-book again. "Here?"

"I don't know yet" Colin said, frowning. "No, not here, I shouldn't think."

"But I must have a telephone number for you" Marques said peremptorily.

"Give me your number in Lisbon, and I'll let you know as soon as I know myself" Colin said—he wrote the number down.

"What name are you using at present?" Marques asked them.

"My own—it's all been too much of a rush to fix up anything" Colin replied. "This wasn't a pre-arranged job, on our part."

When Colonel Marques had gone Colin went up to his room, sat on the edge of the bed, and considered. Where *was* he to stay, if he did stay? Really the obvious place was the Montefiore, he thought,—both Julia's and the Spaniards' rooms were vacant! He giggled a little at the idea. But the first thing was to report to the Office; he put in a call, and then, to fill in that exasperating hour's delay, he began to pack. Presently there was a knock at the door, and de Carvalho came in.

"Has he gone?" he asked at once.

"Yes—I expect they're nearly at the airport by now" Colin said, glancing at his watch.

"Well, he may be a very able man, but for myself, I find him *peu sympathique* to a degree" the doctor said with energy. "Did you manage to conceal all word of Sir Paircy from him?"

"Yes, I think so. It was touch and go in the hotel, though, when the Spanish boys found that the films were missing." Colin described the scene, and how he had put the Colonel on to looking for the aerial. Suddenly de Carvalho noticed the half-filled suitcase on the bed.

"What do you do? You leave Madeira?"

"I've just put in a call to London to ask for orders" Colin said. "I'd much rather *not* go just yet, till I see how my wife gets on" he added.

"She is ill? What is the matter with her?" the doctor asked. Colin told him briefly that she had had a rather severe bout of hysteria the previous day, and was now under sedation—the doctor's professional interest was at once aroused. "Who gives her this?" he asked. Dr. Urquhart, Colin told him.

"*Ah, le vieil Ecossais!* Yes, he knows what he is doing." The doctor sat down and proceeded to ask a number of rather searching questions: Aglaia's age, how long they had been married, any children?—and in his worry and isolation Colin found himself pouring out the whole situation, as he saw it—his long absences from home, the lost baby; Aglaia's dangerous indiscretions, which so conflicted with her ambitions for him; and her passionate desire to play some sort of part in his actual work. "She was frightfully hurt because while I've been here, though it was her idea my coming, I wouldn't stay at the Quinta, nor even let her know where I was; but I simply can't be in the same house with her while I'm on a job—she'd ask questions, and want to *do* things. She can't understand—" he broke off abruptly.

"She shall also be jealous of Madame Jamieson, *sans doute*" de Carvalho said drily.

"Yes, she is—though I didn't realise that till yesterday. But I don't think it's—well, so much an emotional jealousy as being vexed that Julia *can* work with me, and she can't. She doesn't understand" he repeated, rather helplessly.

"Madame Jamieson is of course a very exceptional woman, and, as I gather, with considerable experience of Intelligence work" de Carvalho said.

"Yes—and she has tried to explain to my wife that even so, a lot of the time she had to sit back and let her husband get on with the job—and keep *quiet* about everything" Colin said, almost wistfully. "But it doesn't seem to do any good."

De Carvalho was silent for a moment or two.

"I think I begin to see" he said at last, rather slowly. "May I make a rather disagreeable point, which nevertheless might help?"

"*Anything* to help—don't mind me!"

"*Eh bien,* it looks to me as if you had been rather self-indulgent about this. You have been afraid of your wife's *exigeances,* and demands on your time and patience and nervous force, and so have run away from them, and from her, when you felt that your work demanded it. She has realised your fear, and that—naturally, though irrationally—has increased her *exigeance,* her clutching at you: and so of course she has used hysteria as a weapon, though probably subconsciously."

"What could I have done, then?" the young man asked.

"Faced up to it, when you were in fact together; slapped her face if she made you a scene!" the doctor said vigorously.

Colin looked startled.

"That's what Julia said!" he exclaimed.

"Did she? She has much commonsense" de Carvalho re-marked, again drily.

"Well, she didn't tell me to; she just asked if I had" Colin amended.

"*Enfin,* I think you can do a good deal to cure your wife, by conquering your own fear of her moods—which of course is itself nervous in origin" de Carvalho pronounced. "Much she must do herself; but you have your own part to play." He got up. "Please stay here for as long as it suits you" he said then, putting a hand on Colin's shoulder for a moment. "Your company is a pleasure. And we who run nursing-homes don't like empty rooms!" he added, with a gold and white flash of teeth, as he left the room.

When he had gone, Colin, with a certain relief, unpacked what he had already packed, went out onto the balcony, and sat down. At least he need not worry about where to stay, he thought; but Dr. de Carvalho's words had given him plenty of other things to think about. The bottle of Sir Percy's special Madeira, on the side-table, caught his eye; he glanced at his watch. Ten to twelve —quite a reasonable time for a drink; he got up, poured out a glass, and lit a cigarette. *Had* he been self-indulgent, he wondered—the idea that failure to slap one's wife's face was a form of self-indulgence made him grin rather wryly. But Dr. de Carvalho was certainly right about his fear of Aglaia, and her moods and demands, when he was on a job—probably he was right about everything.

The telephone rang. He went into the bedroom, shutting the French window after him, and lifted the receiver. "Colin" he said.

"Good. Well, our old boffin's safely back—my word, what a haul! It's a terrific show—I do congratulate you."

"I didn't do much" Colin said.

"No need to be modest!—and it won't wash, either. We've heard different!" Major Hartley said. He was obviously in tremendous spirits. "What goes on at your end? Did the Great Man come himself? He threatened to."

"Oh Lord yes—he came, and he's gone again—taking his sheaves with him" Colin said more cheerfully.

"Did you say 'sheaves' or 'thieves'?" Hartley asked.

"Comes to much the same thing—two bad eggs, anyhow; and very fairly inefficient ones! But look—you won't forget that the Great Man knows nothing about the King Boffin being here, nor what he took with him, will you?" Colin said, rather urgently.

"Oh, you got away with that, did you? I can't think how—I should have thought such a super-sleuth would have nosed that out of someone" Hartley said.

"Julia" was Colin's only reply to this.

"Ah yes—no doubt! I'm longing to hear the whole story. When do you come back?"

"Well, I was going to ask about that. I wondered if I could stay on here for a bit; my wife isn't too well."

"Oh, I'm sorry about that. Nothing serious, I hope?"

"We hope not, but I'd sooner be on hand for the next few days."

"Of course. Yes, do stay—take some leave. I'll let them know in Madrid."

"Thanks very much. By the way, the Super-Sleuth said they might want me to go over there presently; I gather they're going to have a top-level conference about this business."

"I should damn well think they would! Our people will want to be in on that too—in fact they're taking steps about it now. Our friends in the metropolitan capital, as you call it, may be asked some pretty awkward questions about how much longer they would have sat with their eyes shut, while you-know-who calmly did a *Pueblo* in their waters, aimed at *us,* unless you and Mrs. Philip had come along" Hartley said indignantly. "Yes, of course you can go if they want you."

"Thanks. And could you ask 'Henry', as you call him, to let the Great Man know that this number is all right for me for the moment?"

"Why didn't you tell him that yourself?"

"Because I didn't know till he'd gone that our medical friend would keep me on as a patient" Colin said—"*nor* that you would let me stay on!"

"O.K.—You win! Congratulations again" the Major said, and rang off.

Colin went out onto the balcony again, and continued to think about Aglaia. Yes, he had been cowardly where she was concerned—de Carvalho was quite right. He would have to try, somehow, to be with her more, and to behave more firmly and sensibly when he was. Should he ask for a job in London?—now would seem to be a good time to ask for anything he wanted, with the Office in this receptive mood, he thought. Anyhow he had better see Ag as soon as possible—begin as you mean to go on, he told himself; he would ring Julia and find out when he would be allowed to. He got up and went in; as he entered the bedroom the telephone rang—it was Julia.

"The Colonel gone?" she asked at once.

"Yes—bag and baggage! He did it all very neatly."

"No trouble for poor Da Silva?"

"No, except about his bill. Gosh, I hope Fernandez did remember to pay that!" Colin exclaimed.

"Oh well, if he forgot we'll twist it out of the Colonel" Julia said easily. "Well, that bird seems to be dead!—good-oh. Now look, could you come up here? Dr. Urquhart wants to see you."

"Why? Is she worse?" Colin asked anxiously.

"Not in the least. He just wants to get an overall picture of her surroundings, I think. I've told him all I can; now he wants to see you."

"When? And where?"

"Today, if you can. He rang up to say you'd find him at the Golf Club."

"All right—I'll go right away."

"He's fearfully nice, and madly sensible" Julia said.

"There's a Greek word for expressions like that!" Colin said, beginning to giggle.

"Like what? Oh, madly sensible. Yes—oxy—something" Julia said, quite untroubled. "Where are you staying, by the way?"

"Here, *pro tem*. Right—I'll be on my way. I'll look in when I've seen him."

Colin's interview with Dr. Urquhart took place, not at the Golf Club, where the young man duly found him, but in the comfortable and very unprofessional-looking study in the doctor's small house close by. Here too there were eucalyptus trees, and their medicinal scent, strong in the midday sun, came in through the windows—for years the smell of eucalyptus was to bring that room back to Colin.

"I start at a disadvantage in treating your wife" the doctor began, "because I have never seen her when she was in normal health. But your cousin tells me—and I am inclined to trust her judgment—that even when she is well, Mrs. Monro is inclined to a degree of impetuosity and indiscretion that you find very inconvenient in your profession. Would you agree with that?"

"Yes" Colin said at once. "That is so."

"Which do you put first, your wife or your work?" the old man asked, peering at him from under grizzled eyebrows.

"My work" Colin said, again without hesitation. "One has to, in my job. I thought—" now he paused. "I thought I had explained that at the beginning, when I asked her to marry me; I did tell her that until I had to retire I didn't mean to live at our place in Scotland—I was going to leave my sister and her husband to run that, because I should have to be all over the place. She seemed to understand at the time, and said she didn't mind. But it hasn't worked out" he ended gloomily.

"Do you feel she has let you down?"

"Not really, I don't think; we were both rather young, and probably pretty silly to think it *could* work. I'm most to blame about that, because I am so much older—but you see I was accustomed to women who did understand about that sort of thing."

"Meaning your cousin?"

"Yes—and my sister."

"Both very disciplined people, I imagine?"

"Yes—and of course a good bit older than either of us."

"I am not sure that age per se has much to do with self-discipline—upbringing is usually more important. What sort of people were your wife's parents?"

"I never knew her father—he died when she was in her teens. He was Mr. Terence Armitage's uncle. Her mother was Greek;

she married again, a South American, and went to live out there —I only saw her when she came over for our wedding."

"There have of course been very high-principled Greeks; even noble" Dr. Urquhart said, reflectively.

"Well, Aglaia's mother wasn't one of them" Colin stated flatly. "She ran away from Armitage with this dago, leaving the child, long before he died."

"Then who did bring her up?"

"A widowed Armitage aunt, in London. I expect she was all right, only a bit dim, I thought. Aglaia went to school, of course —I don't remember where."

"I see—umm. Yes, children from broken homes start with a very considerable handicap, and if you add prettiness such as hers! Unless circumstances, like great poverty, for instance, impose some sort of discipline—umm?" the doctor said again, now interrogatively. "I suppose not, since her father was an Armitage."

"It was worse than that—her Greek grandfather was a millionaire, and left it all to her" Colin said, dismally. "She has had a great deal against her, as far as character-forming goes. And I see now that I haven't helped" he added, slowly.

"How so?"

"I've been cowardly where she was concerned. If she was being spoilt and tiresome, instead of reasoning with her, or putting my foot down and telling her to shut up, I just threw my hand in, and kept out of her way. That's one reason why, on this job here, I stayed in Funchal instead of at the Quinta, and wouldn't even let her know where I was—I felt I *couldn't* work with her butting in, or asking questions, all the time."

"How soon will this present job be finished?—or can you not say?" Dr. Urquhart asked.

"Oh, it's done—all cleared up this morning, thank God."

"And what do you do next?"

"That's what I should like your advice about" Colin said. "I've got a bit of leave, just for the next week or two; but I don't know what to aim at after that."

"How do you mean, 'aim at'?"

"Well, this show hasn't gone too badly, and I think if I asked the Office now to let me have a year working at home, they would probably agree" the young man said. "Then we could settle down in London and try to—to make a fresh start."

"You putting into practise these fresh ideas about your own behaviour?"

"Exactly that. What do you think?"

Dr. Urquhart didn't answer for a moment or two—instead he watched the handsome black-haired, white-faced young man who sat opposite, looking at him with such a humble, appealing gaze.

"Why are you holding your left hand with your right?" he asked suddenly. Colin blushed, laughed, and removed his right hand.

"It's my thumb" he said. "When I'm nervous it jerks out—it's double-jointed, you see." And indeed his left thumb, freed, jerked backwards and outwards with the familiar small sickening sound.

"Umm—very interesting. How long has it done that?"

"Ever since I can remember. But it irritates people, so I try to stop it" Colin said.

Again the doctor was silent for a little while. At last—"Go on trying to stop it" he said. "As to your question, I think it may be a very good idea. How much of a hurry is there about making your request to your Office?"

"Oh, any time in the next week or two."

"Good. Well, I will talk to your wife—probably tomorrow —and then I will let you know what I think."

"And when can I see her?"

"After I have talked to her" said Dr. Urquhart.

17 IN FACT IT was not till two days later that Dr. Urquhart judged Aglaia Monro fit for the conversation he proposed to have with her. He ordained that she should stay in her room, and see no one but Nannie Mack; he had a brief talk with Nannie in the day-nursery about this.

"Just talk to her about nursery matters, or clothes, or that" he said. "If she asks any questions, say ye don't know." (With his fellow-countrywoman he relapsed slightly into his native idiom.) "Give her one of the wee yellow pills three times a day, after her food. Can she knit?" "Well, teach her to; or sew—let her use her hands." "Och aye"—in reply to a question—"she can see the wee boy if he runs in; but no adults." He gave the same instructions to her hostess—"I just want her to keep absolutely quiet for forty-eight hours. Yes, she's doing fine so far—sleep is what she needs. Books? Well, if she wants to read, give her a good thriller; they put the mind to sleep! But give it to yon nurse to give her."

"It's funny he won't let anyone but Nannie Mack see her" Pauline Shergold said, when recounting this conversation to Mrs. Hathaway.

"I fancy Dr. Urquhart knows what he is about" said the old lady.

"I hope so. Anyhow Terry rang up just now to say that she can go back to the Quinta as soon as she's well enough, so that's one mercy. I wonder why on earth he was so keen on shipping her off here" Mrs. Shergold speculated.

"I imagine Mr. Armitage generally has very good reasons for whatever he does" Mrs. Hathaway said blandly.

"Yes, but why all these mysteries?" Pauline said impatiently, "and all this rushing about? Julia dashing off to stay in Funchal, and then coming back in the middle of the night!—and Ag being dumped on us at no notice! You must admit, Mrs. H., that it's all most peculiar."

"You have been wonderfully kind to everyone, my dear Pauline" was all Mrs. Hathaway said.

Dr. Urquhart looked in on Aglaia next day, and told her to be up and dressed the following morning by eleven o'clock—"I'm going to take you out for a while." Then he went in to see Mrs. Hathaway, whose chest he pronounced to be in perfect order again. He mentioned his plan. "I want to have a good talk with that child, so I'm going to take her home with me for an hour or two; we shan't be interrupted there." As if to point his words, a deafening burst of mixed screams and laughter came up from the garden at that moment—Mrs. Hathaway smiled.

"Yes, a *real* bear-garden is tranquillity itself" she said. "I've often been to the one in Berne." Dr. Urquhart laughed, and went away.

As he and his patient got into the car next morning—"Where are we going?" Aglaia asked rather nervously.

"Down to my house; I have a proper consulting-room there." In the pleasant room where he had talked with Colin he gave the girl a brief physical examination, and told her to go and put on her frock again. When she returned he told her to sit down.

"Your body's fine" he said. "Nothing wrong with it at all. Now, is there anything you want to ask me?"

"I don't think so" Aglaia said hesitantly. "Yes—there is one thing."

"What's that?"

She was silent for a moment, scraping the carpet with the toe of her little white shoe. At last—"Can I have another baby?" she asked without looking up.

"God bless the child!—you can have ten if you want them" the old man said. "Do you want children very much?"

"Colin wanted a boy" she said. "The baby I lost was a boy."

"I know—I was very sorry to hear about that. But an only child is usually a bad plan, you know."

"Because it gets spoilt? Mrs. Shergold has four, and if they aren't spoilt, I don't know what a spoilt child is!" Aglaia said, with sudden energy. Dr. Urquhart laughed—she could be shrewd enough.

"Mrs. Shergold has a theory about that" he said. "It's to do with Portuguese nannies. "But you—do you, yourself, want children? Two or three, say?"

"I shouldn't mind, I don't think. I don't know if I should be much good at bringing them up, but I suppose I could manage if I had someone like Nannie Mack. Colin wouldn't like it if they weren't brought up well" she said, again scraping the carpet with her shoe.

"In fact, about having children it's more a case of your husband having what *he* wants, eh?"

"Yes" she said, now looking full at him with huge brown eyes. "I'd do *anything* for him to have what he wants!"

"But only about children? Not so much about his work?"

"What do you mean?" she asked, startled and nervous.

"Simply that the way you have been behaving just lately doesn't look as if you cared very much about the work" he said, slowly. "When your husband is in the middle of a very difficult job, and you do happen to meet him, you make a fearful fuss about not being allowed to take more part; and when you can't get your way, you lose your temper, and lash yourself into hysterics. Can that help him? Did you really not see that it would only worry him, and distract him from doing his job well?"

Aglaia began to cry.

"I *did* want him to do it well! It was I who had him sent for. You've been talking to Julia!" she brought out angrily.

"And to your husband; and to other people too. Do you know why Mr. Armitage had you sent up here?"

"Penelope was vexed because I locked myself in my room" she said.

"Oh no; that wasn't the reason. At that time there was actual danger from strangers coming round the Quinta and asking questions; he could trust his farmhands, ignorant peasants and their families, to keep quiet if he told them to—but he couldn't trust *you*. So he sent you away."

"Oh—oh—*oh!*" Aglaia sobbed.

"Yes—that's a terrible thing. But has no one ever told you that it was indiscreet, and wrong of you to talk about your husband and his affairs?"

"Yes, Julia did, and Terence too, and I did promise her not to."

"Did you keep your promise?"

"Well, partly."

"But not altogether? But this is very serious, Mrs. Monro. Do you know that your husband thinks he may have to resign from the Service?"

She looked at him appalled.

"Oh *no*. Oh, he mustn't do that!"

"I assure you, he thinks he may have to—purely because of your unreliability."

"Julia said that, but I thought she was just trying to frighten me" the girl said, beginning to cry again. "Oh, what shall I do?"

"Be a good girl and stop crying; wipe your eyes, and listen to me" the doctor said. "I'll wait awhile, till you're quiet."

Aglaia did as she was told; she even began to restore her face, using, the doctor noticed, a platinum compact with a monogram in diamonds. "Who gave you that? Your husband?" he asked.

"Oh goodness no!—I bought it for myself. I saw one like it in Aspreys, so I had it made with my own monogram. It's pretty, isn't it?" she said, hopefully.

"Very pretty. But tell me, how many girls do you suppose there are in Britain—or in Europe, for that matter—who can just go out and buy themselves a thing like that?"

"I've no idea" she said, doubtfully.

"Perhaps twenty or thirty, in Britain, out of twenty *hundred thousand* girls who use powder, and like pretty things" he said. As he saw her lips begin to quiver—"I'm not saying that you did wrong to buy it" he went on, "but I do want you to think very hard about one inescapable fact—that this world is a most unequal place. Will you try to do that? It's very important that you should."

"Yes, I will try—but why?"

"Because in this unequal world the only way to be either good or happy is to be content with what one has got, and do the best one can with it; but never, never to be jealous of those who are better off than oneself. You need never be jealous of anyone where money is concerned, but there are other things far more valuable, that money can't buy. There is health, for example, and good looks; well, you are middling well off in both of those" he said, smiling. "But you aren't very rich in some other very valuable possessions."

The girl looked earnestly at him.

"Do you mean I'm not very clever?" she asked.

"Partly—though that isn't one of the really important things. As far as intelligence goes you have got quite enough to live on! No, where you are really badly off is in self-discipline and self-control. And in magnanimity—largeness of mind and heart. Did you ever guess that?—have any doubts about yourself?"

"Yes, I have done sometimes; I mean I've felt somehow *smaller* than some other people" she said slowly.

"Well, you were quite right! You are rather a small person in some ways. But small things can grow, you know" he said gently, "and even a little person can be *good*. How much importance do you attach to trying to be good? I get the impression that you don't think about it very much."

"I don't believe I have thought a lot about it—no" she said, with an attempt at candour.

"Well, you ought to, or you will ruin your life, and your husband's too."

"How do I begin?" she asked.

"Think!" he said pleasantly. Then, as she was silent—"Do you remember what I said just now about the only way to be either good or happy, in this unequal world?"

"Not to be jealous of people who've got things that I haven't" she muttered, rather unwillingly.

"Yes. But you aren't doing that, are you? Are you not very jealous of Mrs. Jamieson, for one?"

"Well, I didn't see why she should do all the driving—I can drive cars perfectly well. I've been kept out of everything Colin was doing, since he came here!—although it was I who had the idea of sending for him" the girl burst out bitterly.

"Mrs. Jamieson gives you full marks for that. But my dear child" the old man said, leaning towards her with a benevolent earnestness, "can't you see that in intelligence and character Mrs. Jamieson is an absolute millionairess compared with you?—as well as having years of experience in this work? That is a fact you must accept—it *is* so." He watched her face; no, she hadn't accepted it. "That's a bitter pill" he said. "Chew on it; taste it and swallow it. Once you have swallowed it, accepted it, the bitter taste will go gradually."

Aglaia remained silent, looking down. He decided to try another tack for the moment.

"I'm going to tell you a story—a true one" he said. "In the last war I was a doctor with the Highland Division, and a lot of us were taken prisoner by the Germans and put in one of those prison-camps. Some of us decided to escape."

She looked up. "Did you dig a tunnel, like in that film?" she asked. Her relief at escaping for a moment from the pressure he had been putting on her was evident.

"Just so; we dug a tunnel. But we knew that after we got out we should have to walk nearly two hundred miles through Germany, talking German, before we reached the frontier."

"Do you talk German?"

"I did then, pretty well. Well enough to pretend that I was Swiss—and so did five or six of the other officers. And we were all strong men, and good walkers. My best friend was in the same camp with me—the best friend I ever had. He was desperate to escape; he was newly married, and his wife was rather ill. He longed to come."

"And did he?" she asked eagerly.

"No. He was still a little lame from a leg-wound he'd got in France; and besides he didn't speak German. We couldn't risk taking him. But I think telling him that we couldn't was one of the hardest things I ever had to do in my life."

"When did he get out?" Aglaia asked.

"Not for five years."

"Oh, how awful! And did his wife get better?"

"Yes, thank God; and she waited faithfully for him, which was more than some of those war-time wives did! But how do you suppose he passed those five years?" Doctor Urquhart asked, bending his eyes on her from under his grizzled brows.

"Well, worrying, I suppose; it must have been frightful for him."

"He spent them keeping the camp laughing and cheerful" the doctor said. "He was a bit musical, sang quite nicely, and he had a big repertory of songs by heart; he was a bit of a comic, too, and could take people off. Numbers of the ones who were there all through the war have told me they thought they owed their reason to Jock Cameron and the turns he put on in the evenings." He got up. "Come on" he said. "I'll take you back now."

Aglaia was silent throughout the short run back in the car, and the doctor didn't interrupt her silence. At the Shergolds he said —"I'll be in to see you tomorrow morning. Tell Mrs. Shergold you can come down to meals now; but go to bed early, and go on with your pills."

"I will—thank you very much." She lingered by the car, fiddling with the door-handle. "I'll try to remember that I'm lame, and can't speak German" she said suddenly, and ran into the house.

As Dr. Urquhart was turning his car on the broad stretch of gravel Julia and her little son appeared from the garden; she waved, and went over to him—the doctor stopped his engine.

"How did it go?" she asked at once—"If I may know, I mean."

"Rather better than I expected" he said. "I gave her what I believe the Irish call 'the length and breadth of my tongue', and she took it reasonably well. I have told her that she may come down to meals, and lead a normal life."

"When can she go back to the Armitages?"

"Oh, any time now."

"Good. I think that might be a good plan; after all, it's where she belongs" Julia said—the old man gave her a keen look, but said nothing. "And how soon can her husband see her?"

"Also any time, provided he takes everything absolutely normally—no going over what's happened, or that" the doctor said. "At least not at first."

"Oh well, the job's finished, so he can give all his time to her" Julia said cheerfully, "till he goes back to London."

"Aye. But he told me he would not be going back for a week or two; they could do worse than start trying to live together on new and better terms" the old man said.

"Oh fine. Do you want to see him again?"

"No need. Just tell him that, from me—you'll be seeing him, I take it?"

"Yes, this afternoon, I expect."

"Thanks—then you'll do that. Make everything norrmal" the old Scotsman said, rolling his R's, as he drove away.

Julia took the child in—he was due for his early dinner with the other two little ones. In the hall she came on Aglaia, lingering doubtfully. "Are you looking for Pauline? I think she's out" Julia said.

"Yes—I wanted to tell her I can come down to meals now."

"I'll tell the maids—and Nannie. I'm so glad you're better. Come through and have a drink with Mrs. Hathaway" Julia said, and led her out onto the verandah, where the old lady sat reading *The Times*. Then she went through and told the maids that the Senhora Monro would be downstairs for luncheon and dinner; she passed on this information to Nannie Mack when she took small Philip upstairs.

"Well, that's an improvement" Nannie said. "Yes—go into the bathroom and try to wash your own hands, like a clever boy" she said to the child—"Little pitchers have long ears" she added to his Mother. "Did she see the doctor?" she asked then.

"Yes. He thinks she'll be all right now; I expect she'll be going home soon."

"Well, I hope she'll keep on with her knitting—she's made quite a good start" Nannie said. "She needs something to do; that's as much what's wrong with her as anything, in my opinion —nothing to do but think about herself."

Julia managed to catch Pauline Shergold before she went out onto the verandah for drinks, and told her that Aglaia would be down to luncheon, and what Dr. Urquhart had said about keeping everything normal—"Don't ask her how she feels, or anything" she said.

"When does she go back to the Quinta?" Mrs. Shergold asked, throwing off her hat.

"I'm going to see Terence about that this afternoon—tomorrow, I should think. Of course I'll let you know at once."

"I wish we'd seen more of Colin" Pauline said. "He's a charmer."

"I dare say you will, now" Julia said easily.

"Why, is this mystery job finished?"

"Yes, practically, as far as Madeira is concerned."

"Julia, what *has* been going on?"

"Pauline, I wish I could tell you, because you've been so frightfully kind—to Mrs. H., and me, and Ag—but you know I can't."

"I *don't* know. *You* aren't in the Secret Service! Or are you?" she asked, with sudden suspicion. Julia gave her slow laugh.

"No—only rather closely related to it!" she said. "Come on—I'm dying for a drink."

Julia drove down to Funchal the moment after lunch, and went straight to the Shipping Office; Terence Armitage was in, and she was shown up to his room.

"How's Ag?" he asked at once.

"Much better—back to daily life. She had a long session with the old Doc this morning."

"So she can come back to us, now?"

"Yes, rather. Only he thought she and Colin ought to start trying to live together as soon as possible."

"Well, they can do that at the Quinta; it's always his home when he comes here, he knows that. They have their own rooms, sitting-room and all—it's only that we all eat together."

"Sounds perfect" Julia said—and again added what Dr. Urquhart had insisted on about everything being kept normal.

"I'll tell Penel. Did you hear whether he had given her the works?"

"I gathered so, from what he said; of course I haven't said any-

thing to her. Oh, by the way, do you know whether the wretched
da Silva ever got paid?" Julia asked.

"For the Spanish thugs' bill, and the hire of the car? Yes, he
did; that Portuguese Major found masses of escudos when he was
clearing out their room, and settled the bill before he left the
hotel. Da Silva came round to tell me."

"Good. Talking of hiring cars, or rather not hiring but bor-
rowing cars, hadn't you better have yours back now?"

"Don't you need it any more?"

"No, I only wanted it to cart Colin and Sir Percy about, and to
get to and from my bed and breakfast; now I shall be staying put
at the Shergolds'. I'm *so* grateful for it, though—it's been an absolute boon, and to them too."

"When do you want to turn it in?" he asked.

"Well, I want to see Colin now at the clinic, and I thought he
could drive me up to the Serra, and perhaps bring Aglaia down
to you in it tomorrow—if that's all right by Penel."

"I'll fix that with her, and ring you up tonight."

"No, don't." As he looked at her in surprise—"I don't mean
that, exactly" Julia said. "I mean, I think it would be better if
Penelope rang up Aglaia herself, and asked when she was coming
back?—and if Colin couldn't come too?—and how nice it
would be, and so on. After all that door-locking nonsense, I
mean."

He smiled on her with much affection.

"As usual, you are perfectly and blessedly right. All part of
what that American President called 'normalcy', only with a few
shining knobs on! It shall be done that way."

At the clinic Julia asked for Colin. She was standing in the hall
while the girl telephoned up to his room when Dr. de Carvalho
emerged from his consulting-room.

"*Ah, bonjour,* Madame! Can you spare me two instants?" he
asked.

"He is not there—there is no reply" the telephonist said at
the same time.

"Yes, certainly" Julia said, and followed the doctor into his room.

"How is Madame Monro?" he asked, pulling forward a chair; seeing the surprise in her face—"Your cousin has told me something of his difficulties in his marriage" he added. "And I am concerned on his account."

"So am I" Julia said, sitting down. "At least, I have been. But Dr. Urquhart has had a long talk with her—she is quite normal again now—and he has seen my cousin too. He thinks they should settle down together and make a fresh start—I've come to give my cousin that message. Do you agree?"

"Start here?—in Madeira?"

"Yes, at the Armitages' Quinta. They've often stayed there before."

"Yes, I do agree" he said. "But what do you think of his plan of working in London for a year or more?"

"I—I'm not sure." Julia was startled; this was the first she had heard of any such plan. "I expect it would be a good idea, for her" she said thoughtfully. "Rather a waste of him, perhaps."

"Why a waste?"

"Oh well, his languages are his strong suit; I can't imagine him doing desk-work! But if his superiors can find a job there for him, and they approve, it might be a good plan. He's got plenty of time ahead of him."

"Good." But Dr. de Carvalho had another surprise for Julia. "And you?—What do you propose to do with yourself now?" he asked earnestly, leaning over the desk towards her.

"I? But bring up my little child, of course" she said, with a smile—she was as much embarrassed as surprised by this sudden initiative.

"Madame, to concentrate your powers on one infant will be as bad for him as it would be inappropriate for you" the Portuguese said, firmly. "You talk of waste!—but this is absurd!"

"What do you suggest, then?" she asked, now amused at his enterprise.

"But that you work regularly, professionally, for British Intelligence! Earn a salary, but far more important, have an occupation, an involvement, which will keep you happy, busy, and protect your child from that terribly dangerous thing, maternal over-concentration!"

She stared at him, now deeply astonished, and also touched.

"Perhaps you've got something there" she said slowly, after a pause. "I hadn't thought of it in that way." She smiled again. "People are always saying that" she added.

"That you should be regularly employed by British Intelligence? What sort of people?"

"Oh, my friends—some of them in Intelligence themselves" she said, with her slow laugh.

"Then why not do it? They must realise your capabilities" he pressed her.

"I'll think about it" she said, getting up. "Thank you very much for your advice—it is good of you to think of it—of us both." As he too rose—"And now, how can I find my cousin?"

Colin was in the garden-house. While he was driving her up to the Serra she told him the upshot of her talks with Dr. Urquhart and Terence, stressing the importance of "normalcy"—she quoted Terence's use of the ridiculous word—and how Penelope Armitage was to do the inviting.

"Yes, that's the best way" he agreed. "And that being so, I think I won't come in this evening, or Ag may suspect that it's all been arranged beforehand. No, I'm not funking it" he said, as Julia looked at him questioningly. "Just make sure that she lets me know tonight, when Penel has spoken to her."

"But she hasn't got your telephone number" Julia reminded him.

"Oh ah, nor she has! How do we get round that one?"

"Can't you go into the Golf Club and write a note on *blank* paper, and send it round by a boy, giving the address and number of the clinic, and telling her to give you a ring?"

"I'll do that thing. Bless you, J. dear. And when I hear from her I'll ring Hartley and tell him where I shall be, and ask him to pass the Quinta number on to Marques." He began to giggle. "And this time I really *will* drop you at the gate!"

This small intrigue was successfully carried out, and the following morning Colin came in very breezily, kissed his wife as gaily as if he had seen her only the day before, hullo'd Julia and Pauline, threw the luggage into the car, and drove Aglaia away.

"Well, I *hope* that goes all right" Pauline Shergold said, waving from the steps. "She seemed much nicer last night, poor little thing."

After this life at the Shergolds' resumed its old gentle tempo—walks with Pauline, playing with the children, prolonged chats with Mrs. Hathaway. But some days after Colin had taken Aglaia back to the Quinta the telephone rang, and Mrs. Jamieson was summoned to it by a hail from Pauline—"Julia! It's for you." She hurried in from the verandah—"Take it in the study; Elvira's Hoovering out here" her hostess said. Julia went in to Gerald's study, expecting to hear Colin's voice, but it was Dr. de Carvalho. "*C'est bien Madame Jamieson?* A message from the Colonel—*de toute urgence!* He has tried to ring your cousin at the other number he gave, but he is out—so he calls me. *Les experts arrivent ce soir.*"

"What experts?" For once Julia's ready memory failed her.

"But to examine the sheep! The Colonel said he would send them—*c'est idiot,* but he has this idea!"

"Ah yes, I remember. Tonight, you say?"

"Yes. So will Madame please make all the arrangements, since the cousin is not available? I disinterest myself from this nonsense, I!"

"Where are they staying?" Julia asked.

"Wherever Madame chooses to put them! These I do not accommodate as patients!" the doctor said sharply.

"Of course not." Julia began to laugh. "I'll send them to the Montefiore!" she said. "Did the Colonel give their names?— hold on, I'll write them down." She went over to Gerald's desk and fetched a pencil and pad. "The Senhor Doctor Francisco Figueiredo, and the Senhor Ingenheiro Lopes" she wrote down. "Are they coming on the plane? All right, I'll see to it."

"There is also a parcel arrived for Madame," de Carvalho said.

"Oh, could you keep it? I will ask Monsieur Shergold to call for it."

"*Très bien.*" He rang off.

Julia went out into the hall. Pauline Shergold was still there; Elvira had finished Hoovering the rugs and was polishing the floor.

"May I ring up Terence?" Julia asked.

"Yes, of course. Do it in the study again—this thing shishes so."

When Julia got Terence she explained what was going on. "The Colonel tried for Colin, but he's out. So I said I would see to it—but really I'm afraid I want you to."

"Quite like old times!" Terence said. "All right—give me their names." Julia spelt them out—"Though why an engineer should know about sheep's diseases I can't think."

"Half the men in Portugal are *ingenheiros*—it covers a multitude of scientific skills" Terence said.

"Oh well. Can they go to the Montefiore? I thought that would cheer da Silva up."

"I don't see why not."

"And can you have them met?"

"Yes, of course—da Silva can send one of his cars. There's no secret about these people, I take it?"

"I suppose not. Oh, and the hammock-men, Terence—they'll need those; can you get them for tomorrow?"

Julia heard the study door open, but paid no attention.

"Yes, I'll send Tomás up on the mo-bike. Won't they need someone to show them the way from the car-turn through the tunnel, and up to the cliffs?"

"I suppose they will."

"Well, I simply can't go tomorrow" Terence said definitely—"I've got a board meeting. But I expect Colin will go. If not, do you think Pauline could bring you over?"

"I'll ask her—hold on." She turned round and saw her hostess standing just inside the door. "Pauline, could we go up to the Paúl da Serra tomorrow? Some scientists will want to be shown the way."

"Yes, certainly. Where will they start from, Funchal? If so, we can pick them up and take them all the way."

Julia passed this on, and it was settled that da Silva would let her know when the experts had arrived. "Tell him they'll have to leave at quarter past seven, and take lunches" Julia reminded Terence.

"Yes, Ma'am. Hammocks the usual time, I suppose? Does Pauline want one? No?—all right, just an extra one for you. 'Bye."

"What is all this?" Pauline asked, as Julia put down the receiver.

"Some experts from Lisbon are being sent to look at the sheep."

"But I thought Pereira and de Carvalho had sent specimens of blood and things already?"

"Yes, they had, and Dr. de Carvalho thinks it all a great nonsense their coming—that they won't learn anything fresh. But you know what governments are" Julia said tolerantly.

"Well, they've taken their time about coming" was Pauline's only comment.

Julia always remembered her final expedition to the Paúl da Serra with particular pleasure. They fetched the "experts", two smallish, stoutish men, typical Portuguese intellectuals, very polite and rather formal, from the Montefiore; they seemed slightly surprised to be met by two ladies—was the Senhor Pereira, one of them asked, not going to come too? Julia bit her lip—she ought to have thought of Pereira, the vet, but it was too late now. It would probably be possible to see him later, she said smoothly, but he was very busy, and this was a long expedition—meanwhile she and the Senhora Shergold would take them directly to the sheep, which were, she presumed, what the Senhores wished to see.

As they neared the car-turn she saw the little Austin pulling up ahead of them—Penelope, Aglaia, and Colin got out of it. Almost before Pauline's car had stopped Julia sprang out and darted over to her cousin.

"They expected Pereira; I said he was busy" she said hurriedly. "Can I introduce you as from Intelligence? That may cheer them up."

"Yes, of course" Colin said. "Do they speak French?"

"We haven't tried—I expect so."

In fact Dr. Figueiredo did speak French, though his assistant didn't; they both appeared much relieved at the presence of someone from British Intelligence. Colin took the doctor aside and explained to him that "these Senhoras" knew about the sickness of the sheep, but not its cause—which he, and he understood Colonel Marques also, believed to be a nerve gas of a new type; he asked the doctor not to refer to this in front of the ladies, and to warn his colleague not to do so. This "top secret" atmosphere seemed to reassure the two scientists still more, and they set off up the ridge in good spirits. These were slightly dashed by the walk through the tunnel, which they found both alarming and unpleasant; however, Mrs. Armitage had her customary haversackful of torches, and took Dr. Figueiredo by the arm; that obstacle was passed all right.

But the two urban intellectuals were again daunted by the aspect of the cliffs, and still more by the sight of Julia and Aglaia lying down and being fastened into their hammocks—"By this fashion we also ascend?" Dr. Figueiredo enquired incredulously of Colin.

"Unless you can climb as well as the two ladies" Colin replied, indicating Mrs. Armitage and Mrs. Shergold, already climbing carefully up the bare vertiginous ridges of the face—with a slight shudder, the two Portuguese resigned themselves to being parcelled up and slung aloft.

At the top the four hammock-borne passengers were undone, and the party set forward across the plateau, Penelope taking the lead, as usual. "Better go first to the picnic pool; there are usually some sheep there" she said to Colin.

"Whatever you say."

Towards the pool they accordingly walked, Mrs. Armitage describing to the newcomers, in her fluent Portuguese, the dismal aspect and unnatural tameness of the sick sheep. After a few minutes the pool came in sight. Sure enough, some half-dozen of the leggy creatures were standing by it, drinking—but at the sight of the party of strangers they started, and then bounded away, running like deer across the short grass and bracken.

"Well, I'm damned!" Mrs. Armitage exclaimed. "They must have got over it, whatever it was. What an extraordinary thing!"

Pauline Shergold burst out laughing. "What a sell!" she said, glancing at the astounded faces of the two experts. "I told you they'd taken their time" she muttered to Julia.

But Julia had taken her little diary out of the pocket of her dress, and was studying it; then she went over to Colin. "Twenty-eight days" she murmured in his ear. "Would that be about right?"

"Are you sure? Yes, I suppose that's what they were working for" he said. "It would give them as much time as they needed, I imagine. Of course we don't know *when* the brutes recovered."

"I wonder if Dr. de Carvalho has tried knocking off Marcusinho's atropine?" Julia speculated. "If not, he ought to do that at once."

"What are you two nattering about?" Penelope Armitage asked rather sharply; she was vexed that this expedition was turning out such a flop.

"I was saying that I think we ought to go on a bit, and see if all the sheep are well again, or only just this lot here" Julia lied easily.

"Yes, we had better, I suppose."

As before they divided into two parties, one of the Portuguese in each, and walked on for about another mile; they saw plenty more sheep, but only from a distance—all fled at their approach, apparently in full activity. Rather dejected, they returned to the pool, ate their picnic lunches, and started homewards. On the track below the cliffs Colin, who had been talking with Dr. Figueiredo, stepped forward to join Julia and Aglaia, who were walking a little ahead.

"Ag, I must report this performance to London at once" he said, "and I think I'd better do it from Funchal; it's quicker, and I get a better line. If Pauline can give me a lift in, I'll come out with Terry this evening."

Julia watched the girl's face. For a minute it clouded over; then, with an effort, she smiled.

"All right, darling" she said. "Why are they in such a hurry to know? No, never mind" she added hastily. Do do that. They'd better hear it from you."

"This probably ties in with your original idea, Aglaia" Julia said, warming to her—"so Colin had better be the one to tell them."

Pauline Shergold's car was much roomier than the little Austin, so there was no difficulty about giving Colin a lift. He asked to be dropped off at the clinic—"That infernal hour!" he said; "I don't want to delay Terry." Julia said she would like to go to the clinic too.

"Whatever for?" Mrs. Shergold asked.

"There's a parcel for me there—I forgot to ask Gerald to collect it. And besides I want to ask about the little boy; if the sheep are better, he may be better too."

"So he may! Right, I'll call for you after I've left these good people at the Montefiore."

At the clinic Colin immediately put in his call to the Office, while Julia went in search of Dr. de Carvalho. He was in his consulting-room—when the secretary asked if he could see the Senhora Jamieson he sprang up and came out.

"Come in! Come in! The very person I wished to see! I tried to telephone, but you were out." He ushered her in and closed the door after them. "The child is well!" he exclaimed.

"So are the sheep! I came to tell you, so that you might stop his atropine."

"Is it not strange?—I decided this morning to omit the dose, and there was no reaction, so I omitted it again at midday, and still nothing. He is well."

"I'm very glad. Had you tried leaving it off before?"

"Yes, two days ago—but the headache came on again then with great violence."

"That's perfectly splendid—now we know to within forty-eight hours how long the stuff lasts" Julia said. "Of course we didn't know when the sheep had recovered."

"So *ces messieurs* have had their trip for nothing! What did I tell you?" de Carvalho observed, with sardonic triumph.

"May I tell my cousin? He's put in a call to London, so he can tell them that too."

"Of course."

"Oh, and my parcel—could I have it?"

"It is here." He opened a drawer and handed her a small parcel, very heavy for its size; it had no postmark, Julia noticed. "May I open it at once?" she asked. As he nodded she did so. Inside the wrappings was a small metal cylinder stamped with Russian lettering—an exact replica of the *cofrezinho;* there was also a note from Major Hartley. He began by complimenting her on "young Colin's immense success, to which I feel sure you contributed largely, as usual." He went on: "Sir Percy was insistent that you should have this at once, so I persuaded Scotland Yard to get their forensic people to see to it in a hurry. I send it via the Consulate—we here feel that the youthful finder of the original deserves everything."

"Oh how nice!" Julia exclaimed.

"What have you there?" the doctor asked, looking up from his case-notes.

"A copy of the child's *cofrezinho*—I told Sir Percy I must have one to give him."

"May I see?" he asked eagerly; he examined the thing closely.

"This is what it was like?" he asked.

"Yes, *exactly,* so far as I can see; I think they must have taken an impression from the real container."

"They go to all this trouble for a peasant child?" he asked.

"Well, why not? After all, he got the actual specimen of the gas concentrate for them."

"Ah yes—does your letter speak of this? In what form it was, I mean?"

"No, not a word. They wouldn't put that in a letter, of course; we shall have to wait till my cousin goes home to hear about that. Dr. de Carvalho, may I take this up to Marcusinho now?"

"Certainly. But should you not first find out how he is to get home?"

"A good idea. May I use your own telephone to speak to Mr. Armitage?"

Terence laughed hugely when Julia told him of the sheep's recovery, and the dismay of the wretched experts at the hammocks. "And what about Marcusinho?" Terence asked.

"Yes, he's perfectly fit too—by accident, the doctor stopped the antidote this very morning. Now he wants to know how he's to be got home?"

"I can take him tonight."

"Can you take Colin too? He came in to ring the Office with the glad tidings."

"Of course. I'll pick them both up."

When Julia went up to see the child the doctor came with her, and told the grey-haired nurse to get him dressed.

"He goes home? He does not have the evening dose?" the woman asked.

"No, no more doses, ever—he is completely cured" de Carvalho said, with a sidelong smile at Julia.

"*Gracias a Deus!*" the nurse said. "But this is wonderful!—and most strange" she added.

Julia gave the child the heavy little metal box—"There you are, Marcusinho." He clutched it eagerly.

"*Muitissimo obrigado, minha Senhora!* But why was my mother so slow in finding it?"

"She found it at once; but then I mislaid it—it was my fault" Julia said happily, thinking that she had lost count of how many lies she had told that day. "And now you are quite well again, and are going home."

18 "SORRY I'M LATE" Philip Reeder said, coming into the dining-room at Glentoran—"I met Menteith, and he wanted to discuss the County Council's plan for this new road up to the Forestry Commission's hutments. Is that tea hot?"

"No, I'll make some fresh" Edina said, turning up the flame under the big silver kettle. "Give me the small pot off the sideboard." As she scooped tea from the caddy into it—"Did you get a decent price for the pigs?"

"Yes, smashing—and for the old moos too. It pays to go to Stirling, every time, in spite of the petrol. Where's Julia?"

"Gone to London."

"London? What on earth for?"

"She had a phone call from her lawyer just after you left yesterday about letting Gray's Inn, and she decided to dash down and see about it. I gather there's a chance of letting it furnished for a couple of years."

"But if she lets it, where will she live?—after she leaves here, I mean?"

"Well, we talked about that a bit—she didn't go till after lunch. I suggested that just for a couple of years she could leave Nannie Mack and the Philipino here; they get on like a house on fire with our nursery party, and it's much better for him than being an only. I hope you don't mind?" his wife asked.

"Not in the least" Mr. Reeder replied, piling butter and honey onto a scone. "But that doesn't settle where Julia is to live. Or is she to stay here too?"

Edina laughed.

"No, not all the time. We both feel that when Mrs. H. comes back from Madeira she oughtn't to be alone so much with those two spoiled old trouts of maids—anyhow they're both getting pretty rocky. And there's masses of room in the flat."

"Yes, that's quite a good idea. Only I should have thought Julia would want to be with the child."

"She talked of getting a job" Edina said, filling her husband's outsize cup from the fresh pot of tea.

"What sort of job? She doesn't need the money, anyhow."

"She didn't say. I suppose she might work at those papers of hers, that she writes for: *Ebb and Flow,* and whatever the other one is."

"Can't think why Intelligence don't take her on, if she feels free to take a job at all; that's really her line" Philip Reeder said. "When does she get back?"

"She said she'd telephone. Before Colin and Aglaia come, in any case."

"Is she staying with them?"

"No, she was going to her Club."

"All the same, it seems a bit dotty to get rid of the Gray's Inn chambers, when she hasn't got anywhere else of her own to live" Philip said.

"I believe she really funks going near the place at the moment" Edina said. "No, I think a couple of years furnished let is a good idea; she need only just collect her clothes and books, and dump them at Mrs. H.'s flat. It will all be much less—less raw —in two years time."

"Perhaps you're right. Only Julia never seemed one to run away from anything before."

"She never lost a husband before" Mrs. Reeder said with finality.

Julia returned to Glentoran a few days later.

"Yes, it's all fixed" she said, in answer to a question from Edina. "They seem very nice people—he's a lawyer himself, so that's quite appropriate; he used to know Philip's old legal uncle, that he got the top set from originally."

"What 'set'?" Philip Reeder asked.

"The set of chambers—that's what they call them in Gray's Inn. I think they'll look after the furniture all right too—she was thrilled with it."

"Did you see Colin and Aglaia?" Edina asked.

"No—I just had a chat on the telephone. They'll be up day after tomorrow, as of course they've told you."

"Is Colin settling into his London job all right? It seems such an odd move for him, after always being abroad" Edina said.

"Yes, they're very pleased with him" Julia said thoughtlessly; then wished she hadn't, for Edina at once asked—"Why? Did you see them? Who, Torrens?"

"No, I had dinner with Major Hartley."

Philip Reeder, whose attention to other people's conversation was very much of the stop-go variety, now looked up from his paper.

"Hartley, eh? Did he tell you anything about this terrific *coup* Colin's supposed to have brought off in Spain?"

"No" Julia said, for a moment in genuine astonishment. "What *coup*, Philip?"

"Oh, when I was in Edinburgh day before yesterday I ran into Watherston, and he said young Colin had done something quite spectacular—he's the number one white-headed boy at the moment, it seems."

"No, Major Hartley didn't tell me" Julia said coolly. "They don't talk much, as you know." She realised that Colin's brief dash to Madeira—after all he had only been there just over a fortnight—had, in the vagueness of Service rumour, been comprised under the general heading of "Spain", where he was known to have been for some time. "I'm so glad" she added.

"Yes, it's twice as different again from what he'd heard last time" Philip said. "Good show." He returned to his paper.

Julia at once became preoccupied with how to get hold of Colin and Aglaia and warn them not to speak of Colin's having been in Madeira before they encountered the Reeders; if the rumour that Colin's "coup" had taken place in Spain was the version preferred by the Office, that version should be stuck to by Colin himself. Telephoning from Glentoran wasn't very private, since there was an extension in every sitting-room and bedroom, and in that huge house it was hard to know where everyone was at a given moment; Edina even complained, half-laughingly, that her mother, old Mrs. Monro, spent half her time in her own wing listening-in to the rest of the family's telephone calls. She asked Edina next day how the young people were coming out from Glasgow—"Boat or plane?"

"Oh, they're coming by the little plane." Edina looked at the huge engagement-block on her desk. "Twelve ten" she said.

"Would you like me to meet them? I can, easily."

"D'you know, that would be rather a boon. I've got to go in to Tarbert to take some honey to the hotels, and to pick up some things off the steamer, and she may be late. Do you mind taking the Daimler?—I shall want the station-wagon."

"Not a bit—good practice for driving a hearse!" Julia replied blithely.

Next morning, accordingly, she was waiting at the small local airfield when the plane touched down; driving back towards Glentoran up the blue-grey road beside the sea, with Aglaia beside her, she said over her shoulder to Colin—"Do you remember this Watherston person?—Philip sees him when he goes to Edinburgh. He's somehow connected with the Service."

"I know who you mean—I barely know him."

"Well listen, both of you—" and she repeated what Philip Reeder had said.

"But that's nonsense—he didn't bring off any *coup* in Spain!" Aglaia objected.

"No, we know that; but if that's the story that's going round, mightn't it be better to stick to it? What do you say, Colin?"

"Yes, of course" the young man said at once. "I'm surprised it's got out at all—but not in the least that it should have got a bit garbled! Yes, Ag—stick to that. But I don't suppose they'll ask you any questions; they know well enough we can't talk—all but my mother," he added.

"But we can't pretend you weren't *in* Madeira; Mrs. Hathaway is sure to have written to Aunt Ellen, at least."

"No, of course not; I just went to Madeira for a spot of leave, and nothing whatever happened!" Colin said. "Thanks for the tip, Julia."

At lunch, sure enough, Philip Reeder, dividing woodcock into halves with great speed and skill, came out with—"Well, Colin, I hear we have to congratulate you on some quite top-hole piece of work. Good show. I suppose you can't tell us what it was?"

"Philip, you *know* he can't!" his wife expostulated.

"Oh well, I thought he might give us a hint what to look out for in the papers, when it all comes to light" Philip said. "Everything seems to be turning pretty sour in Spain, especially with the Russians trying to butt in and get a ROTA for themselves. The Russians are always at the bottom of trouble these days."

Aglaia turned a startled gaze on her husband, but said nothing. Colin said "Too right, Philip," and pushed the tray with brown crumbs and bread sauce towards his hostess.

After lunch Forbes, Mrs. Monro's aged butler, appeared in the library with a message to say that Mrs. Monro hoped young Mr. and Mrs. Monro would come to tea with her at half past four.

"Yes, thank you, Forbes—we'll be there" Colin said. "That will give you nice time to get unpacked, darling" he added to his wife.

When the party dispersed, Aglaia to her unpacking, the two Reeders to their various avocations, "Come up the glen" Colin said to Julia.

"Yes, rather—I'll just get a coat." She ran upstairs, and looked in on the nursery party. "Master Philip's nearly finished his rest; then we're going down to the farm with the others to see the calves" Nurse Mackenzie said. "I must say, Madam, it is a pleasure to be in a *proper* nursery again. Those twins!" Julia laughed and went downstairs.

As she and her cousin strolled up the glen, where the leaves of the sycamores, mottled and golden, were beginning to fall among the dark shapes of the rhododendrons—"There's so much I want to hear, I don't know where to begin asking" Julia said.

" 'The choice is yours', as no Government department will ever dare to say again" Colin replied easily, tucking his arm through hers. "Oh, it *is* nice to be back" he said, looking round him with a contented sigh. "There's nowhere like Glentoran."

"Dead right."

"Well, ask away" he said.

"Well, if you've *heard,* I'm dying to know exactly what was in the *cofrezinho*" Julia began.

"Oh yes, I saw Sir Paircy, as our friend calls him, and he told me. It was really damned ingenious—the gas concentrate was in little granules, for all the world like that sago stuff—*very* small."

"Oh yes, pearl tapioca; it made my least-favourite nursery pudding."

"Mine too. Well anyhow, the Russian chemists had somehow contrived a substance to cover it, that disintegrates when it gets touched by some solar ray—that's why it had to be kept in lead-lined containers. Then, here in Britain, it was to be distributed at night, calm and easy; and as soon as the sun got up the gas would be released, just as it was on the plateau—with precisely the results that you saw on the sheep and the child."

"But suppose it was an overcast day?" Julia objected.

"Doesn't matter—this thing, the ray or what-have-you, penetrates cloud-cover. Sir Percy tried to explain, but I couldn't begin to understand it all, still less pass it on intelligibly. He did use some queer expression like "photo-synthesis in reverse," but that didn't help me—does it you?"

"No, not a bit. Anyhow go on."

"Well, that was it. Chemically apparently fool-proof, if they could only have managed to see the results. But you see, thanks to us they never *got* any results—so their whole experiment has been a complete failure. We've got the films, and the tapes; they've got damn-all. But best of all, for us, is that Sir Percy and his team know the precise chemical composition of this new gas, so that they can make an antidote to counter it that can be air-borne too, for mass distribution. They're working on that at Porton now."

"Yes, you couldn't very well go round injecting even the armed forces with atropine three times a day!" Julia said. "But you said tapes—there were sound-tapes too, were there, to record the coughing and wheezing?"

"Yes—in fact that machine was a brand-new Jap one, that records sound along with the film. Marques' dogs-body told me all about it in Lisbon."

"Poor Major Fernandez!" Julia said laughing. "Oh, what happened in Lisbon? Of course I haven't seen you since."

"Oh, there was a tremendous pow-wow. They got Terence over to give evidence; that let you out—that, and the fact that the two Spanish boys had made a full confession."

"What happened to them?"

"Imprisonment for life—*and* there won't be any remissions for good conduct!"

"Imprisonment where?"

"In Portugal—they were caught red-handed, spying on Portuguese soil. The Spanish and the Portuguese see pretty much eye to eye over Communists, so there was no trouble with the Dons over that. No, the people who were a bit nasty were our own high-ups; they made it clear that they thought the authorities in Madeira had been a bit casual."

"In what way? You can't stop trawlers prowling, can you?"

"No, of course not; our own fishing-fleets can hardly *move* for Russian trawlers round the Orkneys and so on! But you needn't let them put people ashore in strength to poison sheep, and no questions asked!—nor make their accomplices welcome guests!"

"Poor Maderenses! I still don't see quite what they ought to have done" Julia said.

"Well, you said yourself that you'd seen the trawler inside the three-mile limit; they could have kept their eyes a bit wider open, and reported her to Lisbon. And letting those ten types land was a major howler. I expect they'll tighten things up a good bit now—in fact I know they're going to."

"And were the Portuguese Government ever told about Sir Percy coming out, and the *cofrezinho?*"

"Sir Percy, yes—he came to Lisbon himself, and brought the tapes with him. But so far as I know he kept the *cofrezinho* under his hat. After all, the Russians aren't proposing to attack Portugal with gas—not with this gas, anyhow, because the climate is all wrong; it's much drier than Madeira."

"There is just one thing" Julia said thoughtfully, as they turned up into the azalea glen—"If the North Koreans could board the *Pueblo* and imprison her crew, why couldn't the Ports impound the trawler?"

"Because the *Pueblo* was a naval vessel, and the Yanks were at war with North Korea; these bloody trawlers the Russians send out are technically civilian fishing-boats, and pretend to be unarmed."

"What nonsense it all is!" Julia said. "Let's sit" she added, as they came to one of the wooden seats above the stream in the little side glen.

As they sat down—"This is the very seat we were sitting on when I asked you to go to the Bank in Geneva and see about Ag's grandfather's numbered account, I do believe" Colin said.

"So it is."

"The azaleas were in bloom then" he said.

"They're pretty now" Julia replied, pulling off one of the pale yellow and pale pink leaves which covered the bushes—"And do you notice the scent?"

Colin sniffed.

"Yes I do; not strong, but it's there. Can there be some flowers still out?—a second blooming?"

"No, it must be from the plants themselves. I've often noticed it." She turned towards him, twisting the leaf round her finger. "Colin dear, don't tell me if you don't want to, but I'd love to know how Aglaia is—well, getting on."

"I do want to" he said, putting his arm round her shoulders in his old easy fashion. "It's all going ever so much better. Whatever old Urquhart said to her, it made a terrific impression; she's trying tremendously hard to be sensible and unexacting. I'm trying hard, too" he said, smiling a little shyly at her.

"To do what?"

"Actually to follow de Carvalho's advice—he told me I was being self-indulgent about her, and frightened, really. So now if she does start being silly, I stand up to her. He was very sharp, was our doctor."

"He seems to have been a great one for dishing out advice" Julia said, smiling too.

"Gosh, did he have the nerve to advise you? What on earth about?"

"How to occupy myself, now that I'm on my own" Julia said slowly. "He said it would be frightfully bad for the Philipino if I concentrated all my time and energies on him—and I'm pretty sure he's right about that."

"Could be, I suppose. So what did he suggest?"

"That I should take a job."

"Did he have the nerve to suggest what sort of job?"

"Yes. He thought I should work regularly for Intelligence, on a salaried basis."

"Good gracious! And how were you to set about getting such a job? Had he got bright ideas about that, too?" Colin asked, almost indignantly.

"Don't be nasty about him—it was really very sweet of him to worry about us at all" Julia said.

"More sweet to worry about me than about you!—but you're right, really. I'm sorry."

"Anyhow he didn't make any suggestions about that—I just said I'd think about it, and he let it go. But when I was down in London clearing out Gray's Inn I rang up Major Hartley to ask if the Office would like any of my Philip's maps and tropical kit, and so on—I thought they might be useful to some impoverished young agent being sent abroad—and he asked me to dinner, and did offer me a job."

"Good God! What sort of job?"

"I thought he might have told you. Tangier for a bit, because I know it. Perhaps Casablanca later on."

"Good God!" Colin said again. "What's your cover-job to be?" he asked then.

"We didn't get as far as that—I said I'd think it over. I wanted to talk to you about it first. You see he said they would want me to put in a few weeks in the Office to learn about the way they work at this end, and to be taught the drill generally. But I wondered if it would upset Aglaia to have me working there?—with you in the Office too, I mean" Julia said, her ready ripe-apricot blush appearing. "I wouldn't like her to be upset, just when everything's going so well, on the new lines."

He turned and faced her fully.

"Let's get this straight at once" he said firmly. "The basis of what you call the 'new lines' is precisely that Ag is dropping all that nonsense of being jealous of you because you can do things, with me and for me, that she can't. Old Urquhart had all that out with her—she told me about it. He actually said to her that where that sort of capacity was concerned, *you* were the million-airess."

"Good gracious!" was all Julia found to say.

"*Yes*—and she has accepted that. So forget about it. Certainly go ahead and take this job if you're sure you'd like to. *Would* you like to?"

"I think I'd like to have a stab at it. I'm fairly sure it would be better for the child, and Edina says they could keep him and Nannie Mack up here, where he's not the only pebble on the beach."

"Does she know about this plan, then?"

"No—she said I could leave him here when I had to make a snap decision about letting Gray's Inn for two years. But that would leave me free to go abroad when the Office wanted me to. I told Major Hartley I couldn't take on anything whole-time—only come and go, like Bonnecourt does."

"Both based on Glentoran!" Colin said, laughing a little.

"Well, no one could have a lovelier base" Julia said, looking down the pink-and-yellow vista of the little glen, where the azalea-bushes overhung the water.

"Where shall you live while you're in London?" he asked. "Stay with us?"

"No, I don't think so. When Mrs. H. comes back I think I'd probably stay with her; Edina and I agree that she oughtn't to be too much alone now."

"And till then?"

"Oh, there's always my Club. But I rather thought of suggesting to Mrs. H. that I might move in and keep the flat warm for her beforehand. I always suspect those old maids of hers of profiteering—drinking her Burgundy and selling the dripping!"

"So you'll take the job on?"

"Yes, I think so. I must go down and see the Major again and hear a bit more about it, but I expect I shall."

"Well, good luck to you, darling! I'm sure you'll do it superbly, whatever it is. Let's go back and ring up Hartley before tea."

"And I'll write tonight to Mrs. H. and ask about staying in the flat—then the letter can go on the early bus tomorrow. Oh, how much can I tell her?"

"Say you're going to work in the Foreign Office—that's what one says to everyone."

"Won't she guess?"

"With Mrs. H. it doesn't matter if she does" Colin replied.

A few days later it was Colin who drove the Daimler down to meet Julia at the small airport on her return from London. In the car—"Well?" he asked.

"Yes, it's all settled. I go down and start next week, and probably go out to Morocco just after Christmas. I told Major Hartley I wanted Christmas up here, with the child, and he was so nice about it. I do think he's a nice man" Julia said. "I'm sure I shall like working for him; he's so—so accommodating."

Colin burst out laughing. "That's the last thing most people would say about Hartley! I expect you've mopped him up, as usual."

"Nonsense!" Julia said, vexed—her blush appeared again. "Don't be so silly, Colin."

"Sorry" he said, putting an appeasing hand on her arm. "Go on—tell me why you call him accommodating?"

"Well, actually that had to do with what you vulgarly call 'mopping-up', as well as about Christmas" Julia said, still blushing a little. "At one point he said—'I'm sure after all this time you must know quite a lot of the people in the Office fairly well. Is there anyone you'd rather *not* work under, while you're learning the ropes?' Now that was what I call considerate."

"Very percipient, anyhow" Colin said, grinning.

"No, *considerate*" Julia persisted.

"Have it your own way. And what did you say?"

"I said yes, that there were two" Julia said, laughing a little herself.

"Me and Torrens, I suppose?"

"No, Torrens and someone else. I'm not going to tell you, so you needn't ask!" (If Colin had not realised all the misery about John Antrobus in Switzerland, long ago as it was, she was certainly not going to inform him.) "But I'll send him a postcard telling him to add you to the list!" she added briskly.

"Well, I'm very glad you like him, and I'm sure he'll be delighted to have got you right into the Service at last" Colin said. "You know he always calls you 'the wonder-girl'? And so you are, darling."

She was silent for a moment. At last—"I think really he is chiefly glad to give me a chance to try and carry on, a little bit, where Philip left off" she said slowly. "He did say—" she paused.

"Yes?" Colin asked.

"He said that in Madeira we had brought the Central Asia trip to a successful conclusion" she said, turning to him, her eyes full of tears.

"Oh darling!"

"Yes. And he said he was sure I would do a lot more frightfully valuable work."

They had reached the Glentoran gate—Colin swung the car into it and up the drive; by the big beeches near the turning down to the saw-mill he pulled up.

"Let's finish talking here" he said. "There's no hurry. And after Christmas is it to be Tangier?"

"Probably. He asked if I still knew people there, since the take-over by Morocco, and of course I do; old Lady Tracy and

Madame la Besse are still there, I know. But there's just a chance it might be Portugal. Either would be heaven!"

"You really are like the war-horse in the Bible, hearing the trumpets and shouting Ha-ha!" Colin said, shaking her elbow affectionately.

"Well, I do like those sunshiny places, and being on a job" Julia admitted. "Have you told Aglaia I'm going to work in the Office, and take a job in the F.O. after?"

"Yes, and she was tremendously pleased. Oh, we've got a bit of news for you, too. She's started another baby."

"*Has* she? Oh, how splendid."

"Yes—and Nannie Mack is helping her to knit every single thing for it herself! By the way, have you heard from Mrs. H. about occupying her flat?—because if not, Ag would love you to come to us."

"There's hardly been time for a letter, but in fact I telephoned to her, and it's all right—she'd like me to stay there."

"Telephoned?" Colin was startled; it was not like Julia to be needlessly extravagant.

"Yes. Major Hartley wanted to be sure that everything was settled quite definitely, so he made me ring from the Office."

"Good God!" Colin bit back a remark about the Major obviously wanting to make sure of an extra hour in his cousin's company, and merely chuckled inwardly to himself.

In fact a letter from Mrs. Hathaway arrived two or three days later, before Julia left Glentoran; after running through it herself she read it aloud to Colin.

" 'My dearest child,

It was a lovely surprise to hear your voice on the telephone this morning, and I write at once to say what a *very* good plan I think it is that you should do regular work for the Foreign Office, on a business basis—it will be better than just writing for your newspapers.'

"She puts Foreign Office in quotes" Julia interjected, laughing. "Isn't she comical?"

"I tell you it doesn't matter" Colin said. "Go on."

Julia read on. " 'I quite agree with your doctor friend that it is probably better for the child, at this stage anyhow; provided you make it clear that if he is ill, or needs you, you must be released at once. In *your* case, he must come first. But nothing could be more wholesome for little Philip than to be with Edina's children at Glentoran, one of a big, happy, nursery-ful, instead of a London child alone.

As for you, my darling child, this will give you a pleasant, *useful* occupation, to fill the huge gap in your life; and I think Colonel Jamieson would have wished you to do just this. I know how much he admired the work you had been doing, even before you and he became engaged; he spoke to me about it more than once."

Julia stopped reading, and dabbed at her eyes. "That's nice, isn't it?"

"Yes, very, darling. I know it's a fact, too. Is there any more?"

"Oh yes. She confirms that she's glad to have me use the flat; she says—'It will be better for Ada and Dora to have someone to look after; be sure to make them give you everything you want. To have nothing to do is rather disintegrating, as well as boring.' And she asks how Edina and Aunt Ellen are, of course," Julia said, shuffling the thin airmail sheets—" 'Poor Ellen' is what she says; she always calls your mother that, you know."

"She's quite right. That the lot?"

"No, there's a P.S." Julia began to gurgle a little with her slow, warm laughter. " 'Working for the Foreign Office is of course what I shall tell Pauline, who is sure to want to know, and that nice Mr. Armitage, who asks for you every time I see him. But the Foreign Office, like our Heavenly Father's house, has many mansions, and I feel sure that you will be put in one which will suit you.' "

"Good for Mrs. H." said Colin Monro.

ABOUT THE AUTHOR

The wife of a British diplomat, Ann Bridge has travelled around the world and has lived in China, Switzerland, Portugal, Italy, Hungary, and France. Drawing upon her unique international background and upon her formidable amount of knowledge about a vast variety of things, from botany to mountain climbing, she writes with the spell-binding detail and precision of a widely travelled, sensitive, and observant author. Her dramatic stories of the diplomatic world and of international intrigue and her brilliant discussions of everything from menus to rare wild-flowers have made such books as *The Lighthearted Quest, The Portuguese Escape, The Numbered Account, The Episode at Toledo,* and her recently published "Literary Recollections," *Facts & Fictions,* great favorites among her enthusiastic public here and abroad.